Samuel Chandler, Thomas Amory

Sermons on the Following Subjects

Volume 3

Samuel Chandler, Thomas Amory

Sermons on the Following Subjects
Volume 3

ISBN/EAN: 9783337797881

Printed in Europe, USA, Canada, Australia, Japan

Cover: Foto ©Andreas Hilbeck / pixelio.de

More available books at **www.hansebooks.com**

SERMONS

ON THE

Following SUBJECTS,

VIZ.

The immoderate Love of Pleafure.

The great Evil and fatal Effects of it.

The Defign of Chrift's Appearance.

On our Lord's Temptation.

The Folly of cafting off religious Principles.

On keeping the Heart.

The Paths of the Lord are
Mercy and Truth.

Chrift the Friend of his obedient Difciples.

Godlinefs explained and recommended.

Glory, Honour and Immor-
tality, the Chriftian's great
End.

BY THE LATE REVEREND

SAMUEL CHANDLER,

D. D. and F. R. and A. S. S.

Publifhed from the Author's MANUSCRIPT.

VOL. III.

LONDON:

Printed by Samuel Chandler, for the Author's Widow;

And fold by J. Buckland, in Pater-nofter-Row;
E. and C. Dilly, in the Poultry;
And T. Cadell, in the Strand.

M.DCC.LXVIII.

CONTENTS

TO THE

THIRD VOLUME.

SERM. I. THE immoderate Love of Pleasure described. 2 Tim. iii. 4. *Lovers of pleasure, more than lovers of God.* p. 1.

SERM. II. The great Evil of this Passion. *The same Text.* p. 23.

SERM. III. Voluptuousness destructive of real Piety. *The same Text.* p. 50.

SERM. IV. Voluptuousness destructive to Men's Families and secular Interests. *The same Text.* p. 94.

SERM. V. The Design of Christ's Manifestation. 1 John iii. 8. *For this purpose the Son of God was manifested that he might destroy the works of the devil.* p. 126.

SERM. VI. The Goodness of God in this Manifestation. *The same Text.* p. 157.

SERM. VII. VIII. Our Lord's Temptation in the Wilderness explained. Matt. iv. 1. *Then was Jesus led up of the spirit into the wilderness, to be tempted of the devil.* p. 175.—201.

SERM. IX. The Folly of casting off religious Principles. Psalm xiv. 1. *The Fool hath said in his heart, there is no God. They are corrupt, they have done abominable works, there is none that doeth good.* p. 225.

SERM. X. XI. The Importance of keeping the Heart diligently. Prov. iv. 23. *Keep thy heart with all diligence, for out of it are the issues of life.* p. 261.—279.

iv CONTENTS.

SERM. XII. All the Paths of the Lord are Mercy and Truth unto the sincerely pious. Psalm xxv. 10. *All the paths of the Lord are mercy and truth, unto such as keep his covenant and his testimonies.* p. 299.

SERM. XIII. Christ the Friend of his obedient Disciples. John xv. 14. *Ye are my friends, if ye do whatsoever I command you.* p. 320.

SERM. XIV. XV. Godliness explained and recommended, as essential to present and future Happiness. 1 Tim. iv. 8. *Godliness is profitable for all things, having the promise of the life that now is, and of that which is to come.* p. 345—366.

SERM. XVI. XVII. Glory, Honour, and Immortality, the Reward of a patient Continuance in well doing. Rom. ii. 7. *To them, who by patient continuance in well doing seek for glory, honour, and immortality, eternal life.* p. 388—417.

SERMON I.

The immoderate Love of Pleasure described.

2 TIMOTHY iii. 4.

Lovers of pleasure more than lovers of God.

NOTWITHSTANDING the great excellency of the Christian, religion, in those perfect rules of morality which it delivers, and the very powerful motives it offers to our confideration to enforce the practice of them ; yet it could not be reafonably expected, either that all would embrace it, to whom the evidence of it should be offered, or that it would conftantly produce thofe good fruits of piety and virtue, it was calculated to promote, in all who might profefs to believe it. Principles, however certain and important, as they do not irrefiftibly operate by any phyfical or natural neceffity, prove too often ineffectual to convince and influence men ; fuch efpecially who are prepoffeffed by ftrong prejudices, and under the government of corrupt paffions and inveterate habits of vice. If they will give themfelves up to a worldly difpofition, and an eager purfuit of fenfual gratifications, they muft either lofe all ferious regard to the obligations of true religion, or by fome methods or other, fhape it according to their favourite inclinations and practices ; fo that they may have no uneafinefs from their courfe of life, nor any interruption in the pleafures they are determined to indulge.

St. *Paul*, who without infpiration was a very good judge of human nature, and who by the prophetick fpirit that he received forefaw many future events, exprefsly declares, that there fhould in procefs of time be very great corruptions amongft Chriftians themfelves. This know alfo, that *in the laft days perilous times fhall come ; for men fhall be lovers of their own felves, covetous, boafters, proud, blafphemers, difobedient to parents, unthankful, unholy, without natural affection, truce breakers, falfe accufers, incontinent, fierce, defpifers of thofe that are good, traitors, heady, high minded,* and in the words of my text, *Lovers of pleafures more than lovers of God* ; and yet amidft all thefe corruptions, *having a form of godlinefs,* whilft their whole practice was a *denial of the power of it. From thefe,* fays the Apoftle, *turn away.* Have nothing to do with them, as fcandals to Chriftianity, and *enemies of the crofs of Chrift.*

But

But though the *love of pleasure* is here reckoned amongst the moft enormous *crimes*, it muft not be underftood as though this was *univerfally* cenfured and condemned. The love of pleafure is *natural* to us, and implanted in our very conftitution ; and there are certain pleafures which we may *reafonably* and *innocently* purfue. The fenfes with which God hath furnifhed us, were not given by him in vain, nor opened by his hand only to be fhut up by us againft the admittance of all thofe gratifications which he hath rendered them capable of conveying to us. And it is as unneceffary in point of religion on the one hand to bind ourfelves to perpetual feverities and abftinences, as it is contrary to it on the other to devote ourfelves wholly to fenfual purfuits and indulgences. Pleafure is far from being abfolutely and in itfelf unlawful, and the inclination to it need not be entirely fuppreffed. The duty of a Chriftian is wifely to regulate it, and keep it within the bounds that God and nature hath prefcribed it. And whenever in the purfuit or indulgence we tranfgrefs thefe limits, we act inconfiftent with our reafonable and Chriftian characters. The thing cenfured in the words of my text, is not abfolutely the love of fenfual pleafure, but *the living in it*, the *immoderate* love of it. *Lovers of pleafure more than lovers of God*, or perfons who are lovers of pleafure *rather* than lovers of God. In fpeaking to thefe words I fhall

I. Con-

I. Confider the *character* itfelf defcribed. And

II. Shew the *unreafonablenefs* and *evil* of it.

I. I am to confider the *nature* of the *character* itfelf, or who may juftly come under this denomination of loving fenfual pleafures *more than God.* One would indeed fcarce think it poffible that this could be true of any reafonable creature, capable of confidering and underftanding the perfections and works of God, the relation he bears to him, and the numerous and ftrong obligations he is under to his power and goodnefs. The character of God implies in it all that is amiable and lovely, all that deferves efteem, or can attract affection; and the command *of loving God with all the heart and foul and might and ftrength,* carries in it an unalterable and indifpenfible fitnefs. And therefore the loving any thing in oppofition to God, or fo as to extinguifh that love which we owe him, muft be extreamly unnatural and criminal. And yet it will be found that it is the too prevailing difpofition amongft mankind. For

1. When the minds of men are fo *entirely engroffed,* and their hearts fo fully poffeffed with the love of fenfual pleafure, as to *exclude all confiderations of God,* and fhut out all manner of regard to his being and perfections, they may juftly be faid, to be *lovers of pleafure rather than God.* He, as the author of our beings

beings, our abſolute proprietor, our ſovereign
Lord, our kind benefactor, our conſtant
friend, our daily inſpector, our final judge,
our only happineſs, is worthy ſometimes to
employ our moſt ſerious thoughts, and an acquaintance with him in the attributes of his nature, and the conduct of his providence, cannot but be both our duty and intereſt. Our
own frame, every thing that is around us,
invites us to the contemplation of this infinitely glorious and bleſſed being, and Heaven and earth conſpire to put us in mind of
him that ſpoke them and us into being, and
by whoſe conſtant viſitation we are upheld
in life. To a well diſpoſed mind 'tis impoſſible there can be a more grateful reflection, nor is there a ſingle character or attri-
bute in God, that can give the leaſt uneaſineſs
or pain to one who is not diſordered by
unnatural paſſions and criminal affections.
If true reaſon were to guide us, and a juſt
regard to obligation and happineſs, to be the
rule of our conduct, there would not a ſingle
day of life be ſuffered to paſs away, without
employing ſome of our moments in this ſacred and delightful work of converſe with
God, and conſecrating part of our thoughts to
the meditation of his glory and goodneſs. *How
precious*, ſaith the Pſalmiſt *, *are thy thoughts
unto me, O God? How great is the ſum of them?
If I ſhould count them, they are more in number
than the ſand. When I awake I am ſtill with*

---

* Pſalm cxxxix. 17, 18.

thee,

thee. And yet of how many is it true, that *God is not in all their thoughts?* They have no more sense of his being and perfections than if he had no manner of existence, or there was nothing in the whole frame of nature to introduce the remembrance of him into their minds, all they seek after is the gratification of their passions, all the pleasure they relish is what comes by the avenues of their senses, and their whole life is one continued round of amusement and vanity. Just reflection is entirely banished. Considerations of a serious nature are absolutely discarded. They never enquire *whence they are, for what end brought into being, to whom they are accountable,* or what *their ultimate and principal happiness.* They live absolutely by sight. Invisible objects scarce ever appear to them real. This poor span of life bounds all their hopes and views, and though they exist in the immensity of God, and dwell amidst ten thousand proofs of his being, they have no knowledge of or expectation from him. The one care that possesses them is, how they shall *make provision for the flesh to gratify the lusts thereof* †, and secure that succession of pleasure in which they have placed their happiness. An evident demonstration that they are *lovers of pleasure, rather than lovers of God.* But

2. When men so *closely follow* after the *sensual pleasures* of the present life, as to ren-

---

† Rom. xiii. 14.

der

der their minds *incapable of all right dispositions and affections towards God*, they are juftly
chargeable with the guilt of *loving pleasure
rather than God*; becaufe their fenfual difpofition, and their eager fondnefs for prefent
gratifications, fuppreffes all due efteem for
him, and is the principal caufe why the *love
of God dwells not in them.* The prevailing
love of pleafure, and the genuine love of God
are inconfiftent principles, and can neither of
them flourifh or live, but upon the decay
or deftruction of the other. If our affection
and veneration for God be fincere, and entirely
poffefs and influence our minds, the paffion
for other inferior objects will leffen, the inclination to all fenfual indulgences will be brought
under due government and reftraint, and the
fondnefs for all criminal gratifications will
be abfolutely fuppreffed and extinguifhed. In
confequence of this, the life will not be a perpetual purfuit of amufement and vanity, nor
wafted away in the continual queft of worthlefs or criminal pleafures. The abiding fenfe
of God, a due reverence for his majefty, an
high efteem for his infinitely amiable character, and the delighting in him as the center and fource of all perfection and excellency, will infpire the nobleft fentiments,
exalt and purify the mind, turn off the paffions from the vanities of life, and introduce
thofe refrefhing pleafures and facred fatisfactions into the foul, as fhall create a rational
indifference towards all earthly perfection,
and caufe us to look upon all the unnatural

B 4 gratifications,

gratifications of fenfe, with a fovereign contempt and abhorrence. On the contrary,
when the fenfual difpofition entirely prevails,
when the love of pleafure and perpetual attention to it, engroffes all the paffions, be-
witches the affections, and keeps the foul faft
bound in its foft and deceitful inchantments;
fo that all the fears of God are extinguifhed,
all reverence for his authority is loft, all
efteem and affection for him die, hope and
truft in him ceafe, and the ambition to pleafe
him, and the defire to be accepted of him is
no more : When this is the cafe, pleafure
is fubftituted in the place of God, and excludes him from that heart that fhould be
confecrated to his love and fear. It argues
the fame difpofition

3. When men are become fo abfolutely
the property of pleafure, and fo thoroughly
immerfed in fenfual gratifications, as that for the
fake of them they entirely *forfake the folemnities of God's worfhip, both private and publick*,
and caft contempt on all thofe inftitutions,
by which we are to exprefs our dependence
on God, our fenfe of his authority and providence, and to ftrengthen in our minds the
neceffary purpofes of a fober, righteous and
godly life. The reafonings of natural light
on this head are as clear and as certain as
any can be ; that if there is a God he is
to be worfhipped ; and the directory for this
worfhip, in the gofpel of our Lord Jefus
Chrift, is the moft rational and excellent
that can be given ; that *God is to be worfhipped*

in spirit and in truth ; by the exercise of pure affections, by the acknowledgment of our dependence on him, by offering our grateful praises for the innumerable benefits we have received from him, and by humbly imploring the continued protection and blessing of his providence and grace, through every future period of our lives. I presume all men, who can draw any conclusions at all, may see the real force of this, and that nothing but unreasonable prejudice, or criminal prepossessions and affections can prevent their owning the truth of it. The *love of God*, in the judgement of Christ, is *the first and great commandment*, and this love of God can never be rightly cherished and maintained in its proper warmth and vigour, without the assistance of a serious and regular piety and devotion. To worship him is one of the most natural dictates of conscience and reason, a duty of eternal and unchangeable obligation, of primary importance and absolute necessity in its very nature. And therefore there can be no affairs of the present life so pressing and urgent, as to be a reasonable excuse of men in the habitual neglect of it. Much less can the pretence of pleasure, which ought never to be considered or made the business of life, justify them in such an omission, it being the highest absurdity to imagine, that pleasure, which ought always to give way to affairs of moment and importance, can ever be a just plea for a constant disregard to
the

the primary and moſt ſacred obligations of our being.

Human nature and the imperfection of the preſent ſtate, doth indeed require a diverſity of objects to employ and relieve our minds, and 'tis not to be otherwiſe expected but that at proper ſeaſons we ſhould unbend from the more ſerious concerns of our being, that we may renew our ſtrength, collect new vigour, and return to our proper buſineſs with recruited ſpirits, in order to the more effectual diſcharge of it. And as there are no duties of more certain and indiſpenſible obligation, than thoſe which immediately reſult from the characters of God, and thoſe certain relations which we bear to him; the caſting off all regard to theſe, and indulging ourſelves in a perpetual neglect of them, for the ſake of any diverſions and pleaſures whatſoever, is an inſtance both of folly and wickedneſs, and argues ſuch a preference of leſſer things to thoſe which are greater, as we ourſelves in almoſt any other caſe would readily condemn. And I ſhould think, that before men ſhould ſo much as attempt to make themſelves eaſy in ſuch omiſſions as theſe, they ſhould firſt ſee if they can fairly diſprove the being, perfections and providence of God, or clearly demonſtrate that the obligations to piety and devotion are intirely precarious and miſtaken, or elſe plainly ſhew that there can be any kind of pleaſures of ſuch importance and neceſſity, as to diſcharge them from theſe obligations,

gations, and which they can hereafter avow
and juſtify, when God by Chriſt ſhall bring
them into judgment.

Men may poſſibly through great ſtupi-
dity, long inattention, or the prevalence of
a ſenſual diſpoſition, overlook all conſiderations of this nature ; or they may find out
ſome excuſes to palliate this irreverence for
God, and to quiet and ſatisfy themſelves in
ſo very criminal a negligence. But ſurely
ſuch expedients as theſe are very falſe and de-
luſive, and it becomes reaſonable beings to
act upon a foundation of greater certainty
and ſafety, and to form their judgment of
things by an impartial conſideration of and
attention to their reſpective natures and conſequences, and not as they are falſely repre-
ſented by prejudice, paſſion and inclination,
which will always biaſs the mind, and lead
men into the moſt miſtaken and dangerous
concluſions. Though the very notion of God
includes in it all that is venerable and excellent, and the moſt natural poſture of the ſoul
towards this infinitely glorious being, is that
of adoration and worſhip, and though the
moſt genuine ſatisfaction reſults from a rational and fixed devotion ; yet when men
are become almoſt wholly ſenſual, when
they have ſuppreſſed all inclination to this
ſacred exerciſe, or when the call of pleaſure
allures and ſeduces them, they are ready
and quick in finding out excuſes, or elſe
blindly follow the inſtinct of their appetites,
without ever conſidering where they lead
them,

them, or into what criminal and dangerous neglects they fall for the fake of indulging them. And by thus *alienating themselves from God*, and entirely divesting themselves of all care and concern about a religious temper and life, they demonstrate, as far as actions are sure proofs of what men most esteem and habitually prefer, that they are *lovers of pleasure rather than God*. Again,

4. This is most evidently the case when men *pursue* such kind of *gratifications*, as are strictly *criminal* in their nature, expressly contrary to the will of God, and *forbidden* either by the *natural law of reason* in our minds, or the *revelation* he hath given us by the Lord Jesus Christ. This argues not only the want of a sincere affection and veneration for God, but in the significant language of sacred writ, is *being enemies to God by wicked works* *. 'Tis indeed I think scarce possible, that men can bear a real enmity to God in their minds, considering him as possessed of infinite perfection and excellency. As such he is the object of love only, and not of aversion and hatred. But then as these pleasures of sin, obstinately followed and habitually indulged, do certainly argue a real opposition to the authority and will of God, as the supream Lord and Governor of the world, as they are a contradiction to the rectitude of his nature, and the holiness of his law, and as they tend to frustrate the great ends of his pro-

---

* Colof. i. 21.

vidence

vidence and moral government, in thefe views they certainly argue a prevailing hatred of and unnatural averfion to him. And therefore when the pleafures of men are directly and intrinfically criminal, or attended with any unqueftionably finful circumftances, this is the fureft evidence that they prefer the pleafures of fin to the favour of God, and that their love of thefe pleafures hath extinguifhed in them all due reverence and affection for him, and that they are under the influence of a moft unnatural averfion and enmity towards him.

Obedience to the laws of God is fo infeparable an effect of the *love* of him, as that the Apoftle tells us, *This is the love of God, that we keep his commandments* *. This is the moft certain evidence, this the neceffary fruit and confequence of loving God. And therefore if men indulge to a voluptuous life in direct violation of the commandments of God, *how dwells the love of God in them?* In this view the words of our Lord Jefus Chrift carry in them the fulleft evidence and conviction : *No man can ferve two mafters, for either he will hate the one and love the other, or elfe he will hold to the one and defpife the other* †. No man's affection and love can be fixed at once upon two oppofite and contrary objects, and therefore the prevailing love of finful pleafure is abfolutely inconfiftent with, and wholly deftructive of the

* 1 John v. 3.   † Mat. vi. 24.

love

love of God. Now of this kind are all thofe fort of gratifications,

1. Which cannot be indulged without a *manifeft injury* and *lafting prejudice to others;* efpecially without doing them hurt in their deareft and moft valuable intereft. All thofe pleafures therefore which are at the expence of the property of others, which are incon-fiftent with the honour, peace and union of families; all fuch as are built upon the ruin of the virtue, the natural fhame and modefty, the future ufefulnefs and happinefs of thofe we bend to our inclinations, all fuch as na-turally tend to confirm others in their vices, and to render them hardened, abandoned and profligate, are pleafures contrary to the na-ture of things, the dictates of compaffion, the fentiments of generofity, the pleadings of humanity, the will of God, and irrecon-cileable with the loving him. For there is nothing that is more evident, than that the *communicating happinefs,* and the endeavouring to confirm others in thofe difpofitions, which are perfective of human nature, and con-ducive to the welfare and dignity of it, muft be *agreeable to the will of God,* the *moft bene-volent* of all beings; and that therefore the rendering others miferable, and willingly drawing them into the complicated ruins of vice, for the fake of our own perfonal grati-fications, is one of the higheft offences againft the Majefty of Heaven, and abfolutely fub-verfive of the ends of his government. And

2. When

2. When the pleasures we pursue are *inconsistent with our own true welfare and happiness*, they are unjustifiable in their nature, and contrary to the will of God. The consulting our own welfare is a natural dictate, implanted in us by the great author of our nature, and we have no more right, as the subjects of the divine government, to injure and destroy ourselves, than we have to corrupt and ruin others. Reason and religion both strongly oblige us to be provident for our own welfare, and carefully to guard ourselves against every thing that may be in the least detrimental to our natures, inconsistent with the true possession and enjoyment of our beings, or that may incur the forfeiture of the happiness for which we are designed. We hold our natures from God, the universal Proprietor and supream Lord, and therefore have no right to make any waste in his creation, nor to destroy what he hath reserved for his own immediate use and service. And therefore all kind of sensual gratifications, that are destructive of the interests of the present or future state, are criminal invasions of his right, inconsistent with the subjection that we owe him, and irreconcileable with that affection and esteem he deserves from us.

If therefore men indulge to pleasures that are of *too costly and expensive* a nature, and thereby waste and dissipate their own substance, to the ruin of themselves, the impoverishing their families, the straitening themselves felves in bufinefs, the with-holding from or defrauding others of their juft dues, or the rendering themfelves incapable of the great duties of charity and mercy; fuch pleafures are in thefe circumftances abfolutely unlawful. What is a plainer dictate of reafon and prudence, than that men fhould be careful to *provide for themfelves and families* the fupports and conveniences of life? A dictate this, ftrengthened and enforced by numerous precepts of divine revelation. What is a more effential virtue of human life than *juftice?* How can the greater or leffer focieties of mankind profper without *benevolence* and *charity?* Whatever gratifications therefore are inconfiftent with a regard to thefe obligations, are contrary to reafon, and all the maxims of religion and virtue. By this fame rule all the expences of mens tables, families, and equipage, ought to be carefully regulated. For how agreeable foever to the fenfual tafte and inclination, the luxury and pomp of life may be, yet the gratifying fuch a tafte, to the impairing our fubftance, the involving ourfelves and families in inextricable difficulties, and the rendering ourfelves incapable of anfwering the juft demands of others, is an unpardonable folly and madnefs, and a crime both againft God and man. This confideration fhould alfo make men cautious in the choice of their private recreations and *diverfions.* Some there are, which how ever lawful in themfelves, and how fit foever they may be for perfons of larger fortunes, yet are *too coftly* *costly* for thole who are in lower situations of life; who therefore ought to be content to abide in the stations in which providence hath placed them, without aiming at and coveting the pleasures of richer men, which require greater plenty to furnish and support them. But especially it should make men extreamly cautious how they give into those very expensive and prodigal vices of intemperance, luxury, lewdness, gaming and the like; vices that scarce any plenty can support, and by indulging which men contract double guilt, as they allow themselves in practices absolutely criminal in their natures, and as they reduce themselves generally, and those for whose happiness they should have the most tender concern, into circumstances of the greatest distress and misery. So true and pertinent is the observation of the royal preacher: *He that loveth pleasure shall be a poor man, he that loveth wine and oil shall not be rich* *.

Or if men gratify themselves in such indulgences as are *prejudicial to their bodily health,* as well as waste their substance, they act contrary to the law of God, and their *love of pleasure* is *superior* to their *esteem and reverence* for him. As health is one of the most valuable blessings of providence, and the comfort and usefulness of life depend on it, we ought to be very frugal of so excellent a gift, and by all prudent methods to preserve it intire, that we may be the better capable of rightly dif-

* Prov. xxi. 17.

charging the many duties of our station in the world. And therefore the breaking in upon our constitutions, weakening our frame by bodily diforders and pains, and shortening the natural period of life, by criminal indulgences, voluptuous excesses, or irregular pleafures, is an unjustifiable folly, and criminal breach of the divine constitution and order. It is in reality a kind of *suicide* or *self murther*, and oftentimes proves as fatal to men, as if they destroyed themselves by the sword or poifon. Sometimes men *immediately reap* the fad fruit of their debaucheries and vices, and die at once as *martyrs* to their lusts and pleafures. At other times they destroy themfelves in a more *gradual* and *lingering* manner, though not lefs effectually, and befides the diforders they bring upon themfelves, propagate wretchednefs and mifery amongst their unhappy defcendants, whereby they perpetuate the remembrance of their crimes, and leave behind them monuments of their own infamy and guilt.

The fin is still greater, when men are habituated to pleafures that are immediately and in their nature *hurtful to their minds*, and that tend to weaken or pervert, or vitiate their nobler powers. Of this kind are all thofe gratifications which tend to obfcure their understanding, and corrupt their judgment ; to render them averfe to, or incapable of confideration and reflection, to harden and stupify their confciences, to wear off that tendernefs, fhame, modefty, fenfe of honour, and fear of offending, that God hath implanted in our frame, as guards upon our paffions, and to ballance the inclinations and ftrong propenfities of our fenfual appetites. This is offering the greateft poffible violence to ourfelves, debafing and proftituting our fouls, which are made after the image of God, laying ourfelves open to certain mifery and irretrievable deftruction, and to extirpate out of our minds all fenfe of God, and reverence and affection for him.

Or if mens indulgences are fuch, as *feed and enflame their paffions*, heighten their fenfual appetites, and ftrengthen thofe animal inclinations which they fhould keep under perpetual reftraint and government; this is nourifhing in their breafts irreconcileable enemies to the love of God, which is a plant of too tender and delicate a nature to thrive and profper in the foil where thefe noxious weeds are harboured and encouraged, which as they grow and encreafe will draw from it all that kindly fap which fhould bring it to its full perfection and beauty, or by their deadly fhadow foon deftroy it. Wherever this heavenly gueft dwells as a fixed companion, fhe clears the breaft of thefe troublefome invaders, or with a fovereign voice commands them peace, be ftill, calms every tempeft of the mind, reduces all the inferior powers within their bounds, reftores reafon to its exercife, and confcience to its authority and proper jurifdiction; renders the foul an habitation fit for the God of peace, introduces the pureft,

the

the calmeſt ſatisfactions, and opens the heart to *joys unſpeakable and full of glory.* And therefore all thoſe gratifications that *ſenſualize the mind,* and bring it under the dominion of animal affections, and that ſtrengthen the force and influence of inſtinctive paſſions, have an irreconcileable enmity with the love of God.

And finally, when men for the ſake of the momentary pleaſures of ſin, *live in an habitual neglect of the goſpel ſalvation,* and *receive* all the promiſes and offers of the *grace of God by Chriſt in vain,* they incur this grievous cenſure of my text, of loving pleaſure rather than God. The method of the goſpel redemption is a ſcheme of divine mercy and goodneſs, and the ſtrongeſt poſſible demonſtration of the ſincere and tender love that he bears us : Love to our ſouls dictated the gift, that comprehenſive gift, the only Son of God, to be the *propitiation for our ſins,* and to reſcue us from the power and condemnation of them. The *ſalvation* he offers us is from *the preſent evil world,* the wickedneſs in which it lies, the vanities and follies with which it abounds, and the deſtructive pleaſures it offers to ſeduce and deceive men into guilt and ruin. To accept this ſalvation God entreats and beſeeches us by the Lord Jeſus Chriſt, by the manifeſtations of his mercy, by the tenderneſs of his compaſſion and the greatneſs of his love, by every motive of his grace and goodneſs that can win upon our hearts, or kindly conſtrain us to embrace his offers and live. And if this love of God is rightly apprehended,

hended, if it makes the genuine and kindly
impreffions on our minds, enters into our affections and gains our hearts, it will awaken
in us all the ftrongeft fentiments of gratitude,
and the juft return of the warmeft affection
and efteem. The confequence of this will
neceff.rily be, a thankful acknowledgment of
the grace that hath appeared to us in Chrift,
and a moft willing and chearful acceptance
of that falvation by him, which is the nobleft
inftance and proof of this grace. All the
advantages of the prefent world, all the pleafures of fin, which are but for a feafon, when
offer'd in lieu of this falvation, will be looked
on with contempt, and rejected with the
fcorn they deferve. Whatever would render
us indifferent to the heavenly offer, or divert
us from our endeavours to fecure it, will be
looked on with jealoufy, and avoided with the
utmoft care and caution. Even the lawful
comforts of life will be ufed with the greateft
moderation, and the guilty gratifications of
finners fhunned as worfe than a deftructive
plague or immediate death. In a word, when
under a warm fenfe of the love of God to us,
and the facred impulfe of a fincere and affectionate love to him, we are in good earneft
follicitous to obtain falvation, and prevailed
with heartily to accept it, even the moft
grateful and favourite indulgences of life,
that are inconfiftent with the obtaining it,
will be wholly renounced, and nothing will
be thought too dear to facrifice to this infinitely more important concern, the falvation

of

of our fouls. How utterly void therefore of the love of God muft the voluptuary and and fenfualift be, who neglects this great falvation, and turns a deaf ear to all the tender invitations of God, and feels no charm in that facred voice, that perfuades him to accept of eternal grace; who, for the fake of a momentary gratification, the indulging an unworthy paffion, the unmanly pleafures of fin, the fhadowy amufements of life, the fantaftick vanities and gilded follies of the world, contracts an indifference to the moft fubftantial offers of divine goodnefs, and grows infenfible to all that mighty fum of bleffednefs, comprehended in thofe truly important words : *Eternal Redemption.* What is there in the pleafures of life that thus fafcinate and bewitch the minds of men ? Are there any real fubftantial bleffings that flow from a voluptuary courfe? Is private happinefs, or the publick good to be promoted and fecured by indulgences of this kind ? Any one valuable intereft of time or eternity connected with them ? No. 'Tis a courfe productive of innumerable evils, inconfiftent with all principles of true honour, publick fpirit, prudence and happinefs, as will be fhewn you, God willing, the next opportunity.

SERMON

SERMON II.

The great Evil of Excefs in the Love of Pleafure.

2 TIMOTHY iii. 4.

Lovers of pleafure more than lovers of God.

I Have, in a former difcourfe on thefe words, largely defcribed the *character* here mentioned by St. Paul, and fhewn who may be juftly charged as *lovers of pleafure rather than God*; fuch whofe minds are fo entirely engroffed with the love of fenfual pleafure, as to exclude all confiderations of God, or who hereby render themfelves incapable of all right difpofitions and affections towards him, or who on this account contract an indifference and averfion to all the inftances of piety and devotion, or who purfue fuch gratifications as are ftrictly criminal in their nature, and therefore expreffly contrary to the will of God; fuch as cannot be indulged without a manifeft injury and prejudice to others, efpecially in their moft valuable interefts, or confiftently with our own happinefs and ufefulnefs; fuch as diffipate our fubftance, or

C 4   deftroy

our health, or make wafte in our minds and
confciences, or enflame our paffions, and make
us negligent and carelefs as to our final and
eternal falvation.

II. I now proceed to the fecond general,
which is to fet before you *the great evil* of
fuch a difpofition as this, and the *many bad
confequences* that attend the immoderate love
and criminal purfuit of pleafure. There is
nothing more fatal to all the valuable interefts of our beings, or that carries in it
more certain deftruction to private or publick
happinefs. This I would prove under two
heads.

I. Offering to your thoughts fome confiderations in *direct proof* of the great guilt of
indulging to this fenfual difpofition. And

II. Reprefent in a more extenfive view the
evil of an immoderate love and purfuit of
pleafure.

I. I would offer to your thoughts fome
confiderations in direct proof of the folly, fin,
and danger of the particular temper condemned in my text, of *loving pleafure more
than God.* And one would think that the very
mention of the thing fhould carry fuch a
conviction of its unreafonablenefs and impiety, as no one who gives himfelf any room
to reflect fhould be able to refift. For

1. The love of God is a duty of the very
firft and higheft obligation. This is expreffly
afferted by our Lord. *Thou fhalt love the Lord
thy God with all thy heart, and with all thy
foul, and with all thy mind. This is the firft
and*

and great commandment * ; superior to all others in its importance and influence. And it is evidently so, not only upon the foot of authority, but upon all the principles of the most certain truth and reason. For if God be the *best* of all beings, if every possible excellence dwells in him in the most absolute and perfect manner, and if there be nothing in him to create indifference, to awaken aversion, to excite enmity, or to inspire horror and dread in the mind of any reasonable being, 'tis as evident that he is to be *loved with supream affection*, as it is that what is lovely should be loved at all, or that what is most lovely deserves to be loved best. Besides the reasonableness of loving God above all other objects, appears not only from his own infinitely amiable character, as founded in the most perfect rectitude of his nature, but from the *many obligations and benefits* we have ourselves received from him, upon which account this supream veneration and esteem for him is a debt of gratitude and justice. Whatever there is of natural and moral excellency in our frame is originally his gift. All the real blessings of our lives, that contribute to the welfare, happiness, and honour of our beings, we possess by the permission and under the direction of his providence. So that all the characters of Creator, Preserver, Benefactor, gracious Governor, Father, Friend, and Redeemer, conspire to excite in our minds

* Matt. xxii. 37, 38.

the

the warmeft affection towards him, and render him every way worthy of the higheft veneration and efteem of the whole rational
creation.   If therefore there are any arguments capable of perfuading us, or any motives of fufficieut power to influence us, they
all unite to engage our hearts in the love of
God.   What then muft be the ftate of that
mind where this facred paffion finds no admiffion !   What fubftantial darknefs muft
poffefs it, if it difcerns no excellency in this
moft adorable being ! What horrid perverfe-
nefs, if acknowledging his unparallelled perfections, it efteems and loves the fenfual
pleafures of life in preference of him ? How
defperate muft that ingratitude be, where under innumerable obligations for the moft valuable bleffings, the hand that beftows them
is never regarded, and a greater value put
on the bleffings themfelves, than on the goodnefs that confers them ? Can any thing argue
a more perverted judgment, a more degenerate
mind, or a more unnatural difpofition, than
fuch a fondnefs for the gratifications of fenfe,
as eftranges the heart from infinite, eternal,
and immutable perfection, and fills it with
an incurable enmity to the great original,
and indefectible fource of good.   Efpecially
confidering

2. The *nature* and *kind of thofe pleafures*
that are thus *preferred* by fenfual men before God.   Were the pleafures they purfue
ever fo excellent in their nature, and even
of the higheft confequence to the happinefs
of

of the prefent life, yet ftill this could not juftify the loving them more than God, and preferring the enjoyment of them to his acceptance and favour. But this is far from being the cafe. The pleafures they fpend their lives in queft of, have *no* peculiar *worth* and goodnefs in them, and are by no means *neceffary* to the welfare and enjoyment of our beings. Thoufands are without them, who to fay the leaft are equally happy with thofe who have them in the greateft abundance, and oftentimes unfpeakably more fo. Many who have it in their power to purchafe them, look on them as contemptible, as mere empty amufements, as criminal gratifications, and know by experience that true happinefs hath no dependence on them, and that the more they can live abftracted from them, the more they ftrengthen their relifh for every rational fatisfaction and enjoyment. They are in many inftances the pleafures only of *imagination, fancy,* and *falfe opinion,* that have no reality and truth in them ; that owe all their power of pleafing to a bad tafte and a perverted judgment, and are therefore the very loweft and meaneft that men are capable of enjoying. They are pleafures fuited only to the *mere animal life,* the inferior, fenfitive part of our frame, in many of which the very brutes themfelves have a large fhare, and probably oftentimes a much ftronger relifh of them than themfelves, which never enter into the mind, and have not the leaft tendency to exercife and entertain the rational facultics of our natures. Yea, they

are

are fuch too often, as true reafon directs men
wholly to fhun, and their beft intereft leads
to fupprefs every kind of inclination to them.
They are frequently extreamly *diſhonourable* to
thoſe who indulge them, fill them with infamy and guilt, render them averfe to all the
nobleſt pleaſures of life, make them enemies
to their own true perfection and happinefs,
and prove in their confequences bitternefs
and forrow. 'Tis for the fake of thefe imaginary, fantaftick, fpurious and adulterous
pleaſures, that fenfual men contract an habitual fettled indifference to him, whofe perfection renders him worthy the higheft veneration, and that they forfake him, from the
knowledge and love of whom they might
derive the pureft, the moft durable and worthy fatisfactions.   And

3. This folly is ftill the more inexcufable
and amafing, in that men may enjoy *every
valuable pleaſure* in life, that they can reafonably defire, or wifely wifh, and yet at the fame
time *maintain that fupream affection* which they
owe *to God*, and fecure all the valuable fruits
of his friendfhip and favour.   God hath not,
that I can find, any where abridged men of
any fatisfactions, that they can in judgment
and prudence, and confiftent with their duty
and beft intereft, allow themfelves.   Even our
bodily appetites, as far as regular and moderate, are implanted in us by the great author
of our frame, and are his wife provifion for
the fupport and comfort of the prefent life ;
and there are gratifications peculiar to them,
which

which when enjoy'd with a becoming temperance can never be criminal in their nature, and therefore not offensive to the God of nature. The senses which he hath inserted into our frame, plainly appear to have been intended by him to be so many various sources of pleasing entertainment to us. He hath opened the eye, that we might contemplate the magnificence, and take in the innumerable beauties of the creation all around us. He hath formed the ear to receive the harmony of sounds. The food that supports us is designed as well to please the taste as to satisfy our hunger. And therefore it can be no part of true religion to open the eye only to deformity, and the ear only to harsh and unpleasing discord, and the taste only to that which is bitter and offensive. The external blessings of plenty and riches, that God in his providence hath bestowed on some, more liberally than on others, were given them as means to purchase more of the advantages and conveniences of life, than fall to the share of those in more contracted circumstances. And they have a right to use them for their own benefit, and procure every thing, that properly falls within the compass of them, that may contribute to the ornament, elegance, or even splendor of life, as well as to supply the mere necessities of it ; provided the spirit of true piety and goodness be not lost amidst these amusements and gratifications, nor the disposition and ability for any of the important duties of our Christian

character

character injured and deftroyed by them.
And how many valuable fatisfactions are
there of the prefent ftate, that may be enjoyed confiftent with all the interefts of religion and virtue ? Where doth the law of
Chrift abridge us of any thing that is reconcileable with integrity, and that care to fecure
better bleffings, which every one, that will allow himfelf ferioufly to confider, knows to
be his unqueftionable intereft ? And is not
this a demonftration of the folly and madnefs
of an entirely fenfual and voluptuary life,
that banifhes God from the heart, and renders the mind incapable of the exercife of
all right affections towards him ? If a regular, fober, and prudent enjoyment of the world
be reconcileable with the love of God, true
reafon cannot poffibly defire more. If all
the valuable fatisfactions of the prefent ftate
may be had, without leffening that veneration
and efteem we owe to him, and even made
fubfervient to eftablifh and increafe this facred difpofition, the pleafures that are deftructive of it muft be exceeding irrational,
criminal and pernicious. To be wholly abandoned to fenfual gratifications, to furfeit ourfelves with pleafures, to eat to excefs, to
drink to drunkennefs, to enjoy the good things
of life 'till we forget that God who gives them,
and to contract fuch a prevalent affection towards fenfible objects, as renders us reluctant
to converfe with him, incapable of the exercife of gratitude for his benefits, and raifes
in us a fettled oppofition to his government
and

and will ; this argues high ingratitude to the
great Author of all good for the liberal al-
lowance he hath made us of the comforts of
life, is a monstrous abuse of the favours of
his providence, and shews a temper utterly
loft to all ingenuity and sense of honour.   I
add farther

4. That if there be any *solid and substantial
pleasures* which human nature is capable of
enjoying, and which are of *superior estimation
and worth*, they are such as *result* from the
love of God, and from that religious and virtuous life which is the natural and genuine
fruit of it.   Let any man but impartially enter into the nature of things, and weigh the
pleasures of sense and reason in a fair balance
against each other, and he can never be at a
loss to form a true judgment concerning
them, nor where to give the preference. Supposing the gratifications we pursue are from
things in themselves lawful, the mere amusements of life, and our pleasure to arise from
elegance of dress, the plenty of our tables,
splendidness of equipage, magnificence of furniture, gay assemblies, and the fashionable
diversions of the polite and rich ; what sort
of pleasure and satisfaction is it that arises
from all this ? Is it manly, lasting, and that
will bear cool reflection ? Will the review of
it please in retirement ? If we have no other
source of happiness, will it last and supply
us in all the various changes and great emergencies of our being ? If our great employment be the adorning our bodies, and we
                                    study

ftudy principally the exactnefs of mode, and
the elegance of fafhion in our drefs, and when
viewing ourfelves in the flattering mirrour,
we grow enamoured with our own form, and
admire our choice of ornaments, their exact
difpofition, the help they are to feature and
complection, the luftre and gracefulnefs with
which they embellifh us, and their power to
make us fhine in an affembly, and to attract
the eye and draw the admiration of others
that behold us, let us enquire what kind of
fatisfaction all this is. Is it not the little
irrational pleafure of childhood, that all wife
parents endeavour early to correct ? Whence
doth it arife ? From any thing internal,
from moral perfection, the comely habit of
a good mind, and the true elegance of a
wifely ordered and well governed heart ?
No. All comes from the worm that cloaths
thee, the imagination that adorns thee, the
eye that beholds and the tongue that flatters
thee. But are thefe the things that rational
beings fhould pride themfelves in ? Are thofe
the only pleafures that we fhould live to purfue, that we fhould be eternally fond of, and
place all our happinefs in ? Run through the
whole circle of thefe amufements, and when
made the bufinefs of life, they will appear in the light of truth, to be nothing
better than pleafing follies, and the entertainments only of little and uncultivated
minds.

But the pleafures of men addicted to criminal gratifications deferve an infinitely worfe
name.

name. They are really the extravagancies of
madnefs, or the defperate adventures of men
with bankrupt confciences, or the thoughtlefs follies of perfons deftitute of reafon and
wholly void of underftanding, and are no
more to be numbered amongft the genuine
pleafures that belong to human nature, than
thofe which diftracted perfons and ideots
enjoy, as the effects of a wild or weak imagination. Whereas the fatisfactions that arife
from confcious piety and virtue, flow from
the moft perfect order and fulleft poffeffion
of the mind. They are the genuine dictates
of fober reafon, an enlightened confcience,
and a clear underftanding ; that proceed from
cool and deliberate reflection, and therefore
fpring out of the mind itfelf, are the pleafures properly of the reafonable being, and
for this reafon the moft fubftantial and worthy. To contemplate God as the creator and
governor of the univerfe, as the common
father of the whole reafonable creation, as
the author of all the various powers and perfections that are difperfed throughout the feveral claffes of beings, and all the kinds and
degrees of happinefs that the living refpectively poffefs ; to converfe with him as over-
ruling all things by unerring wifdom, as
making all things conduce to the general
advantage by an irrefiftible power and un-
wearied goodnefs ; to confider him as immediately interefted in all the concerns of our
beings, and as by inclination and promife engaged to make all things work together for

our good ; and on thefe accounts to adore and magnify his name, to celebrate his goodnefs, to own our dependence on him, and eftablifh our faith and truft in him by fervent prayer, to love him for his unparallelled excellencies, to exercife habitual gratitude for his conftant benefits, to reft in him as our portion and happinefs, and to yield all the fubftantial fruits of thefe facred difpofitions, by a prevailing conformity of our actions to the example and will of God, and to have the teftimony of our own hearts to the fincerity of fuch a temper and fuch a life ; the pleafures that flow from thefe fources are pure without mixture, real without deceit, fatisfactory without difappointment, permanent without change, grateful in review, conftant in every poffible alteration of circumftance, and the earneft of thofe fubftantial and incorruptible pleafures that are at God's right hand, and laft for evermore. How amazing then the folly of bartering away thefe fatisfactions for the delufive pleafures of fin ! To exclude the love of God out of our hearts, and thofe exalted fatisfactions that receive their being and nourifhment from this heavenly principle, for the fake of more freely indulging the gratifications of fenfe and imagination ; what is it but to exchange *folid enjoyment* for mere *empty amufement*, and the nobler entertainments of a *rational* and *divine life*, for the low, fordid, precarious gratifications of a *merely animal* and *brutal* one. And finally,

5. What

5. What fhews the infinite danger of fuch an habitual temper and courfe is, that even thefe pleafures that now fo entirely captivate men, and engrofs their affections and time, will *in the end be productive of bitternefs and forrow.* It is, I think, impoffible that men devoted to a life of fenfitive indulgences can be eafy in their own minds, but either as the effect of a fixed refolution to banifh all thought about the confequences of their actions, or through the opiate of falfe principles, fubftituting fomewhat in the room of true piety and goodnefs, or by running wholly into infidelity, and making an intire fhipwreck of faith and a good confcience. By thefe methods men may attain to a great deal of infenfibility, and keep themfelves tolerably free, in a voluptuous courfe, from the reproaches and terrors of their own confciences. But how truly wretched is the condition that needs thefe remedies ? How falfe that fecurity of mind that is derived from fuch caufes ? Is a man's danger *ever the lefs*, merely becaufe he is refolved *never to think of it* ? Or is his diftemper like to be the *lefs fatal*, becaufe he *ftupifies himfelf* that he may never feel his pain, or be fenfible of his danger ? Or will his eternal fhipwreck be the lefs certain and fatal, only becaufe he throws away his compafs, and laughs at the thought of a ftorm of future vengeance.

Every object in nature demonftrates a God, and upon this principle nothing is more abfolutely certain than the obligations of religion

and

and virtue. Our reafonable natures declare us accountable, and a future ftate of rewards and punifhments ftands infeparably connected with thefe great articles, which no reafonings can ever difprove, nor the moft fubtle arguments ever render in the leaft improbable. In how dreadful a fituation do thefe reflections place the fenfualift and libertine ? What account can he give of life, that neglects all the effential duties of it, and lives only to indulge the inftincts of appetite, and feed the follies of a diftempered imagination ? How will he like and endure the figure he muft make in a future world, when his mind fhall appear furnifhed with nothing but images of fhewy trifles, gaudy vanities, and fplendid delufions ; and his whole life one continued purfuit of fhining bubbles, golden dreams, and gay diverfions ; abfolutely unconfcious to all the worthieft difpofitions of human nature, and wholly void of all thofe fruits of righteoufnefs, without which no man can be beheld by God with approbation ? But how dreadful, how loathfome a fpectacle to God and man will the wretch be, on whom fhall be found the deep imprinted marks ‡, furrowed in his foul by criminal gratifications, and the horrid ftains of guilty pleafures ? How will he be amazed at the judgment feat of God, when every act of intemperance, luxury and luft, fhall be brought to view, and fet before his eyes ; when all his expenfive vices, and coftly

‡ Vid. Lucian.

indu'gences

indulgences of fin, fhall be recalled to his remembrance ; when he fhall be charged home
as the tempter and corrupter of others, and
as the inftrument of their ruin to fubferve his
own paffions, and ftand bowing under the
tremendous weight of his own and other mens
crimes ? The man of pleafure may fmile at
this reprefentation as fictitious and imaginary.
But yet he knows he cannot difprove it, no
nor wholly get free from the apprehenfion and
terror of thefe poffibilities. And fhould they
at length prove real, what can fave him from
this complicated guilt, or deliver him from
the lowest depths of everlafting perdition ?
Surely *thefe ungodly fhall not ftand in judgment,
nor finners* of this rank *in the congregation of
the righteous !*

In this light, what can we think of the
pleafures of fin ? Doth it not immediately
diffolve the charm, and fhew the infinite hazard of being beguiled and bound by the foft
enchantment ? What judgment muft we
pafs on the character of my text, *Loving
pleafure more than God ?* Is it not departing
*from the fountain of living waters, and hewing
out to ourfelves broken cifterns that can hold no
waters ?* Is it not *forfaking our own mercy*,
cherifhing deftruction in our bofoms, and
for the fake of a momentary, agreeable de-
lufion, madly expofing ourfelves to the moft
fubftantial and durable mifery ? But thus
much as to the *firft* thing, the *evil, folly,* and
danger of loving pleafure more than God. I
now proceed

II. To the *fecond*, which is to confider in a
little *more extenfive view* the evil of an *immoderate love* and *purfuit of pleafure*, facrificing
all other interefts to this, or making it the
one great object of our view, and bufinefs
of our lives. The *man of pleafure* is no rare
character in the times in which we live. How
few families are there comparatively to be
found, in which there is not one or more of
this complection? How numerous are the
opportunities for and incentives to pleafure,
that abound every where in the midft of us,
to catch thoughtlefs minds, and deceive them
out of their time, their fubftance, their virtue, and their happinefs? And are not perfons
of all ranks and degrees, in all focieties and
communions, entering into the common fnare,
and adding ftrength and authority to the
growing evil, by the countenance of their example? Where muft thefe things end, or who
can be at a lofs to foretel their confequences,
if fome fpeedy check be not put to them, by
the prudent interpofition of the legiflature, or
by a feverer but more fovereign remedy, the
rebukes of providence? If indeed men would
but impartially confider the nature of things,
and enter ferioufly into the bad effects of fuch
a temper and practice, effects that all hiftories
furnifh them with, and that are every day vifible amongft us at home, one would think
they fhould need no other motives to check fuch
a difpofition in themfelves, and difcountenance
it in others, as far as their influence and authority will reach. You will not take it amifs,

if

if I repreſent to you the nature and conſequences of ſuch a ſpirit, as they appear to my
mind ; and indeed they appear to me in every
circumſtance of terror and ruin. Conſider,

1. How *contemptible* and *low* the character
of a *man of pleaſure* is ! How mean the figure
he makes in life ! a little, poor, inſignificant,
uſeleſs creature, made up of ſelfiſh views,
ſordid ſchemes, and diſhonourable purſuits !
His mind an uncultivated waſte, in which
nothing manly, generous, amiable, and good,
proſpers, void of knowledge in every thing
uſeful, ſtript of all benevolent paſſions, and a
ſtranger to all thoſe excellent virtues, which
are the great ornaments of human nature :
One who is continually in queſt of impertinent amuſements, or who rejoiceth in nothing
but the indulgence of his appetites, or who
is continually ſinking himſelf deeper into the
guilt of the moſt criminal gratifications. He
is one whoſe mind is entirely diſabled from
all the nobleſt exerciſes of reaſon, who looks
on the ſtudy of all ſerious things with contempt and averſion. His thoughts run no
higher than the caprice of faſhion, the elegance of dreſs, the gay diverſions of the
times, to kill reflection, and waſte away the
tedious hours of life ; and are oftentimes
much worſe employed, in ſtudying to deceive,
betray, and ruin others, by drawing them in
to be partners in his pleaſures, and miniſter
to his vileſt paſſions and inclinations. Your
men of pleaſure, in converſation, are the moſt
empty and unfurniſhed creatures in the world,

or the moft offenfive and fhocking. They
want ideas to bear a part in the folid entertainments of men of fenfe and reafon, and
as to all fubjects of importance in human
life, are as little capable almoft of entering
into them as ideots or children. If they fhine,
it is only by their drefs or equipage, by plaufi-
ble impertinence, by exactnefs of tafte in
trifles, by depth of judgment in fafhionable
follies, by a little wit and raillery in favour of
vice, or at the expence of decency, good
breeding, religion and virtue. And frequently
their converfation is much lower than this,
and defcends to fubjects that a good mind
fcorns to think of, modefty and fenfe of honour blufh at the very mention of, and to delight in which argues the moft abandoned
and profligate confcience; in which the name
of God is never mentioned but to profane and
blafpheme it, nor religion introduced, but to
fhew they are mad enough to infult and renounce it.

And are not there amongft the very loweft
of the human fpecies, and even amidft all
the advantages of fortune and birth, worthy
the contempt of every fenfible perfon that
beholds them; who, to confider them in the
moft favourable light, are a compofition of
ignorance, dulnefs, affectation, impertinence,
indolence, and folly; who mean nothing
good, who aim at nothing great, who live
for no valuable ufe and purpofe, and are in
truth the mere cyphers of human life; and
who, to confider them in another view, are

in

in reality, how strong soever the expression may be, the *miscreant part* of the human species, who sacrifice not only all that is valuable in themselves, but as far and as often as they can, all that is sacred and excellent in others to their own gratifications and pleasures.

2. But this love of pleasure is not only low and contemptible, but extreamly *dishonourable* and *infamous*, which no splendid titles, no elevation of condition, no height of fortune, can extenuate or conceal. Ask even a civilized *heathen* in what true worth and dignity of character consist, what renders any man truly noble and great ; and he will tell us, 'tis not birth, or ancestors, or titles, or wealth, or any of those external circumstances, in which men so greatly pride themselves ; but that *virtue is the only true nobility*, and that *real greatness* consists in the possession of *moral excellency*, in *sanctity of character*, in the *love of justice*, and in an *universal regard to truth* in conversation and practice. Nor is there any one thing that the *wisest* men of *antiquity* have stigmatised with more odious characters, and severe reproaches, than the intemperate love and indulgence of pleasure. 'Tis in its nature *brutal ⁎*. A man of pleasure is wholly degenerated into sense and appetite, and lives by

⁎ Illud tamen arcte tenent, accurateque, defendunt, voluptatem esse summum bonum. Quæ quidem mihi vox pecudum videtur esse, non hominum. Tu enim, cum tibi sive Deus, sive mater, ut ita dicam, rerum omnium, natura, dederit animum, quo nihil est præstantius, neque divinius, sic te ipse abjicies atque prosternes, ut nihil inter te, atque quadrupedem aliquam putes inter esse ? Cicer. Paradox. c. 4.

no other or better principle than the beasts
that perish. 'Tis mere bodily instinct that
governs him, imagination that perpetually
deludes him, caprice and humour that are
the sole rules of his conduct. He is in a state
of the most abject *slavery*, and in bondage
to the most imperious and cruel masters. The
habits of sensuality destroy the natural freedom of the mind, and eradicate the sentiments and love of liberty, and leave men in
full possession of the vilest and most infamous
affections ; insomuch that though frequently
honour, sense of duty, conscience and interest
all exclaim against their practices, they are
almost irresistibly drawn into their accustomed
indulgences, in spite of all the consequences
of ruin that are before them. It naturally
tends to indolence and sloth, to unnerve and
unbrace the vigilant and active powers, and
frequently throws men into that indolent state,
creates in them that indifference to exercise,
and fills them with that hatred to all diligence
and labour, as renders their whole lives an
inglorious state of rest and idleness, except it
be when some new scene of pleasure awakens
them out of their lethargy, and their appetites stimulate them on afresh to some irregular
and criminal gratification.

And how *base* and infamous are the *methods*
by which they generally pursue these. If we
place the man of pleasure in the most favourable light we can, and consider him only as
continually busied in and delighted with the
glare, ostentation, the pomp, and splendid
amusements

amufements of life, how fcandalous is the
wafte of time confumed in them, how fhame-
fully is the improvement of the mind neglected
for the fake of them, how monftroufly the
great end of life forgotten and perverted,
through an attention to them.   If the love
of pleafure leads men further than thefe, into
really criminal exceffes, the infamy of a voluptuous courfe is in proportion much greater,
and throws the fouleft ftain upon thofe who
indulge them.   How loft to all decency are
the men that live only to fatisfy the cravings
of an intemperate and luxurious appetite,
and fpend their time and eftates in the feafts
of a delicious and extravagant table.   Oh !
how is human nature debafed, and all the
dignity of it proftituted and trampled under
foot, by the debauches of wine, by riot and by
drunkennefs, when the powers of reafon are
all laid afleep, and the man transformed into
fomewhat more wretched and vile than the
moft defpicable infect ; when every impious
fuggeftion takes place, when all the brutal
paffions feize him, and he becomes fitted to
perpetrate every enormity of vice, without
reflection to preferve, or confcience to controul him ; when fools and madmen laugh
him to fcorn, and thoughtful and fober men
look on him with a mixture of abhorrence,
indignation and compaffion.   Other pleafures
of vice there are, which are purfued and purchafed by fuch means as are abhorrent to all
principles and fentiments of honour, which
fhew

fhew men deftitute of every thing great and good in their minds, and whatever be their titles, dignity, rank, and plenty in life, de-monftrate them to be men of the moft abject difpofitions ; and as to moral excellency and worth, entirely divefted of it. Such are the men of pleafure, who lay fnares to ruin in-nocence, who condefcend to entreaties, per-fuafions, bribes, oaths, flatteries, promifes, threatenings, and all the accurfed arts and methods that their own perfidious and cruel hearts can infpire them with, to corrupt others, for their own gratifications, into fhame and guilt, and irretrievable deftruction ; men that are the abhorrence of God, and the fhame, the reproach and curfe of human fo-ciety ; who are relentlefs to all the miferies they caufe, and fpread ruin wherever they can prevail, without fhedding a tear over the wafte of which they are the authors ; who enter into families frequently only with a view to undo them, and put an end to their peace ; and to diffolve the tendereft and moft endearing relations of life, or to render thofe between whom they fubfift, the moft fubftantial plagues and torments to each other, as long as ever they continue. The treachery and bafenefs of fuch a character, though I want words to exprefs, yet God hath abundant vengeance in ftore, by *terrible things in rightcoufnefs*, to repay. The truth is, that a life of mere ienfual pleafure, in every view of it, is be-neath the dignity of human nature, and the

the character of *a man of pleasure*, a perpetual infamy and reproach to him that deserves it.   But

3. A life of pleasure is the most *useless* and
unprofitable *.   There is not a more insigni-
ficant creature that breathes than the habitual
senfualist.   He doth not merit the air he
draws, nor deserve a place on the earth that
sustains him.   They are the mere *excrescences*
of human life, that add no comelinefs, strength
or safety to it, but deform and often prey
upon the founder parts of society, and by the
corrupt humours they nourish and spread, endanger the welfare of it.   How unprofitable
is the life they lead to themselves, as to all
the valuable purposes and views of living!
Wholly funk in sense, they forget they have
a mind to cultivate, or a foul to save.   Being
the mean property of bodily appetites and
animal passions, what generous affections,
what manly dispositions, what virtuous habits
can they cherish and strengthen? Being able
to relish nothing but what is grofs, or fantaftick and imaginary, the taste for knowledge
is loft, the desire of moral improvement
ceafes, and the disposition and ability for every
great and valuable attainment languish and
die.   To futurity they are almost absolutely
blind, accustomed to live by fight, they ridicule all the objects of faith, think Heaven at

* Ut tribuamus aliquid voluptati, condimenti fortasse non
nihil, utilitatis certe nihil habebit. Cicer. de Off. l. 3 in fin.

too great a diftance to deferve their care, and
are too impatient and fond of prefent enjoyments, to govern their conduct by the expectations and hopes of any thing that is hereafter to come. So that they are born, and
live and die without wifdom, carry out of
the world with them as little valuable intellectual furniture as they brought into it, and
enter that eternal ftate, which employs the
thoughts and cares of every prudent mind,
without having ever guarded againft its poffible miferies, or acquired one fingle qualification that can fecure them the happinefs and
glory it may be capable of yielding them.

Confider them in a *focial* view, and they
will be found abfolutely incapable of ferving
the interefts of thofe they are united with.
The very example they give in the private
relation of a family, tends to infect and deftroy the feveral branches of it. What tender
concern can they have for the real happinefs
of others, who have no knowledge of or
concern for their own ? How can it be expected that they fhould form the minds of
their children into fentiments of truth, love
of virtue, or difpofition for ufefulnefs, in
whofe own hearts the love of pleafure hath
deftroyed thefe ? In what can they affift them
by inftruction and difcourfe, who know how
to converfe about nothing beyond the diverfions they are fond of, and have no tafte for
any kind of rational entertainment and improvement. As to real friendfhip, men of

pleafure

pleasure are never to be trusted, 'tis impossible they can support it, the love of pleasure
being destructive of all those benevolent and
social affections on which it is founded, and
so engrosses them for the pursuit of what
is grateful to their own senses and imaginations, as that they have no leisure or inclination cordially to consult how they may
serve the advantage of another. Or if they
profess a friendship for others, 'tis a friendship
which must be fatal to those who embrace
it, and carries in it the most powerful temptation to draw them into a sensual and voluptuary course. As to all the valuable arts and
sciences of life, they can be of little or no
possible assistance to cultivate and improve
these ; this requiring serious thought, close
application, diligent study, abstractedness from
the amusements of life, and a fixed attention
of mind to the subject in pursuit, to all which
the sensualist is naturally averse, and cannot
but be under an habitual and strong aversion. In all the great emergencies of state,
what benefit can the publick receive ? How
can he assist by counsel and advice, who
hath all his life been disused to grave
and manly reflection ? What resolution can
be expected from him in times of danger,
who hath contracted an habitual indolence,
and grown into an aversion to all the services of a vigorous and active life ? How will
he appear and act as a magistrate ? Can he
be otherwise than remiss in the execution of
                                              those

thofe laws, that are a reftraint upon his own
conduct; or favourable to offenders, for whofe
crimes he hath an apology in his own breaft?
Can he bravely ftem the torrent of abounding
vice, who is himfelf a pattern of it, or with
authority correct tranfgreffors, who fhares
an equal or perhaps fuperior guilt with
them. I wifh that the example of the paft or
prefent times did not abundantly convince
us, that *men of pleafure* cannot act as *ma-
giftrates* with integrity, nor the publick virtue
ever be fecured, whilft they are intrufted
with the excution of thofe laws, which are
formed for the protection and encouragement
of it. The many excellent ftatutes that we
have amongft ourfelves for the difcourage-
ment of vice and immorality, one would
think fhould be fufficient to put fome check
to the abounding of it. And therefore one
would be apt to wonder whence it comes to
pafs, that all the extravagances of vice are
fo frequently committed in the midft of us.
If indeed profligates and libertines prefide
over thefe laws, 'tis eafy to be accounted
for; when wickednefs fits in high places,
it will naturally foon fpread its dire infection
through every inferior ftate around it; the
confequence of which general corruption of
manners muft be fooner or later the diffolution of the publick peace and order, which
will draw after it other confequences fub-
verfive of the welfare and liberties of thefe
kingdoms.

But

But this would lead me into another head of difcourfe that would furnifh many ufeful reflections ; *viz.* the unfpeakably *bad confe-quences* of this immoderate love of pleafure, and that to the caufe of religion, to all the private interefts of particular perfons, and the being and continuance of the publick hap-pinefs, which will deferve a farther particular confideration.

SERMON III.

Voluptuousneſs deſtructive of real Piety.

2 TIMOTHY iii. 4.

Lovers of pleaſure more than lovers of God.

I Have in two former diſcourſes from theſe words ſhewn you, the *nature of the cha-racter* here deſcribed, of loving pleaſure more than God, and the *unreaſonableneſs and folly* of ſuch a diſpoſition ; becauſe the love of God is a duty of the very firſt and higheſt obligation ; the ſenſual pleaſures that men are ſo criminally fond of, are by no means worthy the preference which is given them ; men may enjoy every valuable and reaſonable pleaſure in life conſiſtent with that ſupream love for God which he deſerves, if there be any ſolid and ſubſtantial pleaſures which human nature is capable of enjoying, and which are of ſuperior eſtimation and worth, they are ſuch as reſult from the love of God, and that religious and virtuous life which is the genuine fruit of it ; and

finally,

finally, becaufe thefe immoderate and irregular pleafures muft, in the end, upon all true principles of religion, be productive of bitternefs and forrow.

I have alfo fhewn you the *evil* of this inordinate love of pleafure in a more *extenfive view* from thefe three confiderations; 'tis *contemptible* and bafe, 'tis *difhonourable* and infamous, 'tis wholly *ufelefs* and unprofitable. I now proceed to reprefent to you the farther evil of fuch a difpofition and conduct, in the innumerable *bad confequences* that attend it, and the deftructive influence of it, upon every valuable intereft of human nature and life. And let us here confider it particularly,

    I. As it affects men in a *religious* view. And

    II. In the *fecular* concerns of the prefent life.

    I. Let us confider this *voluptuary* temper and life as it affects men in a *religious* view, and we fhall find there is nothing more *unfriendly to true piety*, or more abfolutely inconfiftent with the life and power, the fpirit and practice of it.

When I fpeak of religion and piety I would be underftood to mean that reverence and regard which is due to God, both in difpofition and practice, which is founded in principle, and to which he hath a juft claim, upon account of the infinite perfection and rectitude of his nature, the character he fuftains, and our own unqueftionable dependance on

and

and relation to him ; agreeable to the plaineſt dictates of our conſciences and reaſon, the doctrine taught and the directions given us in the goſpel revelation.

There is nothing more evident, than that Chriſtianity abſolutely condemns this difpo-ſition and character I have been reprefenting to you, and particularly declares it irrecon-cileable with its governing defign, and the due care of our ſalvation and eternal happi-nefs. It is deſcribed as exceeding criminal. Theſe *lovers of pleaſures* are numbered amongſt the moſt profligate and impious part of man-kind, *covetous, proud, blaſphemers, difobedient to parents, without natural affection* *, and others the moſt abandoned and criminal offenders, as you may ſee a few verſes before my text. St. John tells us, that *all that is in the world* ‡, every thing that the world can afford ſenſual men, may be comprehended under theſe three, *the luſts of the fleſh*, all the gratifications of impure and intemperate men ; *the luſt of the eyes*, or the immoderate love of riches, ſplen-did habitations, coſtly furniture, ſumptuous cloathing, gay equipage, and the like, with which the generality feed and feaſt their eyes ; *and the pride of life*, or thoſe high ho-nours and dignities, places and preferments, ſplendor and pomp of appearance, which are the great objects of an ambitious temper, and frequently inſpire men with inſolence and pride. *All this*, ſaith the Apoſtle, *is not of*

* 2 Tim. iii. 2, 3, 4.   ‡ 1 John ii. 16.

the

the father. All passions and affections of this nature are neither excited by him, nor agreeable to his will. And therefore he adds, *that if any man loves the world,* if the love of these things be the prevailing passion, and engrosses his heart and affections, *the love of the father is not in him* * ; it is impossible he can have any becoming affection and esteem for God. Nay, we are assured in stronger terms, that *the friendship of the world is enmity with God, and that whosoever will be a friend of the world, is the enemy of God* † ; because that imitation of and conformity to a wicked world, in their criminal indulgences and pursuits, which is implied in friendship with it, argues a real alienation from him, and hatred to the design of his providence and moral government. Hence this sensual disposition and voluptuary course of life is expressly forbidden. *Take heed,* saith our blessed Lord, *to yourselves, least at any time your hearts be overcharged with surfeiting and drunkenness, and the cares of this life* ‡ . *Be ye not conformed to this world* ‖ , says the inspired Apostle, *let us walk honestly, with decency and dignity,* as the original word signifies, *as in the day, not in rioting and drunkenness, nor in chamberings and wantonness, and make not provision for the flesh, to fulfill the lusts thereof* § . It is also severely threatened. *Rejoice, O young man in thy youth, and let thy heart chear thee in the days of thy youth, and walk in the ways of thy heart, and in the sight of thine eyes* ** ; gratify

---

* 1 John ii. 15.   † James iv. 4.   ‡ Luke xxi. 34.
‖ Rom. xii. 2.   § xiii. 13, 14.   ** Eccles. xi. 9.

all

all thy paſſions, and take thy fill of pleaſure ; but take this along with thee if thou doſt : *Know thou, that for all theſe things God will bring thee into judgment* * ; ſo that the words are an exhortation to follow their pleaſures at their peril, and therefore are in reality the ſtrongeſt prohibition of ſuch a courſe. And St. Paul after mentioning ſome of the criminal gratifications of voluptuous men, ſays, *for theſe things ſake the wrath of God cometh on the children of diſobedience* †. And the Apoſtle James, ſpeaking of the corrupt ſtate of the Jews, aſſigns it as one grand cauſe of the ruin with which he threatened them : *Ye have lived in pleaſure on the earth, and been wanton* ‡, or as the word more properly ſignifies, fared deliciouſly and lived in luxury. *Ye have nouriſhed your hearts as in a day of ſlaughter,* or rather, as for, or againſt a day of ſlaughter ; elegantly comparing them, as fitted for vengeance by their criminal indulgences, to beaſts that were fattened up for the ſlaughter. To ſave us as Chriſtians from all corruptions of this kind, was one principal reaſon of the death and ſufferings of our bleſſed Lord, *who gave himſelf for our ſins, that he might deliver us from this preſent evil world, according to the will of God even our Father* § ; *and the grace of God that hath appeared to us* in and by him, *teaches us to deny all ungodlineſs and worldly luſts, and to live ſoberly, righteouſly and godly in the preſent evil world* ||. The great principle

---

* Luke xii. 19, 20. † Coloſ. iii. 6. ‡ James v. 5.
§ Gal. i. 4. || Tit. ii. 11, 12.

that

that should animate and influence the disciples of Christ is, that of faith ; a steady belief of and regard to the invisible God and a future judgment and world and recompence. *We live by faith and not by sight, we look not at the things which are seen, but at the things which are not seen* *, *for the things which are seen are temporal, but the things which are not seen are eternal* † ; and accordingly we are exhorted to *seek those things which are above, where Christ sitteth on the right hand of God,* and to *set our affections on things above, and not on things on the earth* ; *and to have our conversation in Heaven, and to have respect to the recompence of reward* ‡ ; precepts which are absolutely irreconcileable with an habitual fondness for, and constant pursuit of sensual pleasure. Indeed almost the whole of Christianity is directly and on purpose calculated, to recover men from the low pursuits and the criminal indulgences of the present life, to exalt their affections, and terminate them on superior objects, to prepare them for and secure them the possession of pleasures and satisfactions of a quite different kind, from the animal and brutal, and such as depend merely on imagination, and a disordered and perverted judgement. So that the thorough sensualist can never be a real Christian ; his disposition is altogether the reverse of the spirit of the gospel, and his life influenced by quite other principles, and a constant pursuit of quite

* 2 Cor. v. 7. † iv. 18. ‡ Colof. iii. 1, 2

E 4

dif-

different objects, than those recommended by
the revelation of our blessed Saviour. Indeed
there is nothing so unfriendly to, and destructive of the great end and design of all
true religion, as may be made appear by many
considerations.

1. Confider the *bad influence* which the *voluptuary* disposition hath on all kind of *good
principles* whatsoever, and how impossible it
is that they should ever prosper in, and have
any firm possession of the minds of those,
who are under the power and dominion of it.
If we attend to *facts*, what are, generally speak-
ing, your men of pleasure and gaiety, whose
lives are one perpetual round of diversion and
sensuality ; what are they but poor, empty,
thoughtless, unprincipled wretches, who
know nothing of truth, who are incapable
of all just reasoning upon the most important
subjects, who cannot see the force of the
clearest evidence, nor draw the proper inferences and conclusions from the most un-
questionable premises ; who will scarce allow
the being of a God, and are sometimes impious and fools enough to ridicule it ; who,
as far as they can, have banished his inspection and providence out of the world, laugh
at the thoughts of a future account, and
censure all the doctrines and great duties of
religion as precarious and irrational, and
having no other foundation but superstition
and credulity. As to Christianity, they seem
to be in general agreed, that 'tis nothing but
a mixture of imposture and priestcraft ; and I
believe

believe all who rightly underftand the nature
of it will fo far agree with them, that 'tis
a religion perfectly unfuitable to them, and
that they have no other way left to make
themfelves tolerably eafy in the courfes they
are determined to purfue, but to difcard and
renounce it. For

1. It is impoffible in the nature of the
thing, but that they muft be *prejudiced* in their
own minds againft all the *genuine principles of
true religion,* and cherifh a fecret difpleafure and
averfion to them. *They cannot receive the love
of the truth that they may be faved by it.* For
there is nothing fo oppofite as thefe principles
and their practice, and the maxims they lay
down for the regulation of their own conduct. Inclination and paffion, bodily inftinct
and appetite are with them the great rules
of conduct. What pleafes their eye, gratifies
their vanity, feeds their luxury, indulges their
pride, contributes to their mirth, and minifters
to their fenfual gratifications, thefe are the
things that poffefs their hearts, that conftitute
their happinefs, and which they imagine ef-
fentially neceffary to the true relifh and enjoyment of life. Separate them from thefe, and
you take away from them the very fources of
felicity ; they are uneafy, difcontented and
reftlefs, they know not how to poffefs themfelves, every hour of life is tedious, every
other engagement is a burthen. They lan-
guifh, they pine, they almoft die for want of
their accuftomed gratifications, and 'till they
are reftored to thofe amufements, follies and
indul-

indulgences, which alone have power to en-
teitain and pleaſe them. Now what reliſh
can men of this compleation have for religious principles, which in the very nature of
them tend to check the paſſions, to correct
the ſtrong tendencies of our animal nature,
to curb and reſtrain all the lower inclinations
and appetites of our frame, to render us fuf-
picious as to the final conſequences of a ſenſual
conduct, and to fill us with anxiety and fear,
as the fruit of forbidden, immoderate indulgences ? Religious principles call men to
converſe with quite different objects, and
point out to them a courſe of life quite contrary to what ſenſualiſts are fond of. They
expreſſly condemn their way as folly, and
hold up to their view the moſt aggravated
and ſubſtantial ruin, from the diſpleaſure of
the almighty being, and the puniſhments of a
future ſtate, as the ſure recompence of a life
of habitual, bodily, and criminal pleaſure.
How then is it poſſible that they can approve, or think favourably of, or have any
eſteem or regard for principles that are perpetually thwarting all their favourite inclinations, checking thoſe appetites to which they
want to give the freeſt indulgence, and conſtantly raiſing ſcruples and jealouſies, and fears
about things, as to which they would be entirely and abſolutely at liberty ? Who loves
to be made perpetually uneaſy ? Who can
endure a monitor that is perpetually controuling and chiding him ? Who can be fond
of, or have any prevailing affection for companions

panions, that are always reproaching and cenfuring of him ? Who will cherifh in his own breaft, reflections that are every day preying on his heart and confcience, and that will never fuffer him to enjoy himfelf, and gratify his defires in peace, whenever he attends to them ? On thefe accounts, religious principles cannot but appear to men of plea-fure in the moft difadvantageous and unfa-vourable view. They have an intereft with which they can never be reconciled. They muft be enemies to them in inclination, and ever look upon them with an inward averfion and hatred.

2. Hence it becomes almoft impoffible, that they can ever * *examine* them with that *care and impartiality*, which are neceffary to form a proper judgment concerning them, and to enable them to difcern the real evi-dence and proof attending them. The truth is †, men of this caft feldom fearch with any defire of being convinced at all, or find-ing out fuch evidence as would carry con-viction with it. They had much rather ne-ver be convinced, and therefore their inquiries relate only to the difficulties of religion. They are always in queft after objections, fome appearance of contradiction, fomewhat that may furnifh them with matter of ridi-cule ; in a word, they are not follicitous to underftand the foundation of thofe truths that

* —— Male verum examinat omnis Corruptus Index. Hor. Sat. l. 2. Sat. 2.

† Acclinis falfis animus meliora recufat. Hor. ibid.

difpleafe

difpleafe them, but to provide themfelves with
fuch fpecious arguments againft them, as may
at leaft put them out of all pain upon account of them. And as the prejudices and
vices of men will eafily furnifh them with
topicks of this nature, a fuperficial enquiry
is beft for this purpofe, and that curfory carelefs view of things will be fufficient to help
on the ends of fcepticifm in religion, which
will by no means ferve to form a clear and
impartial judgment as to the great principles
of it. For

Though religious truths have the moft
certain foundation to fupport them, and may
be made appear, to minds rightly difpofed,
with the fulleft conviction, both as to their
certainty and importance ; yet they are of
that nature as to deferve and require very ferious confideration, to be maturely weighed,
and with a mind free from all prejudice and
biafs, otherwife the evidence, however near
to us, and fufficient in its own nature, will
efcape our obfervation, or at leaft not enter
into our minds with that clear light and force,
as to carry a fuitable conviction. If the paffions and appetites be allowed any fhare in the
decifion, the judgment cannot fail fo far to
be miftaken and falfe, the leaft objections
againft truth will heighten into very formida-
ble difficulties, and gradually arife to unan-
fwerable arguments againft the moft facred
principles, and the beft and moft fatisfying
folutions will be received with great indifference, and treated as unfatisfactory and deficient

cient. If the enquiry into them be flight
and fuperficial, and men choofe to take the
reprefentations of fuch as have themfelves
contracted an incurable diflike and averfion
to them, inftead of being at the pains of ho-
neftly examining for themfelves; it is no wonder, that when truth is mifreprefented to
them either by being fet up to fcorn in a *ridiculous* drefs, as abfurd and contrary to all
reafon; or fhewn them in a very *forbidding*
and *frightful* view, as creating groundlefs terrors, as inconfiftent with liberty, and deftructive of the pleafures and enjoyments of life;
or reproached and reviled as a wicked thing,
the creature of impofture, and the invention
of crafty and defigning men, to fubdue the
world, and keep others in the ftate of dependence on themfelves; I fay, 'tis no wonder, that truth under thefe difguifes fhould be
treated with contempt, or abhorrence by thofe,
that have never had time or inclination, to
give it any ferious examination themfelves,
and who are too much interefted againft it
to hear with patience a different account of
it from others, and too conceited of their
own knowledge and ability, to think they
need any farther information and inftruction.
Now on all thefe accounts men of pleafure
feem to be the moft incompetent judges of
truth, and the leaft likely ever clearly to difcern it. For it is a thing fo foreign to, of
fo quite a different nature from a pleafureable fenfual life, that 'tis impoffible they can
have any inclination to thofe feverer ftudies,
or

or the labours of reflection and enquiry, which are neceffary to underftand it. The continually hurry of diverfion, and their con- ftant purfuit of what amufes and gratifies them, employs their whole time, fo that they have no leifure for ferious thought, no fpare hours of life to enter into any confiderations becoming the dignity of human nature, and worthy the character of reafonable beings ; fo that nothing is more evident, than that their contempt of and rejecting the principles of religion is not the effect of mature delibe- ration, impartial enquiry, folid judgment and fuperior underftanding.

And indeed no one can imagine this, who confiders what fort of perfons they are, who now appear amongft us, to fhew the greateft difregard and moft fovereign contempt for all the great and effential articles of natural and revealed religion. They are generally fpeaking, *young perfons,* juft flipt into the character of men, educated either in all the hurries of fecular bufinefs, or amidft all the negligences, corruptions, luxuries and bad examples of riches and plenty, who have fcarce ever converfed with men of learning, knowledge and principle, who have read lit- tle, and thought lefs, who can never be fup- pofed to have formed any mature judgment, nor indeed ever had the proper time and op- portunity for entering ferioufly into religious fubjects, and who appear to be really incapa- ble of reafoning upon them, and almoft wholly ignorant of the nature of them. All
they

they know is what they have been *told* by
fome of their elder brethren in infidelity, who
began the world juft in the fame circumftances with themfelves ; or what they have
gathered from a few modern writings, in
which the doctrines of religion have been
wickedly blafphemed, or ridiculed, or impu-
dently condemned, as irrational, abfurd, and
contradictory, or through weaknefs mifiepre-
fented and perverted. And all they have,
many of them, learnt is, an air of affurance
and importance, great intrepidity in profanenefs, and the art of being profligate and vile,
withour fear of God, or remorfe of confcience. Thefe are infidels at fecond hand,
upon the foundation of credulity and implicit
faith ; and their arguments to defend themfelves are a feafonable jeft, a little borrowed
ridicule, a fmart invective, or a few properly
placed names of reproach on thofe who profefs to believe the principles of religion, and
efpecially on thofe whofe character and office
'tis to teach, and inftruct others in the knowledge of them. The cry of *enthufiafm, impofture, faith, credulity, bigotry, fuperftition,
prieftcraft,* and the like *magick* terms, doth
wonders with them, difarms reafon of all her
power, deftroys the force of demonftration,
difpoffeffes the evil fpirit of religion, transforms
piety into a mere creature of imagination,
turns Chriftianity into a fable, and all the
powers of the world to come into a dream, a
vifion, a romance. Would to God all that I
have faid in this defcription was a mere imagination

gination, and that there was no room for this complaint or reproach. But the thing is fact, it appears uppermoft in their converfation, and is the only ftrength of the infidelity of many, who have neither years nor knowledge, nor acquaintances enough with men or books, to render them competent mafters of the things, as to which they pertly decide, and pafs the moft fevere and pofitive judgment. As the firft part of their life hath been fpent in learning the affairs of trade and commerce, fo they have no fooner become their own mafters, but they have chofen the gay, the pleafurable part, and fallen into acquaintances, and contracted friendfhips with thofe, who have led them into all the fafhionable follies and extravagances of the times; whereby it hath been abfolutely out of their power to cultivate their minds, to improve their under-ftandings, or make any confiderable progrefs in wifdom and true knowledge. So that wherever religion be in its own nature, 'tis impoffible they fhould know much of it, either of the real and main difficulties, or the force and fufficiency of the evidences that attend it.

3. Hence this immoderate love of pleafure, this fenfual difpofition is the natural *preparative* for *downright infidelity,* and generally ends in it. *They believe not the truth, becaufe they take pleafure in unrighteoufnefs.* Inclination leads them to hope there is no God, and that all the principles of religion may be falfe. Their paffion for pleafure will not endure any curb or

or reftraint, and makes them determined enemies to truth and righteoufnefs; puts them
upon ufing violence to all the fobereft dictates
of confcience, renders them incapable of all
ferious confideration and reflection, hardens
their minds againft all poffible convictions,
creates an utter inattention to every kind of
evidence, and makes them the property of
wretches, who take a devilifh pleafure in
corrupting their principles and morals, and
bringing them to be as profane and wicked
and profligate as themfelves. *This is the condemnation, that light is come into the world. But
men love darknefs rather than light, becaufe their
deeds are evil.* And let it be obferved as a
ftanding mark of infamy, and eternal reproach
upon this voluptuary temper and courfe, that
it is, as will be fhewn, abfolutely inconfiftent
with all the valuable interefts of the prefent
life; fo that there is *one* path to *infidelity and
ruin,* and the fame way that leads to impiety
and contempt of principle, carries them on,
however fmoothly, yet infallibly, to all the
worft diftreffes and miferies of human nature. But

4. If through the ftrong and clear evidence
with which the great truths of religion are attended, men cannot thoroughly get rid of
their principles, fo as entirely to throw off
the belief of them, and renounce them as
wholly precarious and abfurd; yet the habitual
love of pleafure will render them *incapable of
attending* to them; fo that they will almoft
abfolutely lofe fight of them, and think of

them to as little purpofe, as though they intirely difbelieved them. Downright infidelity
is a length that even all bad men neither profefs nor dare to go ; they have fome general
fecret perfuafion, that there is fome truth in
religion, and there is generally fome feafon or
other in their life, fome interval of cool and
fober reflection, when their apprehenfion and
conviction of the reality of religious truths is
more affecting and lively. And notwithftanding their habitual wickednefs, and living as
though they had wholly difcarded all manner
of principles, yet they would reckon themfelves extreamly injured, fhould they be reproached as unbelievers, and warmly refent
and ftifly deny the charge of impiety and
atheifm. Allow them to be believers. Let
them keep poffeffion of their principles, yet
this muft be granted, that if they have them,
'tis *as though they had them not* ; if they are believers they are extreamly thoughtlefs ones,
and feldom if ever, but when fome kind of
unavoidable neceffity or other forces them,
reflect on what they believe, or confider the
proper influence and tendency of it. And
indeed how fhould they ? 'Tis impoffible the
mind fhould be attentive to two abfolutely
contrary fubjects at once, or equally divided
and ferioufly fixed at the fame time on Heaven
and earth, religion and pleafure, fpiritual and
fenfible objects, the improvement of the mind,
and the gratification of the bodily appetites and
paffions. *They that are after the flefh will mind
the things of the flefh, and they that are after the*
fpirit

fpirit will mind the things of the fpirit †. The prevailing difpofition will fuitably employ the thoughts, and in a great meafure exclude all other confiderations that are diffimilar to, and tend to interrupt and check the general biafs. What therefore fignify principles ? The fenfualift's head is engroffed by thoughts of a quite foreign nature, and as to them he hath laid them afide as ufelefs lumber, of no fignification and value ; as things with which he hath no concern, or much too dull to be admitted to any fhare of his converfation and friendfhip. Gayer fcenes attract his eye, and more fprightly images are perpetually fluttering before his imagination, that will not give him leifure to receive any other impreffions, or admit fuch confiderations, as have a tendency to check the pleafing profpects, and cool the warm defires of his heart. And therefore,

5. The confequence of this will certainly be, that whatever his *principles* are, they will have *no influence* on him, or power fuitably to affect him ; whereby he will be juft the fame man, as to his moral temper and conduct, as though he had intirely difcharged them, and given them up as altogether groundlefs. For if principles, though ever fo good, are kept conftantly out of fight, they muft be as conftantly difregarded, and the effect of fuch an habitual neglect and contempt of them muft be an utter incapacity in them to excite an-

† Rom. viii. 5.

fwerable

fwerable difpofitions, and to produce any valuable and worthy fruits. Nothing can operate
where it is not, and therefore abfent principles
muft, in the nature of the thing, be wholly
ineffectual ; and you will always find it true,
that inconfiderate and thoughtlefs men, or,
which is the fame thing, men that never think
of any thing but their pleafures and fenfual
gratifications, are ever irreligious and bad
men. Principles influence the mind, not by
any natural or phyfical force, or neceffarily as
pleafure or pain affect the body, and make
men attentive to them whether they will or
no ; but in a quite different manner, and for
their agency depend on the permiffion of the
will, the confent of the heart, and the leave
of the governing inclinations and paffions.
They muft be placed before the mind in the
cleareft view, and held up to conftant infpection and attention. They muft be difcerned in their full evidence and certainty, in
all their connections and confequences, and
in their unfpeakable and infinite importance
to us. They muft be again and again impreffed on the heart and confcience by the
moft fixed and frequent confideration, and
they fhould be ftrengthened and quickened
and warmed by the moft ferious prayers unto
God, that he would enable us to preferve a
lively fenfe of them in our minds, and fubject
ourfelves intirely to the facred guidance of
them. Whatever paffions or affections tend
to weaken our regard to them, or fupprefs
their natural influence, fhould with the utmost

most caution be guarded against, and nothing
allowed in us that can offer the least violence
or injury to it. With principles thus cultivated, thus diligently tended and nourished,
we shall *neither be barren nor unfruitful in our
knowledge.* They will prosper and thrive in
the mind that thus receives them, and discover their genuine worth and powerful influence in all the substantial fruits of real
piety and goodness. But can such an improvement and management of principles ever
be expected from a man of pleasure? His attention is led off to a thousand different objects. He studiously avoids and flies from all
reflections of this kind. He is uneasy whenever by chance they steal or force themselves
into his mind, and ever thinks their visits
unseasonable and impertinent. He studies
his face more than his heart, his glass oftener
than his creed, the fashion, the colour, the
garnish of his dress, more exactly than the
habit of his mind, the call of his passions
rather than the dictate of his conscience, what
pleases and regales instead of what may profit
him, what may keep up the elegance, the
splendor, and luxury of life, instead of what
may add to the perfection, rectitude and dignity of his rational being ; in a word, how
he may *kill the time* by seasonable successions
of amusements, follies, and vices, rather than
how he may improve it in fixing right sentiments of truth in his mind, and securing the
proper influence of them over his conduct. So
that should such a one profess to believe the

best

beft principles, and to be ever fo firmly perfuaded of them, his belief muft be abfolutely
ineffectual and dead, and wholly ufelefs as
to all the purpofes of true religion and virtue. But

6. In confequence of this difbelief of, inattention to, and inefficacy of principle, which
is the conftant attendant of this immoderate
love of pleafure, there will be farther *an utter
want of that rational regard to God,* of all thofe
right affections and 'difpofitions towards him, in
which the very effence of true piety confifts,
and without which all external fervices whatfoever will be of no value in the nature of
things, or in the eftimation of God. This
awful fenfe of Deity cannot poffibly be duly
cultivated and rightly cherifhed, unlefs we
are at proper feafons abftracted from every
thing of a fenfual nature, divorced from all
the pleafing amufements of life, and wholly
attentive to the moft grave and fober, and ferious reflections. The general belief of the
being, perfections, and providence of God,
is of itfelf of but little confequence in religion,
and unlefs actually and habitually prefent to
the mind, can never excite that reverential
fear, that warm affection, that ftrong gratitude,
that chearful truft, that firm confidence, that
fixed delight in, that defire to pleafe, and
that ambition to be accepted of God, which
are all indifpenfible ingredients of a rational
piety. Faith in him is indeed the root of all
other graces; but unlefs the ground in which
'tis planted be duly prepared, cleanfed from
every

every thing offensive, and the root itself in it carefully cherished by a due proportion both of moisture and warmth, 'tis impossible it can live, send forth fresh fibres, open into bloom, or bring forth any of its fruits to maturity and perfection. Fixed and frequent consideration on the perfections and character of God, is one of the most effectual means that carries nourishment to this sacred principle, enlivens, quickens, and renders it vigorous and active, conveys its influence to the several affections and passions, and thus exalts them above their natural state, and transforms them into the more excellent and worthy dispositions of genuine piety. But what room for reflections of this kind in one, that hath no sort of relish but for sensual pleasure, and resigns himself entirely to the possession of it ? How can he be attentive to the considerations of Deity, how can *God dwell in him*, and fill his mind, and employ his powers, when the whole current of his thoughts is drawn into a quite different channel, and directed into a course that terminates at the utmost distance from him ? But unless we thus set God continually before us, and solemnly introduce him into our souls, in all the substantial and affecting glories of his being, what possible sentiments of piety can arise in our breasts, or what one right affection can we exercise towards this most excellent and adorable object ? What possible veneration and reverence can there be in us for his majesty, if a thousand gaudy

F 4 images

images are erected in our souls, which we are continually admiring and adoring ? What room can there be for the love of God, or for complacency and delight in him, if we are professed votaries of *Mammon*, *Belial*, and other the foul idols that vice and vanity have erected in opposition to him ? How can we exercise that humble trust and chearful hope in his power and goodness, which are essential to the character of a religious man, if sensual gratifications constantly banish from our minds all thoughts of those divine perfections, which alone can support the exercise of those graces ? What biass can there be in the soul towards God, what tendency to rest in him, as its portion and exceeding great reward, whose affections bind it down to earthly objects, and entirely estrange and separate it from its great original ? Supposing the objects on which men thus immoderately set their hearts were in themselves lawful, and the pleasures that engrossed them could not be said in their own nature to be criminal, yet 'tis impossible that truly religious sentiments and dispositions of real piety could ever prosper in such a state of mind, because the affections can never center with *a superior force* on two directly contrary objects; no, nor embrace them with an equal ardency and warmth. All fixed dispositions and prevalent habits in favour of the lower pleasures, that are relative only to the body and the present world, do necessarily weaken and retard the flow of the passions towards invisible and spiritual things ; so that in an

exact

exaɛt and unalterable proportion as our affections tend to created and corporeal good,
they will withdraw themfelves from and grow
cool towards him, who as the fupreain perfection and excellency deferves our beft and
higheft regards. What then fhall we fay to
the pleafures of fin, and to the habits that
men contraɛt of criminal gratifications ? If
the love of pleafures, in their nature innocent, may gain fuch an afcendency in us, as
almoft to fupplant all right affeɛtions towards
God, how is it poffible that thefe affeɛtions
fhould ever fubfift in the midft of paffions di-
reɛtly and unalterably finful, or flourifh in
minds that aie enfiaved by habits of wickednefs and vice ? In the former cafe, the root
of faith is impoverifhed and ftarved, by drawing from it all the kindly juices and nourifhment that fhould invigorate and fupply it ;
in the latter cafe, it is really killed by thofe
poifonous and deftruɛtive weeds, which fuffer
no feeds of piety whatfoever to live around
them. And indeed the love of pleafures, di-
reɛtly finful, eradicates the awes of God,
defaces all impreffions on the mind arifing
from the fenfe of deity, wholly fuppreffes all
tendernefs of confcience, fteels the heart
againft the terrors of the divine anger, con-
ceals from the view every pleafing profpeɛt of
God, and creates a dreadful incapacity for
loving and delighting in him ; ftifles every
tendency to ingenuous gratitude, and is abfolutely inconfiftent with the exeicife of it ; fub-
verts the very foundation of hope and truft in
God,

God, takes of every biafs of the foul tending
to him as its proper happinefs ; and, in a word,
intirely indifpofes and difables it for all acquaintance with God, and extinguifhes thofe
facred affections towards him, in which the
life and power of real religion and godlinefs
confift. But farther,

7. Another bad effect of this voluptuary
and fenfual difpofition, and which fhews
how inconfiftent it is with the life and
profperity of true religion, is : Its *bad influence* in reference to all the *external expreffions, means and inftruments of real piety*, by
which the inward principles are difcovered,
and the religious fpirit and temper is preferved, cultivated and improved. All inward
difpofitions have natural and proper methods
of manifefting themfelves, vifible fruits that
indicate of what nature they are, as certainly
as the tree is known by what it produces ;
and there are fuitable means for cultivating
difpofitions and habits of a moral and religious nature, without which they will not
thrive, nor even become fuperior in their influence to the impulfes of our animal affections and paffions. Thefe, as natural to us,
are infeparable from us, and need nothing
of art, endeavour, or ftudy to ftrengthen
them. 'Tis the bufinefs of a wife and good
man's life to fubdue, reftrain and regulate
them. The other, the fentiments and habits
of true piety and goodnefs may be truly faid
to be adventitious ; that do not, like the other,
fpring up out of the foil of unimproved nature,

ture, but are the fruits of cultivation, and that need therefore perpetual care, watchfulnefs and induftry to maintain their life, their vigour and their beauty. 'Tis I believe fcarce poffible to imagine, how inward fentiments and habits of piety can difcover themfelves, by external correfpondent actions, otherwife than by fixed meditations on God, folemn adoration of his infinite perfections and majefty, fuitable praifes and thankfgivings for his benefits, fervent fupplication and prayer for his continued protection and favour, care to imitate him, and by a chearful attendance on all thofe inftitutions which are proper in their nature, and appointed by God, to keep up the life and fpirit of true devotion and piety. Thefe things are both genuine expreffions of an inward reverence and efteem for God, and help to confirm them ; and I apprehend that an internal principle of true religion and godlinefs will fhew and exert itfelf in fruits of this kind, as naturally and invariably, as every feed arifes into its diftinguifhing production, and can be expreffed by no other figns and evidences whatfoever.

1. But how *heartlefs* and *indifpofed* to all exercifes and fervices of this nature, muft the *man of pleafure* naturally be ? How is it poffible he fhould fo far abftract himfelf from the world, and all the concerns of it, as is neceffary to his having any relifh and tafte for employments of this kind, who hath wholly accuftomed himfelf to converfe with fenfible objects only ? If he be taken up with the
impertinences

impertinences and follies of life, which cannot be termed directly and in their nature
criminal; if the gay, the polite, the fashionable world is his great study and care, and
his thoughts habitually employed on the
splendid trifles and shewy amusements, to
which the noble, the great, the rich in general attend, for which alone they almost
think themselves made, and for a more liberal
indulgence in which they imagine their titles,
their honours and their fortunes to be their
peculiar priviledge; if, I say, the inclination
to these impertinences of life becomes the
prevailing passion, and the fancy and imagination be fully and constantly possessed with
them, the effect must be a settled disinclina-
tion and inability to all the exercises of godliness. For sober reasoning and thought upon
abstracted subjects and invisible objects, can
never employ the head that is crowded with
material and sensible images; and if the world
hath always free admission into the heart, God
must necessarily be excluded from it. Converse with him will be a difficult task. 'Tis
an exercise so foreign to what the sensualist
hath habituated himself, that he will neither
know how to set about it, or by what means
to carry it on. The faculty is obtained by
experience and use, and can be improved only
by frequency and application. Whenever he
attempts any thing of this nature, 'tis impossible his heart can be fixed, his thoughts
coherent, his reasonings connected, or his apprehensions clear; and therefore as impossible
that

that his affections can be warmed, or any
fuch pleafure experienced in it, as is neceffary
to reconcile him to the work and render it
an entertainment to him. The effect of
which muft be a growing reluctance to fuch
engagements, the becoming weary of them,
the looking on them as an unpleafing tafk
and burthen, the framing to our minds ex-
cufes and apologies for the neglecting of
them, the gladly laying hold of every opportunity that offers to omit them ; 'till by
frequent omiffions, the uneafinefs arifing from
fuch omiffions gradually ceafe, whereby they
become more and more frequent, and at laft,
which is frequently the cafe, they are entirely
thrown up, without any remaining remorfe of
confcience on account of it.

2. Yea, fometimes this fenfual, pleafureable
difpofition fo far prevails over and deceives
men, as that they are at laft taught to *defend
themfelves in fuch omiffions* by fpecious reafonings, and appearances of argument. If they
are preffed to that folemn converfe with God,
which is implied in prayer to him, and in
the facrifice of thankfgiving and praife, they
will tell us ; " that God knows our wants
" without our telling him, that he is immu-
" table, and our prayers cannot change him,
" that he doth not want our praifes, and
" can receive no benefit by them, and that
" morality and a virtuous life, are the beft
" recompence we can make for all the di-
" vine benefits ;" as if we were not to *acknowledge our dependence* on God becaufe he
knows

knows we are dependent, or as if God could
not be immutable if, according to his own
immutable perfection, he varied the external
methods of his providence, and vouchfafed
his favours according to the moral circumftances of his creatures; or as if God's not
wanting any thing from us could make any
alteration in our relation and duty to him,
who want every thing from him; or morality
could be compleat if men forget their obligation to God ; or the practice of moral virtue to men could excufe us from a right
difpofition and conduct towards him. Objections of this kind are not founded on *reafon*, but fpring out of *difinclination* and prejudice to thefe great duties and expreffions of
piety, which if regularly attended to, would
check that inclination to pleafure they are refolved to cherifh, and indulge freely. In like
manner, the attendance on all the publick
fervices of the houfe of God, they look on
as quite unneceffary, and a periodical worfhip they imagine hath nothing to fupport
it. They are exceeding wife themfelves,
and know as much as the preacher can tell
them. Or they can read a good book at
home, or meditate abroad with equal devotion as in the church. Every day is alike
proper for religion, and they know not why
they fhould be more religious one day than
another ; with other objections of like force.
But a man need not be very acute to fee
through the fallacy of thefe arguments. If
they are fo very *knowing*, do they never need

to be *put in mind* of what they know ? Do
not men of pleafure need it almoft above all
other men ? Can *publick worfhip* be fupported
without *fixed times* and feafons, and is not pe-
riodick worfhip therefore as neceffary as any
publick worfhip at all ? Is devotion that is
altogether private equally conducive to the
publick good as *focial ?* Is not the publick
expreffion of reverence for God a publick
teftimony in favour of religion, and therefore
a very great encouragement to it, and one
method of putting fome check to national
impiety and vice ? Is not a nation, as fuch, one
political body and perfon, that hath its blefs-
ings to afk of God, and is to be thankful for
the receipt of them ; and therefore why are not
expreffions of piety as neceffary and proper
from the publick perfon as from individuals ?
Suppofing *fome few* could gain as much benefit
by a good book at home as by publick inftruction, can this be faid of *all*, or the ma-
jor part ? Is there not therefore fomewhat
due from every one by way of example to
the publick ; doth it not anfwer a good end
to lead and invite and encourage others to
attend on thofe publick fervices, which are
neceffary to their inftruction, and to preferve
alive in them any fenfe of God, any regard
to principle and the practice of true virtue ?
And fuppofing for once, that there are fome
peculiar advantages in publick worfhip, that
are to be expected no other ways, fuppofing
it to be an *inftitution of God*, and that his
prefence and bleffing may reafonably be hoped
for

for in the uſe of it ; what will all theſe pretended arguments againſt it prove ? What,
that ſocial worſhip is an impertinent and unneceſſary thing ? Or that God hath done
wrong to appoint or expect it ? Or rather,
that men themſelves are in an extream bad
diſpoſition, who are thus entirely diſaffected
to it, and ſtrive to impoſe on themſelves,
and by fallacious arguments to juſtify a conduct, that I am perſuaded may be proved contrary to the moſt certain principles of natural
and revealed religion.

From theſe ſort of arguments, which are
the main pleas of your men of liberty and
pleaſure, 'tis evident that the great thing they
want and aim at, is, wholly to baniſh all expreſſions of regard to and reverence for God
and his providence, both out of publick and
private life. If prayer and thankſgiving to
God be unneceſſary for the reaſons they urge,
the devotions of the cloſet, and the beſt part
of thoſe of the church muſt abſolutely ceaſe
at once, and in truth almoſt every thing of
religious worſhip, God, the object of it, and
every thing relative to him be wholly diſ-
carded from amongſt mankind. And in conſequence of this, all inſtruction muſt be thrown
by, or become an exceeding poor, lifeleſs,
and impertinent thing ; for if men are not
to be taught their duty to God, nor led into
the veneration of his majeſty, nor morality to
be urged on them by the authority and awes
of God, every thing elſe that can be taught
them will be of little conſequence to morality ;

rality ; which without this will want the beft
and fureft motives to fupport and encourage
the practice of it.

3. Hence 'tis no wonder, that under the
influence of fuch a difpofition, they fhould
never themfelves *appear in an affembly for re-*
ligious worſhip, and take as much care to keep
out of a church, as they do out of a charnel
houfe or fepulchre. Nothing that is regularly
tranfacted there can be the leaft entertainment
to them. They are barbarians as to the very
language made ufe of in the houfe of God,
and cannot conceive the meaning of the
terms with which devotion cloaths itfelf.
Pray they cannot. They have neither the
knowledge nor the heart to do it. The blefs-
ings that good men afk are to them undefirable, and many of them fuch as they are
determined never to accept at the hands of
God. The exercife of gratitude to God they
are ftrangers to, know not whether or no they
are indebted to him for thofe external blefs-
ings in which they place their happinefs ; and
as to others, they neither have them, nor
wifh to have them, and therefore owe nothing upon account of them, and thus in
their own imagination have as little reafon,
as in reality inclination to be thankful. And
therefore the offering praifes to God muft,
upon their principles, appear an unneceffary
and impertinent fuperftition. As to all publick inftruction, they hold it in the moft fovereign contempt. A difcourfe concerning
religion is enthufiafm and cant. Morality is a

dry, infipid fubject, of which they have no
relifh. Their ears are too delicate to hear
any thing about a future judgment and the
punifhments of a life to come, and they
would be apt to charge the preacher with want
of decency and politenefs, fhould he, if they
were accidentally prefent, grate their ears
with fuch harfh and unpleafing founds. To
reproach them for their fins would be rude-
nefs. To prefs them to repentance, impertinence. To threaten them with divine vengeance, nothing fhort of prefumption and
infolence : And therefore to avoid all uneafinefs on thefe accounts, they feldom come
near the places where thefe difagreeable fubjects are made mention of. And for this
reafon the weekly day of worfhip is perverted
by them into quite a different ufe and purpofe from its original intention, either wafted
in fleep and floth and indolence at home,
or partly loitered away in houfes of refort,
kept open for the men that have nothing to
do with Almighty God, and think their own
fouls of too little worth to deferve any care
to fave them ; or partly trifled away in the
impertinences of drefs and vifit; or proftituted in private diverfions, games, and entertainments, that in the manner they practice
them are fcarce lawful on any day ; or abufed
in adjufting and fettling their worldly affairs
and accounts, becaufe they have no thoughts,
or views, or hopes as to a future ftate. In
a word, as 'tis a day, in which no publick
diverfions are as yet authorifed, I know not
what

what time may produce, 'tis an almoſt loſt day to them, which they ſcarce know how to fill up, which lies tedioufly upon their hands, and on which they are glad of any thing, except the exercifes proper to the day, to paſs away the time, and keep themfelves from the plague of reflection, and the hated drudgery of worſhipping God.

4. Or if through cuſtom, or ſome remaining tendernefs of confcience, they cannot wholly abſtain from the houſe of God, how can it be that they ſhould receive any *real benefit* from the fervices of it ? For

1. They are *incapable of attending to them.* Frequently the foregoing evening is ſpent by them in ſuch entertainments, as have filled their minds with ideas but little favourable to the ſpirit of piety, and in ſuch company and diverfions, as no one ever imagined would contribute any thing to the life and fervour of true devotion ; amidſt fcenes, the impreffions of which are not eafily forgotten, and which cannot but frequently crowd in upon them in thofe folemnities, where men ſhould be entirely abſtracted from all the vanities of life, and wholly intent upon much more excellent and intereſting objects ; fo that their minds are abfent, and they ſcarce bear any part in the fervices at which they are prefent ; on which account they deferve a ſhare in that character which God hath fo feverely threatened : *This people draws near me with their mouth, and with their lips do they honour me,*

me, but have removed their heart far from me †.
If through fullnefs, or the fatigue of diverfion, they are not oppreffed with drowfinefs,
and heavy with fleep, the remembrance of paft
entertainments takes up their minds, or future affignations and parties of pleafure warm
their hopes, and are enjoyed by lively anti-
cipation ; or the drefs of the audience attracts their obfervation, fo that Heaven hath
no more of their eyes than their hearts ; or
by fecret whifpers, and the indecency of
laughter in the countenance, they betray an
inward contempt for the fervices they fhould
be engaged in, and too plainly difcover that
God is not in all their thoughts. In a word,
their reflections are diffipated, their attention,
if there be any, diftracted, and their affections utterly fenfelefs and unmoved ; fo that
they cannot unite their hearts to fear God,
and if they offer him any thing, what muft
it but the *facrifice of fools ?*

2. If they could attend to the fervices of
the houfe of God, yet they could not bear
any *hearty willing part in them.* How is it
indeed poffible, that they fhould cordially
join in any of the folemnities of religious
worfhip, when all of them tend to awaken
and fix a difpofition directly the reverfe of
what influences and governs them ? Can
they with fincerity fay Amen to prayers,
that God would *create in them clean hearts, and*

† Ifaiah xix. 13.

renew

renew right fpirits within them, that he would
fave them from the vanities of life, and the
delufions of pleafure, and enable them to *fix
their affections on things that are above, and not
on things that are on earth?* Will not habit
and paffion reluctate rather to fuch an affent?
Will not fuch requefts appear to them unneceffary, and favouring of fuperftition, four-
nefs, and precifion? Or will they not through
partiality and felf deceit forget their own immediate concern in prayers of this nature,
and imagine, that however reafonable they are
in themfelves, they do not affect their character and conduct, as feeing nothing criminal
in themfelves, and being unwilling to believe
that what they love is inconfiftent with religion, or offenfive to God? If fuch fubjects
are infifted on, in the courfe of publick inftruction, as tend to cenfure their conduct,
and reprefent the folly and danger of it; either they are offended with the preacher as
ufing indecent liberties, and levelling his difcourfes immediately againft them, meddling
with things quite out of his fphere; or treat
him with contempt, as inveighing againft
pleafures he is not able to come at, and
finding fault with innocent gratifications, in
which through intereft, or morofenefs, or
needlefs fingularity he refufes to partake; or
fortify themfelves againft all that he can
fay to them, by refolving immediately to
forget it, or by fheltering themfelves in fome
faving opinions, that may give hopes of final
mercy without repentance and reformation.

3. If

3. If on thefe accounts perfons are not at laft prevailed on wholly to abfent themfelves from the folemnities of worfhip, yet they effectually *prevent* all manner of *good influence* and *ferious impreffions* on themfelves in the ufe of them. Heedlefs, inattentive prayers can never affect the mind, nor derive any fupplies of grace from God. They are mere ufelefs breath, blown away long before they reach his throne ; or if they find their way thither, appear only as arguments of the infincerity and hypocrify of the offerer ; fo that as they do not proceed from, fo they leave no traces of a ferious fpirit behind them, nor contribute any thing to fix the difpofition of piety by their acceptance and prevalence with Almighty God. In themfelves they are lighter than vanity, and in his account they are foolifhnefs and an abomination. Nor will the inftructions of religion find their way into the confcience, quicken the active powers, be attended with fuccefs, or conduce to the purpofes of real religion, however pertinent and clear they may be in themfelves, and with whatever warmth and ferioufnefs they may be enforced, if the firft attention to them be negligent, or the after remembrance of them be entirely excluded. What fignifies preaching, if the minds of the hearers be not engaged ; or what would even an Apoftle be, as to any good effect, better than founding brafs or a tinkling cymbal, if the ear was entirely difaffected to the mufick of his inftruction, or if that was heard through a medium

dium that would render it indistinct or grating ? It is confessed, that the preaching of the gospel is too frequently wholly ineffectual, and the number of converts it makes to religion and virtue comparatively but small. And there are many causes that contribute to this evil. But is not the principal one frequently in the indisposition of the hearer ? Doth he come with that temper which is necessary to his profiting ? Doth he attend to publick instruction as an institution appointed by God for his. improvement in the life of faith and piety ? Doth he ruminate on what he hears, and digest it by serious reflection, and a faithful application of what he hears to his own condition and character ? If he receives at any time any good impressions or right convictions, doth he cherish them and fix them by proper consideration ? If the love of pleasure be uppermost in the heart, this can never be done. Impressions of this kind, in a sensual disposition, cannot be permanent. The prevailing habit will soon efface them, and when neglected they will instantly die.

Our blessed Saviour hath well compared the truths of his religion to *good seed*, and the different sort of hearers to different kinds of ground, on which the seed falls. *Formal* and *heedless hearers* he likens to the *way side* and *the seed falling on it*, because as such seed never enters the ground, so the doctrines of religion never enter into the understandings and hearts of such persons ; *the wicked one catches*

away

away the word, as the fowls of the air do the feed fcattered on the high road. Other hearers are compared to *ground full of thorns* on which the feed is fown, which indeed may come up, but cannot thrive or live long, becaufe kept down and deftroyed by the foul-nefs of the ground on which it fell ; repre-fenting thofe who having heard his word, *go forth and are choaked with cares and riches, and the pleafures of this life, and fo bring forth no fruit to perfection* *. Both the feed muft be good, and the foil proper and well cleanfed, or the hopes of a confiderable harveft muft be difappointed. Hence the inefficacy of the Chriftian doctrine, and the inftructions of the houfe of God, on fuch large numbers who wear the Chriftian name, may be moft certainly accounted for, without fuppofing any defect in the doctrine itfelf, or internal inaptitude and impotency to promote the ends of religion and virtue. A love of moral truth and a firm belief of it, are the proper difpo-fitions to receive the doctrines of Chrift. It is this that makes the ground, the *heart good.* If it falls on any other foil, or meets with a contrary difpofition, 'tis impoffible it can live, take root, fpring up with vigour into real and permanent good habits, or produce any valuable increafe, any genuine fruits of righ-teoufnefs in due proportion or abundance. Or if there be any natural goodnefs in the foil, any native ingenuity of mind, or origi-

* Luke viii. 14.

nal

nal tendency to truth and righteoufnefs, yet
if through an habitual and criminal neglect,
fenfual affections have been fuffered to prevail, and a long courfe of indulgence to appetite and inclination hath fixed and rivetted
the love of pleafure, fo that the mind is filled
with lively images and ftrong defires, paffionately fond, and eagerly bent to the purfuit
and enjoyment of it ; the natural goodnefs
of the ground in fuch a cafe will be of no
avail, whilft thefe thorns and briars, thefe
noxious and deftructive weeds are encouraged,
and fuffered to grow at liberty and unmo-
lefted. The beft principles that can be offered to fuch a one's confideration can carry
but little conviction, nor the warmeft and
wifeft inftructions, how well foever adapted
to do good, make any deep or lafting impreffions ; becaufe of the return and prevalence of ftronger paffions, that foon efface
all weaker traces on the mind, or prevent it
from receiving any in favour of Chriftian piety
and goodnefs.

This is an effect that arifes out of the very
nature of things, and the narrow capacity of
the human mind, which cannot retain, nor
fteadily view at once a multiplicity of objects,
nor be equally impreffed and affected at the
fame time by fuch as are of a quite different
and contrary nature. As a ftream can never
run contrary to itfelf, fo neither can the inclinations and paffions; and therefore if they
flow with their full ftrength to fenfible appearances, the gratification of the appetites,
and

and thofe pomps and pleafures of the world,
which are all the heaven and happinefs that
the generality defire ; all other tendencies will
be too feeble to refift the impetuous ftream,
and be eafily borne down by the prevailing
current. So that if we confider only the
frame of our own being, and attend to the
natural workings of thofe paffions that are
inferted into it ; men of pleafure can reap no
advantage from any of the fervices of the
houfe of God, and the temper they bring
with them into it will either render them abfolutely ftupid and infenfible under every perfuafive that revelation can offer to a religious
life ; or enervate and fupprefs every rifing fentiment and difpofition in favour of it, before
it gains root and ftrength enough to bring
forth fruit to maturity.

4. Or if we confider the inftitutions of
publick worfhip as appointed for the *communication of the divine affiftance and grace*, and as
means of deriving from God any peculiar
aids and fupports, fuitable to the fpecial difficulties of a religious life, in which view I
think all the inftances both of private and
publick devotion fhould be confidered ; what
profpect or hope can men under the influence
and power of a fenfual difpofition reafonably
form of obtaining any fuch influences from
the God of grace ? Or what likelihood is
there that impreffions of this kind, if received, fhould be permanent and effectual.
I know indeed what God can do in this refpect if he pleafes, and poffibly fome few in-

ftances

ftances of extraordinary converfions may be produced, by fudden ftrong impreffions on the mind that have been happily fuccefsful. But there is no reafoning from what God *may do*, to what *he will do*, nor from a few *extraordinary* cafes to the *common* and ordinary courfe of his dealings with men. God can produce an harveft out of the ground by his almighty power without the hufbandman's labour and care, if he faw fit to do it. But fhould the hufbandman refufe to fow his ground in expectation of fuch a miraculous harveft, would any one wonder at his difappointment? What is it to men in fuch inftances to confider what God can do, when the obvious thought that fhould poffefs them is, what God ufually doth, and what he hath given them reafon and encouragement to hope he will do. If the *good feed* be, like that fcattered by *the way fide*, that never falls into the ground, is fuffered to make no impreffion at all upon the heart and confcience; where hath God promifed to make it fpring up? Or to prevent the evil one from catching it away? Or if it fhould ftrike root, yet if it falls into an heart poffeffed with the love of riches, and a prevailing fondnefs for fenfual pleafures, hath God undertaken by an extraordinary power to prevent its being choaked up and wholly deftroyed? God's grace is unqueftionably *free*. But doth it therefore follow that God will give it where 'tis *neither offered*, nor defired, nor the means of obtaining it rightly *improved*? Or that he will beftow it on men who,

who, by being immerfed in pleafurable indulgences, are really incapable of receiving
and gaining any advantage by it. Senfualifts
are of all others the moft unlikely to receive
grace from God, and to find a bleffing from
him in the inftitutions of worfhip, becaufe,
generally fpeaking, there is nothing in them
on which religious impreffions can faften, no
hold to be taken of their confciences, nor
any room for the admiflion of principles to
operate in their minds, nor any one of their
affections but what is ftrongly engaged in favour of their pleafures, and deeply prepoffeffed
in prejudice of every thing of a religious
nature. And if you make your obfervations
you will find, that few of this complection
and character, comparatively fpeaking, are
ever recovered, either by extraordinary or
ordinary means, to real piety and virtue ; becaufe nothing renders the mind fo incapable
of and averfe to thofe fentiments and difpofitions, which are effential to the life and
power of godlinefs, as a ftrengthened, confirmed habit of fenfual indulgence. So that
divine influences falling on fuch perfons would
be like the fruitful fhowers, or the warming
beams of the fun falling on a rock, or the
fand, or the furface of the fea, that make no
kind of vifible alteration in them, and cannot,
in the nature of the thing, produce either
verdure or fruitfulnefs. So that in every view
men of pleafure preclude themfelves from all
the advantages that may be otherwife expected
in the ufe of the feveral means and inftruments

of

of religion and virtue, and cherifh within themfelves a temper that renders all the provifions of the grace of God wholly ineffectual to recover them to a fenfe of their duty and a proper meetnefs for their higheft and moft durable happinefs; and which therefore muft be allowed to be a temper highly differviceable to the caufe and intereft of ferious piety and godlinefs. And this will farther appear if we confider,

IV. The bad influence which a prevailing love of pleafure hath upon mens families; and I am convinced that the confequence muft unavoidably be an increafing difinclination to every thing of a religious nature, and at length an abfolute want of all manner of concern and thought about it; and that nothing fhort of this can be expected, according to the ordinary courfe of things. But of this in the next difcourfe.

SERMON

SERMON IV.

Voluptuoufnefs deſtructive to Mens Families and fecular Intereſts.

2 TIMOTHY iii. 4.

Lovers of pleaſure more than lovers of God.

IN fome preceding difcourfes I have defcribed this temper, and proved it to be
very criminal, and fhewn its fatal influence
in feveral important inftances. To thofe I
have named, I would now add,

IV. The *bad influence* which a prevailing
love of pleafure hath upon *mens families.*

'Tis natural to think that if parents are fo
fond of pleafure, as to neglect the cultivation
and improvement of their *own minds* in religious habits, principles and difpofitions, they
will be but little follicitous of inftilling them
into *their children,* and never think it worth
while to excite in them a relifh for what they
have no tafte of themfelves ; much lefs for
that to which they have contracted a ftrong
difinclination or real averfion. Frequently
they have neither time nor ability to give their
children

children any rational information. They have a multitude of *important trifles* on their hands, that are of too great moment to be neglected for the fake of that part of education, which they don't think of any great confequence or neceffity, and which, as they have been without, or at leaft got rid of, as to any abiding effects, they cannot be perfuaded is any ways effential to the welfare and happinefs of their families. Many of them indeed, have not fo much as an idea of the common principles of religion, or if they have, hold them in the moft fovereign contempt, and never think or fpeak of them but with derifion ; and therefore are fo far from any defire or care to inftil into their childrens minds any knowledge or reverence of thefe things, that they breed them up in the deepeft ignorance of thefe, or with an hereditary averfion and enmity to them. Yea, too many, who have had themfelves the advantage of a religious education, yet having loft almoft all the good impreffions of it, by entering into the acquaintances and practices of the fafhionable and well bred, look upon themfelves as under a kind of obligation to bring up their children according to the prevailing tafte, and give them an education that we ufually call a genteel and polite one. They are oftentimes at great expence for mafters to inftruct them, and begrudge nothing they can lay out to refine and accomplifh them. But then piety, morality, and the principles neceffary to fupport the practice of thefe are never confidered as part of a polite

polite education, as real accompliſhments of
human nature, and neceſſary to ſhine and appear with advantage in the world. Theſe
kind of things are quite grown out of faſhion
and repute, and ſhould any one venture to
appear with accompliſhments of this nature,
amongſt the gay and elegant part of mankind, they would look upon his dreſs as
much out of all mode and character, as though
he had cloathed himſelf with *the antiquated
habit* of a century or two paſt. To poliſh the
mind, to refine the manners, and to teach
moral elegance of behaviour, is not the art
nor turn of the preſent times. The artiſts
and inſtructors now ſought after, are not men
that can teach wiſdom, or inform the underſtanding, that will read lectures on the reverence due to deity, the government of the
paſſions, the obligations of benevolence and
juſtice, the rules of honour, publick ſpirit,
the love of our country, the contempt of indolence and pleaſure, the foundations of moral virtue, or on any ſubject that may render
them bleſſings in private, and ornaments in
publick life : No. But ſuch as can inſtruct
the feet to move, and give *a graceful air* to
the body only ; ſuch as can teach the fingers
to play, and the voice to bear a part in any
harmony but that which is employed in
praiſing the univerſal Creator : Such as have
an exquiſite taſte and ſkill in the ſcience of
faſhion, great depth of judgment in forming
their pupils into an external elegance of appearance, richneſs of fancy and invention in
the

the ornaments of dress, the furniture of our houses, or the disposition of a table; such who can provide new entertainments for the publick, or nicely and exactly regulate and conduct them, or form others into the behaviour that may make them appear with advantage in them. Education in families of fortune, pleasure and gaiety is almost universally confined to these and the like particulars; and though I am far from censuring every thing of this nature, as criminal, or improper for persons of fortune or station, yea, though I think them in their measure truly ornamental, and such as ought not to be wholly omitted, where the rank of life requires it, and there is a due affluence of fortune to support it; yet when education is wholly imployed in these things, and all the care of parents is only to instruct their children in the nature and use of these *fashionable elegances*; every one must see that children must grow up wholly destitute of all better principles, and almost without so much as a distant tendency of mind to true religion and virtue.

Especially when there is not only *a want of due cultivation* and instruction, but the constant influence of *example*, leading them almost from their very infancy into a life of pleasure, indulgence and sensuality; whereby the natural inclination to these things is heightened, and grows into such a fixed and permanent habit, as to become almost incurable. Pleasure is in itself an artful enchantress, grateful to sense and inclination, and the earliest care should be taken to check the tendency to it, and prevent an immoderate fondness for it. We need no incentives to pursue it, no examples to lead us into the love and indulgence of it. If nature be left to itself, to follow its own dictates, and gratify its own passions and affections, we shall find it prone enough to animal gratifications. All her original instincts and propensities are after these, long before the faculties of reason open, and judgment and conscience can have power to curb and restrain them. But if those who have the care of children never concern themselves to call the powers of reason into exercise, nor assist them in forming just sentiments of the valuable ends and true improvement of human life ; but leave them merely to the instincts of appetite, and the government of their senses, and even educate them in the arts of vanity, initiate them into all the reigning follies and extravagances of the times they live in, and countenance and encourage in them the natural bent and disposition to these things, by their own practice and daily example ; how is it possible in such a situation, that they should have any apprehension of principles, any understanding of moral excellency and worth, any relish for the entertainments of reason, or the least inclination to enter into the spirit of true religion, and practice the virtues that are essentially and inseparably connected with it ?

There is nothing more boasted of in the present age, than *reason.* Its absolute sufficiency

ficiency is so magnified as to decry all the affiftance of divine inftruction and revelation. It is, it seems, of so divine and all perfect a nature, as to be fit for any thing, and capable of every thing. I am not at all difpofed to run down reafon, nor have fo much malice in my heart as to defame it, in revenge for the blaf-phemies that others have thrown out upon divine revelation. It is unqueftionably an excellent thing, exalts us into fome refem-blance with the firft and greateft of beings, and is the foundation of every thing that is great and valuable in human nature. But do we rightly underftand what is meant by reafon?

Do we mean by it the rational *powers and faculties?* Thefe unqueftionably are fufficient for every valuable purpofe of human life, be-caufe they are our only capacities for every rational act and duty, and nothing, in the nature of things, can be required of any man, which he hath not powers to enable him to know and do. But *how are they fuffi-cient?* What without opening, *without culti-vation and improvement?* How have thofe charming and admirable youths of the prefent age, who are the moft perfect adepts in the philofophy of drefs, fafhion, politenefs, and all the various arts of gay life, how I fay have they gained their important knowledge? To what do they owe this their fingular ele-gance of tafte, and exactnefs of judgment? Is it mere nature, or the improvement of na-ture? Have they it by the mere unaffifted ufe

of

of their own excellent reaſon, without being
beholden to any human inſtruction, revelation,
and example ? Is it not the effect of critical
obſervation, being bred up amidſt the moſt
improving patterns, converſing with maſters,
valets, powderers, and the like noble pro-
feſſors in theſe belles arts and ſciences ? Yea
have not many of theſe hopeful and incom-
parable youths travelled for the ſkill they have
into foreign countries, expoſed themſelves to
many hazards by ſea and land, endured the
ſcorching heat and pinching cold, viſited the
courts of princes, and the palaces of the great
and noble, and returned bleſſings to their native country, finiſhed by travel, furniſhed
with knowledge, and capable of dictating
laws of good breeding, and ſettling every
punctilio of a genteel behaviour and dreſs ?
Is it not owing to what they have learnt
abroad, and the curious obſervations they have
made on foreign men and manners, that they
have ſo much ſkill in the air and attitude of
the hat, the ſhape, the length and breadth of
the bag, the trim, the ornament, the cut, and
colour of the coat, the fall of the ſword, and
many other the like things, the grand objects
and only improvements of modern travelling ?
What would mere reaſon have done for theſe
gentlemen without this ? Much more, what
can it do in the more dry and unpleaſing
ſubjects of religion and virtue, without cultivation and direction ? How can it be expected that the knowledge and habits of either
ſhould be attained, unleſs the reaſonable

powers

powers be kindly led to them, affisted in their
inquiries, and in the most tender and friendly
manner encouraged in their pursuit of and
regard to them ? Or

Do we understand by reason, that which
is the effect of a right use of these powers,
truth, the *reason of things*, their connections,
repugnances, and the consequences of each ?
But the great question is how to come at this ?
What art or science is there, that *self-sown*, ever
rises up in the mind and flourishes without some
friendly hand to plant and water it, and help
forward its increase and perfection, and bring
it to maturity ? Are religious and moral truths
to be clearly discerned, in their nature, obligations, and importance ? Can they be im-
pressed on the heart, and embraced as the
genuine principles of a rational and moral
conduct, if the education be such as wholly
keeps them out of the mind, and the example set before our eyes, from our earliest
infancy, calls off our attention from them,
and leads to maxims and practices that are
directly the reverse of them ? To you I ap-
peal, the rich and honourable, to you who
boast yourselves as the polite and fashionable
part of the human species, to you, the lovers
of pleasure, and devotees to inclination ;
who have had the singular advantage of being
educated to every thing but religion and virtue, and been brought up in high life, and
blessed with the fair examples of a splendid
and pleasureable anceftry ; what noble principles inspire you, what high sentiments of

H 3   deity

deity poffefs your minds, how juft your
thoughts, how profound your reafonings upon
all religious fubjects ? It muft be confefied,
indeed, your principles are not of the *fupernatural kind*, nor are you at all beholden to
the borrowed affiftance and grace of divine
revelation. No. Nature is your oracle, and
the great originals you have copied have
ftrengthened her propenfities, encouraged her
inclinations, offered no violence or reftraint
to her appetites, nor engrafted any thing of
Chriftian fuperftition on it to debafe and corrupt it. Sublimer fentiments elevate your
minds, and nobler paffions in confequence
animate and infpire you ! In that early part
of life, in which ancient philofophy taught
men filence and modefty, you enter into the
world, out of all the foftneffes of an indulgent education, exquifitely formed, and compleat in every kind of liberal and elegant
qualifications. To you the moft difficult fubjects appear in all the lively demonftrations
of day-light, and others that the generality
of mankind, and thofe who have been the
moft laborious enquirers after truth, have
efteemed as the moft certain and felf-evident,
you have found out to be entirely precarious
and ill-grounded, and learnt, without fear or
fcruple, to reject as impertinent abfurdities.
You peremptorily decide this grand world was
all formed of atoms, without the direction of
an intelligent caufe, that every thing is fubject to the neceffary laws of matter and motion, or the arbitrary caprice of undefigning
chance

chance ; that providence is the fiction of enthufiafm, and all reverence and fears of a
deity mere contemptible fuperftition : That
whatever is in man is entirely material, that
at death he perifhes like the ignobler brute,
hath no being or fenfation beyond it ; nothing
to hope for, nothing to be afraid of after
it. In confequence of this you difmifs the
deity from all your cares, and are too polite
to trouble him with the impertinences of your
worfhip. The difpofitions of piety are perfect ftrangers to your breafts, and have no
place amongft the gayer images that continually poffefs you. And O what fanctity
of manners, what an invariable rectitude of
conduct, what perfect elegance and amiablenefs of behaviour, what high regard to deco-
rum, character, title, ftation, fortune, and
every valuable confideration of human nature
and life, flows from fuch an education and
fuch fentiments ! Who that obferves them,
or hears their publick characters, can help
imagining them to be *the improved difciples* of
a *Socrates*, a *Paul*, a *Locke*, or *Woollafton ?* Go
on ye rich and great thus to polifh and
refine your children. Bred up in all the arts
of high and pleafureable life, they will inherit
all your virtues, never difgrace your blood
and families, nor degenerate from the fair
examples you fet before them. You and they
will be an eternal proof how extreamly
friendly the love of pleafure is to true religion,
and of the vaft probability, the abfolute certainty there is, that it will thrive and flourifh

without

without any kind of education or example in favour of it.

And was the influence of fuch examples confined only to their own children, it would be more tolerable, and one would be apt to leave them in quiet poffeffion of their own madnefs and folly, and give them up *as in-curables.* But the mifchief fpreads farther, and the *infection reaches to all around them.* They are living peftilences in fociety, they blaft whatever they breathe on, and fpread diftemper and death through every perfon almoft they converfe with. What are the domefticks and menial fervants in the families of men devoted to pleafure, but either the mean and infamous affiftants to their vices, or elfe as execrably corrupt as thofe they attend on ? What is the whole family, from firft to laft, but a mixture of profanenefs, ex-travagance, luxury, intemperance and de-bauchery ; amongft whom innocence never enters, but 'tis immediately betrayed, or in-ftantly forced to fly with fhame and horror, as from infamy and deftruction. The ma-fter's pleafures, the fervants in their turns pur-fue, enter into all their diverfions, and prac-tice in their lower ways all the fame enor-mities and extravagances of fafhionable vice ; whereby they become daring and infolent, and grow fearlefs both of God and man ; fit to ferve in no families of moral reputation and characters, and incapable of being ufeful as to any valuable purpofes of private or pub-lick life. How fhould they, when they have

feen

seen nothing but impiety and profaneness in thofe who have cloathed and maintained them, have oftentimes been made confcious to their worft debaurheries, been carried by them to every publick scene of pleafure, been accuftomed by them to idlenefs, fed to ex- cefs, kept from all publick inftruction, and thus prevented from every poffibility of know- ing more, or acting better than their keepers? Wretches thus led and formed by fuch ex- amples, and allowed and encouraged in fuch practices, cannot but be extreamly profane, and run the utmoft lengths of the moft daring impieties. And by thefe means

5. The mifchief *fpreads wider* and *irreligion gains ground,* as it hath numbers, fafhion, no- bility, power, and riches, to countenance and fupport it. There is in many a ftrong inclination to be like the reft, or the generality of the world; and without enquiring whether what they do is right, and agreeable to rea- fon, they follow too implicitly their exam- ple, and are efpecially fond of imitating thofe whom they efteem perfons of fortune, cha- racter, and education; whofe example they think adds a kind of dignity and fanction to the like practices in others. They imagine that cuftom is reafon enough for any practice, and that they need not be more fcrupulous than the great and rich; that there is no living in the world, if one muft not be like it, nor enter into the ways and manners of it, and that *fingularity,* either in principle or practice, is *a ridiculous precifion,* that fhews a

man

man abject, and renders him contemptible.
Hence, becaufe there is too general a difregard to all the principles of religion and morality amongft mankind, they think principle,
and a regard to it, almoft unneceffary accom-
plifhments, treat the principles of religion at
beft with coldnefs and indifference, oftentimes with great freedom and difrefpect, and
at length, that their conformity to the patterns they copy after may be more exact, and
they may fhew how much they have improved
by them, they venture not only to call their
truth into queftion, but reprefent them as
abfurdities, and laugh at them as impertinent
and ridiculous. And as to all religious inftitutions and obfervances, becaufe the regard
to them is not *fafhionable*, and the attending
on them not practiced by thofe, who are
efteemed as the patterns of elegance and politenefs, they are in a great meafure entirely
neglected by thefe *fervile imitators*, and held
in great difefteem, merely for this poor and
contemptible reafon, becaufe they would not
be thought *fingularly devout*. Yea fome are
mad enough to fmother their own convictions,
and act contrary to the dictates of their own
confciences, through a wicked complaifance
to cuftom and example, and a defired conformity to the manners of the profligate, rich
and great, whofe company they are fond of,
and whofe acquaintance and converfation they
are fools enough to think an honour to them ;
though the almoft only poffible effect of being admitted to intimacy and freedom with
                                            them

them is, the being laughed out of their principles, the corruption of their morals, the
waste of their time, and the ruin of their
fortunes. And though *our ancient nobility* and
persons of *real quality* and fortune, would
have thought it beneath them, and a reflection upon their honour and character, to
have made *mechanicks* and tradesmen *their
companions* and intimates ; yet in our times,
when almost every thing *runs dregs, the coronet*
and *the counter* harmoniously associate, *the peer*
puts himself on a level with *the cit* ; they
swear, they drink, they game, they whore
together. The fool of *a cit* thinks 'tis polite
to be like *my lord,* enters into all his extravagancies, joins with him in his impious ridi-
cules, receives his profane wit with approbation, laughs when he blasphemes, and becomes at length as *finished a wretch* as his
right honourable instructor.

When thus qualified and formed, and tu-
tored into the knowledge and love of the
pleasures and vices of those he counts his bet-
ters, he becomes fit for extensive mischief,
and sets up for polishing and improving in
the same arts he hath himself learnt, those
of like employments, circumstances, and stations. To these he relates with pleasure and
boasting his acquaintance and intimacy with
this man of quality, that person of fortune,
and such a gentleman of distinction and family. He entertains his companions with an
account of this adventure, such a party of
pleasure, such a night's frolick and gallantry.
He

He gives the shocking account of his profuse-
ness and extravagance, his profaneness and
vices, with an air of satisfaction and exulting
pleasure, and insensibly instils the soft and
pleasing poison, the passion for pleasure and
the love of criminal indulgences, into the
hearts of his associates *. If at first his impiety and wickedness create an horror in any
of his companions, whose education hath
led them to a disapprobation of such extravagances, and in whom there are any remains of tenderness of conscience, sense of
deity, or knowledge of good and evil ; frequent converse gradually takes off that horror. At length they can hear every thing
without trembling, after this, with a kind
of approbation and pleasure. Then they enter into the first measures of vice, gradually
grow dexterous proficients in it, and at last
learn to practice all the pleasures of iniquity
with full approbation and greediness. If any
lesser fears should for a while continue, and
conscience should shew any reluctance to the
desperate measures into which they are drawing ; banter and ridicule will in time entirely
suppress them, and the bold and daring examples of those they converse with, fortify
them against all their apprehensions, and render them every hour more and more insensible.
They will be taught to call their reluctance

---

* ———— Ye little think how nigh
Your change approaches, when your virtuous joys
Shall vanish, and deliver ye to woe.

Milt. Par. L. B. 4. v. 366.

to

to vice, squeamishness ; their fears of God
and a future state, superstition ; and the history and principles of religion, old women's
fables ; or by that all controuling name, which
by a kind of magick power crushes all the
force of demonstration and truth, and over-
throws the credit of all past histories ; I mean
the dreadful name of *priestcraft*.

Thus the love of pleasure and the vices and
impieties attending it, enter into mercantile
life, and spread themselves through all the
various ranks and degrees of men engaged in
trade and commerce. One wretch that is
deeply sunk into them, infects all he can
within the compass of his acquaintance, and
lays snares to debauch and ruin all that are
around him. When he is once become a
finished profligate himself, with *a devilish
malice* he beholds virtue in another, and is
uneasy and restless till he hath destroyed it *.
And as his own criminal pleasures have made
it necessary for him to renounce all principles, he not only becomes a professed enemy
to all without exception, that profess to instruct and ground others in the knowledge of
them ; but sets up for an instructor in the

---

* Like Milton's Devil. — League with you I seek
And mutual amity, so strait, so close,
That I with you must dwell, or you with me.
And should I at your harmless Innocence
Melt, as I do, yet publick reason just,
Honour and Empire, with revenge enlarg'd
——— ——— compels me now,
To do, what else, though damned I should abhor.

Par. Lost, B. 4, v. 375 —388, &c.

scheme

fcheme of infidelity, propagates impiety, fpreads contempt of religion, and endeavours to feduce young and unfettled minds into an utter difregard to all the moft facred obligations and duties. So fovereign is the averfion of men of this caft to truth and principle, that they wifh them utterly difcarded from human fociety; that none might remain to preferve the ungrateful remembrance of them, and reproach their conduct by a different and better behaviour. And 'tis to the affiduous endeavours and vile infinuations of thefe pefts of fociety, that we owe the early corruption of fo many of the youth of the prefent age, in all claffes of life, who are beguiled into deftructive pleafures, and too eafily and naturally led into fcepticifm and infidelity, in order to quiet their minds, and render themfelves eafy in their criminal indulgences. And 'tis a remark that will ever hold good, that as the love of pleafure prevails, impiety will fpread; and the circumftances of our own age abundantly confirm it, in which many of all ranks and degrees feem devoted to the purfuit of pleafure, and in confequence of it are grown indifferent to, and have difcarded all belief of the moft unqueftionable and facred principles.

For this love of pleafure, and that profanenefs which is the effect of it, hath gone down even to thofe who are in the *loweft claffes* of life. That men of fortune and affluence fhould fink into luxury and foftnefs is lefs to be wondered at, not only becaufe they have

the

the means to gratify all their paffions and inclinations, but becaufe they are generally bred
up without employment, and even with an
averfion to the labour and fatigue of bufinefs,
and becaufe they are taught no other ufe or
value of riches, but as the price and purchafe
of every fenfual indulgence, and as they procure all the various gratifications, in which
the thoughtlefs part of mankind place the true
happinefs of human life. But one would think
that nature and providence had excluded thofe
of ftraiter circumftances from many of the
criminal pleafures of the rich, and that their
poverty and difficulties would be a powerful
reftraint upon their paffions, inure them to
frugality and good œconomy, reconcile them
to labour and induftry, and naturally lead them
into fuch reflections, as might help to ballance
the difadvantages of their condition, and put
them upon ferious endeavours to fecure the
advantages and pleafures of religion. Had
they this wifdom, they would foon learn to
pafs the proper judgment and eftimate upon
the guilty follies, and mad indulgences of
the debauched and profligate rich, be convinced that a religious and virtuous poverty, is
infinitely preferable to all the finful pleafures
of grandeur and plenty, and look down upon
profperous finners without envying their
lot, with a fuperior air of pity and contempt.

But even the rich and great are fcarce
guilty of more horrid enormities, or chargeable with greater impieties than the loweft
and

and poorest of mankind. These two classes, how different soever their circumstances, seem to vie with each other, who shall be most desperately wicked and profane. The servants and domesticks of great families enter into all the passions of their superiors, and think they have nothing to fear from imitating their masters in their pleasures. The conversations they are accustomed to hear at their tables, and in the hours of revelling and mirth ; such as frequently transgress all the bounds of decency and honour, and as truly *polite and well bred gentlemen* would be ashamed of ; prepare them for all the excesses of vice, and wipe out of their minds every impression and sentiment in favour of religion and virtue. And by conversing with tradesmen in lower life, and with those who are bred up in laborious and servile employments, they tempt and reconcile them to excesses and debaucheries, render them blasphemers and fearless of God, and teach them a contempt of every thing that is sacred and good. As all the various conditions and relations of life are connected with each other, from the highest to the lowest, as they have a mutual dependence, and as there is a constant intercourse and commerce between them ; as this is unavoidable to circulate the affairs and carry on the business of life ; 'tis impossible, but that if any one branch be thoroughly corrupted, the infection must gradually spread, and at length diffuse the contagion amongst great numbers in every different state of life. Especially
cially

cially as a fondness for imitating others is a
very powerful and prevailing paffion of human nature, and moft powerful when the
example given hath the luftre and dignity of external circumftances to recommend it.

Let it be farther confidered, that in an
age of pleafure, and when the love of it becomes the general paffion, there muft be
great numbers employed as proper inftruments
and minifters to provide for the gratification
of the publick tafte, and to procure and regulate thofe diverfions and amufements, that
are fo eagerly and generally fought after. The
rich will not fail to encourage thofe who can
ferve them in this refpect, and whatever be
their characters, to carefs and reward them
as the moft valuable and ufeful members of
fociety. At the fame time perfons of defperate or broken fortunes, who cannot bear the
confinement of bufinefs, or who have ruined
themfelves by neglecting it, will fet themfelves
to contrive new entertainments, and furnifh
out frefh fcenes of pleafures. As thefe multiply and grow, new trades and occupations
arife, and gradually employ confiderable numbers, who fubfift upon the publick follies
and vices. And as fuch kind of employments
are generally very lucrative, thofe who engage
in them will fcarce entertain a bad opinion of
thofe pleafures by which they live, and frequently gain confiderable fortunes ; and are
indeed too often themfelves as unprincipled
and profligate as thofe whofe creatures they

are, and to whofe vices they are fubfervient.
And by thefe means pleafure becomes an almoft neceffary evil in fociety, the encroachments of it grow wider and wider, great numbers are engaged in intereft for the fupport of
it, numerous families fubfift by it, and the correcting or retrenching it by wholefome laws
becomes a very difficult and dangerous thing,
and cannot oftentimes be effectually done,
without injuring property, bearing hard upon
families, depriving them of the means of
maintenance, raifing clamours, creating dif-
affection to government, and endangering
the peace and welfare of civil fociety. I may
add, that too often government itfelf makes
its advantage of thefe corruptions, and draws
them in as fources to the fupply of its expences ; whereby the difpofition to pleafure
receives the publick fanction and encouragement. For I think nothing is more evident,
than that the fo taxing luxury and pleafure,
as to leave the people full liberty to indulge
thefe, is a kind of political approbation of
them, and little lefs than countenancing and
eftablifhing them by law. And I am afraid
that few governments are fo virtuous, and
managed upon fuch principles of integrity
and honour, as that when they have found
the way to fupply their own neceffities by the
extravagances and follies of the people, to be
eafily perfuaded to part with their funds, or
over defirous of a publick reformation, that
would leffen the fources of their own reve-
nues. And when thus publick and private
interefts

interests unite to encreafe the fpread of fenfuality and pleafure, the love of thefe muft
make large advances in a nation, and irreligion and vice triumph by a neceffary confequence and proportion.

What hath greatly helped to fpread this evil
amongft ourfelves, and to draw in perfons of
all characters, ranks and employments, from
the greateft to the leaft, is, the numerous
places of pleafure that are opened all around
us, to which all the various claffes of mankind
may refort ; in which there are diverfions of
every price, fuited to the meaneft circumftances, and the very refufe of the people.
Plays and interludes, which a few years ago
had an appearance of fomewhat of dignity in
them, when the number of houfes where they
were acted were fewer, and they were regarded as the proper entertainments of the
fafhionable and rich, are now performed
almoft at every end of the city, and received into fcandalous and dirty houfes of
entertainment, for the fcum of mankind to
haunt. Our publick papers abound every
day with advertifements of this kind. The
diverfions of mufick, more innocent in themfelves, and that carry lefs *immediate danger* of
debauching mens morals and principles, are
by the low prices affixed to them, and the
many places where they are to be found, become little lefs than a publick nuifance and
grievance. For as fuch fort of entertainments
relax and unbend the mind, difpofe to foftnefs and indolence, and powerfully inftill the

love

love of gaiety and pleasure, so when they become general, they must have their share in vitiating the taste, and corrupting the manners of the people; and too often prepare them for indulgences of a more extravagant and criminal nature, especially as there are never wanting at these entertainments persons who frequent them for the worst of purposes, and to make a prey of the simple and unwary. It would be endless to mention the various kinds and places of pleasure, that are now furnished out in and about this city, for the gentleman and tradesman, the rich and poor, masters and servants. Every man's taste and purse is consulted, and nothing omitted that may tempt and beguile all without exception to countenance by their presence and example, that fondness for pleasure, which is the reigning taste of the present age, which hath almost put religion out of countenance, and which if it grows in proportion as it hath done for some years past, will grow near to extinguish the very appearance and form of it.

But this is an effect of pleasure, that many would rejoice to see real, and if no worse fruits arise from it than this, we shall never persuade them to lend their assistance towards suppressing or retrenching the spread of it. I beg leave therefore to consider the bad consequences of such a prevailing disposition in another view : And that is

II. In reference to the *secular concerns* of the present life, and all the valuable interests of
time

time, that call for and deserve our attention.
There is nothing that hath a more fatal influence on all these, than the temper and practice I have been arguing against. And
this will demonstratively appear, if we
consider,

1. The certain consequences of this prevailing love of pleasure on *particular persons.*
On what doth their present welfare depend,
but on their right behaviour in the several
ranks and situations of being, in which the
God of nature hath placed them, their dis-
charging the proper duties incumbent on
them, the securing a reputation and interest
amongst those, whose good opinion and friendship may be highly serviceable to them, their
preserving their bodily health and vigour, their
attending their proper business, and managing
it with diligence and care, such an œconomy
and frugality in their expences, as may enable
them to carry it on with comfort and honour,
knowing the right value of their time, watching favourable circumstances of advantage,
and dexterously and skilfully improving them
for those valuable purposes for which they
offer themselves to them. 'Tis evident that
the comfort and success of life, and the business of it depend on these and the like things,
and he that hopes to be prosperous, easy or
happy in his circumstances by any other
methods, will find himself miserably disappointed. Now the love of pleasure, suffered
to become habitual, and growing prevalent in
the mind, is absolutely irreconcileable with

such

fuch a conduct, and utterly deftroys all thefe
evident and conftant fources of profperity.

How frequently do men by a conftant attention to pleafure, *injure their health*, and *impair their conftitutions*, bring upon themfelves
lownefs of fpirits, acute diftempers, or chro-
nical diforders, that often fhorten life, or that
render it miferable whilft it lafts, and greatly
unfit them for the regular management of
their own affairs, and making thofe improvements in fortune, which otherwife they might
eafily do. The pleafures of mere indolence,
when they engrofs the whole of life, are inconfiftent with eftablifhed health, which is
fcarce ever to be maintained without fuitable
exercife, and a due proportion of vigorous
action and labour. The immoderate gratifications of the appetite, in the luxuries of the
table, and the exceffes and riots of drinking,
make a more fpeedy confumption of the bodily ftrength and vigour, open the conftitution to innumerable diforders, prepare it for
lingering decays and torments, or more vio-
lently rend and diffolve it. *Who hath woe,
who hath forrow, who hath contentions, who hath
babling, who hath wounds without caufe, who
hath rednefs of eyes? They that tarry long at the
wine, they that go to feek mixt wine. Look not
on the wine when it is red, when it giveth its
colour in the cup, when it moveth itfelf right:
At the laft it biteth like a ferpent, and ftingeth
like an adder* *. Immoderate diverfions, pro-

* Prov. xxiii. 29—32.

tracted

tracted to irregular hours, and indulged without regard to the bodily conftitution, or fitnefs
of time and feafon, however otherwife lawful,
often bring on diftempers, which if they do
not prove fatal, leave bad effects behind them
that are never to be thrown off, and which
fometimes put a fpeedy end to life. I omit
to mention thofe more criminal pleafures,
which nature punifhes with confequences the
moft fhocking and deteftible ; confequences
the moft infamous in their nature, as well as
prejudicial to the bodily welfare. *His own
iniquities take the wicked, and he fhall be holden
with the cords of his own fin* †. In a word,
pleafure, how enchanting foever the perfuafions of it be, and in whatever form it appears, is a dangerous as well as fweet deluder ;
and when fhe is not attended and guarded,
and under the direction of prudence, wifdom,
religion, and virtue, feldom fails, fooner or
later, of preying on the vitals of the conftitution, and feeding herfelf with the fpoils of
the fpirits, health and vigour of it. *He that
goes after her goes like an ox to the flaughter, or
a fool to the correction of the ftocks, 'till a dart
ftrike through his liver, or as a bird that hafteneth
to the fnare, and knows not that it is for
his life.*

Again, the love of pleafure *waftes and confumes mens time,* and engroffes many of the
beft opportunities, which ought and might be

† Prov. v. 22.

I 4   improved

improved to the most valuable purposes. This is the grand season for securing all the best advantages of life, and is amongst the number of those blessings, which when once lost, are never to be recalled ; 'tis therefore equally a point of wisdom and interest to husband it well, and not prodigally waste and trifle it away, in impertinent amusements of no consequence to rational beings, and which cannot be the least subservient to the true ends and interests of life. The improvement of the mind by principles of useful knowledge, by cultivating the dispositions of rational piety, and strengthening the habits of justice, benevolence, temperance, and all the private and social virtues, demand a proper share of the time of life, and can never be carried on to any great perfection, unless some considerable portion of it be allotted to this purpose. In business and the affairs of commerce, 'tis of the utmost importance to watch every favourable season that offers, to be always in the way of transacting our own concerns, with those that may choose to have any dealings with us, and to contrive and manage so, as that we may carry on the correspondence of life with integrity, reputation, and honour, with ease and comfort, and prosperity. Especially when persons first enter into the world, business requires the strictest and closest attendance, must be dexterously invited, and courted, and cherished by frugality, application, and constant diligence. Pleasures
should

should scarce ever enter into the head of a man of business, and all the sollicitations of it should be looked on as so many attempts to rob him of his time, *i. e.* his fortune and success. Few wise persons will chuse to have any transactions with men that are frequently absent from their own concerns, because in such they can never expect that punctuality which is the life of business, and they will justly reason, he that neglects his own affairs can never be careful in those which belong to others. The keeping accounts with order and exactness, the providing for the payment of just debts, the seasonable gathering in those that are due in the course of business, the watching proper opportunities for buying, and the observing the most advantageous seasons for disposing of what is purchased; these, and other like incidents in commerce, will find men full employment for all their time, if they are not wanting to their own interest, and if they rightly consider, abundantly convince them, that business and pleasure are absolutely inconsistent, and irreconcileable with each other. For what is there that destroys and wasts men's time more than pleasure? Both cannot, in the nature of the thing, be minded at once. The time that is devoted to the one must be lost to the other. If the tendency to pleasure prevails, the very inclination to business must lessen, and if that be pursued, the other must be proportionably neglected. And the truth of this is demon-
 strated

ftrated by a thoufand facts. To what is the
failure of fo many in the common concerns
of life owing, but their facrificing thofe hours
to diverfion and unneceffary amufement, that
fhould be appropriated to their fecular employments ? From the afternoon of every Fri-
day to the Tuefday morning following, is
the common portion allotted by tradefmen in
low life, to idlenefs and recreation, efpecially
for eight or ten months in the year ; when
they leave all their concerns in the city, for
the pleafures of the country, to the management of fervants, who often neglect their
truft when their mafters are abfent, and often
enrich themfelves at their mafter's expence.
Whatever affairs of importance they have to
manage, they will either wholly neglect them,
or do them in a very curfory and imperfect
manner, that they may not be prevented from
enjoying what they are continually hankering
after, their weekly retreat from the burthens
and cares of their ordinary occupations. And
this defire will be ftill the ftronger, if they have
families to engage their affections ; wives
and children too frequently encouraging abfence from bufinefs, and drawing in the eafy,
good-natured hufband and father to omit the
care of his own affairs, to indulge and gratify
their own fond and unreafonable defires and
inclinations : Whereby, befides the days that
are profeffedly condemned to pleafure, many
other hours, mornings, afternoons, and whole
days are wafted away, without confideration

of

of any confequences whatfoever. And if the computation was fairly and impartially to be made, it would appear that the time thus fquandered and fooled away, would amount to above one half of the whole time of life, to the irreparable injury of themfelves and families. For the effects of fuch a conduct often appear in the lofs of bufinefs, the making capital miftakes in it, the confufion of their accounts, great perplexity and difficulty in managing affairs, and too often in total failures and final bankruptcies. Befides,

As pleafure thus thieves away our time, fo it really confumes men's fubftance and property. It is in its nature a *coftly* and *expenfive* thing. Among the lower orders of mechanicks, the expences of *one* day of pleafure amount to more than they can allow for *three* days fubfiftence of their families. And among the higher rank of artificers, with whom 'tis grown cuftomary to convert the Lord's day into a day of fenfual indulgence ; the expences of their excurfions into the country, with the contempt of the grateful worfhip which they owe to the Giver of all their good, and in defiance of his laws, confume *half* the gains of the preceding week. 'Tis not neceffary to carry the eftimate into higher life. They who know the fafhionable world want no farther information ; and they who are ftrangers to it, would hardly believe the moft moderate calculation. And all who are converfant with the affairs of our ruined traders and gentry know, that three parts

out

out of four of thefe, owe the diftrefs and want to which they and their families are reduced, to their compliance with the follicitations of this *fyren* pleafure.

Can it then be neceffary to offer any more confiderations for convincing you of the malignant nature, and deftructive effects of voluptuoufnefs, which, wherever it prevails, extinguifhes all fenfe of religion, and every noble and generous affection, difqualifies perfons for attending to or relifhing the manly and exalted fatisfactions of knowledge, goodnefs, and devotion, and fwallows up the time and money, which fhould be employed in acquiring and enjoying thefe. Which deftroys men's conftitutions, confumes their fubftance, debauches and finks their families, and having made men wholly regardlefs of any future interefts, either of this world or the next, and reduced them to extream want here, turns them naked into the invifible and everlafting ftate, deftitute of all moral worth, with eager and infatiable cravings after bafe pleafures, which they can no more enjoy, and utterly incapable of the divine enjoyments of Angels and of Heaven; and doom'd to fuffer the juft punifhments of their inexcufable folly and guilt, tortur'd by fruitlefs remorfe and utter defpair, and the victims of *everlafting deftruction*. He who *likes fuch an end* may *chufe fuch a life*.

But let thefe confiderations determine you, my friends, to reftrain fteadily the inclinations to fenfual pleafures, and to cultivate the

the nobler defires and affections of your fouls ; that having been in a high degree *lovers of God* here, and delighted to converfe with him in the exercifes of devotion, and having refembled him in generous goodnefs and extenfive beneficence, you may fhare in the largeft communications of the divine favour to eternity : *In his prefence where is fullnefs of joy, and at his right hand, where are pleafures for ever, Amen.*

SERMON

SERMON V.

Of the Purpose for which the Son of God was manifested.

1 JOHN iii. 8.

*For this purpose the Son of God was manifested,
that he might destroy the works of the devil.*

IN the beginning of this chapter, the
Apostle having spoken with admiration of
the greatness of the love of God, in calling,
owning, and treating us as his children, and
assured us that one happy effect of it should
be, our becoming *like* Christ, at his second
appearance, *by seeing him as he is*, draws this
important practical inference from it. *Every
man that hath this hope in him, purifieth himself,
even as* Christ is pure *. Of the purity of the
master the disciple must be partaker, and we
must be conformed to his image in holiness,
now, otherwise his future appearance will be
no comfortable sight to us, and we shall have
little reason to expect to resemble him here-

* Verse 3.

after

after in heavenly glory. And the neceſſity of this purity the Apoſtle farther enforceth, by informing us, *That whoſoever committeth ſin is of the devil,* is under his influence, and belongs to his family, and that the very end of Chriſt's coming into our world, was to reſcue mankind from his power, and recover them from thoſe vices they had ſo long practiced in obedience to his ſuggeſtions : As in the words of my text : *He that committeth ſin is of the devil ; for the devil ſinneth from the beginning. For this purpoſe the Son of God was manifeſted, that he might deſtroy the works of the devil.* In ſpeaking to theſe words we may conſider,

    I. What *the works are* which the Apoſtle
      here refers to, and in what ſenſe they are
      the *works of the devil.* And
    II. *How Chriſt was manifeſted to deſtroy them.*

    I. *What works* the Apoſtle here refers to, under the character of the *works of the devil.* And here the context will fully inform us. For the Apoſtle tells us, *He who committeth ſin is of the devil, for the devil ſinneth from the beginning* *. *Whoſoever is born of God doth not commit ſin* †. *In this the children of God are manifeſt, and the children of the devil* ‡, *whoſoever doeth not righteouſneſs is not of* God. The *practice of righteouſneſs* argues men to be the *children of* God, *and whoſoever is born of God doth not commit ſin.* Whereas, on the contrary, they *who commit ſin,* and do not righteouſneſs,

* Verſe 8.   † 9.   ‡ 10.

                                        are

are the *children of the devil.* And this is the
great *distinction* between thefe *two great fami-*
lies, by which it may moft certainly be known,
who they are that belong to each ; they who
are of God's houfhold, and the children of
him their heavenly Father, *doing righteoufnefs*
as God is righteous, and abftaining from all
habitual, wilful, prefumptuous fin, becaufe
they are born of God ; they who are *of the*
devil, and belong to his family, being enemies
to truth and righteonfnefs, and indulging
themfelves in the practice of thofe fins, which
argue men to be in a ftate of real oppofition
and enmity to God, and to be of the fame fpirit
and character with him who finned from the
beginning. Now as *the Son of God was ma-*
nifefted, that he might deftroy the works of the
devil, thofe works which he himfelf did from
the beginning, and by the love and practice
of which, all who belong to him diftinguifh
themfelves ; they muft be the works of fin ;
becaufe he hath been an old, hardened, habitual, incorrigible finner himfelf, and all his
children give themfelves up to commit iniquity
with greedinefs and pleafure. This then is
that character of infamy, which the fpirit of
God in revelation fixes on all fin, that it is
the work of the devil ; that is, all *wilful and*
habitual fin ; thofe prefumptuous crimes, and
tranfgreffions of the law of God, which corrupt and fenfual men are chargeable with.
They are not the works of truth and reafon,
which thefe either dictate or juftify. They
are not the works of God, *for he is not tempted*

to do evil himself, neither tempts he any man to do it, nor is he chargeable with doing it; but *loves righteousness, hates iniquity,* and will finally manifest his displeasure against it, by the punishment he inflicts upon impenitent and incurable offenders. Sin therefore is the work of folly, presumption, and madness, and of those who are under the leading of these dreadful guides. It is in all instances the work of mischievous, impious, abandoned spirits, and of him emphatically, who is at the head of the apostacy from God, and who, enraged at the loss of his own original happiness and glory, and impatient at the thought, that any part of God's rational creation should be happier than himself, not only continues his own crimes, but takes pleasure in those who follow his example, and fall under the same condemnation with himself.

But though *all* sins are thus characterised as the works of the devil, yet there are *some,* which are in a more *especial manner* stigmatised in divine revelation as his works, done by himself, or by others under his instigation and influence ; particularly, *wilful ignorance and unbelief* of the *gospel* revelation, under the proper means of information and knowledge, which the Apostle expressly ascribes to their *minds being blinded by the God of this world, least the light of the glorious gospel of Christ should shine into them* *. Our blessed Saviour gives it as part of the character of this evil spirit, that

* 2 Cor. iv. 4.

he abode not in the truth, because there is no truth in him †; and therefore they who have no principles of truth in their minds, or who having once received and believed them, renounce and defert them, and fuffer them to have no farther influence, refemble him who is deftitute of all truth, in difpofition, and do thofe very works, of which he gives them an example, by his having apoftatifed from, and rebelled againft it. In like manner, a *violent and obftinate oppofition to the truth*, in order to prevent the progrefs and reception of it, whether it be by fraud or force, or by endeavouring to obfcure and corrupt it, argues a very diabolical difpofition, and that men are under the influence and actuated by the counfels of the great enemy of truth, and the fubtle deceiver and feducer of mankind. Thus St. *Paul* tells *Elymas* the forcerer, *who withftood him*, and *endeavoured to turn the deputy* governor of *Paphos from the faith :* That *he was a child of the devil* ‡, both becaufe he was an *enemy of all righteoufnefs, and ceafed not to pervert the right ways of the Lord.* The particular fins of *envy, ftrife* and *contention*, that occafion confufion and every evil work, are declared by St. *James* to proceed from *that wifdom, which is earthly, fenfual, and devilifh* ||. *Subtlety* and craft *in doing mifchief* conftitute perfons children of the devil, according to St. *Paul* § ; the *malicious* and *murtherous* difpofition, efpecially againft the preachers of truth

† John viii. 44.   ‡ Acts xiii. 10. || Jam. iii. 15.
§ Acts xiii. 10.

and

and righteoufnefs, argue men to be *of their
father the devil, and that they will do the lufts of
their father,* according to Chrift *. The *love
of lying,* and *fpreading of falfehood,* he alfo declares to be the employment of the devil,
who when he *fpeaks of a lie, fpeaks of his own* †,
from his natural difpofition to falfehood, as
being *a liar, and the father of lies.* Hence alfo
calumny and *defamation* ftand in the fame lift
of diabolical crimes ‡, as they are the effects
of an envious, malicious heart, are pernicious
lies, and the genuine dictates of falfehood.
And as there is nothing more villainous and
execrable than *treachery* and breach of truft,
and an intention to betray and ruin, under the
pretence and guife of friendfhip, hence our
bleffed Saviour expreflly calls *Judas, who betrayed him, a devil* ‖ ; and the Apoftle obferves,
that juft before this unhappy wretch determined to betray his Lord and Mafter, *Satan,*
or the devil, *entered into him* § : And indeed
nothing but a devil incarnate could have been
guilty of fo atrocious, heinous and aggravated
a perfidy. I cannot help adding, that the
wars which are carried on by the kings and
princes of the earth, through the luft of ambition, to enlarge their dominions, and through
an avaricious view to gather in the riches of
the world, and the fpoils of nations to themfelves, without neceflity and juftice, and contrary to the rules of humanity and honour,
argue fuch a diabolical fpirit, and are attended

* John viii. 4.   † Ibid.   ‡ Ibid.   ‖ John vi. 70.
§ John xiii. 27.

with

with fuch ravages, defolations, cruelties and murthers, as that it is no wonder they are afcribed, by the fpirit of prophecy, *to the in-ftigation of the fpirits of devils, gathering the kings of the earth to battle* *, and caufing them to delight in, and unnaturally fport themfelves with the miferies and deftruction of mankind. In a word, *hatred to religion, enmity to righteouf-nefs,* and the *taking pleafure in iniquity,* are the proper characterifticks of the *ferpent and his feed,* and 'tis with the utmoft propriety, that fin, in all the various inftances of it, is ftiled the work of the devil.   For

He was the *firft* who *introduced fin* into the creation of God ; the firft himfelf in the re-bellion againft his maker, and who by his inftigation drew in others to fhare his guilt and condemnation. The expreffion imme-diately before my text is remarkable. The *devil finneth from the beginning,* plainly afcribing the *origin* of fin to him, and pointing out his obftinate *perfeverance* in committing it. *He finneth from the beginning* is much more than to fay, he *finned.* He might have finned, and repented ; but to affirm *he finneth from the beginning,* is to affirm, that he *continues* the fame, and ever fince he began to fin, he hath never changed his conduct, but perfifted in-curably to multiply his offences againft God. 'Tis difficult to determine the precife meaning of the expreffion *from the beginning.* It may mean, in the beginning *before ever the world*

* Rev. xvi. 14.

began, as the fame expreffion certainly means
in *John*, *In the beginning was the word, i. e.*
before the creation of the worlds, becaufe *all
things were made by him, and without him nothing
was made that is made.* And in this fenfe the
expreffion will refer to that early rebellion
againft God, by which many of the Angels
loft their original perfection and dignity of
nature, and were deprived by God of their
native happinefs and glory; to which the
Apoftle *Jude* refers, when he writes concerning fome of the Angels, *that they kept not their
firft eftates, but left their own habitations* †, and
who have therefore been *referved in everlafting
chains, unto the judgment of the great day.* The
whole angelick order was undoubtedly created
in a ftate of proper perfection; but ftill muta-
ble; and in their nature, and by the neceffary
law of creation, liable to natural and moral
evil. The perfection of no created being is
fo high and abfolute, as to be without limita-
tion and defect. *God* only in this fenfe is perfect, and who therefore *can never be tempted
to evil.* There is nothing that he can want,
and therefore he can have no defire after more.
He hath nothing that he can fear, and therefore can never be anxious about lofing what
he hath. He hath none fuperior to him,
and can have nothing of the difpofitions of
jealoufy and envy. He knows every thing,
and can never be miftaken. He can do what
he pleafes, and therefore can never be pre-

† Verfe 6.

K 3   vented

vented from doing what his wifdom directs him to effect. So that he hath nothing in his own nature that can induce him to evil, and therefore cannot be tempted from himfelf, and therefore muft be above and free from all external temptation, becaufe there can be no place for this, unlefs there was fomewhat in his nature anfwerable to the temptation, and which might render it proper to influence and perfuade him. But thefe things can be faid of *no created beings* whatfoever ; becaufe being created, they are neceffarily *limited* and *dependant*. They have their wants, to which they are unavoidably fubject, and there may be kinds of happinefs of which they are not in poffeffion ; and therefore they may be liable to the uneafinefs of defire, and to be tempted by that defire to purfue the object of it, by fuch means as they imagine the moft likely to obtain it. And as they are defective in power, they are fubject to apprehenfion and fear, either that they may not obtain the good they defire and covet, or may lofe the good they poffefs ; and therefore may be moved by fear, either to right or wrong meafures, to get what they have not, or fecure what they have. Their very perfections, and height of dignity may infpire undue elevation and hauteur of heart, and expofe them to be tempted by vanity and pride. As they are not in the firft rank of being, and do not poffefs the higheft degres of dignity and honour, they are liable to the ftrong temptation of envy and ambition. This very ftate of fubjection to a fuperior may make them

afpire

afpire after independency, and tempt them to free themfelves from the uneafinefs of obedience to thofe who are above them. As all created knowledge is defective, they may be betrayed and deceived into a very wrong and criminal conduct ; and as their power is limited, they may not be able to guard themfelves from evil, and fecure themfelves either from guilt or mifery. So that the *origin* of *moral* and *penal* evil is to be derived from the *natural imperfection* of every *created* being, which expofes them to the power and influence of temptation, and by confequence to fin and guilt, and the punifhments and miferies that attend them. So that whatever may have been the original perfection of Angels, it had its mixture of imperfection ; they were therefore liable to change; they had in their very frame and conftitution what fubjected them to temptation to moral evil, and rendered them liable to natural and penal evil. And when the Apoftle tells us, that *the Devil finneth from the beginning,* it feems to point out his early apoftacy from God, and that he foon became an offender againft him, to whom he owed his very being, and the diftinguifhing privileges and honours of his nature. Or his finning from the beginning may relate only to the *beginning of this world,* and that original temptation by which he feduced our firft parents into fin and ruin ; the forfeiture of their innocence, and the lofs of their happinefs. He then finned by falfhood and lying, by telling them *they fhould not die* if they eat

K 4   the

the forbidden fruit, but that they *should be like Gods* † ; upon which account our Saviour declares, that *from the beginning he abode not in the truth, becaufe there is no truth in him ; and that when he fpeaketh a lie, he fpeaketh of his own, becaufe he is a liar, and the father of it.* And as by a lie he deceived our firft parents into fin, he deceived them into deftruction ; and fo in our Lord's expreffion, he was a *murtherer from the beginning*, the deftroyer of the whole human race, as by his falfe infinuations he brought them under the condemnation of death. Sin therefore is with great propriety faid to be the work of the devil, becaufe he *firft* difordered and defiled the creation of God by this execrable evil, falling from his original integrity, involving himfelf in the guilt of fin, and becoming the great example and pattern of it to the whole reafonable creation. And what fhows, that he ftill continues obftinate and impenitent as a finner, and takes pleafure and delight in it, as his proper employment and daily woik, is,

That not content with finning againft God *himfelf*, he is in a very criminal refpect, *the author* of *mens fins*, by affiduoufly and artfully tempting them to fin, and doing whatever he can to feduce and perfuade them into guilt and ruin. It is at firft view furprifing, that *reafonable beings*, whofe poweis and faculties of reafon were given them, to render them capable of the very high and elevated

† John viii. 44.

fervices of religion and virtue, of imitating
God by works of righteoufnefs and goodnefs,
and fecuring their beft and higheft happinefs,
in the acceptance and favour of the greateft
and beft of beings, fhould become fo intirely
corrupt, fhould fo wholly degenerate from all
moral excellency and rectitude, and be fo
abfolutely loft to all fenfe of and regard to
their own welfare and honour, as to be wholly
funk into the infamy of fin, and delight to
make others as vile as themfelves : Efpecially,
that beings of fuch fuperior powers, privileges and endowments, as *angels* are, fhould
fo far degrade themfelves, and be fo dread-
fully changed from what they were, when
brought into being by God, as not only to
continue in their *apoftacy* from him, and habitually delight in thofe crimes which are his
abhorrence ; but fhould condefcend to become
a kind of traders in vice, the mean and vile *feducers of others* into all kinds of wickednefs,
and by lying, falfe infinuations, deceitful,
treacherous impofitions, and by all the methods of fraud and iniquity, fhould make it
a proper bufinefs to propagate corruption and
mifery, and fpread that ruin in the creation of
God, which reafon, the dictates of juftice,
and every fentiment of compaffion and goodnefs, would excite them to prevent. But the
wonder will in fome meafure ceafe, if we confider what not infrequently *paffes amongft mankind.* For how often have we feen perfons
of the greateft abilities, natural endowments,
fprightlinefs and wit, who have made great
improvements

improvements in science, and must be acknowledged by all that know them to be
persons of superior genius and understanding :
I say how many instances have we seen of
such, who, notwithstanding all these advantages, have been the most profligate and abandoned, both with respect to their principles
and morals ; without one right sentiment to
guide them, or one valuable disposition to
influence and govern them, in whom reason
hath been wholly overcome by sense and appetite, and who seem to make little or no
other use of all their valuable abilities, but to
become more desperately wicked themselves,
and to spread with greater success the dreadful
contagion of infidelity, and all the most
scandalous enormities of vice amongst others.

When men become wicked themselves,
there seems to be in them an unnatural desire
to corrupt others, and a real but execrable
pleasure that they take in destroying innocence
and virtue wherever they can see it, in rooting
out all principle where they have any influence, and in rendering human nature in others
as contemptible, scandalous, and sordidly vile,
as 'tis in themselves. And what are these
but *real fiends in human shapes,* the destroyers
of men, and the murtherers of their souls,
by false insinuation and lying suggestions, and
so acting the part, and doing the works of
the devil, and doing it more effectually under
the appearance of men. For 'tis one of the
prevailing characters of this evil spirit in the
sacred writings, that he is a *tempter* to sin.
Undoubtedly

Undoubtedly he feduced many of the angels to be partakers with him in his guilt. He entered paradife, tempted and actually feduced our firft parents, and by them introduced fin and death into the world. He infolently tempted our bleffed Lord, but there found himfelf abfolutely difappointed, and Jefus was the only inftance amongft the fons of men, where his temptations were wholly ineffectual. He hath been the great patron of fin, and the mean and vile inftrument of drawing men into it, in all ages and nations of the world; and doth not yet ceafe to go on in the fame deteftable employment, and to practife on the paffions and imaginations of mankind, in order to deceive, corrupt and deftroy them. And on this account fin is properly the work of the devil, as wicked men commit it by his fuggeftion, follow his example in doing it, and are employed by him as the avowed patron and original introducer of it. So that mens crimes are his works, as he acts by them, he is fo far the author of them, and the guilt of them imputable to his account, as they are committed by his inftigation, and he derives his fatisfaction and pleafure from them.

But then it muft be carefully obferved, that whatever fhare evil fpirits may have, as tempters and feducers in the fins of others, this by no means *takes away,* or *diminishes the guilt of finners* themfelves; and that maxim of the Apoftle ftill remains true, *that every man is tempted, when he is drawn away of his*

own

own lust, and enticed *. *i. e.* They are mens own paſſions, affections and deſires, by which they are properly tempted or inſtigated to evil, and without which they would be incapable of all external temptations. *When lust*, or the inward appetites and deſires *conceives*, grows warm and ſtrong, fires and ſwells the imagination, and becomes big with the proſpect of gratification and indulgence, *it brings forth ſin*; ſin is and will be the effect and fruit of it. And every man finds it ſo by continual experience. He finds himſelf prompted to ſin by his own inclinations ; the call of his appetites is what he follows, and when he coṃes to reflect on the crimes he hath been guilty of, he naturally condemns himſelf, knows that the fault is chargeable on his own content and choice, and that no one could have forced him to have done wrong without it. He who tempts another to do evil, immediately diſcovers his own wickedneſs, and that his intention is to enſnare the perſon he tempts to his own ruin : And this is ſo far from being any reaſon why he ſhould comply with the temptation, that it is one of the ſtrongeſt in the world why he ſhould reject it, and reſolve never to have any thing more to do with the perſon who offers it ; though the *tempter* is *accountable* for *ſoliciting* another to ſin, and ſo far partaker in the guilt of it, yet as the complying with the temptation intirely depends on the determination of every man's

---

* James i. 14.

own will, the conſent of which the temptation cannot force, that *compliance* muſt be *voluntary*, and the ſins committed, in conſequence
of it, become properly his actions who doth
them, *he is accountable* in the nature of things
for them, and juſtly liable to all the penal
conſequences attending them.

Nothing therefore can be weaker than to
alledge the being tempted by the devil, as an
excuſe or *alleviation* for mens ſins, when it is
really one of the circumſtances that aggravates
and renders them more heinous. For what
is *his character*? Is it not that of a rebel and
offender againſt God? That of an enemy to
truth and righteouſneſs? That of a ſeducer
and deſtroyer of men? Conſiderations that
ſhould make them reject his ſuggeſtions with
abhorrence, and abſtain from the evils to
which he ſollicits them, as from death and
damnation. If ſin be *his work*, for that very
reaſon it ſhould *not be ours*. If he will perform
the mean and criminal office of a tempter and
ſeducer, leave him to his guilt, but don't be
partaker in it ; let him go on to expoſe himſelf to an aggravated vengeance ; but be not
the fool to be enſnared by an enemy who
ſeeks for thy deſtruction, and who is mad
enough to damn himſelf doubly, if ſo be he
can but prevent thy ſalvation. Bring thy
paſſions under government. Guard againſt
the habits of ſin, let reaſon, conſcience, and
principle be attended to, *put on the whole ar-
mour of God*, and uſe the means appointed for
thy ſafety, and his temptations will be entirely
harmleſs,

harmlefs, and have no power and influence over thee. *A bad heart* is the *moft dangerous tempter*, and no man is ever fafe, who is in poffeffion of it. He is liable every moment he lives to be enfnared and overcome by it. He cherifhes in his own breaft an enemy, againft which it is almoft impoffible he fhould ever guard himfelf. Every folicitation from without, will be ftrengthened by the traitor within him, and rendered effectual by his in-fluence and perfuafion. Expel this fecret ad-verfary, and all is fafe. Evil fpirits may tempt, but they can make no impreffion on a good mind. *God* himfelf is concerned for the fafety of an upright man, and he, *under every temptation, will find out a way for his efcape.*

How doth this account *heighten the evil of fin*, and how ftrong a character of infamy and guilt doth it throw on thofe who take plea-fure in and wilfully commit it, in *that they do the works of the devil. He who committeth fin*, faith the Apoftle, he who lives in the habitual practice of wilful and prefumptuous fin, *is of the devil*, he is one of his children, impreffed with his temper, refembles him in difpofition, imitates his example, fubmits to his authority, and is employed in his fervice. Upon which account our bleffed Saviour tells the Jews, for their oppofition to the truth, their hatred of his perfon, and the envy and malice with which they perfecuted him and fought his death †, *Ye are of your father the devil,* and

† John viii. 44.

the

the works of your father ye do. He forms by his fuggeftions, and influences their moral nature, difpofition and character, upon which account they are, in the *moral* fenfe, as properly his offspring and children, as in the *natural* one we are the children of earthly parents, from whom we derive our bodily frame, and thofe lineaments and features of our face, by which we refemble them, and are oftentimes known to be their offspring. And indeed how ftrong is this refemblance that men bear to this evil fpirit, by the difpofitions and habits, and practice of fin ! This wholly defaces the image of God, cuts off their relation to him, as children, and renders them utterly incapable of his approbation and acceptance. *For whofoever is born of God doth not fin**, *i. e.* wilfully and habitually, with pleafure and delight ; *for his feed remains in him* ; the good feed of his word, the principles of truth, and the ingrafted difpofitions of piety and virtue ; fuch a one *cannot fin, becaufe he is* thus *born of God.* A man may have the natural power of doing, what may be juftly faid he cannot do, in a moral fenfe. There is no man, who lives in this world, but is liable to fin, and therefore may actually fin. But yet he *who is born of God,* formed into the Chriftian temper, under the influence of the principles of divine truth, and in poffeffion of all thofe facred difpofitions, which are effential to the character of God's children, fuch a one *cannot*

* i John iii. 9.

fin,

fin, i. e. delight and perfevere in the practice
of it ; becaufe it is what he abhors and detefts,
what all his beft principles and convictions
oppofe, and what all the governing difpofitions of his mind, and the good influences
of the fpirit of God, which he is under, do
in the moft powerful and effectual manner
caufe him to reject. And therefore the
Apoftle adds : *In this the children of God, and
the children of the devil are manifeft* *. *Whofoever doth not righteoufnefs is not of God, neither
he that loveth not his brother.*

You fee here Chriftians the *grand divifion*
made of *all mankind* : They are either *the
children of God,* or *the children of the devil.*
What conftitutes them God's children is the
love of truth and charity, and the practice of
univerfal righteoufnefs. What renders them
the children of the devil is, oppofition to the
truth, enmity to goodnefs, and the love and
practice of fin. But would any wife man
choofe to be the children of fuch a father,
and to be the members of fo infamous, accurfed, and deteftable a family ? Can it be
for our own reputation to refemble him,
who is the moft monftrous and deformed being in the whole univerfe of God, and the
features of whofe face are all compofed of
pride, envy, revenge, malice, hatred of God
and goodnefs, cruelty, and every difpofition
that can diftort and blacken it ? And can any
thing be faid to paint out in a ftronger light

* Verfe 10.

the

the intrinfick evil of fin, than that fo far as
it prevails, it defaces the glorious image of
God, and imprefles on thee a refemblance of
a fiend, and transforms the man into a devil.
This is not my reprefentation, but that of the
fpirit of God and truth. And it is not a figurative, but a real defcription, agreeable to
nature and fact. For if the devil be, according to the Scripture account, a finner from
the beginning, and continues to be fo, is the
great promoter of, and the tempter of others
to do it, then all thofe who live in a courfe of
fin are really like him, imitate him as their
example, and are in the moral fenfe his children, and belong to that family of which he
is really the head and father. Are there any
of you here, who are *habitual flaves* to the
power of fin ; whofe confciences reproach
you, with allowing yourfelves in any of thofe
grofler crimes, which argue enmity to God,
which are inconfiftent with the love and
practice of righteoufnefs, and difcover you
to be deftitute of all reverence and affection
for God ? You would perhaps count it a breach
of decency and good manners, fhould I tell
you in plain terms, what you really are, and
to whom you belong. I will not tell you,
that I may not offend you. But I will tell
you what the fpirit of revelation fays, and if
you are offended it muft be at your own pe-
ril. And it is this in plain words : *He who committeth fin is of the devil* *, and that it is this

* Eph. ii. 2.

evil spirit, who works in the children of disobedience. You see from hence whose influence you are under, if you are workers of iniquity, whom you are to call father, and from whom you are to receive your final portion and inheritance. And shall any of us thus choose to be numbered in his family, who is a rebel and an apostate from God, an exile from Heaven, and an outcast from celestial glory, proscribed to eternal death by the just vengeance of the Almighty, and who wants to influence and tempt thee sinner to partake in his guilt, that thou mayest finally share in his damnation. Retreat therefore timely from the paths of sin. Scorn to imitate the father of lies and wickedness. Apply to the grace of the Redeemer, that he would rescue thee from the power of the evil spirit, form thee into his own image, reconcile thee to God, and give thee a right to the inheritance of his children. Blessed, for ever blessed be God, who manifested his Son in the world, to destroy the works of the devil. Blessed be thy name, thou benevolent Saviour of the world, who came on this errand of compassion and goodness. Oh ! deliver us all from the works of this destroyer, and in imitation of thy example and obedience to thy commands, may we work the works of God, and be found in the habitual practice of righteousness, that we may become the *children of God*, and the happy *heirs* of eternal life and blessedness. Amen and Amen.

But

But there is *another evil*, which ſtands in cloſe connection with *ſin* ; which is attributed to and the proper work of the devil, and which *the Son of God was* alſo manifeſted to deſtroy, and that is *death*. And that the Apoſtle had this alſo in his thoughts, appears from the context, in which he tells us, that the goſpel doctrine obliges us to be of a different ſpirit from *Cain, who was of the evil one and ſlew his brother* *. He was like that evil ſpirit, a *murtherer*, and by his inſtigation ſlew his brother. Deſtruction and death therefore are from the evil ſpirit, and equally his production as ſin itſelf. And this ſentiment is plainly confimed by the author to the Hebrews ; and the expreſſions are ſomewhat parallel to thoſe before us. For as Chriſt is here ſaid to *be manifeſted to deſtroy the works of the devil* ; he is there ſaid to have *taken part of fleſh and blood* †, that *through death he might deſtroy him that had the power of death, that is the devil*. It was a ſettled opinion amongſt the *Jews*, that *Samael* or *Satan* was the *Angel of death* §, and received commiſſion from God to execute it. If the meaning of this be, that *all* who die are deſtroyed by this Angel of death, or by the *immediate hand of Satan*, 'tis an aſſertion that hath nothing in reaſon and ſcripture to ſupport it. Diſtemper, old age, a thouſand accidents will occaſion death, without any immediate interpoſition of this Angel of death.

---

* Verſe 12. † Heb. ii. 14. § Maimon. M. Nev. p. 398.

for

for their deftruction. Not to add, that with
refpect to all fincere Chriftians, this evil fpirit
hath no power over them, God having difpoffeffed him by Chrift of his dominion in
this refpect, and given *the keys of Hades and
death* into the hands of *Chrift.* And therefore
this expreffion of the Apoftle, of the devil's
having the power of death, cannot fignify,
that he ever had fo the power of it in his
hands, as to inflict it at his pleafure, that
every difeafe of which men died was of his
fending, or that every accident which put a
period to men's lives was owing to his contrivance and power. The great events of life
and death are under a *better difpofal* and management, and the Chriftian need not give
himfelf a moment's uneafinefs about the power
which Satan hath to take away his life, or
haften his death. He hath none at all over
him ; for by being recovered from fin by
the word and fpirit of God, he is no longer
under the dominion of the deftroyer, who
cannot take away a fingle moment from the
period of his life, and is not the executioner
of the divine vengeance to deprive him of
life, when he leaves this world, and ex-
changes it for an eternal one. For he is under the perpetual guardianfhip of the power
of God, and interefted in thofe gracious promifes of the Redeemer, which affure him,
that *Satan fhall be trodden under his feet*, that
the *good guardian Angels* fhall watch over and
minifter to him living and dying, and convey
him fafe in his departing moments, into thofe
facred

facred receptacles of reft and peace, that God hath provided for his faithful fervants, there to abide under the immediate cuftody, and in *the prefence of Chrift,* 'till their refurrection to a blefled life and immortality. However, there is a proper fenfe, in which death is the work of the devil, and in which he may juftly be faid to have the power of it. For

He introduced death into the world, as the fruit and punifhment of fin, and as *fin* was his work, as he was the original feducer of mankind to it, fo alfo *death is his work,* becaufe it is *the wages of fin.* And it is upon this ac- count that our blefled Saviour declares of him, that *he was a murtherer from the begin- ing* * ; becaufe by tempting and feducing our firft parents into fin, he fubjected them to immediate death, and involved all their po- fterity in the fame condemnation and ruin ; *for as by one man fin entered into the world, death alfo entered by fin, and fo death paffed upon all men, for that all have finned* †. Death in- deed was the penalty annexed by God to tranfgreffion, and which the evil fpirit never could have inflicted on mankind without this permiffion and conftitution of God. But as he knew the law under which man was cre- ated, deceived him out of his obedience, and prevailed with him to violate the condition of his life and happinefs ; he became pro- perly the deftroyer and murtherer of the whole human fpecies, and introduced all the

---

* John viii. 44.   † Rom. v. 12.

ravages

ravages and defolations of death, throughout all the various ages and nations of mankind, and fo laid wafte this fair and beautiful creation of God, which was originally formed to be the dwelling of innocence, the garden of life, and the paradife of enjoyment and pleafure.   It is *objected* to this account :

That *Adam was formed out of the duft*, as to his bodily frame, and that the *materials* of it were *corruptible* and *feparable*, and could have no principle of immortality in it.   That he had as real need of the recruits of fleep and proper food in Paradife, as we have, for his nourifhment and fupport, and muft have died fooner or later whether he had finned or not, without fome powerful provifion to guard him from mortality and death, and to repair thofe defects and decays of his animal frame, to which in the nature of things it was liable ; all this is very true, but an objection nothing to the purpofe.   Nor is there any difficulty in fuppofing, either that God at firft formed the *original conftitution* of man of a *more durable and firm* contexture, than that we all experience it to be at prefent ; or that he could, and did caufe the earth in her primitive ftate of unwafted vigour to produce trees, plants and vegetables, originally with fuch *medicinal* and powerfully *reftorative virtues* and qualities, as fhould prevent all fatal diforders, recruit the conftitution from time to time, guard it againft all inward decays, revive the wafting fpirits, and lengthen out life to any fuppofeable term of duration ? The
longevity

longevity of the *Antediluvian Patriarchs* is
expreflly afferted in the facred writings, and
confirmed by many intimations of the moft
ancient profane hiftory. And there are now
many things in the vegetable, mineral and
animal worlds, that have reftorative, ftrength-
ening qualities, free the body from diforders,
and tend to the prolonging and enjoyment of
life. Let now the fagacious naturalift inform
us, how the life of man, in the firft ages of
the world, was *lengthened* out to a period fo
largely exceeding that of the prefent generation; or if he will, by what means it *en-
dures even to the prefent term* ; and we may
venture to affure him, that we, in our turn,
will inform him, with equal certainty, how
it may be protracted to any fuppofeable term
or period whatfoever. For I imagine that
the fame author of nature, who formed man
for fo much longer a duration than the infect, who lives and dies in a day, or a month,
or a year, could with equal eafe have created
man to endure the whole length of the antediluvian race, which is not the life of an
infect when compared to eternity ; or for
any longer term, or period of duration that
can be affigned. And if it can be fairly explained, how our prefent food repairs the
daily wafte of nature, and preferves the
animal œconomy in due vigour, or how the
virtues of medicine preferve from the fatal
effects of bodily diforder, or repair the conftitution when emaciated and enfeebled by
it ; I believe we fhall then be foon able to

L 4 makg

make the difcovery, how the food of our firft
parents in Paradife, when all the fruits and
productions of the earth muft have been particularly falutary and nutricious, might have
perpetually preferved the vigour of the conftitution ; or at leaft how the medicinal virtues of certain fruits and vegetables might
have done it, had their ordinary food been
infufficient for this wonderful and vivifying
purpofe. And that there was fuch a *provifion* made, for originally *perpetuating* the life
of man, had he preferved his innocence, is
extremely plain from revelation ; which affures us that *Eden had its tree of life* ; and
that when man had finned, and the perpetuating his life muft have proved the utter
ruin of the world. *God drove him out of
Eden, leaft he fhould put forth his hand, and
take alfo of the tree of life, and eat, and live
for ever* * ; i. e. leaft by having perpetual re-
courfe to the fruit of this tree, he fhould
guard himfelf againft diftemper and mortality,
and thus perpetuate his life in a ftate of guilt
and mifery. And I fee no more wonder and
miracle in this, than that by food and phy-
fick we fhould now be able to guard off
difeafe, and continue our exiftence to fixty
or feventy years, or any longer or fhorter period of human life. Man therefore was originally created with all the natural means of
prolonging and perpetuating his prefent life ;
at leaft *'till God fhould pleafe to tranflate him* into

---

* Gen. iii. 22.

a beta better, *without the pains of dying.* And that God would thus have tranflated him, feems to me at leaft extreamly probable, from the inftances of *Enoch* and *Elijah*, whofe tranfla-tions feem to fhew us, what would have been the privilege of all men, had they not cor-rupted and deftroyed themfelves by fin. Death was therefore an evil man had it in his own power to avoid; and though he made himfelf fubject to it by his own fin and folly, yet as he was *deceived* into fin by the lies and perfidy of the wicked *tempter,* with an intention to deftroy him; both fin and death are equally the works of this malignant fpirit; and on the one account he is the *corrupter* and *feducer* of mankind, and on the other their malicious and implacable *deftroyer.*

And as he was thus a *murtherer from the be-ginning,* fo by tempting men to fin he is *con-tinually employed* in the fame cruel and de-ftructive fervice, and makes their paffions and vices fubfervient to their prefent and eternal ruin. How often are the crimes to which they indulge fatal to life, and all the valuable interefts of it; whereby they cut themfelves off in the midft of their days, either by thofe bodily diftempers which they contract, or expofing themfelves to the ven-geance of human juftice. The horrid deftruc-tions and ravages of *war,* carried on by ambitious and revengeful *princes,* with im-placable and unrelenting hatred againft each other, facrificing thoufands and ten thoufands in the fury of their rage and madnefs; Is not

the

the *devil* executing by them his murthcrous purpofes, and glutting his fpite and malice in the innumerable cruelties they commit with pleafure and triumph ? Are they not *his in-ftruments*, and do his works and act by thofe infernal paffions which he infpires, heighthens and enrages ? Could men act thus did humanity poffefs them ? They may ridicule the notions of a devil, and his tempting and inftigating mankind to vice ; but they themfelves too ftrongly prove the reality of his agency, and what manner of fpirit they are poffeffed by ; a fpirit not human or divine, but a fpirit fierce and deftructive, that delights in the carnage of mankind, and that fports itfelf with the mifery and flaughter of the innocent and helplefs, and which therefore demonftrates, that they are influenced by a fpirit and policy *earthly, fenfual, and devilifh*. For what can the policy of the devil himfelf influence them to befides, or worfe than this : Or how can they more effectually prove themfelves his children, than by imitating his example, and doing thofe works which are the moft perfect copies of his own, and of all others the moft agreeable to his will ?

The truth is, that the entire dominion of this evil fpirit is upheld and continued by the prevalence of fin and death. He is the author and father of both, as he tempted, prevailed, and deftroyed our firft parents, and involved all their pofterity in the confequences of their fall. And therefore in the fame fenfe

as

as sin is his work, so is death ; of which he may be said to have the power, because whenever he prevails with men to sin, he as certainly prevails with them to destroy themselves, and renounce the invaluable blessing of eternal life. *He that sins against me,* says wisdom, *doth violence to his own soul, all they that hate me love death* *. Death therefore attends his pleasure, 'tis his inseparable companion, it strikes the mortal blow wherever his suggestions are admitted and prevail ; and will triumph over mankind to the end of the world, who are all involved in the original sentence, justly and that because all here are in their natures obnoxious to sin and guilt, and must therefore submit to the penalty annexed to it by the wisdom and justice of God, which is death. And this ruin would have been irrecoverable and eternal, had not the mercy of God interposed. As he was the person in a peculiar manner offended by sin, he only could forgive it, and remit in any part the penalties attending it. As he is the sole author and lord of life, he only can give it originally, or restore it when lost. Every man therefore that dies, for any thing that created power can do, dies eternally, and can never revive to life and happiness. And whether as sinners, the penalty of death shall be everlasting, or finally reversed, must depend on the *good pleasure of God,* and can only be known to us by the revelation of his will. And

* Prov. viii. 36.

blessed

bleffed be God we are affured, that neither fin nor death fhall be permitted to triumph univer-fally or for ever, over mankind, that the power of the evil fpirit fhall be broken, and his do-minion come to a perpetual end. And this brings me to the more pleafing part of this fubject, which is

II. To reprefent to you the *benevolence and grace of God* towards a finful world, in the manifeftation of his Son, in order to deftroy the works of the devil. But of this in the next difcourfe.

SERMON

SERMON VI.

The Goodnefs of G O D in the Manifeftation of his Son.

1 JOHN iii. 8.

For this purpofe was the Son of God manifefted, that he might deftroy the works of the devil.

IN a preceding difcourfe I gave you a view of thofe works of the devil, which the Son of God was manifefted to deftroy, *fin* and *death*. I am now

II. To reprefent to you the *grace* or *benevolence* of *God*, towards a finful world, in the *manifeftation of his Son*, in order to his deftroying the works of the devil. *For this purpofe was the Son of God manifefted, that he might deftroy the works of the devil.*

Confidering this evil fpirit as the enemy of God, and the feducer and deftroyer of man; how could God more effectually confult our peace and welfare, than by fending fo great and excellent a perfon to prevent the effects of his perfidy and malice ? If *fin* be the *reproach* of human nature, if it *alienates* us from God, the *eternal fource of happinefs*, and if it creates

in

in all, that are fubject to the power and flaves
to the practice of it, a real indifpofition and
incapacity for ever attaining their ultimate
and fupream felicity ; the deftruction of the
love of fin in us, and our reconciliation to
God by faith and love, and holinefs of heart
and life, is bleffing us in the moft fubftantial
and durable manner, and is infinitely more
defirable and valuable, than all the treafures
of the earth that can be put into our poffeffion.   If *life* is highly to be prized, and *immortal life* and *bleffednefs* are the greateft objects
to which our ambition, or moft partial wifhes
can reach, what muft *death* be ! How formi-
dable an evil ! How uncomfortable the profpect of it ! How immenfe the lofs we fuftain
by it ! The abfolute lofs of ourfelves, of
every thing we poffefs, and of all that we can
hope for ! The deftruction of death is it not
the reverfal of our own deftruction ! To
overcome this enemy, how glorious the victory ! To return to life and happinefs, how
pleafing will be the furprize ! What fatisfaction and triumph will attend it ! Oh who
can fufficiently adore the exceeding riches of
the divine grace, in raifing us to the hope
and giving us the promife of fo fignal a redemption ! The Son of God was manifefted
to deftroy both fin and death, both of them
the works of that evil fpirit, who tempts men
to fin, eternally to ruin and deftroy them.
Confider here

  1. The *perfon* employed to abolifh thefe
evils is of no lefs a character than that of the
Son

Son of God. Undoubtedly this title is given to our blessed Lord to set forth the *dignity* of his person, and to represent to us how *fit* he was to be employed in this errand, and how capable of effecting the purpose, for which his heavenly Father sent him. This adversary of God was grown wise by his experience, was well versed in the arts of deception, had grown insolent by success, was one of those beings who excelled in strength, and was not to be dispossessed of his usurpations, to be defeated in his policy, or prevented in his future schemes of destruction, by one of inferior capacities and powers. How unequal would the contest have been between one of the angelick order, and this insinuating and mighty spirit, who drew in the third part of the Angels themselves, to be partakers of his crimes, and sharers in his condemnation ! As to men, they were all of them become guilty before God, and inevitably subject to destruction and death, from which they knew their recovery to be by themselves absolutely impossible. Who then was sufficiently mighty and able to save them ? God would not undoubtedly employ an improper instrument to accomplish his own design of goodness ; either one too weak to accomplish it, or who by a transcendently superior dignity of person and character was above being sent on an errand, that would have been successfully managed by one of an inferior nature and station. And therefore God fixed on him to be his substitute in this affair, who is by nature the *express*
image

image of his person, and the *bright representation of his glory*; on him, who was his great agent in the formation of man, to rescue him from the power of him who had deſtroyed him; that both in the works of creation and redemption he might have the pre-eminence, who is the *only Son of God*, i. e. the Son of God in ſuch a ſuperior ſenſe, as cannot be affirmed of any created being whatſoever. A choice this, that ſhews both the importance and difficulty of deſtroying the works of the devil.

2. To effect this, the Apoſtle tells us, the Son of God was *manifeſted*. The manifeſtation here ſpoken of refers to his *incarnation*, when he firſt came into the world and tabernacled in our fleſh, and to the whole of his after miniſtry, when *he came* publickly *to his own* people, and *manifeſted his glory* by the miracles which he performed, the doctrines he taught, the precepts he gave, and the promiſes he made, in order to perſuade them to believe in him and obey him, and gave himſelf up to the death, to accompliſh the ſcheme of his Father's goodneſs, and perfect the redemption of thoſe that were given him. And there is this intrinſick evidence of the truth of Chriſtianity, that though the ſcheme of ſalvation by Chriſt conſiſts of many parts and branches; yet there is ſuch a mutual connection of all of them, and ſuch an entire dependence of every one of them on each other, as that they all concur to produce the one great confeſſed deſign; inſomuch that take

away

away any one single essential branch, the
whole will appear confused and imperfect,
and incapable of effectually answering the
avowed intention of it.   This intention of
the gospel revelation, and the appearance of
Christ in the world, as expressed in the
words of my text, is to destroy the works of
the devil.   And when the several parts of
our blessed Lord's mediation are duly considered, they will all of them appear to be of
very great importance, and even absolutely
necessary to bring to perfection this benevolent purpose of the divine providence and
government.   Let us consider here

1. *That the Son of God was manifested to
destroy the works of the devil*, by putting a stop
to the *prevalence* and *dominion of sin*, and re-
scuing men from their subjection to the influence and power of it.   Our blessed Saviour,
in *his own person and conduct*, foiled this great
deceiver in every attempt to seduce and ensnare him.   He maintained his obedience and
fidelity to his heavenly Father, notwithstanding the most artful endeavours to beguile and
corrupt him, and was the only person of
the human race, who escaped the pollution
and guilt of sin, and secured himself from
the condemnation due to it.   So that the
Son of God may be said to have destroyed
the works of the devil, as in his own behaviour he was perfectly free from sin,
broke the force of all his temptations to it,
trampled the tempter under his feet, rendered
wholly ineffectual all his arts to seduce and

corrupt him, exhibited a noble example of an uniform, fteady piety and virtue, and thus gave a fignal check to his ufurpations, and the triumphs of fin over mankind. But farther,

Chrift was manifefted to deftroy the works of the devil, as the intention of his appearance was to *put an end to the impious idolatries and fuperftitions,* which had prevailed for fo many ages almoft among all the nations of the world. That *barbarous* and *uncultivated nations,* who had no arts or learning to civilize and polifh them, fhould fall into miftaken fentiments of deity, and practice abfurd and ridiculous rites of worfhip, perhaps is not fo much to be wondered at ; though I confefs it lowers my opinion of the *great fagacity* and *boafted perfection* of *human reafon,* to reflect that any, who have reafonable powers, fhould fo utterly miftake the nature of God, as the heathen world did, introduce fuch a rout of deities, as they fet up for objects of adoration, and give into fuch methods of worfhipping them, as argued the want of common fenfe, and bid defiance to decency, truth, piety, and every juft fentiment of the nature and perfections of God. But how much more aftonifhing is it, that *nations* and *cities,* where all the *liberal arts and fciences flourifhed,* who reafoned and judged well in almoft all other affairs relating to the conduct of human life, and amongft whom there were men of the fineft genius, and well verfed in all parts of literature. I.

fay

fay how truly aftonifhing it is, that *Athens* and *Rome*, in their highelt period of glory, and with all their advantages for wifdom and knowledge, yet fhould continue in such a ftate of ftupid ignorance with regard to the firft principle of all religion, and not excel the wildeft barbarians on the face of the earth in. the modes and ceremonies of their religious worfhip ! This is moft unqueftionably fact, and abundantly fhews that the *wifdom of this world* could not deftroy this mighty fabrick of the powers of darknefs, this chief, this mafterpiece of all the works of the devil, Idolatry ; into which all the nations of the woild had been deceived, and out of which no human power had been able to recover them. But *our Lord was manifefted to deftroy this work* of the great corrupter of men ; for he appeared to *reveal the father* ; to form men into worthy fentiments of God, to recal them to the worfhip of him, and to difcover that good and acceptable manner, in which they were to pay the worfhip which was due to him. And as the Son of God came with this view, fo he forefaw his fuccefs, and rejoiced in the fure profpect of it : Thus he fays to his difciples, upon their rejoicing that the *devils were fubject to them through his name : I beheld Satan, as lightening, fall from Heaven* *, i. e. divefted of that majefty and power which he had ufurped, by being worfhipped as God, and caft out from Heaven,

where the ignorance and fuperftitious folly of
men had placed him, as lightening, i. e. fud-
denly, and by the fpeedy prevalence of my
doctrine and religion.   And in another place
he tells his difciples.   *Now is the judgment of*
this world *.   God will foon decide the fate
of it, and refcue it from thofe vile idolatries
that have fo long overfpread it.   *Now fhall*
the prince of this world, who by the fuperftitions and vices he introduced reigned over
mankind, *be caft out,* be ftript of his dominion, ejected from his employ, and be no
longer worfhipped as God by the nations of
the earth.   And as the great intention of St.
Paul's miffion to the Gentiles was, to *open*
their eyes, and to turn them from darknefs to
light, and from the power of Satan unto God †,
fo wherever the doctrine he taught prevailed, idolatry immediately became the abhorrence of mankind, they renounced all the
infamous works of it, reconciled themfelves
to the true God, and worfhipped him through
the mediation of Chrift in fpirit and in truth.
And this muft, in the nature of things, be
the perpetual effect of the reception and
fuccefs of the gofpel doctrine, to expel idolatry wherever it hath been fettled, and to prevent the return of it wherever it hath been
rejected.   Again farther,

The Son of God was manifefted to deftroy
the works of the devil, as the great intention
of his appearance in our world was, to *re-*

* John xii. 31.   † Acts xxvi. 18.

cover

cover men from their *slavery to sinful passions and habits*, to bring them to repentance, to enable them to break off their sinful courses, and to return to God by the regular practice of all the duties of righteousness. This is the express doctrine of our blessed Lord himself. For he tells his disciples, *I am come, not to call the righteous, but sinners to repentance* †. And when the Jews boasted of their freedom, he tells them, *that if the Son should make them free*, viz. by saving them from the bondage of their vices, *they should be free indeed* ‡ ; partakers of the most necessary and valuable liberty. And indeed the whole of his doctrine is calculated to represent to men the danger of sin, the necessity of obedience to God by doing his will, and the practice of righteousness, and the folly of, and final ruin that must attend the substituting any thing in the place of real religion, and the virtues of a good life. And with this evident intention of his doctrine the whole of his life and character corresponded; for in him there was no unrighteousness at all, nor could any of his most inveterate enemies charge him with, or *convict him of sin.* How should they ? For it was *his meat to do the will of his heavenly father*, and he continually *went about doing good* to the bodies and souls of men. And by giving us such an amiable and perfect pattern he evidently discovered the end of his manifestation to be to save men from their sins, and

† Matt. ix. 13. ‡ John viii. 36.

from

from his power, who is the cruel tempter and
seducer of them to sin, and by obedience to
God to reinstate them in his favour, and secure them the glorious inheritance of his
children. His Apostles after him assert the
same important doctrine, that the end of
Christ's appearance was to rescue mankind
from slavery to their vices, and purge them
from all dead works. Thus Peter to the
Jews. *Him hath God sent to bless you, in turn-*
ing away every one of you from his iniquities *.
And St. John, a verse or two before my text :
To know that he was manifested to take away our
sins †, i. e. as appears from the whole context, to recover and preserve us from the
works of sin, that herein we might resemble
him ; for the Apostle immediately adds :
And in him there is no sin. This also is the
burthen of St. Paul's epistles : Who tells us,
that *this is a faithful saying, and worthy of all*
acceptation, that Christ came into the world to
save sinners ‡ ; both from their sins and the
condemnation due to them ; and that *the*
grace of God hath appeared to us, *bringing sal-*
vation, by teaching us, that denying ungodliness
and worldly lusts, we should live soberly, righte-
ously and godly in the present world, looking for
the blessed hope and glorious appearance of the
great God, *and our Saviour Jesus Christ, who*
gave himself for us, that he might redeem us
from all iniquity, and purify unto himself a pe-
culiar people, zealous of good works §. This is

* Acts iii. 26.   † 1 John iii. 5.   ‡ 1 Tim. i. 15.
§ Tit. ii. 11—14.

also

alfo farther evident from that abundant provifion, which the mercy of God hath made
to accomplifh this great work of men's falvation from fin. All the *doctrines of the gof-*
pel are *doctrines according to godlinefs,* that lead
to and powerfully promote the practice of
it, and it is the very end of our believing the
truth to make us free from fin, and thoroughly fanctify and renew us. The *pre-*
cepts of Chrift command us *to mortify every*
finful affection and habit, enjoin us to *repent,*
to *bring forth fruits meet for repentance,* and
to practice every virtue that can refult from
any of thofe relations and circumftances, in
which mankind can be placed. The *example*
of the Son of God is the higheft reproach to all
immorality and vice, and the nobleft recommendation of every thing that is facred, virtuous
and praife-worthy. *His promifes* are given us,
that under the influence of them *we might*
efcape the corruptions that are in the world through
luft, and that we might be effectually perfuaded
to *perfect holinefs in the fear of God.* The good
fpirit of God is offered to us, as the fpirit of
truth and holinefs, and that by his influences
we might *be fanctified throughout, in body, foul,*
and fpirit. The end of his *giving himfelf to*
death for us was, *that he might deliver us from*
this prefent evil world, redeem us from all ini-
quity, and refcue us from the vanity of a finful converfation with his own moft precious
blood, and *that our fouls might be purified by*
our obeying the truth. For this end he is *ex-*
alted to be a Prince and a Saviour, that he might

grant repentance and forgiveness of fins. God *hath appointed a day in which he will judge the world in righteousness by Jesus Christ,* to enforce the commands of *repentance* for pall fins, preferve us from the guilt of future offences, and *establish us unblameable in holiness to the end.* And indeed for what other end, exclufive of this, can we poffibly conceive God fhould fend his Son into the world? Had it not been for fin, we had needed no redemption. There had been no curfe, no mifery, no death. Man would have needed no forgivenefs, would never have afked it, and could have had nothing to fear from the difpleafure and juftice of God his Maker. His innocency would have been his fafety, maintained his confidence in God, and perpetuated his happinefs in the divine favour. 'Tis fin is the one great comprehenfive caufe of all the evils that infeft our world, renders focieties and individuals unhappy, and expofes the doers of it to temporal and eternal miferies. Remove this evil from amongft mankind, the voice of mifery would ceafe, and the world would immediately be converted into a paradifiacal eftate. Reftore to man his innocency, he will be reftored to himfelf, to his God, and to all the loft glory and happinefs of his nature, and God will pronounce him, as at his firft creation, *very good,* behold him with approbation, and fhew that approbation by the uninterrupted effects of his favour. It was therefore a fcheme worthy the infinite wifdom and benevolence of God,

God, to fend his Son into the world, in order to prevent that univerfal ruin, in which
the fubtlety of the tempter had involved
mankind ; by raifing them from the death of
fin, and furnifhing them with the means to
difcover his devices, and overcome all his
temptations to thofe criminal practices, which,
whatever prefent pleafures may attend them,
are bitternefs in the end, and utterly inconfiftent with every valuable intereft of our
beings.   And confidering that all the various
miferies of this life flow from fin, as the
original fource of them, I have no poffible
conception, how God himfelf could provide
for our everlafting welfare, without faving
us from this parent complicated evil, or refcue us from the power and mifery of the
evil one, but by enabling us to *deftroy his
works,* by renouncing all the works of iniquity, and working thofe works of God, for
which God originally made us reafonable
creatures, and *which he hath ordained that we
fhould walk in* as Chriftians, and for which
he creates anew in Chrift Jefus our Lord.   But
farther,

Chrift was manifefted to deftroy the works
of the devil, as he came to deftroy *the con-
demning power of fin,* and fet us free from
thofe obligations to punifhment, under which
he had brought us as finners againft God.
Sin is the one great comprehenfive crime
under the divine government, is a contradiction to all the great ends of it, and a direct
violation of his will.   It is abfolutely a contradiction

tradiction to the purity and rectitude of his nature, what he therefore can never approve, what he cannot countenance and encourage, what he will not permit to dwell in his fight, and what he cannot but punifh in all reafonable beings, where it is inveterate and incurable. And this was the end aimed at by the tempter of mankind, firft to feduce men into an apoftacy from God, and then from what he found as the effect of his own tranfgreffions, to involve them in certain and irretrievable condemnation; imagining, that as he had no hopes of remiffion for himfelf, the unhappinefs and ruin of man, when once become guilty before God, would be as fixed and permanent, and hopelefs as his own. But herein both his fagacity and malice deceived him. God, who knew by whofe devices man was corrupted, had compaffion upon his unhappy and deluded creature, and contrived the method both how to reftore him from the power and practice of fin, and confiftent with the honour and intereft of his own character and government, to free him from that condemnation, under which he had brought himfelf. *He fent his Son into the world, not to condemn it, but that the world through him might be faved, and that whofoever would believe in him, fhould not perifh but have everlafting life.* And to effect this great purpofe, *he received a commandment from his Father to lay down his life for his fheep,* whom the Father had given him, and was fent by him *to be the propitiation for*

their

their fins; that having thus cleanfed us from our fins in his own blood, he might reconcile us to God, deliver us from wrath, and reftore us to the blefied and glorious hope of an happy immortality in the kingdom and prefence of God. Oh! how kind a provifion is this to prevent the everlafting triumphs both of *fin and death*; and when reftored by the word and fpirit of God from the dominion and prevalence of fin, and by the Almighty power of God from the corruption of the grave, and the ruines of death, then fhall thefe works of the devil be entirely deftroyed, his arts no more beguile us, his temptations no more endanger us, nor the fear of final condemnation interrupt our peace, nor give us one moment's anxiety and pain. Let us reflect

What a *mark of infamy* is here fet upon *fin*, in that it is declared by the fpirit of God to be the *work of the devil*, and that the *manifeftation of the Son of God was neceffary to deftroy it!* It is what Satan delights in, what he firft introduced into the creation, what men do by his fuggeftions, what enflaves men to his power, what renders them his children, and from the deftruction it brings, they could never have faved themfelves had not the Son of God himfelf undertaken their deliverance. And is it poffible for reafonable creatures to imagine that this is a trivial and inconfiderable evil, or that God can behold it with indifference, or that he will endure it with impunity? He made man originally
after

after his own image, and can he be pleafed
with thee, when thou defaceft it, and put-
teft on a diabolical refemblance ? He created
thee for his own fervice, and to do thofe
works by which thou mayeft manifeft thy
gratitude and obedience to him. And can
he approve thee when thou enflaveft thyfelf
to his power, who is his implacable adverfary, and doeft his works, by which thou
involveft thyfelf in his crimes, and in his
guilt ? Hath he not fent his Son to reclaim
thee from this madnefs, to warn thee againft
his delufions, to enable thee to overcome his
temptations, and thereby to prevent thy
eternal deftruction ? And wilt thou refufe
this falvation, and by thine actions tell thy
Maker, thou prefereft the fervice of the
devil to his will, and wilt perfevere in doing
his works, in fpite of all he hath done by
his only Son for thy redemption ? Let reflection take place but for one minute, when
an inviting temptation to fin prefents itfelf to
thee, and give thyfelf but leifure to afk : Who
is it follicits me to do this evil ? Whofe work
am I going to do ? And what are the wages I
muft expect to receive ? And when thy confcience tells thee, the devil is thy tempter,
that thou art going to do his work, and that
thy wages muft come from his cruel hand :
Will it not ftartle thee ? Will it not make
thee retreat, and when thou confidereft that
the action is diabolical, and the reward muft
be fo too, will it not excite thy horror, caufe
thee to reject the temptation, and fly from it

as

as from destruction and death, and become
the happy means of preserving thy innocence
and peace?

How *glorious* in itself, and how *worthy* the
infinite rectitude and perfection of the divine
nature, is this professed *end* of God's sending
his Son into the world, *to destroy the works of
the devil,* by turning men from their sins, and
recovering them to the love and practice of
universal righteousness? How strongly doth
this point out the intrinsick *excellency* of the
Christian scheme, and shew its *original* to be
from God? If left in the power of this evil
one, if governed by his suggestions, and employed in his service, we must be unavoidably
undone, and can expect nothing but to share
in his condemnation. But if rescued from
his dominion, superior to his suggestions, and
victorious over all his temptations, we *depart
from all iniquity, yield ourselves to God,* and *become the servants of righteousness;* we are secure
from every possible destruction, have the principle of eternal life and happiness within us,
and *nothing shall be able* finally to *separate us
from the love of God in Christ our Lord.*

Lastly, let us therefore be persuaded to *renounce all the unfruitful works of darkness,* and
*work the works of God, who hath sent us, whilst
it is day.* What wise man would serve a bad
and cruel master, when 'tis in his power to
be under the protection of a benevolent and
friendly one? Who would be a slave, that
can enjoy his freedom; or submit to the vilest
drudgery, when he can employ himself in
services

fervices that are the moft honourable and worthy ? Can any man in his fenfes hefitate one
moment, to which of the two he fhall yield
himfelf to obey ; whether a vile, apoftate,
profcribed fpirit, who hath nothing but death
and damnation to beftow upon thofe whom
he can deceive into fubjection ; or the Son of
God, whofe *yoke is eafy and whofe burthen is
light* ; whofe fervice is reafonable, generous,
and pleafing, and whofe reward is life and
glory, and an happinefs commenfurate with
eternity ? Let therefore no follicitations feduce
us from God, into the paths of fin. They
may feem to be ftrewed with flowers, and
appear to the eye of fenfe all delightful and
joyous. But they are in reality full of fnares,
abound with forrows, and end in deftruction.
But if *we have our fruit unto holinefs, and become
the fervants of God*, our way will be fafe, our
minds be chearful, and the *end everlafting life.*

SERMON

SERMON VII.

Chriſt's Temptation in the Wilderneſs explained.

MATTHEW iv. 1.

Then was Jeſus led up of the Spirit into the Wil-
derneſs, to be tempted of the Devil.

THIS hiſtory of our *Saviour's temptation*
is mentioned by *three* Evangeliſts ; by
Matthew and *Luke* more largely, and in the
ſeveral peculiar circumſtances attending it, and
by *Mark*, but in a more general and curſory
manner, and without entering into the particulars of it ; and is I think evidently referred
to by the author to the *Hebrews* ; who, ſpeaking of Chriſt, tells us, *That he was in all points*
tempted like as we are, yet *without ſin* * ; tempted
to the ſame ſins, and by the ſame inſtruments
and methods, though without falling by the
temptations.

This part of ſacred hiſtory hath been excepted againſt, as *improbable* and incredible,

* Heb. iv. 15.

and

and *Chrift* himfelf hath been reprefented upon account of it, as a fort of *melancholy enthufiaft*, whofe head was filled with brain-fick vifions, and notions of apparitions, and converfe with devils ; fecluding himfelf from the converfe and fociety of men, in deferts, to feed upon his own melancholy difpofition, and indulge the diforder of a perverted imagination. And in order to get rid of this and other difficulties, fome have imagined, that there was nothing *real* in this tranfaction, no proper appearance of the tempter, but that the feveral things related were only tranfacted in a kind of *vifion* or trance ; like what 'tis thought we may find in many inftances relating to the *ancient prophets*, who are faid to do, what was only done in a prophetick trance or vifion. But this is to cut the knot, inftead of untying it ; and 'till the *facts* recorded are fhewn to be *impoffible* or *unworthy the character* of his miffion from God, or *incapable* of anfwering any *valuable end*, I muft continue to regard the *hiftory as real*, and accordingly fhall confider and endeavour to *vindicate* it as fuch. And here the following particulars deferve to be taken notice of.

1. Our bleffed Saviour was *tempted*, folicited to fin, and to crimes of a very heinous nature, as fhall be hereafter explained ; and by this folicitation his ftrength was *tried*, and *proof made* of his firmnefs and conftancy of mind, of his truft in God, and fubmiffion to his will : And this temptation was *extraordinary* in its nature ; not only by the common ways

ways and methods by which men are tempted and feduced, *viz.* by invifible folicitations, addreffed to their fenfual affections and paffions ; but in an *open manner* alfo, by an addrefs to him immediately in perfon, and to thofe affections and paffions of his nature, as were moft likely to be impreffed and excited, by objects fuitable and agreeable to them. For though our bleffed Saviour had none of thofe criminal propenfities and wrong habits, to which the reft of mankind are unhappily more or lefs fubject, yet he had *all the affections effential* to human nature, and thofe capable of being excited and put into action, by the offer and approach of fuch things, as were pleafing and grateful to them ; and which in their nature, like thofe of other men, were capable of becoming exceffive and irregular. And unlefs he had been in this refpect *like unto us*, he would not have been liable to have been tempted like us at all; as no external objects could otherwife have made any impreffion upon him, nor any motives from them had any influence to feduce and pervert him. We may obferve,

2. That the *agent* in this temptation is expreffly faid to be the *devil. Jefus was led up into the wildernefs to be tempted of the devil ;* and undoubtedly by him who is called fo by way of diftinction and eminence, that evil fpirit, who is at the head of the apoftacy from God. And 'tis evident that the temptation was partly carried on by him in a *vifible fhape.* But in what form he appeared, the

hiftory doth not relate, and I cannot inform
you ; but probably *not as himfelf* ; that would
have been at once to have prevented the effect
of his temptation ? but as a *kind and friendly
Angel*, pitying his lonely and deftitute condition in the defert, and in fuch a form, as
might not terrify, but tend to reconcile our
Lord to his perfon and perfuafions ; and that
the bait might be more agreeable, as thrown
out by one, whom he had no reafon to fufpect
as an enemy and feducer. It feems very evident that he had fome apprehenfion of our
Saviour's being the *Son of God*, and that promifed *feed of the woman*, that was deftined to
crufh his own head, to break his power, and
deftroy his authority and kingdom in the
world ; but at the fame time that he was not
abfolutely fure of it. This *fufpenfe* of mind
is evidently implied in the very firft temptation
mentioned : If *thou be the Son of God*, which
he alfo repeats, when he begins the fecond ;
an expreffion that carried in it fome inward
fufpicion, that he might be this Son of God,
and at the fame time a doubt whether he was
or not. However, to feduce and ruin him,
if he could, was his determined refolution ;
hoping, that as by fubtlety and craft he had
deftroy'd our *firft parents*, even in a ftate of
innocency, fo he might prevail by the fame
means againft *Jefus himfelf* ; and who ever
he was, might, by perfuading and deceiving
him to fin, render him obnoxious to the difpleafure of God, and thereby intirely prevent
every thing he had to fear from his character
and

and influence. This seems to have been the ground of this attempt upon our blessed Lord, who was now entering upon his ministry ; the whole of which must have been rendered ineffectual, had he previous to it fallen a prey to the solicitations of this insidious and faithless deceiver. We may remark farther;

3. The *place* where this temptation of the evil spirit was managed, *viz. in the wilderness.* He *was led into the wilderness to be tempted* ; some uncultivated barren desert, far from the society of men, where none could comfort and assist him, and which by its solitude and waste appearance might excite his fear, awaken uncomfortable imaginations, give force to the suggestions that were offered him, and weaken the natural firmness and resolution of his mind. How *different* this from the situation of our *first parents*, when they were deceived by the tempter's subtlety ; who had their dwelling in the *garden of God*, where every thing was pleasing to the eye, and all the various produce of it grateful to the taste, and good for food ; that was frequented by Angels, and honour'd by the immediate presence of God, where almost every circumstance concurred to render them chearful, and so many considerations of duty, interest, gratitude, all presented themselves to their minds, to make them superior to every allurement that could be offer'd them, to transgress the law of their Creator, and neglect the directions he had so graciously vouchsafed them. And yet amidst all these delights, they were

N 2   tempted,

tempted, and they fell. But how great were the difadvantages, how uncomfortable the circumftances in which the *Son of God* was aſſaulted by the fame evil and deftroying ſpirit! When all alone, in an unhofpitable wild, amidſt ſavage beaſts *, without the viſible appearance of God, without any friend or acquaintance to ſuccour him, without any means of ſupplying his wants, or obtaining the food that was neceſſary to ſupport him ; where all was horrid around him, and his own neceſſities pained and pinched him within ; he thus entered the lifts with the deftroyer of mankind, was for a ſeaſon left to be practiſed on by his wiles, and given up to all the force of his moſt artful and infinuating perfuaſions. But though thus tempted, he ſtood his ground, triumphed over his tempter, and made him quit the field, aſhamed of his repulſe, and enraged at his diſappointment. Again,

4. We may take notice, that this temptation was carried on by the *permiſſion* and expreſs appointment and *order of God* ; for the ſacred hiſtory tells us, that *Jeſus was led up of the ſpirit to be tempted.* St. *Luke* ſays, that *being full of the Holy Ghoſt, Jeſus returned from Jordan, and was led by the ſpirit into the wilderneſs* † ; evidently aſcribing his going into the wildernefs to the immediate impulſe of that ſpirit of God, with which he was filled, and which deſcended on him in a viſible ap-

* Mark. i. 13.   † Luke. iv. 1.

pearance

pearance at his baptifm, that he might be fubject for a while to grievous affaults of the evil fpirit, and finally triumph in his victory over him, who had long triumphed in the fuccefs of his temptations, and the victories he had gained over the children of men. So that the pretence of a *melancholy* difpofition, leading him into retirement and folitude, and to fecrete himfelf from all converfe and acquaintance with men, is wholly without any foundation and fupport ; as the facred writers exprefsly affert, that it was under the *impulfe of the Holy fpirit,* that he thus went into the defert. Nor indeed is there any thing in our Saviour's hiftory and character, that gives the leaft ground for fufpicion, that he was of an unconverfable, gloomy, referved temper, that he fhunned the fociety of mankind, loved the folitude of a defert, or knew not how to relifh the pleafures of ufeful and friendly converfation. It appears evidently on the contrary, *that he rejoiced in the habitable parts of the earth, and that his delights were with the fons of men ;* for we find him prefent on occafions of *chearfulnefs* and *feftivity,* a gueft fometimes at the tables of the rich, often fhewing himfelf in the temple of his father, in the midft of the largeft concourfe of people, flocked after by multitudes, feeding and inftructing thoufands, afcending to *Jerufalem* at the yearly feftivals, and fo far from being a reclufe, that he was continually, during the whole of his miniftry, in publick life, and always employed in the moft benevolent and ufeful fervices to

others.

others. What were the particular *reafons*, why God was pleafed to *permit* thefe temptations to befall our blefled Lord, fuppoling we could not give any thoroughly *fatisfying account* of them, it would be no juft *objection* againft the truth of the hiftory, fince I don't know that God is obliged to acquaint us with the reafons of every thing he is pleafed to permit and order. But we are not without fuch as will juftify the divine wifdom and equity in this affair. *One reafon* might be *to do honour to human nature*, and caufe mankind to *triumph* by Chrift over this haughty and fubtle fpirit, and all his powerful and infinuating folicitations ; and to let him know that though he prevailed by mifreprefentations and frauds over the firft parents of the human race, and fo involved them all in the fentence of death ; yet neither craft nor power could profit him, when practiced againft the *man Jefus Chrift* ; who by his intire victory over him, during a more than forty days conteft with him, fpoil'd him of the glory of his former victories, convinced him that he was a conquerable falling enemy, and that mankind through him fhould learn to refift and triumph over him.

It may be farther remarked, that this courfe of temptations was *previous* to our Lord's entering on his *publick miniftry*, the great end of which was *to deftroy the works of the devil*, and fubvert that dominion which he had ufurped over the children of men. Into this work God was pleafed to initiate him by

very

very grievous temptations from him, whofe
kingdom he was to oppofe, that he might be,
inured to difficulty, cloath himfelf with refolution and firmnefs of mind, and by feeing
with what art and determined malice he was,
in the very entrance into his fervice, affaulted
and perfecuted, he might be, with the greater
vigour and zeal, excited to go through that
work for which he was fent into the world;
be ever upon his guard, be ever watchful
over his adverfary, that he might gain no
advantage againft him, expect future temptation, and efpecially arm himfelf for the *laft
and great conflict* he was to undergo, when he
faid to thofe who came to apprehend him :
This is your hour, and the power of darknefs * ;
and when through the extream violence of
the temptation, probably to fave himfelf from
the ignominious and accurfed death that was
now before him, by deferting his poft of
duty, and renouncing his pretenfions as the
Son of God, he was in fuch an *agony*, as caufed
him *as it were to fweat drops of blood* ‡. Thefe
introductory temptations were extreamly proper to harden and fortify him againft the
greater that awaited him, as experience and
fuccefs naturally create courage, and make
men bold and intrepid in future encounters; and
as an enemy, that hath been frequently overcome, is refifted with a kind of affurance of
victory over him in every new conteft, and
the remembrance of paft glory, the difdain

---

* Luke xxii. 53.   ‡ 44.

to

to loſe it, and the ambition of final triumph, all conſpire to render the reſiſtance more reſolute, by final ſucceſs to add freſh laurels to the former.

Another reaſon why theſe temptations were permitted is ſuggeſted by revelation itſelf, and is a very important one, *viz. to teach him humanity*, and *great pity and compaſſion to mankind, under the various temptations of life*, to which they are expoſed in the preſent ſtate, and that he might know by experience the uneaſineſs and danger of a tempted condition, and from the remembrance of his own feelings, be more warmly excited to afford ſuitable aſſiſtance and grace to his faithful diſciples, in every hour of their trial ; *for we have not an high prieſt, who cannot ſympathize with our infirmities, but who was in all points tempted like as we are, yet without ſin* † ; *and in that he ſuffered being tempted, he is able to ſuccour thoſe who are tempted* ‡ ; hath both the *power* to enable him to do it, and the *inclination* and affection, that will effectually excite him to it.   We may add alſo, that theſe temptations were permitted to befall the *great captain of our ſalvation, to teach his followers*, that they muſt *expect* the ſame kind of oppoſition, and from the ſame enemy, that their Lord and Maſter had found in the diſcharge of their duty, and working out their own ſalvation. Every convert to truth and righteouſneſs is a ſubject loſt to Satan's power and authority,

† Heb. iv, 15.   ‡ ii. 18.

and

and every thing that men undertake for the
glory of God, and to advance the kingdom
and intereſt of Chriſt, tends to ſhake and
weaken the foundations of his government.
It is therefore no wonder, that as he is *re-
ſtrained* by the power of God from all acts of
open violence, he ſhould endeavour by *ſecret
temptations,* and the concealed methods of art
and fraud, to prevent the defection of mankind from his cauſe, to recover them, and
retain them in his intereſt ; hinder them by
the proſpect of difficulties, and the terrors of
their own minds, from proſecuting any great
and good deſigns, and if he cannot prevent
them from attempting, yet render the work
as difficult and fatal as he can ; and defeat, as
far as his influence reaches, the good effects
of ſuch uſeful undertakings.   This may be
expected from the conduct of the tempter,
in relation to our bleſſed Lord ; and God
ſuffered his Son to become ſubject to theſe
ſolicitations, to warn and forearm them, to
encourage them to reſiſt ſteadfaſtly, and aſſure
them by his example, that God their heavenly
Father will *out of every temptation find a way
for their eſcape*; that if they maintain their
reſolution they ſhall overcome, that He will
cauſe them to triumph over this tempter and
ſeducer of mankind, and finally reward their
perſeverance with a crown of righteouſneſs
and glory.

5. We may farther take notice of the *continuance* of *theſe temptations* to which our Lord
was expoſed ; and St. *Mark* expreſſly aſſures

us,

us, that *he was in the wildernefs forty days tempted of Satan.* What were the *peculiar temptations,* with which our Lord was affaulted, and the *manner* in which they were carried on, whether in an invifible manner, by fecret fuggeftions to his mind, or by an open per-fonal appearance, or interchangeably, fome-times by the one, and fometimes by the other; as the facred hiftory hath not deter-mined, 'tis impoffible any perfon fhould be able to explain. For as to the three particular temptations expreffly mentioned by *Matthew* and *Luke,* they did not take place 'till the forty days trial were over; and the two laft of the three, as appears by the very nature of them, not 'till Chrift was gone out of the wildernefs. As to the *firft* of them, his being tempted to turn ftones into bread, the hiftory is exprefs, that *when he had fafted forty days and forty nights, he was after this an hungry;* upon which the *devil came to him,* and faid : *Command that thefe ftones be made bread.* And that he was not in the defert, when he was tempted the fecond and third time, is evident ; becaufe during the fecond he was at the *temple,* and during the third on a *high mountain*; and I particularly mention this, becaufe this obfervation will, I apprehend, take away all the difficulty that feems to have attended this tranfaction, and make the whole account of it eafy and intelligible, as I hope will appear in the fe-quel. As to the *methods* made ufe of by the tempter, during the forty days Chrift was left to be practiced on by his art and malice,
they

they were, no doubt of it, fuch as were well
adapted to carry his point, and allure the prey,
he hunted, into his net.   A *wildernefs* carries
in its very appearance fomewhat horrid and
fhocking to human nature.   To be *alone in it*,
without companion or guide, is a circumftance
that muft heighten the apprehenfion and
diftrefs.   To fee one's feif encompaffed *with
wild beafts* in fuch a forlorn fituation, muft
awaken the ftrongeft fenfe of fear and terror ;
and amidft this fcene of amazement and
anxiety, to be left for full *forty days* together
to the fubtlety and management of a mighty
fpirit, who is by employment and office a
tempter and deceiver, and by inclination and
charaĉter a deftroyer ; it is not well poffible
to conceive of a more afflicted, melancholy,
dangerous fituation, than what our bleffed
Mafter was now left in ; and whatever the
tempter could do, to corrupt or imprefs his
imagination, to *terrify* him from engaging in
the work he was now about to enter on, or by
more pleafing profpects prefented to him, to
pervert his mind, and ftagger his conftancy;
no doubt but he exerted all his abilities to
carry his important point, and practiced all his
wiles and ftratagems to deftroy this extraordinary perfon, and prevent every thing he
had to fear from his charaĉter and influence.
But in what way he tried his power and fkill
remains to us an intire *fecret* ; though we know
the *event* was defeat and fhame to the tempter,
but victory and glory to the Son of God, and
the

the Saviour of mankind. But we are farther to obferve,

6. That when thefe *forty days* temptations were over, our Lord, who had *fafted* during this whole period, and fevere conflict with the tempter, *found himfelf an hungry.* *When he had fafted forty days, and forty nights,* fays the hiftory, he *was afterwards an hungry.* God had miraculoufly fuftain'd him thus far, and he felt no weaknefs of body, or faintings of fpirits by this long abftinence from his ufual food. We read alfo of *Mofes,* that he was *with the Lord in the mount forty days and forty nights, and neither eat bread, or drank water* *. In like manner *Elijah* travelled the fame fpace of time without food, unto *Horeb,* the mount of God †; and in this miraculous circumftance, thefe three great prophets, *Mofes,* the founder of the Jewifh polity, *Elijah,* the great fcourge of the Jewifh idolaters, and zealous advocate for the true worfhip of God, and *Jefus Chrift,* the introducer and mediator of the new covenant, *refembled* each other, in their being fuftained without food, by the immediate power of God, and all of them in barren deferts and wilderneffes ; as a teftimony to all future ages, that when God calls men to extraordinary fervice, he will fupport them in it by extraordinary means, when the common and ufual ones entirely fail ; for as *bread* fupports us, only becaufe it receives its *power* and

---

* Exod. xxxiv. 28.   † 1 Kings xix. 8.

efficacy

efficacy to do it *from God*, and becaufe he continues the virtue of it for this purpofe; he can make the *air* or the *light* of Heaven equally fubfervient to this purpofe, or without any external means continue life, and maintain the vigour of it, by his *fole immediate influence* upon the bodily conftitution. It was no wonder however, that our Saviour, after fo long a forbearance of ordinary food, and the divine power that fuftained him was withdrawn, fhould find himfelf an hungry; and on this occafion the great adverfary founds his firft temptation, that the facred hiftory particularly takes notice of. Unwilling to quit the field, though repulfed with difhonour in a forty days conflict, he artfully renews the attack upon an occafion that naturally offer'd itfelf, and in a manner that cover'd over the malignity of his defign, and was well adapted to deceive. *Jefus was an hungred, and when the tempter came to him he faid: If thou be the Son of God, command that thefe ftones be made bread.* Let us here remark, that

1. What gave *occafion* to this temptation was our Saviour's *hunger*, after an abftinence of forty days; and we may very reafonably conclude, that his hunger was very *preffing* and *fevere*. He was probably ftill in the wildernefs, where he faw nothing that could minifter relief to him, and where there was no human hand to fupply his wants. So that as to the ordinary methods of fatisfying his neceffities, he had reafon to defpair of them, and knew that there muft be fome miraculous

interpofition

interpofition of providence in order to fuftain
him. And yet how many thoughts might
occur, on this occafion, to check any expectation of this kind? He found, by the
return and fharpnefs of his appetite, that the
power, which had wonderfully fupported him
for the forty days paft, was intirely withdrawn,
and that nature being now left to her ordinary
courfe and laws, required her ordinary fupplies, and muft, in the common order of
things, fink and faint without them; and
how could he well expect a frefh exertion of
that power, to keep him alive without food,
which by the return of his appetite he actually
experienced to be intirely ceafed; or why
would his Father have witheld it, had it not
been to fhew him, that he muft take fome
extraordinary method to fatisfy and provide
for himfelf. This feems to be the natural
fituation of a perfon's mind in fuch circumftances, and the reafonings that would be
moft likely to arife in any difficulty, or upon
any fuch emergency as this. In this ftrait,
and during this uncertainty, how to obtain
the relief he wanted; the tempter artfully
fteps in, and in fome vifible form and friendly
addrefs, accofts him, and fuggefts to him a
method that would immediately bring him
out of all his perplexities, and fatisfy his
hunger at once. And

2. The *temptation* and fuggeftion was this :
Command that thefe ftones be made bread. You
ought to look for no farther miraculous fupport from God. That now fails you, and
you

you muſt therefore depend upon yourſelf, and procure your ſupply by any other means within your own power, or elſe you will infallibly periſh by hunger in this deſolate wilderneſs. Theſe ſtones, or any of them that lie before you, immediately convert into bread, as the moſt ready and expeditious method of ſatisfying the cravings of your appetite, and eaſing the painful gnawings of the hunger that oppreſſes you. And to enforce this advice, he adds :

3. *If thou be the Son of God*, command that theſe ſtones be made bread. If you are that Son of God as you ſeem to be, that is ſpoken of in the prophecies, you can eaſily convert theſe ſtones into bread, for you may be ſure God your heavenly Father will enable you to do it, and as your neceſſities now ſeem to drive you to this expedient, ſo by this proof of the divine power aſſiſting you, you will have the moſt abundant conviction yourſelf that you are this perſon, and give me the fulleſt ſatisfaction and evidence of it too. It may be ſomewhat difficult to account for it, how this evil ſpirit ſhould *know* any thing about this character of the Son of God, or have any ſuſpicion that our bleſſed Saviour might be *He*. Probably he might hear and gather this *from the voice from Heaven*, which, juſt before theſe temptations commenced, declared him to be *God's beloved Son, in whom he was well pleaſed*. It is certain he is by no means ignorant of ſcripture, as appears by that

appoſite

appofite paffage which he quotes from it,
to prevail with Chrift to throw himfelf from
the battlements of the temple. And in *Da-
niel's* prophecy mention is exprefly made of
him, in what *Nebuchadnezzer* fays to his
Counfellors : *I fee four men, loofe, walking in
the fire, and they have no hurt, and the form of
the fourth is like the Son of God* *, And that
this character was not unknown to the Jews,
appears from the apocryphal *Efdras*, who defcribes the Son of God, as crowning thofe
who have confeffed the name of God ‡.
And in our bleffed Saviour's time, the character of the *Chrift*, or *Meffiah*, and the *Son
of God*, were underftood to denote the fame
perfon, as appears by the adjuration of the
High Prieft to our bleffed Lord : *Tell us, whether thou be the Chrift, the Son of God* †, and
from many other paffages that might be
mentioned. So that the tempter could not
but know, from prophecy, and from the current language and fentiments of the Jews,
that the character of the Son of God belonged
to the Meffiah. And therefore the putting
him upon this proof, that he was this great
and extraordinary perfon, and perfuading him
to exert his power as fuch, to fupply his neceffities in the midft of a barren defert, was
an artful fuggeftion to his appetite and ambition, and had fome appearance of a friendly
concern for his relief, and that he fhould

appear

appear in the full character and glory of the Son of God.

But our bleffed Saviour well difcerned the treachery of the counfel, and was full proof againft the intended deception, and gave a much better evidence of his being the *Son of God*, than by turning ftones into bread, *viz.* by his obedience to his heavenly Fa-ther, and abfolutely confining himfelf within the limits of the commiffion he had given him. Had he in compliance with the fuggeftion given him, attempted to turn ftones into bread, *without* his Father's fpecial direction, and the immediate impulfe of the fpirit of God, whofe conduct he was under, it would have been an unwarrantable prefumption, and an attempt to have wrought a miracle, where he had no occafion, reafon, or leave to do it ; and then the divine influence and power might have *failed him*, and the unfuccefsful attempt would have at once funk his credit, proved him to have loft his Father's affection and prefence, and rendered him utterly incapable of accomplifhing that great work, for which his perfect obedience was an indifpenfible qualification. As to any confirmation to himfelf, that he was the Son of God, our Saviour needed none, and the turning ftones into bread was not a greater proof of it, that what he had already in his breaft, or than what the teftimony he had received from Heaven afforded. And as to any fatisfaction, that the tempter defired in

this article, he deferved none ; and had our
Lord been perfuaded to attempt the miracle
at his bidding, whether he had fucceeded
or not, the devil would have triumphed in
his fuccefs, claimed him as his own, gloried
over him as his conqueft, and turned his
immediate accufer in the court of Heaven.
And as to the motive derived from the prefent hunger of Chrift, it was a fuggeftion to
diftruft his Father's power and goodnefs, of
which he had experienced fuch full proof,
in his miraculous fupport for forty days paft,
and who would immediately himfelf have
fuggefted this method of making bread, had
it been agreeable to his will, that Chrift fhould
have taken it. Befides, as the complying
with the advice would have argued a diftruft
of his Father's power, it would have looked
as though he had fet bounds to it, and imagined that God could not have fupported him
without bread. And on thefe accounts, the
fuggeftion, with what ever appearance of
friendfhip, and concern for the honour and
relief of Chrift it might be made, was infidious and enfnaring, and as fuch it was

4. *Rejected by our Lord*, and upon fuch a
principle, as fhewed the tempter it was impoffible he fhould fucceed in it. For our
Lord gave his refufal, in thofe remarkable
words of fcripture, *It is written : Man fhall
not live by bread alone, but by every word that
proceedeth out of the mouth of God.* It is a ci-
tation from what *Mofes* faid to the *Ifraelites*,

to

to perfuade them to obey, and put their truft in God : *Remember all the way, which the Lord thy God led thee, thefe forty years in the wilder-nefs to prove thee, and to know what was in thy heart, and fuffered thee to hunger, and fed thee with manna, and that he might make thee know, that man doth not live by bread only, but by every word that proceedeth out of the mouth of the Lord doth man live ;* i. e. by every kind of means that God is pleafed to appoint and blefs for this purpofe. Bread, unlefs he fanctifies it will not preferve life, and he can fupport it equally without bread. He hath all power in his hand, and can make every part of nature fubfervient to his will, and whenever the command proceeds from him, though bread fhould be wanting to fatisfy thy hunger, other means fhall be provided for the prefervation of life, and even the defert itfelf liberally fupply thee with neceffary food. And how perfectly appofite was the application of this paffage of fcripture by our bleffed Lord to the circumftances he was in ! How effectual a repulfe of the temptation offered him ! And the anfwer in its full length was this. " 'Tis true that I hunger. But it is by the permiffion of my heavenly Father. And he permits it to prove me, and know what is in my heart. And though I have no bread, nor any vifible means of fatisfying my hunger in this barren and defolate wildernefs, yet I know he is able to find other methods of fuftaining my life, and can immediately fend me down *manna* from Heaven, as he did formerly to his people, when hungry and fainting in the defert.   In his power and goodnefs therefore I truft, will ufe no unwarrantable methods to fupply my wants, and fhall expect my relief in the way, and at the feafon which his wifdom fhall direct." Thus ended the firft temptation that is here particularly recorded.   The impoftor was detected, his craft and fubtlety difappointed, and the Son of God glorioufly triumphed in his full victory over the feducer and deftroyer of mankind.   We may from this account obferve :

1. That even our *innocent paffions,* and the very *neceffary appetites* of nature, fhould be *indulged with great caution* and prudence, and never be gratified at the expence of our duty, and when the doing it will be attended with any real offence againft God. Hunger is a neceffary and very troublefome appetite, and the fatisfying it a very reafonable and neceffary thing, and every wife man will do it, when he can find the proper means of doing it.   But there may be circumftances that may render the doing it extreamly criminal, unbecoming our character, and inconfiftent with the regard and fubmiffion we owe to God.   In the circumftances of our blefled Lord, what more natural for him than to eat when he was hungry, and if he could not procure a fupply without a miracle, how could a miracle be better beftowed,

stowed, and why should not the advice be accepted, to turn stones into bread? But our blessed Lord would not live by any means, that would discover the least diffidence in his heavenly Father's power and goodness, nor work a miracle for his own preservation, without an intimation from him of the propriety and seasonableness of it ; to teach us, that hunger and thirst are preferable to sin, and that there are no passions and affections of our frame, however natural and necessary, but what may be unseasonably gratified ; and that the question with a wise and good man should never be : Will this and the other indulgence suit my present inclination, and be agreeable to my appetite? But, can I do it, consistent with the reverence and duty I owe to God, and so as to give no advantage to the tempter to corrupt, accuse and destroy me ? He often lies concealed in a strong inclination, and works it up into a powerful snare to destroy us. By means of this he drew our first parents into his toils, and made an appetite, innocent in itself, instrumental to destroy them and their posterity ; and by the same method he would have seduced the restorer of mankind, and by one fatal indulgence, to which his necessities strongly urged him, would have deceived him into transgression, and thereby have frustrated all the counsels of God, for the redemption of the world by his mediation and death.   And it is the almost con-

Q 3   stant

ftant method he makes ufe of, and indeed
the only one he can be well fuccefsful in, to
enfnare men into vice by thofe natural appetites and paffions, which are good and ufeful
in themfelves, and inferted into our frames
for the wifeft purpofes ; perfuading them
into immoderate and too frequent gratifications of them ; 'till by long indulgence they
feize the reins, lead away in triumph reafon,
confcience, and principle, captives, and hurry
men into enormities abfolutely inconfiftent
with every valuable intereft both of time
and eternity. *Keep thy heart therefore with all
diligence*, is an advice that fhould never be
forgotten, *fince out of it are all the iffues
of life.*

2. We fee in the example of our bleffed
Lord, that a *conftant fenfe of God* upon the
heart, and the maintaining a *lively, firm and
habitual hope and truft* in his protection and
goodnefs, is the *beft guard of integrity*, the
moft effectual fupport under all temptations,
and the fureft means of obtaining grace from
him in every time of need. It was by this
our bleffed Lord ftood his ground, and baffled the attempts of the evil fpirit to beguile
and pervert him. The heart, that hath no
apprehenfions, no reverence for God, Satan
feizes on as his own habitation, finds it, in
our Lord's emphatical defcription, *empty,
fwept, and garnifhed* * for his reception, fixes

* Mat. xii. 44.

in

in it as his ftrong hold, and foon reduces all
its powers and paffions into his intereft and
fervice. But the prevailing fenfe of God,
the fear to offend, and the defire and ambition to pleafe him, are barriers that will
abfolutely exclude him, either prevent his
fuggeftions, or effectually deftroy their influence ; and when fupported and feconded
by faith in his goodnefs, and hope in his
promifes, will render Satan, with his utmoft
craft and power, an impotent harmlefs
enemy, and fecure us the final victory and
triumph over him. Thefe are difpofitions
and graces of perpetual ufe in the Chriftian
life, and that by daily exercife we fhould
be careful to ftrengthen and improve to their
higheft perfection. And laftly

3. I cannot help obferving, in honour and
defence of a good old cuftom, though
looked on as obfelete, and actually grown
into difufe by many, that fince it is a moft
certain truth, *that man cannot live by bread
alone, but by the word that proceeds out of the
mouth of God*, or by his command, rendering our daily bread effectual for this purpofe, it is a *decent* and a *right thing*, never
to *begin* our meals without *afking his bleffing
on our food*, and always to *conclude them by
thankfgivings* to him, who in feafon provides
them for us. Whilft the principles of religion are true, this will be a reafonable fervice, and whilft there is any regard due to
the *Saviour* of mankind, *his example* will

be thought worthy of imitation, who, previous to his meals, confecrated them by prayer and thankſgivings to his heavenly Father. Be not therefore aſhamed of a practice in which you have him for a pattern, but acknowledge God in all the bleſſings of life, and his favour will make them effectual to your comfort and happineſs.

SERMON

SERMON VIII.

The Hiſtory of our Lord's Temptation finiſhed.

MATTHEW iv. 1.

Then was Jeſus led up of the Spirit into the Wilderneſs, to be tempted of the Devil.

S
T. *Mark* and St. *Luke* aſſure us, that Jeſus *was in the wilderneſs forty days tempted of Satan,* and that *in thoſe days he did eat nothing* ; and St. *Matthew* and St. *Luke* agree in their report, that after this forty days faſt *he became hungry,* and that the tempter took this occaſion to practice on him, and tried to deceive him ; ſaying to him, *if thou be the Son of God, command that theſe ſtones be made bread.* " You are now in a deſert that can yield you nothing, you are pinched with hunger, you have no friend to ſupply your wants. Surely the Son of God ſhould not want neceſſary food. *If you are this Son of God,* ſhew me the proof of it. Exert your power, help yourſelf, turn ſome of theſe ſtones into bread, and this evidence will

will be fatisfying both to you and me." And
friendly as this advice might appear, it was
neverthelefs infidious and deftructive; as it
was a temptation to *diftruft the power and goodnefs of God*; either that he could not, or
would not relieve him in his neceffities; to
ufe unprefcribed methods of fupplying his
want, and dictate to his heavenly Father the
time and manner, when and how he fhould
exert his power, and enable him to do miraculous works. Such a *miracle* as this, had
it been wrought in the wildernefs, would
have been entirely *loft*, and no good end could
have been anfwered by it; as there were
none to convince; Chrift himfelf needing
not this proof of his being the Son of God,
and the tempter not really defiring it; but
rather hoping, by putting him on this experiment, that he would fail in the attempt;
as well knowing, that Chrift's endeavouring
to do an unneceffary miracle at his bidding,
would be no likely method to attain that influence of the divine fpirit and power, that
was neceffary to effect it. Our Lord therefore, who faw into the treachery of the advice, rejected the propofal, by telling him:
*It is written : Man fhall not live by bread alone,
but by every word that proceedeth out of the
mouth of God.* i. e. I feel my hunger, and
know I have here no bread. But I have no
need for this reafon to turn ftones into bread;
becaufe God can fupport me without it, as
he did the *Ifraelites* with *manna* in the defert,
and make whatever means he is pleafed to
appoint

appoint effectual to my relief. 'Tis his pre-
rogative to prescribe the methods by which I
am to live, and my part, to wait for his
orders, and to obey them.   But

II. Being baffled and disappointed in this
attempt, the adversary tries another method,
and applies to a different paffion, that by
the influence of it he might ensnare and ruin
him. In the former temptation he feems to
have endeavoured to infinuate fome *diftruft*
into our Lord's mind, as to his being the Son
of God, upon the account of his hunger,
and being deprived of all visible means of
satisfying it. In this he tempts him to *pre-
fume* on the character, and give an open, convincing evidence and demonftration of it at
once to the whole city of Jerusalem, by an
action that would carry its own proof and
conviction along with it. The historian relates it in the following manner †. *Then the
devil takes him into the holy city, and fetteth him
on a pinnacle of the temple, and fays to him : If
thou be the Son of God, caft thyfelf down ; for it
is written :* He *fhall give his angels charge concerning thee, and in their hands fhall they bear
thee up, left at any time thou dafh thy foot againft
a ftone. Jefus faid unto him : It is written
again : Thou fhall not tempt the Lord thy God.*
Here we are to confider,

The *nature* and *circumftances* of the *temptation,*

And the *victory* of our *bleffed Saviour* over it.

† Verfe 5—7.

As

As to the *temptation* itself, the following circumstances deserve to be taken notice of in it.

The *place* in which it was carried on; which was *Jerusalem*, the *temple* of God, and the *pinnacle* or *battlement* of it. *The devil takes him into the holy city, and sets him on a pinnacle of the temple.* The holy city is *Jerusalem*, and there are some ancient coins remaining of it, which have this very inscription on it. It is stiled so again by the Apostle * ; by *Nehemiah* after its restoration † ; and long before the first destruction of it, by *Isaiah* ‡ ; who tells us, that the Jews, amidst their impieties and corruptions, gloried in this, and counted it their security, that they belonged to the *holy city*. They *call themselves of the holy city, and stay themselves upon the God of Israel, whose name was the Lord of Hosts,* and in other places of scripture. And *Jerusalem* was called by this name of the *holy city*, because of the *temple* of God that was in it, and the sacred solemnities of worship, which were performed there in honour of him, upon which account it was regarded as the place of his peculiar residence ; the temple on Mount Sion being his *immediate habitation and palace*, and under his perpetual and distinguishing protection. Hence it is stiled *the city of God*, the *holy place of the tabernacles of the most high* || ; and *the city of the great king,*

* Matt. xxvii. 53.　† Nehem. xi. 18.　‡ Isaiah xlviii. 2.
|| Psalm xlvi. 4

where

*where God was known in her palaces for a re-
fuge* §. When in this city, he was led by
the tempter into the temple, carried up
by him to one of the battlements of it, and
placed in such a situation, as overlooked
the city, and from whence he might easily
throw himself down into one of the courts
of the temple.

It is enquired here, how the devil *conveyed*
our bleſſed Lord into this ſituation. And the
generality of interpreters have concluded, that
he carried him forcibly *through the air*, and fled
with him 'till he had placed him on the temple battlements ; and becauſe this ſuppoſition
is liable to many objections, ſome interpreters of great note, have imagined that there
was nothing *real* in this tranſaction, but that
it was in the whole of it carried on in a *dream*,
or trance, or viſion. But as this account is
liable to as many real difficulties as the other,
I cannot eaſily come into either, eſpecially
as there is a way of explaining this hiſtory,
which avoids the objections on both ſides,
and to which the hiſtory itſelf, and the terms
made uſe of in it, plainly lead us. When
our bleſſed Saviour came out of the deſert,
after he had refuſed to turn ſtones into bread,
the devil takes our Lord into the holy city,
i. e. prevailed with him to go up to Jeruſalem
along with him ; *took him* as any one *takes his
companion*, whom he preſſes and perſuades to
attend him ; juſt as *Jeſus*, going up to Jeru-

§ Pſalm xlviii. 2, 3.

ſalem,

falem, *took the twelve difciples with him* *, where the word is the fame as in my text, and in which fenfe it is ufed in many places of the New Teftament, and never once for carrying any perfon by force from off the earth, through the air ; a fignification of the word unknown either to facred or profane writers. And when he had thus carried him to the temple, he by the fame perfuafion, and the permiffion of God, prevailed with him to go up to the battlements, and there *fetteth him,* i. e. *brought him* to fuch a part of them, where Chrift might eafily do, what the tempter intended to perfuaded him to do. This is a way of fpeaking common to all languages, and we *carry a friend* with us, when we wait on him to any particular place ; and we *fet* or place him, when we *bring him to the feat* or ftation we have provided for him. And thus the tempter fet or placed our Lord on the pinnacle, or battlements of the temple, by attending him there, 'till he had fixed him in the fituation that he thought proper for his purpofe ; in which fenfe the original word is ufed in feveral places in the New Teftament, and by all writers without exception. The plain and natural meaning of the paffage therefore is : That the tempter, by God's permiffion, attended on our bleffed Saviour, from the defert to Jerufalem, led him into the temple, caufed him to afcend to fome of the battlements of it, and at-

---

* Luke ix. 10.

tended

tended him to fuch a part of them, where
he might perform the miraculous leap, which
he intended to perfuade him to take, in hopes
that it would prove his utter deftruction :
thus he addreffes him :

If thou be the Son of God caft thyfelf down.
It appears very evident, that this was a propofal founded on a fuppofition, that Chrift
thought himfelf the Son of God, and was
made, that he might perfuade our bleffed
Lord to imagine, that this would be the moft
ready and effectual method, publickly to *declare* and *convince the whole city* of Jerufalem,
that he was the *Son of God*, and *their Meffiah.*
*If thou art the Son of God, fhew thyfelf to be
fo*, by fome extraordinary performance, that
may perfuade the whole nation to acknowledge and receive thee as fuch. Why fhouldeft
thou conceal thy pretenfions, why defer the
publickly taking on thee this character ? Here
is now an opportunity that offers itfelf, whereby thou mayeft afford the moft unconteftible
demonftration, that God is thy Father, and
be received at once by the whole body of
the people, and by the priefts who are now
miniftering in the temple, as the promifed
Meffiah, whom they expect. For if thou
caft thyfelf from thefe battlements, and the
nation know, that no real harm accrues to thee
by it, and they fee thee alive and found after it, and this thou mayeft certainly expect,
if thou art the Son of God ; fuch a miraculous prefervation will fhew how dear thou art

to God, and difpofe them immediately to own thee as his well beloved Son."

And to encourage our Lord in this affurance of his Father's protection, *i. e.* more effectually to perfuade him to venture on this prefumptuous trial of it, and thereby moft certainly to forfeit it, and deftroy himfelf; he cites to him a very apt paffage of fcipture, with a defign to infpire him with this falfe confidence, and to perfuade him into the rafh project, into which he would have precipitately drawn him to his ruin. For this deceiver well knew, that the paffage he cites, was never intended to encourage mens hopes in God, when they caft themfelves into needlefs dangers, but only when they were providentially brought into them, and that therefore the application of it to the purpofe he wanted to anfwer by it, was a falfe and a lying one. However refolved to try his ftrength, he will venture for once to become a fcripturift and preacher; and to prevent our Lord's being fhocked at the propofal, tells him; *It is written : He fhall give his Angels charge concerning thee, and in their hands fhall they bear thee up, leaft at any time thou dafh thy foot againft a ftone* *; which words are a quotation from the Pfalmift, defcribing the fingular happinefs of religious men, who fear and truft in God, in that peculiar protection by the divine power, of which they might affure themfelves, as the reward of their piety and virtue. And

---

* Pfalm xci. 11.

the

the paſſage is artfully applied, to perſuade our
bleſſed Lord, that what he perſuaded him to,
he might do without any hazard ; becauſe if
the ſcriptures aſſure all religious men, that
*God will give his Angels charge over them, ſo
that they ſhould bear them up in their hands, leaſt
they daſh their feet againſt a ſtone ;* much *more*
might he aſſure himſelf, that they ſhould bear
him up, and preſerve him from being cruſhed,
ſhould he throw himſelf from the battlements, *if he was the Son of God ;* and eſpecially as ſuch a miraculous preſervation would
be the fulleſt evidence of his divine character,
and enſure his being univerſally received and
ſubmitted to as the promiſed Meſſiah.

But this was too ſhallow reaſoning to impoſe on our bleſſed Lord, who neither needed
this deceiver's memento, to bring the ſcripture promiſes to his remembrance, nor his
advice, when, and how to apply to them
for the encouragement of his faith and hope
in God ; and therefore ſhews him, that he
underſtood the deſign of his ſuggeſtion, and
the fallacy of the argument, by which he
endeavoured to ſupport it, by quoting another paſſage of ſacred writ, which explained
the true meaning of that, which the tempter
had perverted and abuſed, and carried in it an
abſolute refuſal to comply with the propoſal
that he made him. *Jeſus ſaid unto him, it
is written again : Thou ſhalt not tempt the Lord
thy God* *. Our Lord refers to the words of

* Deut. vi. 16.

Moses to the *Israelites*, when he says to them :
*Ye shall not tempt the Lord thy God, as ye tempted
him in Massah ; where they tempted the Lord,
saying : Is the Lord amongst us* † ? They wanted water, and through their impatience for
it cried out with indignation against *Moses :
Wherefore is this, that thou hast brought us up
out of Egypt, to kill us and our children, and
our cattle with thirst ?* Is this a sign, that the
Lord is amongst us ? If he be, let him now
give us a proof of it, by furnishing us with
water for ourselves and our cattle. So that
to *tempt God* is to put him to the proof of his
power and goodness, to demand it from
him for our own satisfaction, and to prescribe
to him the time and means of giving it. If
therefore our blessed Lord had, in compliance with the tempter's proposal, thrown
himself from the temple, depending on God's
giving his Angels charge over him, to bear
him up, and prevent his being crushed by
the fall, it would have been *tempting God,*
and putting him, without any direction and
order from him, to the trial, whether he
would or could deliver him. It was venturing upon a rash, unwarrantable action, and
prescribing to God to prevent the destructive
effects of it, by the immediate interposition
and care of his Angels. But thus to tempt,
and prescribe to God, and put him to the
proof of his power and goodness is real in-
solence and impiety, and so far from being a

† Exod. xvii. 2, 7.

rational

rational inſtance of truſt and confidence in God, as that it it a very high and criminal preſumption and folly. And as this is ex-preſſly forbidden by God, it is the moſt cer-tain method to forfeit his protection, and no other conſquence can be reaſonably expected; but our being left to reap the fatal effects of our own inſolence and folly. And therefore our bleſſed Saviour gives the tempter to un-derſtand, that his deference and regard to the ſcriptures was the very reaſon why he refuſed to comply with his propoſal, backed by the ſcripture ; becauſe as the word of God forbids us to tempt him, by putting him to unneceſſary proofs of his power and goodneſs, he therefore could not, conſiſtent with the duty he owed him, venture upon ſo raſh and deſperate an action ; becauſe that would be to throw himſelf into the extreameſt danger, without any reaſon or neceſſity, merely to put God to the trial, whether he would or could preſerve him. And thus ended the ſecond trial, in the compleat victory of our bleſſed Lord over this practiſed and experi-enced ſeducer. But he was not to be thus ſilenced, nor his malice thus eaſily ſatisfied. He hath yet a farther reſource, and one more experiment to make of our Saviour's conſtancy and reſolution. And therefore,

III. Thirdly, *the devil takes him up into an exceeding high mountain, and ſhews him all the kingdoms of the world, and the glory of them, and ſays to him : All theſe things will I give thee, if thou wilt fall down and worſhip me.*

But

But in this alfo he was as unfuccefsful, as in the former two ; for *Jefus faid to him : Get thee hence Satan, for it is written : Thou fhalt worfhip the Lord thy God, and him only fhalt thou ferve.* To fet this in as clear a view as I can, I would obferve :

That the expreffion of the tempter's *taking Chrift into an high mountain*, is the very *fame, word* for word, with that which this Apoftle ufes on another occafion, and where no interpreters find any thing extraordinary and miraculous ; viz. where he tells us, *that Jefus takes Peter, James and John his brother, and brings them up into an high mountain* * ; i. e. went himfelf thither and ordered them to follow him ; took them with him as his companions to attend him, and be witneffes to the glory of his transfiguration. No one ever here imagined that Chrift miraculoufly conveyed them through the air to the top of this mountain, or carried them there any otherways than on their feet. Nor doth the expreffion convey any other meaning, or is capable of any other interpretation but this. And therefore in the place before us, the tempter took our bleffed Lord into an high mountain in the fame fenfe, by leading him thither, going before him, and by God's permiffion conftraining him to follow him ; or by perfuading and preffing him to accompany him, which our bleffed Lord complied with, by the fecret direction of that fpirit of God,

* Mat. xvii. 1.

which

which he had juft received at his baptifm,
and under whofe influence and conduct he
continually acted. This is the eafy and the
natural interpretation, and hath no difficulty
attending it. *Where* this mountain was, I am
not knowing enough to determine. Our
bleffed Lord was baptized in *Jordan*, and 'tis
probable the wildernefs into which he was
led, was fomewhat beyond, but *near that ri-
ver*, as there were feveral of them towards
Arabia Petræa. And when *Mofes* prayed,
that God would permit him to go over *Jordan*, that he might fee the promifed land,
God would not permit him, but ordered him
to go up to the top of *Pifgah*, from whence
he had a very fine and extenfive view of it;
and 'tis not improbable, that this was the very
hill to which our Saviour was led, where he
might have that pleafing profpect, by which
the tempter intended to enfnare and deftroy
him, by exciting his ambition, and kindling
in him a ftrong defire after temporal grandeur and ambition. But whatever the
mountain was, or wherever fituated, when
our Lord was ftationed on it, it is farther
remarked :

   That the tempter *fhewed him all the kingdoms of the world, and the glory of them*, and
as St. Luke adds, *in a moment of time* *. Every
one here fees, that thefe words, *He fhewed
him all the kingdoms of the world*, if they are
to be underftood of their being fo fhewn to

* Luke iv. 5.

him,

him, as that he could fee them with his bodily eyes, are not to be interpreted *literally*,
nor in the *full extent* of the expreſſion ; ſince
no human eye can take in ſo large a proſpect, could there be any point in the world,
in which all thoſe kingdoms could lie in
proſpect, and much more becauſe ſuch a
view is rendered abſolutely impoſſible by the
globular form of the earth ; and therefore ſome
have imagined, that this evil ſpirit raiſed up,
in the *imagination of Chriſt*, in an inſtant of
time, ſome kind of picture and proſpect of
the kingdoms of the earth, and the glory that
attended them, and ſo made a fictitious re-
preſentation of what he could not really make
him behold. But this is not agreeable to
what the hiſtory affirms, which ſpeaks of
what he *really ſhewed him*, and not what he
deluded him with a falſe and ſhadowy view
of ; and is a ſcheme which offers ſo many
objections to my mind, as that I cannot eaſily
digeſt it.

There are two words by which *Matthew*
and *Luke* expreſs, what we render the *world*,
neither of which lead us neceſſarily to underſtand the *whole world*, or globe of the earth,
but which hath each a more confined ſenſe,
and denote ſome particular province, country,
and kingdom of the earth ; and by way of
diſtinction, either the *Land of Canaan*, or at
other times the *Roman Empire*. Thus 'tis ſaid,
that God gave the promiſe to Abraham, that
he ſhould be *the heir of the world*, i. e. of the
Land

Land of Canaan *. Thus alfo *Auguftus Cæfar* ordered that *all the world fhould be taxed,* i. e. the provinces of the *Roman Empire* †. In this *limited* fenfe, the tempter fhewed our bleffed Lord all the kingdoms of the earth, gave him a view of *fome parts* of the *tetrarchies, kingdoms,* and *provinces,* that lay extended before him, and which were fubject to the dominion of the *Romans.* And it is to be remarked, that the profpect which *Mofes* had before him, from the top of *Pifgah,* was exceeding extenfive and wide, towards all the four corners of the world, as it is defcribed in the laft chapter of Deuteronomy. So that as this view prefented itfelf at once to our bleffed Lord, and the tempter pointed out to him *Judea,* with fome of the neighbouring diftricts, and fhewed him the fruitful plains, the fertile hills, the populous cities, towns and villages, the ftately houfes and palaces, the countries abounded with ; he might well be faid to fhew him all the kingdoms of the world, and the glory thereof, *in a moment* or inftant of time ; as the *profpect,* whatever it was, was *inftantaneous,* and offered itfelf to his view, as foon as ever he was in the ftation fixed on for that purpofe, and could furvey the feveral objects that were around him. Efpecially, as I apprehend, that the fhewing here fpoken of, relates rather to *defcription,* than by ocular fight ; in which fenfe the word is frequently ufed, both in facred and

* Rom. iv. 13.   † Luke ii. 1,

P 4   profane

profane writers. Thus St. *Paul* to the *Corin-thians* : *I shew unto you a more excellent way* ‡, i. e. I inform you of it, and defcribe it to you. And thus when our Lord from the top of the mountain, beheld fuch a variety of coun-tries before him, and had the pleafing view of their fertility, riches, and cities before him, the tempter feems to have fhewn him *the kingdoms of the world*, by pointing to the fituation of others, too diftant to be feen. Look towards the *Eaft*. There is the *Perfian* empire, and the kingdom of *Arabia*, with all its gold and frankincenfe and myrrh. Behold the *South*, there you may fee where the *Egyptian* kingdom lies. In the *Weft* you are to look for *Tyre*, and the *Ifles*, and *Rome* itfelf, the head of the univerfe. Towards the *North* you'll fee *Ga-lilee* and *Syria* ; and then laying hold of the opportunity, gave him fuch a defcription of that grandeur and magnificence, that fplen-dor and pomp, that plenty and riches, which the princes and kingdoms of the world pof-feffed, and which were fo much admired and envyed by the generality of mankind, as he hoped would imprefs his mind, kindle in him the fparks of ambition, and induce him to pay to himfelf homage, as the fovereign Lord and Difpofer of them. And it is evi-dent that fuch an artful well wrought defcrip-tion and reprefentation as this, added to the grandeur and beauty of the profpect before him, would heighthen the temptation, and

‡ 1 Cor. xii. 31.

carry

carry in it much ftronger influence and perfuafion.   And methinks this feems to be
pointed out by the relation itfelf.   For as Luke
reprefents it, the tempter fays to him, *all this*
power will I give thee, and the glory of them.
Power could not be feen, and the glory of
kingdoms not beheld from a mountain.   But
if he had been *defcribing* the power and majefty of kings and princes, and the glory
with which they were furrounded in their refpective kingdoms; nothing could be more
natural and proper than to add : All this
power will I give thee and the glory of them.
This was firft to work up his imagination to
its full heighth, and then artfully throw in
the bait, that he might the more eagerly
feize it, and the dazling propofal be more readily complied with.

And this is what we are next to confider,
viz. the nature of the offer, and wherein the
ftrength of the *temptation* confifted.   *All thefe*
things will I give thee; all thefe kingdoms
which thou haft now in profpect, or I have
pointed out to thee, and the pomp and fplen-
dor that belongs to them.   Or as *Luke* : All
this power, and the glory of them, which
thou haft partly feen, and I have fully defcribed to thee. 'Tis evident that the tempter
fufpected him to be the *Son of God*, or promifed
Meffiah, by the two former temptations, and
it feems plain from this, that he had entertained the common opinion of the *Jews* concerning him, that he was to be a temporal
prince, and probably thought, that by

conqueft

conqueſt and victory over the nations he might
deſtroy idolatry, and profelyte them to the
Jewiſh religion. And in this view the offering him the throne of *Iſrael*, and the kingdoms of the neighbouring nations, and per-
ſuading him to lay hold on the preſent opportunity to appear as *King of Iſrael*, and attempt
the conqueſt of the kingdoms around *Judea*,
was worthy his craft and ſubtlety. Otherwiſe,
it will be hard to account for his making him
this promiſe, if he had no apprehenſion of
his being born to the inheritance of them.
The ancient *prophecies* concerning the Meſſiah
were, *that to him ſhould be the gathering of the
nations*, and that he ſhould *have the heathen for
his inheritance, and the uttermoſt parts of the earth
for his poſſeſſion*. To theſe prophecies the
tempter probably was no more a ſtranger than
to other parts of ſcripture ; and therefore
willing to be before hand with God Almighty,
or rather deſirous to fruſtrate his intentions,
he offers to put our Saviour into poſſeſſion of
them ; well knowing that if he held them
by grant from him, he could have nothing to
fear from his dominion and power ; or hoping,
that if he ſhould be tempted through ambition to accept his offer, God would never
permit him to obtain them, and that hereby
the ſcheme of deſtroying his own kingdom
by the Meſſiah's advancement, would be intirely fruſtrated. The performance of his
promiſe he little regarded. The object he
aimed at was the ſeducing our Lord, which
if he could but happily for himſelf accompliſh,

plifh, he hoped every thing elfe would fucceed to his wifhes.

But leaft our Lord fhould fufpect his power to make thefe glorious affurances good, he adds, as St. *Luke* relates it : *All this power will I give thee, and the glory of them ; for that is delivered unto me, and to whomfoever I will, I give it.* An ill compliment this, to the kings and princes of the earth, that they hold their dominions by the grant of this evil fpirit. But how true foever it may be, as to the *tyrants* and *oppreffors* of the earth, who come to enlarge their dominions, and govern their fubjects by the criminal meafures of fraud, and violence and murther ; yet the affertion, in the general manner in which 'tis made, is falfe, and worthy *the father of lies.* For the kingdoms of the earth are under the difpofal of God, and this evil fpirit, inftead of giving them to whom he will, can give them to none, without the permiffion of God. However, truth was not the thing intended, but to make the offer tempting, and if that could be done by lies and falfhood, it would not be in the leaft fcrupled by this infidious deceiver. Any method was equal to him, provided he could fecure the event he aimed at. However, the boaft feems to be founded on that very antient opinion, which hath a great deal of countenance from the facred writings, *viz.* that the *kingdoms of the earth* had each their *guardian angel,* who prefided over the refpective affairs of them, and had a fort of fovereignty within their own provinces. And if, if, as some have, not without reason, supposed the tempter took on him the form and character of the *guardian Angel of Judea*, he might say with some propriety: It is delivered unto me : This is the province committed more immediately to my care, and which I can give to whomsoever I will. But there was a condition annexed to this promise of putting Christ into the possession of these kingdoms, and the glory of them ; and that was,

If thou wilt worship me, all shall be thine, as *Luke* ; or as 'tis in *Matthew* : *All these things will I give thee, if thou wilt fall down and worship me.* This appears a most *extravagant* and *insolent* demand, for the evil spirit to ask the Son of God to worship him ; and it was so unquestionably considered in itself ; and it would have been as extravagantly weak as wicked a proposal, had the *tempter* appeared *as himself*, or imagined that Christ suspected or knew him to be the person he really was. But supposing he personated *a good Angel*, and took on himself the appearance of the Angel of God's people, there could be nothing extravagant or shocking in the proposal, upon the principles of the Jews themselves, nothing but what even a good man might do, and what in former times they had actually done. For they esteemed the worship of angels a right and commendable thing, and imagined it an instance of respect and veneration that was due to them. And though he demanded our Saviour to *prostrate himself* before him in

token

token of homage and adoration, yet that was no more than what was conftantly practiced, all over the Eaft, by fubjects to their princes, or by inferior princes to thofe by whofe authority they held their dominions. And therefore the evil fpirit promifes our Lord the kingdom of the Meffiah, upon a condition, againft which a *Jew* would have had no objection, with refpect to *a good angel, viz.* the *proftrating himfelf* in his prefence ; and if our Lord, by paying him this acknowledgment and homage, would own him to be *Lord Paramount*, and difpofer of the kingdoms under his charge, and which he governed as his province, he makes him an offer of all, and to put him into poffeffion of his largeft ambition.

But here alfo the tempter's fubtlety and malice *fail'd him*, and he finds himfelf fully difcovered and repulfed. For our bleffed Lord with indignation and authority rebukes him, and fays : *Get thee hence, Satan, or get thee behind me, Satan,* for *it is written : Thou fhalt worfhip the Lord thy God, and him only fhalt thou ferve.* It is remarkable, that in the two former temptations our Lord *calmly* replies to the fuggeftions that were made him, without difcovering to his tempter that he knew him. And the plain reafon feems to be, becaufe what he prompted Chrift to do, carried in it fome *femblance* of doing honour to God, as it was perfuading him to exercife a remarkable truft and confidence in his power and goodnefs. But as the *prefent* fuggeftion was an act

of

of immediate *impiety* againſt God, and to
acknowledge by proſtration and worſhip another diſpoſer of the kingdoms of the earth
beſides him ; our Lord rejeéts it with abhorrence, and with an authority and anger
becoming the Son of God, ſays to him, *Satan*,
thou adverſary of God and man : *Get thee
hence.* " This inſolence I will no longer
" endure. Depart from my preſence, and
" know I underſtand my duty too well, to
" pay thee, or any creature, the worſhip thou
" demandeſt ; for 'tis written : *Thou ſhalt*
" *worſhip the Lord thy God, and him only ſhalt*
" *thou ſerve."* Had our Lord *bowed himſelf*
before him, as the condition of receiving the
kingdoms of the earth from him, it would
have been an aét of *homage* to him, as the *God
of this world* ; which would in reality have
been to countenance his rebellion and apoſtacy
from God. And therefore by quoting this
paſſage of ſcripture, *Him only ſhalt thou ſerve*,
our Lord not only rejeéts his offer and the
condition of it, but lets him know alſo, that
the *power* he claimed of diſpoſing the kingdoms of the earth was *vain* and *preſumptuous*,
that the *Lord only was God*, that he was ſupream over the armies of heaven, and the
kingdoms of this world, and was therefore
alone worthy to be worſhiped and adored as
the Sovereign of the univerſe, who orders all
things according to the direétions of his own
will ; and for his preſumption and impudence
commands him inſtantly to depart, with an
authority which he was not able to reſiſt.
And

And accordingly the Evangelifts remark, that *the tempter immediately left him*, whilft the *good angels came to congratulate* him on his glorions victory, and *minifter* to his wants.

The practical inferences from this fubject of our Lord's temptations are fo various, and of that importance to us, as that they deferve a particular confideration. But I fhall now only obferve : How much it becomes us, as the difciples of our Lord Jefus Chrift, to *imitate his faith and conftancy*, his firmnefs and refolution, in refifting and overcoming the temptations of life. He was tempted by the calls of appetite to improper gratification, and unfeafonable indulgence ; by the love of reputation and fame, to purchafe it by unwarrantable and unjuftifiable methods ; by his very reverence for and truft in God, to rafh expectations, and prefumptuous confidence ; and by the fpirit of ambition, and the profpect of empire, grandeur, riches and glory, to feek after them, without the leave, and contrary to the permiffion of God his heavenly Father. He was tempted under the guife of friendfhip, and with a pretended concern for his fafety, profperity and honour. His temptations were of long continuance, addreffed to all the moft prevalent paffions of human nature, managed with great art and delicacy ; in the very critical feafon and circumftance, in which they were moft likely to imprefs and influence him, and when every thing feemed to concur to render them effectual. But our Lord was not to be moved.

He

He ftood his ground, foiled the great adverfary, and by his principles triumphed in an
honourable and compleat victory. What are
we to learn from hence, Chriftians ? To be
upon our guard, to *watch* our fpirit, never
haftily to litten to the fuggeftions of our appetites and paffions, to *ftrengthen* our *principles*, to have them always *ready* for our
affiftance, and to refift every follicitation to
evil, whatever motives may be offered to us
to perfuade us to a compliance with them.
Tempted to fin we may be, and probably
every one of us have been, and fhall be ; but
we need not be overcome. The victory over
temptation is certain, if we will ufe the appointed means to obtain it. The very fame
method by which Chrift endured, will render us invincible. The fame fpirit of God,
under whofe conduct he was, dwells in us,
Chriftians, and by his aid, and under the
lead and example of the great captain of our
falvation, we fhall be entirely conquerors, put
to flight and to fhame the great adverfary of
our fouls, and nothing fhall be able ever to
feparate us from the love of God in Chrift
Jefus our Lord.

SERMON

SERMON IX.

The Folly of casting off the Principles of Religion.

PSALM xiv. 1.

The Fool hath said in his heart, there is no God. They are corrupt, they have done abominable works, there is none that doeth good.

'TIS a complaint frequent in the mouth of religious and good men, that *infidelity*, as to all the great principles of religion, greatly prevails in the midst of us, and we are apt to look upon and bewail this apostacy, not only as an argument of our great *degeneracy*, but as the *peculiar infidelity* of the times we live in, and as what renders the present generation much worse than the former. But though the complaint is but too just, that there is a growing disregard to every thing of a serious and sacred nature; yet the inference drawn from it, of the peculiar badness of our own times above the former, may not be agreeable to the truth of history, and the experience of wise and observing

VOL. III. Q serving

serving men in the foregoing ages of the world. As long ago as the times of *Job*, probably before *Moses*, there were impious men, *who said unto God, Depart from us, for we desire not the knowledge of thy ways* *. *What is the Almighty that we should serve him, and what profit should we have, if we pray to him? Is not God in the height of heaven? And behold the height of the stars, how high are they! How doth God know? Can he judge through the dark cloud? Thick clouds are a covering to him, that he seeth not, and he walketh in the circuit of Heaven* † : Expressions, that are at least a denial of all providence in God, and of all dependence on providence in men ; and that represent all religion in practice, as an irrational and unprofitable thing. And in the *Psalms* we find frequent *complaints* of this nature, *viz.* of man's casting off all sense of and reverence for deity, and in consequence of it breaking through all the restraints of piety and virtue ; and my text represents this as the state of the generality of persons in his own times. *The fool hath said in his heart there is no God. They are corrupt. They have done abominable works. There is none that doth good.* And in the verses immediately following : *The Lord looked down from Heaven on the children of men, to see if there were any that did understand, and seek God. They are all gone aside. They are all together become filthy. There is none that doeth good, no not one.*

---

* Job xxi. 14, 15.   † xxii. 13, 14.

Thefe

Thefe words point out a very *general cor-ruption* of principles and morals, at leaft ; fo univerfal, as that few or none were to be found, who had efcaped the infection of in-fidelity and vice. So that how bad foever the prefent times we live in, and how much rea-fon foever we have to lament the defection both as to principles and morals, that feems to be fpreading amongft us ; yet the caution of the *royal preacher* feems worthy our regard : *Say not thou what is the caufe that the former days were better than thefe ? For thou doft not inquire wifely concerning this ‡. i. e.* The fact itfelf hath no foundation in truth ; or if it hath, thou wilt not eafily be able to account for the reafons of it.   In *all ages* there have been men of atheiftical principles, and very im-moral lives ; fools who have caft off all re-verence for God, and lived without any regard to their dependence on, and final accountable-nefs to him. *The fool hath faid in his heart there is no God. They are corrupt. They have done abominable works, there is none that doth good.* Which words reprefent to us :

I. The *folly* of *cafting off the principles of religion.*
II. The *confequence of this folly.*   It leads to the moft corrupt and diffolute practices.

I. Thefe words reprefent to us, the *folly* of *cafting off the principles of religion.* The *fool hath faid in his heart, there is no God,* and there

‡ Ecclef. vii. 10.

can

can be *no greater* folly in the world than to
think or say so, *one* instance only *excepted:*
The *believing* there is a God, and yet *living* as
if there *was none.* If the atheist could prove
his point, he would then have a kind of right,
and full liberty to gratify his passions, and he
would have no reason to govern himself by
the restraints of religion, and could have
nothing to fear from the consequences of his
vices in a future world. But if there be a
God, and the principles connected therewith
are true, and we believe them to be true ; *habitual vice* is the *extremest folly*, because the
certain consequences of it are absolute misery
and destruction.

The scheme of *atheism* is indeed the whole
of it *folly*, and a contradiction to the most
certain and evident principles, and hath nothing to support it but the most improbable,
romantick, and self contradictory principles.
The leading principle of it is, that *there is no
God;* no eternal, infinitely wise, all powerful,
unchangeably good being ; possessed of all
intellectual powers, and moral perfections ;
and that therefore there is *no providence* that
concerns itself in the conservation, protection
and government of the world in whole
or part ; no being to whom man stands in
any relation as creator, preserver, father,
friend, inspector or Lord, from whom he
hath any thing to fear or hope, to whom he
owes either reverence, gratitude or love, to
whom he stands obliged for his being or well
being ; to whom he can address his prayers
or

or praifes,or from whom he can expect or receive any kind of good; and in confequence of this that he is under no law to him, and owes him no homage or obedience, to whom he is accountable, or from whom he fhall ever receive either punifhment or reward; *i. e.* that there is no future ftate, or world to come, no future judgement, no Heaven, no Hell ; and, in a word, that all the principles of religion are falfe, and all the duties and practices of it are fuperftitious and abfurd.   Thefe are the confequences that attend this leading principle of atheifm, that there is no God.   The denial of this one truth implies a denial of all the other truths arifing out of and connected with it.

And this the Pfalmift tells us is the language of a *fool's heart.   He hath faid in his heart there is no God.*   It feems they were not arifen to that height of impiety, as *openly* and avowedly to deny the being and providence of God ; but *their actions* carried in them a plain denial of thefe truths, and therefore he reafonably concluded, this was their inward fentiment, what they endeavoured to perfuade themfelves to believe, and what they were fometimes apt to think and hope might be true.

It hath been doubted by many, whether there ever was, or whether 'tis poffible there can be a *fpeculative atheift* in the world, *i. e.* one who is really convinced, and that firmly believes there is no God. 'Tis a difficult matter to determine what really paffes in mens breafts. There have been unqueftionably

fome,

some, who have in words openly and exprefsly denied it. 'Tis uncertain whether this
proceeded from the firm perfuafion of their
minds, but abfolutely certain, that if it did,
that perfuafion could arife from no rational
and moral conviction ; becaufe *'tis impoffible
to prove,* and therefore impoffible to be certain *that there is no God.* When men have an intereft to anfwer by rejecting the principles
of religion, they will try every art and practice
with themfelves, to perfuade themfelves out
of the belief of them ; and I am apt to think
they may fometimes fo impofe on themfelves,
and fo far fubdue their confciences, as that
for a feafon, they may quite get rid of all apprehenfions and fears of deity, and fettle into
a *temporary* atheifm.   But I do not apprehend
that 'tis eafy or common, abfolutely to get
rid of thefe apprehenfions of God.   The
fuggeftions of confcience, and the thoufand
arguments that prove his being, and the fufpicion that he doth exift, I imagine, will return in the intervals of reflection and confideration, and not leave him in quiet and
uninterrupted poffeffion of the atheiftical
fcheme he hath endeavoured to eftablifh in
his own mind.   And befides this, men may,
by habitual vice, and a long courfe of wickednefs, bring themfelves to fuch an inattention,
irreverence, and difregard towards the being,
perfections and providence of God, as that
if they can't be faid formally to have got rid
of the belief of Deity, they may be faid to
be wholly difpoffeffed of *all* manner of *fear of*
Deity,

Deity, and to be no more influenced by any motives that relate to him, than if they had wholly renounced his exiftence. And this difregard to deity may in time grow fo abfolute and intire, as to come little fhort of atheifm itfelf, and as may be reafonably conftrued to be a real profeffion of his belief that there is no God.

'Tis certain, that habitual finners and profligate men can be *fafe* in their practices upon no other fcheme but that of *atheifm*; and if they cannot prevail with themfelves to break off thefe by repentance, and return to religion and virtue, they will do every thing to render themfelves eafy in that courfe they are determined to purfue; and amongft other methods, they will not fail by falfe reafonings and fpecious objections, to endeavour to impofe on, and deceive themfelves into a perfuafion, of the truth of what they wifh to be true. And as we fee often in fact, that there is nothing fo abfurd but what perfons may be induced for a while to credit, efpecially when inclination and intereft prompts them to it; fo I do not know, but that for a feafon at leaft, they may prevail with themfelves to fink down into and embrace that, which is of all opinions the moft abfurd and ridiculous, that there is no God; and bating occafional interruptions of this belief, from the fuggeftions of confcience not wholly wafted, fome occafional events in life, carrying in them ftrong marks and clear intimation of a providence, and from the vifible footfteps of Deity evidently im-

preffed

preſſed on the whole frame of the creation, occurring to their minds, in ſpite of all their endeavours to avoid and reſiſt the force of them ! I ſay excepting ſuch temporary interruptions as theſe, I know not, but their diſbelief of Deity may become habitual and ſettled, and then they may wholly diveſt themſelves of all thoughts and apprehenſions as to the divine Being, perfections and providence. For I cannot think it leſs poſſible for men to come to this height of impiety, and embrace the abſurdeſt imaginations of atheiſm, than it is for them to do what is more abſurd and impious, profeſſing to believe a Deity, and yet *living* as if there was *none*. And as the Pſalmiſt argued, from the vices and corruptions of thoſe in his own time, to which he ſaw them indulge, that they *ſaid in their* hearts, or were apt to perſuade themſelves, that there *was no God ;* ſo we may reaſon from the ſame cauſes in our own to the ſame concluſion. And indeed the impieties and vices that are now practiced by ſome amongſt ourſelves are ſo enormous, that one would be apt to imagine men could never commit them, unleſs they were as fully atheiſts in ſpeculation as in practice. But this *their way is their folly,* whoſoever may approve and imitate them. And this may be made appear by many plain and evident conſiderations. And I would obſerve,

1. That the *caſting off* all the *great principles* of religion, whether natural or revealed, is an *inſtance of folly,* becauſe 'tis

impoſſi. L

impoſſible in the very nature of the thing, ever
to diſprove them, or *demonſtrate their falſhood.*
If this could be done, atheiſm would have
ſome plea, and might have reaſonable perſons
to countenance and embrace it. But this
can never be done. There are no ſelf-evi-
dent, certain principles, by which this can
be fully, or even probably ſhewn. That
there is a God, a providence, a future ſtate,
a judgment to come, a retribution of rewards
and puniſhments in another world ; that there
may be a perſon ſent from God to inſtruct
the world in knowledge and righteouſneſs,
and the belief of a future ſtate, that he may
endow him with a power of working miracles,
raiſe him from the dead, and for reaſons of
the higheſt importance give him power to
confer the moſt valuable bleſſings on mankind, and conſtitute him univerſal judge ;
theſe and the like propoſitions are incapable
of being diſproved, and the falſhood of them
being made appear by any ſubſtantial and
convincing evidence. I know objections may
be raiſed againſt them, and ſo alſo there may
be objections raiſed againſt the moſt certain and
unqueſtionable facts and principles. But an
objection to the truth of any thing is quite a different thing from a *demonſtration* of its falſhood.
To do this, it muſt be ſhewn, that they imply
either a natural impoſſibility, or a contradiction to ſome certain, obvious, acknowledged
principles of truth, or that they are repugnant
and contradictory to each other, or may be reduced to a clear and plain abſurdity. But

1. They

1. They *imply no natural impossibility*. That a being *infinitely more perfect* than we should exist, is no more impossible, than that *we should exist* in so much more perfect a state than a mite or worm ; or that *he* should be *eternal*, any more than the *world*, or the *atoms* of which it consists, or something else should be eternal ; because nothing could have been, if there had. been nothing from eternity ; or that there should be a *divine providence*, any more than that there should be *human foresight* or care ; or that there should be a *future world*, any more than that there should be the *present one* ; or that there should be a *future judgement* any more than that there should be a *present one* ; or that the consequences of men's actions should overtake them *hereafter*, any more than that they do often overtake them in the *present* life ; or that Christ should be an *instructor to mankind*, any more than that I should be *to you*, or *you* to one another ; or that *miracles* should be done by God *through him*, any more than that *God should do miracles by himself*, and that greatest miracle of all, create the world, and all the various objects of it ; or than that, which is a *greater miracle*, in the scheme of atheism, that the *world should create itself*, or be created without any creator, or exist without a cause, or exist from eternity, without one single reason of an eternal existence belonging to it. There is no natural impossibility, that any genuine principles of religion should be true. And

2 There

2. There are *no certain maxims* to which the *principles* of *religion* are a *contradiction*. The being and providence of God contradict no original and clear perceptions and convictions of the mind, but fall in with and arise out of those primary notions and apprehensions. The *possibility* of a *future* state is juft as certain as the *reality* of the *present* one, and 'tis no repugnancy to the conſciouſneſs that *I now am*, that *I may hereafter be.* That there ſhould be future rewards and puniſhments is irreconcileable with no firſt principle of truth, but may be, as demonſtrably, as that we are capable of them in the preſent ſtate ; and the ſuppoſition of them carry no affront to reaſon, nor any contradicton to the condition and conſtitution of our nature ; but it is perfectly conſiſtent with and entirely ariſes out of it. And upon ſuppoſition of the being of a God, it carries *no reflection* upon *his character*, and is contrary to no one ſingle perfection of his nature, that *he ſhould commiſſion*, by peculiar inſtruction, one or more perſons, as the circumſtances of the world required, to make known his will, and recover men to virtue and religion ; any more than it doth, that he ſhould *firſt give them reaſon*, or make men capable of informing one another, or inſtruct them by the works of nature, or lead them to conſideration by the exerciſe of a conſtant providence ; or put them under the obligation of a natural law, or confer on them any one bleſſing whatever of nature or providence. Nor doth it imply the denial of

of any one fingle truth, that a perfon thus inftructed of God, fhould be furnifhed with a fuitable proof of his divine commiffion and authority, or be enabled to prove it by fuch extraordinary and miraculous works, as fhould point out the immediate finger and power of God. The *over-ruling* on extraordinary oc-cafions the powers of nature, and the common courfe of caufes and effects, is *as eafy* as the *firft fettlement* of them, by him that fettled them ; and the doing this for wife reafons is as confiftent as the original fixing of them for other wife reafons ; and as the doing it doth not interrupt the general con-ftitution of things nor introduce any diforder or confufion into the common courfe of na-ture ; fuch a temporary and partial fufpen-fion of them is no reflection upon the fitnefs and wifdom of that original and general con-ftitution, nor of levity, ficklenefs, and want of forecaft in him that ordained it. And finally, that *one man* fhould be conftituted a *mediator*, or medium of conveyance of any fignal bleffings to all men, and be advanced to be univerfal Governor and Lord, is no more repugnant to our plaineft fenfe, and daily experience of things, than that God fhould conftitute *one man on earth* to be a mediator or means of conveyance of any fig-nal bleffing to another, or to a family, or to a nation, or to feveral nations united under his government ; or than that God fhould appoint, as he hath in fact appointed, all the great bleffings of human life to be con-veyed

veyed in private and publick life by the mediation of others. So that all the principles of religion, whether natural or revealed, are incapable of being difproved, as they can never be fhewn to be repugnant to any original, certain, and indifputable principles of truth, to the conftitution of human nature, or the common and univerfal experience of things ; but are in fact entirely confiftent with them, and indeed may be certainly demonftrated to be included in, and confiftent with them. And

3. 'Tis as *impoffible to fhew any real contradiction* between the genuine *principles of religion themfelves,* as to fhew their repugnance to any original notions, or felf-evident and unqueftionable truths ; and therefore as impoffible to evidence and demonftrate their falfhood. Contradictory propofitions can never be both of them true. The certainty of the one demonftrates the falfhood of the other ; and if the great and genuine doctrines of religion were juftly liable to the charge of inconfiftency, fome of them at leaft could have no foundation in truth, but would deferve to be rejected. But here we have no reafon to fear for our religious principles, as they are all reconcileable, and in the moft perfect concord and harmony with each other. The principles of *natural religion* are fuch, as are fuppofed to be the *mere genuine* certain dictates of *natural light* and reafon ; and as true reafon can never dictate contradictions, thofe principles which are

dictated

dictated by it, muſt for that reaſon be all of them reconcileable, and in all things conſiſtent. Nor is the harmony leſs between thoſe of *natural* and *revealed* religion, and one great end of the latter is to confirm and eſtabliſh and enforce the former ; and by conſequence the doctrines of both muſt be as conſiſtent, as the diſtinguiſhing principles of either. And thus they will be found to be, upon the moſt careful examination. The *ſupport* of religion and morality in the world, muſt be the *great deſign* of providence, and the promoting the ends of both is the governing intention of revelation ; and therefore in this view of it, it muſt have the warrant and ſupport of all true principles of reaſon. The *means* of promoting theſe, as ſettled by revelation, are thoſe which alone can with propriety be uſed, inſtruction, and perſuaſion, conviction and evidence, againſt which reaſon can make no juſt objection. The *doctrines* themſelves, which revelation conveys the knowledge of, as peculiar to itſelf, and diſtinct from thoſe of natural religion, are cloſely *connected* with, and *ariſe out* of thoſe *natural principles* ; ſuppoſe their truth, and are impoſſible without it. Natural religion .teaches us, that God who is the Author of our reaſonable powers, and gave us our capacities for knowledge and perception, can as immediately convey the knowledge of his will by direct impreſſions on, and application to our intellectual powers, to any one or more perſons, or to the whole of mankind,

as

as immediately, by the operation of external objects and arguments. Revelation tells us that he hath done this ; and yet as reason affures us, that our intellectual powers were not given us in vain, nor to be rendered perpetually or generally *ufelefs*, by fupernatural and extraordinary impreffions, and by miraculous conveyances of knowledge, fo as to render infignificant the ordinary methods of effecting it ; herein revelation agrees with reafon ; attempts no violence to men's powers, offers itfelf to their confideration, and leaves them to the common methods of drawing inftruction and information from it. As *natural* religion teaches *the eternal and immutable difference* between moral good and evil, and that the true worfhip of God muft be that of the heart, manifefted by the fruits of a good life ; fo *revelation eftablifhes* both. As the one teaches and eftablifhes the doctrine of a future ftate, fo doth the other ; but with this difference, that revelation affures us that this future ftate fhall take place by a real refurrection from the dead ; without which, even upon the principles of true philofophy, it doth not appear how men are ever to recover their proper natures, or as men be either rewarded or punifhed. Reafon evidently teaches a future judgment, or what is equivalent to it, an equitable decifion of men's future lot, according to their refpective characters of good and evil. Revelation eftablifhes this doctrine of a future judgment ; but then as reafon teaches that God is abfolutely

lutely invisible and therefore cannot in any
visible shape or form preside personally in this
great work, revelation assures us this judgment shall be carried on by *a visible president*,
every way furnished with those intellectual
and moral qualifications, as shall abundantly
fit him for this high dignity and office. The
same consonancy and mutual dependency
might be shewn between all the distinguish-
ing, real principles of natural and revealed religion , and therefore 'tis absolutely impossible to disprove the truth of either, by shewing
them to be in any instance self-contradictory
and repugnant. And therefore

4. Lastly, 'tis *impossible* to reduce them to
an *absurdity* ; because this can only be done
by shewing them to be impossible in their
nature, repugnant to plain and self-evident
principles, or repugnant to one another, and
destructive of themselves. And therefore it
must be an argument of the greatest folly to
reject the belief of them, and banish all regard to them out of our minds. For after a
thousand objections that may be raised against
them, the possibility of their truth and cer-
taintn still remains, and whilst this continues,
'tis stupidity and the excess of weakness to
pronounce them false, or live so as if they
were not, and could not possibly be true. And
this will appear with farther conviction, if
we consider

1. That the *casting off the principles of
religion* and the embracing the scheme of
atheism and infidelity, is *a contradiction to the
general*

general sense and reason of mankind, and stands condemned by the almoft univerfal fuffrage of the world. I am as fenfible as any one can be, that there is oftentimes little regard to be paid to common opinions and vulgar notions, which are oftentimes nothing better than common prejudices, and vulgar miftakes ; nor do I in the leaft meafure truth, by the judgments which they pafs on things, or the fentiments they form concerning them. But ftill, if any fentiments can be made appear to have been embraced from the earlieft ages of the world, throughout all the various periods of its duration, amongft all nations in it, barbarous and polifhed, free or enflaved, learned or ignorant, and by infinitely the far greateft part of mankind in every nation, by thofe that have been the moft inquifitive and fagacious, as well as by thofe who have little leifure for enquiry, by men of the higheft abilities, as by thofe of the loweft, by the moft excellent and virtuous of men, infomuch that Cicero *, who well knew the fentiments of his own and paft ages, did not fcruple to fay, with refpect to the foul's immortality, which fuppofes a God : *Nefcio quo modo inhæret in mentibus quafi feculorum quoddam augurium futurorum ; idque in maximis ingeniis, altiffimifque animis exiftit maxime, & apparet facillime.* And I may add, frequently by the moft profligate and vicious, by men that have differed in ten thoufand other fpecula-

* Tufc. Quæft. l. 1. c. 15.

tions, and embraced repugnant schemes of philosophy; by men that have had the strongest enmities, and the deepest personal prejudices against each other; in a word, by men who have been led by personal and publick reasons, by their prejudices and fears, by their interest and views of safety, wholly to deny their principles; and by others who could embrace them, from nothing but conviction of their truth, certainty, and importance; I say when this is the case, when principles come thus universally recommended, they certainly carry with them great authority, and deserve to be most seriously and impartially considered; and the rejecting such principles is not only an opposition to vulgar opinions, but a contradiction to human nature itself, and to the light of reason in general. If it should be said, that by this way of arguing, the greatest absurdities of principle may be embraced, because these have been as universally espoused, and come recommended to us by the general approbation of mankind: I answer, that the cases are vastly different, and that though the general principles of religion have been the common belief of mankind, yet the absurdities attending them have not been every where the same, but been peculiar to this and the other nation, and the absurdities of some been ridiculed and rejected by others.

The general principles of religion are those of the being of one God, a providence, the natural difference of actions, and the rewards

and

and punishments of a future state. These principles were univerfally held. In thefe the general fenfe of mankind concurred, and their fentiments in thofe refpects were uniform. What they differed about were the attributes, circumftances, modes and explication of thefe things. In thefe nations differed from nations, the vulgar amongst themselves, and wife men and philosophers from the vulgar. So that though the general fenfe of mankind, as to the principles themfelves, was uniform, and is therefore a strong prefumption in favour of the truth of them ; yet the like prefumption can never be argued in favour of their fuperftitions and abfurdities of belief, becaufe in thefe there was no unity, but a perpetual variety and difagreement. If it be faid, that this unity and agreement of the principles was the effect of tradition from one age and generation to another, be it fo : But then whence did it firft come ? How was it brought into the world ? And what gave rife to it ? If it was the natural effects of the reafonings of a mind, struck with the magnificence, variety, connection, marks of power, traces of wifdom, and various footfteps of goodnefs, that every where appear from the *effects of power* to an *almighty agent*, from the *figns of contrivance* and art to a *divine contriver* and artift, from the *tokens of goodnefs* to a *benevolent original*, and from the nature of the whole frame of things to a fuitable and proportionable caufe of them ; and from thefe characters of the firft caufe reafoning farther

the certainty of providence, the moral government of God, and therefore the account-
ablenefs of men to him, as their proper judge,
and therefore the exiftence of a future ftate for
the proper diftribution of rewards and punifhments; if this I fay gave the firft rife to the
principles of religion, this is a ftrong recommendation of them, and a probable evidence
of their truth ; and as the general belief of
them amongft all ages and nations hath been
actually fupported by thefe kind of arguments, it fhews that the tradition hath thus
univerfally prevailed, not by chance and accident, not by fraud and power, but by the
appearance of fuch evidence to the minds
of men, as that they have never been able
to refift it, even when wholly free from all
the wrong inducements and motives of force,
or intereft; even when they have been in the
retirements of the clofet, and have had nothing to biafs them, or tempt them to a conclufion in favour of them, but the irrefiftable
evidence of the things themfelves, and the
fulleft conviction in their own minds and
confciences in favour of them. Much more
might eafily be faid on this head ; but from
what hath been already urged, I think it may
be fairly inferred, that to treat thefe notions
as merely imaginary and groundlefs, and to
ridicule them as contemptible and abfurd,
when they have been in poffeffion of mankind univerfally, throughout every period of
their duration, and have been efteemed by
the beft and wifeft of men, as the moft venerable,

nerable, important and facred truths ; is
great prefumption and folly ; and that the
wholly rejecting them as falfe and impofture, is fuch an affront to the common fenfe
and reafon of mankind, as that none but
they who are deftitute of both can be guilty
of. And this is a character more efpecially
due to them, who take on them to cenfure,
condemn, and run riot on thefe principles,
whilft their paffions are ftrong, and their reafon weak and immature ? who have never
been accuftomed to fevere enquiries, and laborious fearches into the fecrets of truth ;
who have read but little, and ftudied lefs,
and of whom by reafon of their age, inex-
perience, want of time, and purfuit of pleafure, it may be certainly faid : They are not
mafters of the fubjects in which they pretend
to decide, and whether their decifions are
true or falfe, yet are in them precipitate and
irrational.   But farther,

2. The great *probability* of the truth of
religious principles, yea the *demonftrative evi-*
dence for the certainty of the capital leading
ones, fhews the extream folly of rejecting
them, and wholly renouncing all belief of
and regard to them.   I have fhewn you already, that to difprove them is in the nature
of the thing impoffible ; and 'till even this
can be done, the treating them as abfolute
falfities is inexcufable, and betrays a very
weak and wrong difpofition of mind.   But
when 'tis farther added, that they are fupported by the ftrongeft probabilities, fuch as

in

in all other cafes would he fufficient grounds
of affent, and thought fo by all impartial and
equitable reafoners ; the folly of infidelity
appears in a ftronger light, and becomes in
every view of it inexcufable. And the true
ftrength of this probability will appear, if we
confider, that all the foundation principles of
it have demonftrative evidence to afcertain and
and fupport them, and may be proved by firft
principles, by indifputable, felf-evident ax-
ioms of truth, by the intuition of our minds,
and by the moft certain experience that we
univerfally have of our own ftate, and the
condition of human nature. And thefe firft
principles, that are the bafis and foundation
of all religion, both in principle and practice,
are thefe three : The being of a God, the
effential and immutable difference of moral
actions, and the capacity of being accountable for our own. The firft of thefe hath been
certainly demonftrated two ways : By the argument called *a priori*, or from the nature
and reafon of the thing itfelf, proving firft the
eternal principle or caufe, and then defcending to the operations and effects of it. And
then from the argument *a posteriori* ; or arifing
from the evident effects and proofs of power,
wifdom and goodnefs, in the formation and
ftructure, and productions of nature, to an
infinitely wife, powerful, and benevolent
original, or caufe of all things. The demonftration in each way is certain, and though
it may be cavilled at, can never be evaded.
That there is an effential difference of ac-

tions,

tions, between good and evil, we plainly
difcern by intuition ; or their difference appears at once to the mind, without any need
of any intermediate idea or thought to afcertain or demonftrate it ; as inconteftibly as
the difference between the oppofites in natural
things, fuch as light and darknefs, fweet or
bitter, hard or foft, hot or cold, or any other
contraries that can be named.   And that all
men have the capacity of being accountable,
is as certain as that they think, can reafon,
are confcious, do remember, and are capable
of choice.   Thus far then we reft upon an
immovable foundation of truth, that nothing
can overturn and deftroy.   From the firft
of thefe principles, the being of a God, *i. e.*
of a being infinitely powerful, wife, and good,
immutable and every where prefent, the caufe
of all things, the univerfal Proprietor, and
Lord of the creation, we immediately infer,
univerfal providence, infpection, and government, fuitable to the nature of every diftinct
being, and therefore managed with the greateft
equity and juftice.   Hence it follows that if
this providence and government be managed
fuitable to the diftinct nature of every individual, *i. e.* fuitable to the refpective powers
and faculties every individual is endowed
with, the diftinguifhing powers of every
being muft be to him the rule of his conduct : That fuch as have only fenfe and inftinct can be actuated by no other principles
than thofe : And that reafon, where that is
implanted, is equally the rule of reafonable

beings : And that where fenfe and reafon both enter into the compofition, both have their proper province, and are to have their diftinct influence on the conduct; and that the lower and brutal principle of fenfe is to be kept in a conftant due fubordination to the higher and divine one of reafon. Hence it follows, that as by our fenfe we difcern, what is wholefome or noxious to the fenfitive part of our frame, and are by this law of our nature to choofe only that which is good, and tends to the prefervation of it; fo by our reafon we are enabled to difcern what is good and evil in actions, or prejudicial or conducive to the welfare and happinefs of our rational part, what refults from our relations, connections, and ftations of being, and to choofe or refufe according to the dictates of this rational fenfe, or our inward convictions concerning thefe things; and that to live by reafon, as we are rational beings, is as truely and as univerfally the law of our nature, as to be governed by fenfe in all cafes, that are immediately within the province of it; and to fubject fenfe to reafon, becaufe the welfare of the whole frame abfolutely depends on it. Hence it follows, that as this difference of moral actions is as certain in itfelf, and as certainly difcerned by all men, who do not wilfully fhut out the cleareft perceptions, as the difference in any objects that the fenfes are the judges of; it muft be the will of God that formed us, that we fhould govern ourfelves by that reafon he hath given us, attend

to

to the moral fenfe he hath implanted in us,
chufe according to our natural perceptions,
purfue that courfe that certainly appears wife
and good, and always do thofe things which
the mind difcerns to be lovely, excellent,
amiable, and good, fuited to our relations,
and conducive to our perfection, welfare and
happinefs, and that we fhould avoid every
thing that is contrary hereto. Hence it follows, that God, who hath formed our natures,
fixed our relations, given us both our natural
and moral fenfe of things, and who by the
immenfity of his nature, and the perfection
of his knowledge, doth and cannot but conftantly obferve us, muft approve or difapprove
us, as we act agreeable or contrary to the
conftitution of our frame, and the law of
our nature. But what is approbation and
difapprobation without effect ? What is government without rewards and punifhments ?
What is wifdom, without wife diftributions ?
What juftice, where there is no juft and
equitable retributions ? What the love of
rectitude, without encouragements of it ?
What encouragement of it, without rewarding it ? What is hatred of fin, without difpleafure againft it, and what difpleafure,
without the proper fruits and effects of it ?
Hence arifes, from the nature of things, the
high probability, the ftrong prefumption, the
irrefiftible conclufion of an impartial judgment ; made more certain by the accountable nature of man, the principles of confcioufnefs and felf-reflection, and the fenfe he
hath

hath of the good or evil of his own actions ; and rendered indifputable by the fure information and evidence of divine revelation. Hence follows the certainty of a future ftate, and a life to come, as there is no proper judgment, no impartial award, no difcriminating marks of pleafure or difpleafure, to the good or bad ; a principle, that natural reafon almoft demonftrates the certainty of ; it being impoffible to confider the nature and character of God, and the rational powers and accountable condition of man, without falling into this conclufion ; that as God doth not here, he will certainly hereafter judge all men in righteoufnefs, and impartially diftribute to every one according to his deeds. And as this is one of the fundamental principles of divine revelation, it ftands upon fuch a foundation of truth and certainty, as carries the moft clear and forcible conviction. Now in this connection and view of things, how foolifh, how contemptibly foolifh doth atheifm appear ? To argue againft the being of God, is arguing againft demonftration itfelf ? 'tis oppofing the moft certain and indifputable truth, and rifing up in oppofition to the ftrongeft evidence that can be brought for the proof of it. None but a weak man can do this. 'Tis equally ridiculous as reafoning againft the exiftence of light at mid day, or the warmth of the fun beams when we actually feel them. And though men may think themfelves wonderoufly wife by oppofing certainty and demonftration,

ſtration, yet with wiſe men the endeavour
will always be treated with the ſovereign
contempt it deſerves. And as all the other
principles of religion, both natural and revealed, ſtand ſo cloſely connected with this
original foundation one, that even this muſt
be rendered uncertain, without theſe others
are true ; as every conception of God muſt
be partial and diſhonourable, that doth not
include the characters of Inſpector, Governor, Judge, and final Rewarder ; the doctrines of providence, a future ſtate, a final
judgment, and the diſtributions of rewards
and puniſhments, muſt appear to every impartial mind in the light of demonſtration,
or with ſuch an high degree of probability,
as tells little or nothing ſhort of it. And if
men diveſt themſelves of theſe principles,
cannot or will not diſcern the evidence of
them, nor acknowledge or ſubmit to the
power and influence of them, 'tis not becauſe
too much knowledge or learning have made
them bad, but becauſe they have too little to
diſcern the truth, or not integrity enough to
own and yield to it.   Again,

The *abſurdities*, *contradictions*, and *impoſſi-
bilities*, that muſt neceſſarily take place upon
the ſcheme of *atheiſm*, are a farther demonſtration of the great folly of rejecting and diſ-
carding the genuine principles of religion.
There is nothing more frequent in the mouths
of unbelievers than the charge of credulity,
bigottry, implicit faith, and ſuperſtition, upon
all thoſe who profeſs to believe, and live by
religious

religious doctrines and rules. They all of
them to a man, if their cenfures be true, believe contradictions, and fwallow down the
groffeft abfurdities ; and there is nothing fo
contrary to reafon, and oppofite to common
fenfe, that they will not embrace, and give
the firmeft affent to. It is but decent and
modeft however, that they who make and
throw fuch charges on others, fhould be of
all others the moft rational and confiftent in
their fcheme of principles, and liable to no
charge of grofs abfurdities, and embracing
a fyftem confifting of a thoufand contradictions. And yet upon comparifon it will
appear, that credulity lies on the fide of infidelity, and that in this fcheme they muft avow
the moft evident and palpable inconfiftences ;
infinitely greater than can with any juftice be
charged on the friends of religion and virtue.
With refpect to the origin of all things, what
is a Chriftian's belief ? Why that there was an
infinitely perfect, active, intelligent caufe, ex-
ifting from eternity, to whofe agency, wifdom,
and power, all beings owe their exiftence.
And this is evidently affigning a caufe proportionable and adequate to the effects produced,
and doth not at leaft appear at firft view to be
fo very romantick and incredible an abfur-
dity. Well, but the wife man of whom the
Pfalmift fpeaks, fays there is no God ; no fuch
infinitely wife, powerful, and good Being that
we fuppofe. What doth he place in the room
of him ? Even the fcheme of atheifm won't
do without allowing fomewhat eternal. And
to

to what doth atheifm allow this glorious privilege of eternal exiftence ? To the world in
its prefent form ? No, this they fee is too
abfurd to be defended.   What then ? Why
to atoms, fmall particles of matter, indivifible
in their nature, and which were the original
primitive feeds of which all things were afterwards formed.   If it is afked, what was
the employment of thefe atoms during their
eternal exiftence ; they anfwer us, they were
dancing in the infinity of fpace, and undergoing
infinite changes of fituation and place ; though
without any internal or external principle of
direction, and abfolutely unconfcious of exiftence, motion, and power.   If it be afked,
how thefe atoms came to make a world, and
unite into the prefent fyftem of things that
we behold, we are told : That after the infinite alterations, as to motion and place, which
thefe atoms underwent during the eternity of
their exiftence, they at laft united themfelves
into all the prefent various combinations and
forms in which we now behold them.   If
through our wonder and furprife we fhould
afk, how thefe combinations came to take
place, Whether by any fuperior direction and
agency ? They tell us, No, for that would be
to own a God.   What, by chance ? Some
fay, yes, and othes no ; affigning not chance,
but neceffity as the caufe of all things.   When
they are afked, what chance or neceffity is,
they anfwer : A caufe that acts without confcioufnefs and intention.   When afked, whether this caufe exifts within every atom, or
without

without them, the answer must be, not without them, for that would be to suppose a cause
existing, independent of and superior to them,
which would be dangerous to them, and lead
to the existence of a believer's God. If this
cause be in the atoms, doth it exist in every
individual one, or only in the whole of them?
If not in each, but in the whole body of them,
did it exist as a cause in them from eternity,
or just from any given period of that eternity?
If from eternity, why did not the present
frame of things exist from eternity? Why
was it not co-eval with the cause that at last
produced it? Why did not this chance or necessity operate and exert itself infinite ages
before it actually did? If it could not exert
itself 'till these atoms came into such a particular given situation, then this internal cause
did not exist in them from eternity, and so
could never be a cause of the existence of the
world at all ; for on all schemes the cause of
the world must be strictly everlasting. Besides,
how came the whole system of atoms to be
endowed with this internal power of chance
or necessity, that was not in each individual?
This is the absurdity of supposing that the
whole is different from its parts, or that mere
motion and difference of situation can produce new powers and properties in matter.
If every individual atom of matter contains
within itself this power or unconscious cause,
how came they without design to unite?
What must we suppose another cause to cause
these infinitely various causes to unite? This
will

will bring us to an original caufe again, *i. e.*
to God, the univerfal caufe, which deftroys
the whole fcheme of atheifm. The union of
fuch an infinite variety of caufes, without intention, defign and contrivance, to produce
one regular, confiftent, connected world, and
without the fuperior direction of an infinitely
wife and powerful agent, is an infinitely
greater miracle than ever was believed by the
moft credulous Chriftian ; or rather an ab-
furdity or contradiction too palpable and grofs
ever to be embraced by any other, but the
fool, who fays in his heart there is no God.
For what doth he fay by affirming this ?
Why, that an infinitely various number of
contradictory principles, powerlefs, unconfcious, roaming through the immenfity of
fpace, that had exifted in eternal diforder, fu-
rioufly contending with each other, repelling,
attracting, defcending, rifing, juftling, uniting,
feparating, and in a ftate of a perpetual, reftlefs difcord, come at laft by fome fortuitous,
happy jumble, to fall into union, harmony
and order, and thus to ftrike out this amazing
uniform frame of things, and combine into
a fyftem of themfelves, of conftant, regular,
uniform caufes and effects. That is, that
difcord produced union, confufion order,
chance defign, fenfelefs atoms a regular world,
unconfcious principles the moft exquifite and
beautiful productions, unthinking matter all
the powers of perception and reafon ; that the
effects of wifdom, contrivance and fkill had
no proportionable and adequate caufe ; in a
word,

word, that the present frame of the world
was not eternal, and that it was not even produced in time; but came into being by an
inexplicable neceffity or chance, *i. e.* by caufes
that had no power, thought, contrivance, defign, or any one fingle qualification to render
them the caufes of the effects they produced.
And is not this an hopeful fcheme? Can any
man help admiring the fagacity and confummate wifdom that appears in it? Or rather
can any thing be more defpicably contemptible? And are thefe the men, who charge believers with credulity? and reproach them
with the belief of contradictions and abfurdities? If we follow them farther, we fhall
find them uniform to themfelves, and not
afraid of embracing the moft credulous fuppofitions. If there be no God, of confequence there can be no infpection and fuperin-
tendency of providence. To what then in
their fcheme is the conftant regularity of
nature owing? What keeps her regular and
uniform in her productions? Why doth not
fhe diffolve, and fly off into her original
atoms? Why doth not fhe change her prefent form and enter into different combinations of things? Why now we fhall be told
of nature, and nature's operations, and her
regular courfe, and fixed order. But what is
nature? according to them fhe is nothing
but a compofition of atoms; and the queftion
returns : How this compofition of atoms fub-
fifts? A true theift, a well inftructed chriftian hath the proper anfwer ready. 'Tis by
the

the fuperintending power, and conftant direction of his providence, who firft fettled the
order of nature.   In the other fcheme all
that can be anfwered is, fate or chance; which
is no anfwer to the queftion, fince both are
fenfelefs names, which they that make ufe
of them can give no rational and fatisfying
defcription or definition of.   So that atheifm
fuppofes, that matter and motion preferve
themfelves, though they have neither confcioufnefs or power to do it ; that matter operates in infinitely various productions, by certain fixed laws of which it is infenfible, and
by which therefore it is impoffible it fhould
direct itfelf ;   and that it neceffarily operates
by thefe, though the neceffity be neither felf
impofed, nor impofed by any external agent
or power.   So that we have ftill marks of
power without a powerful agent, fteady direction, without internal or external power of
direction, contrivance, without confcioufnefs,
art, without defign, and the moft aftonifhing
proofs of fkill, without any thing of wifdom,
and innumerable proofs of a fuperintending
providence, though in reality there be no
providence at all.   Agreeable to thefe abfurdities they proceed farther, and in confequence
of cafting off the belief of God and his providence ; they farther believe, that man hath
no former or maker, his conftitution and frame
is abfurd, felf-contradictory, and made abfolutely in vain ; that all his powers and capacities for knowing, worfhipping, adoring,
loving, and ferving of God, are wafte and

uselefs ; that though he is formed for worfhip, 'tis impertinent and ridiculous ; that
though he hath fears and apprehenfions of
deity, they are groundlefs and abfurd, that
though he can demonftrate a God, the demonftration is falfe, and not to be trufted
to ; though he can prove a providence, the
proof deceives him ; and though he hath a
thoufand probabilities to convince him of a
life to come, and to render him thoughtful
of the confequences of it, yet all thefe no-
tices are vain and delufive, and that he
ought never to think of what he can never
put out of his mind, nor pay any regard to
the moft important fuggeftions and fears of
his own breaft.   Befides thefe evident abfurdities, they are forced to form the moft uncertain and groundlefs fuppofitions, that have
no proof, and are incapable of all proof : *viz.*
that nothing exifts but matter, that there is
no fpirit in the univerfe, that every man is
mere material mechanifm, that the whole of
man is mortal, that he can exift no where
but in the prefent world, nor in any other
manner than in his prefent condition ; that
death diffolves his frame, and annihilates the
whole of his exiftence.   Thefe are very important hypothefes, and to the proof of them
require fomething more than pofitive affertion,
and the confident affuming determinations of
the greateft pretenders to fcience and wifdom.
If the being of a God be allowed, and the
acknowledgment of it extorted by the irrefiftable force of evidence ; the folly of throw-
ing

ing off the belief of the principles connected
with it is ftill more amazing and contemptible. For fee, to believe a God without a
providence, is to believe a God without wifdom or agency. To believe a providence
that doth not regard the actions of men, is
to believe a providence without government,
and without that infpection which is the nobleft end of providence. To believe a divine
infpection that is attended neither with approbation or difapprobation of human actions,
is to believe an infpection that makes no diftinction, and that confounds the natures and
differences of things. To believe that God
doth approve or difapprove the actions of men,
as they are good or bad, and yet that he will
not reward and punifh them, is to believe
that his government is lefs perfect than that of
men, and that he is defective both in equity
and wifdom. And to believe that God will
reward and punifh, without believing a future ftate and judgment, is to believe that
he will reward and punifh, without conferring the one, or inflicting the other, fince 'tis
certain that thefe rewards and punifhments
do not take place generally in the prefent
world. Thefe and others like them are the
abfurdities to which the caufe of atheifm is
driven, and I am not afraid to leave every
man of fenfe and reafon to pafs the proper
judgment on them. None but fools can believe thefe abfurdities, and I think nothing
but vice corrupt any man to believe them.
Treat therefore thefe abfurdities with the

contempt they deferve. Shew yourfelves men
by yielding to the evidence of divine truth, and
let nothing deceive you out of thefe principles, which firmly believed, and made the
rule of your conduct, will guide you into
innocence, integrity and an univerfal propriety
and dignity of conduct in the prefent life,
fecure you the moft refrefhing comforts of
your being, give you courage in the laft moments of life, and fecure you all the advantages your hearts can defire, or God can
give in a more perfect and durable exiftence.

SERMON

SERMON X.

On keeping the Heart.

PROVERBS iv. 23.

Keep thy heart with all diligence, for out of it are the issues of life.

THE government of the *heart,* or the due regulation of the *various passions,* which have as it were their rise from, and their seat in it, is of the utmost consequence to the peace of our minds, and the wise and regular conduct of our lives. The utility and necessity of it, hath been acknowledged and inculcated by the best and wisest of the *moral* writers of the *heathen* world. " Govern, saith one of them †, thy mind or heart. Unless it be taught to obey, it will imperiously command. This, this therefore restrain with bridles and chains." Nothing is more frequent in the morals of the *Roman* Philosopher than the maxim, that the *appetites* should

† Horat. Epist. l. 1. Ep. 2. v. 62, 63.

S 3 submit

submit to *reason.* " The inftinct or force, faith he *, of the mind is double. The one belongs to the appetites, which hurry men away to this or that indifferently. The other belongs to reafon, which teaches and explains to us, what we are to do, and what we fhould avoid. Hence it is neceffary, that reafon fhould prefide, and appetite be made to obey." Many paffages of like nature may be produced from the fame excellent author, and almoft every other, that hath written upon the fubject of morality. 'Tis frequently inculcated by divine *revelation.* And indeed there is no maxim that hath been more univerfally known or inculcated by facred and prophane writers, than this of *watching of our hearts,* or *keeping* under perpetual reftraint or government, all the *various paffions* of our nature, *becaufe out of them are the iffues of life.*

You will remember that in this exhortation of my text, the *heart* is reprefented as a kind of *citadel* or fortrefs, on the keeping of which our entire fafety depends. If we furrender it to thofe enemies, that are continually labouring to get poffeffion of it, and give the government of it out of our hand ; diforder and ruin will neceffarily enfue, our liberty will be foon loft, our beft riches plundered and deftroyed, and we fhall be reduced to a ftate of the moft abject flavery. And as the enemies of our happinefs will be per-

* Cicer. de Offic. l. 1. c. 28.

petually

petually endeavouring by fraud or force, to
wreft it out of our hands, and reduce it
into fubjection to themfelves ; there is a
conftant neceffity of vigilance and care to prevent the fuccefs of their attempts, and their
having any kind of influence over, or fhare
in the government of it.   And here

1. We fhould fo *keep our hearts*, or have that
perpetual watch and guard over them, as to
fecure the entrance of them againft all danger,
and every attempt to invade them ; that we
may not through negligence or inadvertence
admit and harbour any thing that may trouble or defile us.   A fortrefs, how well fo
ever garrifoned, will eafily be gained, and
carried by furprize, if duty be not conftantly
done, and thofe who fhould watch and guard
it, indulge to fupinenefs and floth, and are
not ready upon every occafion to obferve the
motions. of an enemy, and to fecure all the
avenues, by which they may approach and
gain admiffion into it.   A wife and prudent
man will never fuffer an enemy to come too
near him, when he hath it in his power to
keep him at a diftance, and there is nothing
more certain, than that it is much eafier to
prevent evil difpofitions and affections from
intruding themfelves into our hearts, than
after we have admitted them, and fuffered
them for a while to influence and govern us,
to *difpoffefs* them of their power, and utterly
to exclude them.   Here the experiment is
always dangerous, and generally fatal ; and
there have been innumerable inftances of

perfons, who having unwarily put their hearts
out of their own keeping, and thereby loft the
government of themfelves, have never recovered their freedom, nor been able to dif-
intangle themfelves from the fnares they
have been caught in, but who have been finally undone without redemption. The avenues to the heart fhould therefore be well
guarded againft all intruders, and the entrance
barred.

Againft *all evil imaginations and thoughts*,
which are always bad and dangerous inmates,
fubtle, infinuating and deceitful, which, however pleafing they may appear, and whatever
gratifications they may promife and lead to,
yet Syren like, fmile only to beguile us, and
that they may allure us the more effectually,
to our own deftruction. We fhould therefore, if poffible, entirely exclude from our
breafts, fo as that they may never find any
room there, *all thoughts difhonourable to God*,
unworthy his purity, juftice and goodnefs,
that are fubverfive of the certainty, or injurious to the nature of his providence, that tend
to *weaken our regard to the principles*, or *difaffect* us to the *duties of religion*, that tend to
infpire favourable fentiments of fin, and leffen
the danger of committing it, that may excite
lawlefs and criminal paffions, or that may
warm, aggravate and fix them ; we fhould
never admit fallacious reafonings to deceive
us out of our principles, nor the pleas of appetite and paffion to perfuade us to act contrary to them ; but to guard the eye, the ear,

all

all the various inlets to imagination and
thought, as may moſt effectually prevent their
entrance, and carefully ſhun all ſuch objects,
connections, converſations, and occaſions, as
may tend to encourage and excite them.   Or,
if they ſuddenly ariſe in us, without our in-
vitation and conſent,   as we ſometimes find
they will do,   they ſhould be immediately
caſt out with abhorrence,   and the mind di-
verted to ſuch other conſiderations, as may
have the moſt direct tendency to diſſipate and
deſtroy them.

Imaginary wants, and *unneceſſary appetites
and deſires,* are alſo very troubleſome and dangerous gueſts, when admitted into the hearts
of men, and when we ſuffer them to become motives and rules of action to us,
without the neceſſary checks of reaſon and
conſcience.   It was a noble anſwer of *M.
Antonine* the emperor, as related by his ſuc-
ceſſor *Julian* the apoſtate * ; who being aſked,
wherein he thought the trueſt *imitation of
the Gods* conſiſted, replied : " To want the
feweſt things, and to be moſt abundant in
doing good to others."   And indeed how
many things are there that we do not really
want, either for cur comfort, uſefulneſs and
happineſs ! If indeed we judge by our paſſions,
our wants will prodigiouſly multiply upon
our hands.   Fancy, vanity, pride, ambition,
envy, and the love of pleaſure, will make us
uneaſy in the abſence of all thoſe things

* Juliani Cæſ. p. 334. A.

which

which are neceffary to indulge them. This
we fhall want for drefs and ornament, this
for furniture and equipage, this for the plenty
and elegance of the table, this to expend on
pleafure and amufement, this to be upon an
equality with our neighbour, and this to
excel and overfhine him. I have no objection againft men's endeavouring to profper in
the world, and their cherifhing an honeft
ambition to rife as high as diligence and integrity can carry them : Only let them keep
this ambition and defire under regular bounds;
not think this and the other thing neceffary to
happinefs, not be uneafy in what they have,
through an over anxioufnefs for what they
have not, not purfue any meafures of profperity by means inconfiftent with real prudence and integrity, not facrifice their principles and religion to the world, nor fuffer
their defires after the plenty they are in queft
of to be animated by the low, unworthy
views only of more freely entering into the
follies, amufements, gratifications, pleafures,
cuftoms, and manners of an unprincipled,
thoughtlefs world, which never adds any
thing to the real worth and dignity of character, make no one eftimable in the fight of
God, or of wife and good men, and is fo
far from contributing to any one's true felicity, as that it always endangers, and frequently finally deftroys it. All fuch wants
therefore as arife from miftaken opinions,
from irregular affections, or irrational views
and motives, fhould be utterly and forever
                                        excluded,

excluded, if we would confult our peace, fecure our virtue, and obtain the poffeffion of
our real happinefs.

It is farther highly incumbent on us, that
we fhould *diligently watch* over our hearts, to
prevent any wrong habits from being fettled in
us, and all difpofitions to that which is evil,
from having any power and influence over
us.   This is a care abfolutely and univerfally
neceffary, on which the credit, comfort, and
ufefulnefs of this life, and all our hopes of
a better in a great meafure depend.   Tendencies to evil in our natures there certainly
are, and they arife from the very nature,
and indifference of our paffions, to all objects,
without exception, that appear grateful to
them.   But thefe paffions are generally *in
the beginning eafily governable,* and fubmiffive
to the proper reftraints of reafon and prudence, if they are not too early heightened
by indulgence, and ftrengthened by frequent
practice.   It is by thefe means bad habits
are contracted, and rendered inveterate and
too frequently unconquerable.   Generally
fpeaking men have fome *native reluctances* to
criminal indulgencies, when they are firft entering on a finful courfe, and look with a
kind of horror on thofe exceffes of vice in
which they fee others madly plunging
themfelves.   Nor do they oftentimes efcape
the remorfe and reproaches of their own confciences, when firft they venture on forbidden
ground, break through the original reftraints
of education, and do violence to thofe principles

ples and fentiments of honour, modefty, and
virtue, they once looked upon as facred and
inviolable. But by venturing on farther and
farther, adding one tranfgreffion to another,
and frequently fuppreffing the fears of offending, they grow more familiar with fin, the
danger of it leffens in their minds, the
confequences of it are kept out of their fight,
the inclination to it grows ftronger and ftronger, all the motives to refrain from it become
weak and deftitute of all life and vigour, the
very flow of their blood and fpirits feels and
nourifhes the difpofition to it, irregular imaginations inflame and quicken their defires,
perpetual opportunities that offer themfelves
to gratify their paffions, feduce and perfuade
them, and the powerful follicitations of their
brethren in vice, and companions in iniquity,
that have long deferted the path of uprightnefs, and walk in the ways of darknefs, become fo perfuafive and prevalent, as that he
hath no difcretion to preferve him, no underftanding to keep any watch over him. *He
goes after them as an ox to the flaughter, or as a
bird that hafteneth to the fnare*, i. e. without
fhame, wit, or fear, *not knowing that it is for
his life*; or not confidering, that it will end
certainly in his deftruction.

By frequently indulging himfelf in thefe
courfes, the habit is contracted, and grows
every day more powerful and abfolute. Every
thing gives way to the force of it. It con-
trouls all other interefts and views, and by
hardening the confcience, by trampling un-
derfoot

derfoot all confiderations proper to refift it, and keeping intirely out of view all the fatal confequences that will. attend it, it becomes impregnable by any of the regular forces of religion, maintains its ufurped dominion over the foul, fcorns all reftraints, and draws men into the moft complicated and aggravated crimes.

In fuch a difpofition, under the cruel flavery of fuch habits, what hope, what profpect of redemption ! How improbable is the recovery ! How difficult is the cure ! If the fortrefs be thus in the hands of the enemy, and all the avenues of it in his poffeffion, how fhall we be able to oppofe him ! When all the forces that fhould refift his power are op-preffed, or intirely difarmed, how can we ever expel him ? How neceffary, how unalterable muft our fubjection and flavery be ! Every one knows, that even as to trifling and indifferent things, an habit contracted by long ufe is very difficultly fuppreffed and broken. How much more fo the habits of fin, which have fo many peculiar circumftances to ftrengthen and confirm them, and when all the proper means to conquer and extirpate them are become impotent, or rather utterly deftroyed. What God may think proper to do, by any extraordinary influence and grace, I cannot determine ; but I do not apprehend, that if any perfons are refolved to enflave and deftroy themfelves, they have any great reafon to expect, from the gofpel revelation, that God will by miraculous interpofitions prevent

their

their flavery and ruin. 'Tis at leaft a prefumptuous and dangerous expedient. But in
the natural courfe of things, an habitual,
hardened finner, who, having extirpated all
the natural good difpofitions of his mind, and
broken down all the original fences, that fhould
have been his protection and fecurity againft
the deceitfulnefs and power of fin, hath long
indulged himfelf in prefumptuous crimes, and
thereby created in himfelf ftrong and unnatural and permanent propenfities to that which
is evil : I fay, that fuch a perfon, judging of
things according to moral probability, hath
but little chance of ever becoming a real
convert to religion and virtue ; or in St. *Paul*'s
words, *of putting off the old man, which is corrupt according to deceitful lufts, and putting on
that new man, which after God is created in
righteoufnefs and true holinefs.* For in fuch perfons the heart is fo entirely corrupted and enflaved, the confcience fo abfolutely fubdued,
the fenfe of the difference between good and
evil, fo wholly effaced, and the mind fo utterly blinded and fteeled againft all the confequences of a future ftate, as that there is
almoft nothing left in them which the motives
to repentance can take hold of, and by which
any kind of perfuafions to reclaim them from
their vices, and recover them to a better life,
can become effectual. Hence it is that the
fcriptures reprefent the converfion of an habitual hardened finner, as almoft impoffible.
It is in this manner that the prophet reprefents
the condition of the *Jews*, who had been long
                                    proficients

proficients in all manner of wickednefs. *Can the Ethiopian change his fkin, or the leopard his fpots? Then may ye alfo do good, that are accuftomed to do evil* *. Not to fignify, that the one is as impoffible as the other, but the extream difficulty of the thing, that a long accuftomed finner fhould ever be reclaimed and reformed by any of the ordinary means of converfion, and to prevent perfons from contracting fuch habits as are, in the nature of things, fo hard to be cured, and from the power of which there are but few who are intirely recovered, and gained over to the intereft and practice of true religion and virtue. How much need therefore is there of a conftant infpection over our hearts, that we may not fuffer the paffions of our nature to enfnare and feduce us into fuch criminal purfuits and gratifications, as may create and confirm in us the habit of finning. This may be done by daily watchfulnefs and care, by keeping alive in our minds a becoming fear and horror of ever entering into the paths of vice, by immediately retreating from them, if unhappily we have been ever by furprife or perfuafion inticed into them; by avoiding all thofe occafions that may inflame our paffions, and endanger our fafety; by fhunning all familiarity and friendfhip with unprincipled and profligate offenders, and by continually habituating ourfelves to thofe duties and fervices of life, that may employ our thoughts

---

* Jer. xiii. 23.

in

in a better manner, keep us out of the way of temptations and fnares, and help to confirm us in all our wifeft refolutions for the practice of righteoufnefs. But then,

2. Farther, we fhould not only keep a conftant watch over our hearts, fo as to guard it againft the entrance of every thing that may injure us, or endanger our fafety, but fo as to *infpect narrowly what actually paffes in them*, and to become intimately acquainted with their real ftate, and habitual difpofition. This *knowledge of ourfelves* is one of the moft *neceffary* and *ufeful* parts of knowledge that we can feek after, and one would think the moft eafily attainable ; becaufe the object lies immediately under our infpection, and if we but attentively view it, we cannot fail of thoroughly underftanding it ; and we cannot be impofed on and deceived, unlefs we willingly deceive ourfelves. And yet how few are there who thoroughly know themfelves, or care and endeavour to do it. They fuppofe, that all is right in the ftate of their paffions, or they don't choofe to be convinced that there is any thing wrong in them ; or they find a way to palliate and excufe the very exceffes of their paffions, and miftake even criminal ones for fuch as are natural and harmlefs. 'Tis much eafier to let things go on in their common courfe, than to be at the trouble of correcting and amending them ; and they are fo partial to themfelves, as that they are not willing to lofe the good opinion they have entertained of themfelves, or to imagine that their habitual
courfe

courfe can be difpleafing to God, or in the
final iffue prejudicial to their true intereft and
happinefs.   But this is a *deceit* of all others
the *moft dangerous*, and what a wife and prudent man will take the moft effectual care to
guard againft.   He loves himfelf, and cherifhes
a warm rational concern for his own welfare ;
and for this very reafon choofes to be well
acquainted with his own heart, that if upon
good inquiry he hath good reafon to conclude,
that all the affections of it are good in their
nature, rightly directed, and kept under proper
difcipline and government, he may cultivate
and ftrengthen them, and fafely enjoy the
fatisfaction that naturally arifes from it ; or
that if upon the review of himfelf he difcerns
any thing irregular or criminal in the ftate of
them, he may have the opportunity of correcting and amending it ; that hereby he may
become altogether fuch, as the great author
of his nature would have him to be, and that
he may have reafon to rejoice and be thankful
to find that he alfo is in fome good meafure, what he himfelf wifhes and endeavours
to be.

He will therefore be no ftranger to the
imaginations and thoughts that pafs through,
and abide in his heart, or that are dictated by
the feveral affections and difpofitions of it ;
becaufe according to the nature of them, and
the indulgence given them, the heart will be
denominated either good or bad.   *Out of an*
evil heart proceed evil thoughts, they are fuggefted
by fomewhat wrong in the temper of it, and

if they are harboured, and in the fcripture language *lodge* or *dwell in it*, and are cherifhed and indulged with pleafure, they fhew that the moral temper and character of it is habitually evil. And therefore we fhould ever be upon our guard; that, though we may not always be able to prevent their arifing up in us, for they will fometimes enter by furprize and ftealth, and not only unbidden, but againft our confent; we may immediately expel them, as dangerous enemies of our peace, and prevent their defiling the fanctuary of our hearts, that fhould be kept facred to piety and virtue. And indeed there is nothing more unbecoming the character of a good man, or that argues a more real depravity of heart, than the voluntary admiffion of corrupt imaginations, the cherifhing them in our minds, dwelling on them with pleafure, and caufing them to pafs in review before us with fatisfaction and approbation; when all fuch fuggeftions of a profligate imagination and criminal appetites fhould be regarded with the utmoft abhorrence. And there is no good man, who ever recollects the finful indulgences of his paft life, but he deteſts both the thought and thing, and reviews them with humility and contrition of mind, and fecretly but earneftly implores the mercy of God in the forgivenefs of them.

As the moral character of our actions takes alfo its denomination from the *ends* and *views*, that influence and govern us, here alfo we ought to watch over our hearts, that they may

be

be fuch as we can juftify to our own confciences, fuch as may not depreciate our beft
actions, fuch as may inftamp a real worth and
excellency upon them, fuch as the great
fearcher of our hearts may approve, and fuch
as we ourfelves may own without fhame or
dejection at the laft great and impartial day of
our account; all actions *materially* good, are not
always good in a *moral* fenfe. The attendance
on the publick inftitutions of religion, and
even the private fervices of the family or *clofet**,
are for the matter of them good, are commanded by God, and may be made extreamly
profitable to thofe, who with a right difpofition of mind engage in them. But if our
view in thefe things is that we may be feen
and obferved of men, have their commendation and applaufe, may infinuate ourfelves
into their efteem and confidence, and by their
friendfhip the better promote our worldly
views and interefts, this is fo far from being
genuine and acceptable devotion, as that 'tis
deteftable hypocrify, and in the higheft degree
offenfive to God. Or if we practice the external duties of religion, by way of com-
penfation for real immoralities of life, and as a
fupplement to the want of, or our defects in
judgment, *righteoufnefs*, *mercy*, temperance, charity, and the government of our paffions, it argues the moft ftupid ignorance or enthufiafm, or
deep corruption of heart, renders all fuch kind
of pretended devotions contemptible and cri-

* Matt. vi. 5.

T 2   minal

minal, and expofes men to a peculiarly heavy
condemnation. *Charity* may be given for
oftentation, or through the mere dictates of
natural compaffion and good humour †. In the
former cafe, it is wholly worthlefs and unprofitable ; in the latter, it is defective in moral
worth, as it wants a nobler motive to heighten
and compleat it, than the mere dictates of
conftitutional benevolence and goodnefs. Men
may *faft,* and practice bodily feverities, to
gain the character of great mortification and
humility, and felf denial, without real contrition, meeknefs, condefcenfion, and whilft
their hearts are full of fpiritual pride, bitternefs, refentment, and hatred of their neighbour ; and when this is the cafe, there is no
more virtue in thofe things, than in a fool's
going to the correction of the ftocks, or dif-
ciplining his back for his own or others diverfion §. Thefe three cafes are particularly
mentioned by our bleffed Lord, as inftances
of hypocrify and folly, as of no fignification
in the account of God, and that can intitle
no man to a reward from his goodnefs. It is
the fame in all other inftances whatfoever.
Where the motives are low, felfifh or criminal, whatever appearances of good the
action may have, it hath the appearance only
without the reality of goodnefs ; and whatever advantage it may procure the doers in
the prefent life, it is all the reward they are
ever to expect ; for folly can never be recom-

---

† Matt. vi. 1.   § Matt. vi. 17.

penfed

penfed by infinite wifdom, nor the fhadow of piety and goodnefs pafs on him for the genuine body or fubftance of them.

How *diligently* therefore fhould we *watch over our own hearts*, how *intimately* fhould we be *acquainted* with every thing that paffes in them, and how great a point of wifdom is it, in all the duties we perform, and all the good actions that we do, that we fuffer no unworthy views and motives to influence and govern us. True religion is feated in the heart. The very foundations of it are laid in principles of truth, firmly believed, and habitually attended to. It confifts in the exercife of the beft and worthieft affections towards God. Reverence for his authority, fear of his difpleafure, the loving him for his goodnefs, the defire to refemble him, fubmiffion to his will, truft in his power, hope in his mercy, and the firm perfuafion of his being a rewarder of them that feek and ferve him through Chrift, are the unalterable effentials of it ; and all external acts of devotion that are not animated by thofe principles, and dictated by thefe facred difpofitions, want the effential requifites of a truly rational and fpiritual devotion. And as to all acts of moral virtue, when they are performed from a full conviction of their intrinfick goodnefs, as inftances of obedience to God, in imitation of Chrift, and in hope of approving ourfelves to, and being accepted of the Lord ; they then become actions of fubftantial virtue, and genuine piety. And when we are confcious to ourfelves, that thefe are the difpofitions that govern us, in all the great concerns of our lives, and the habitual motives that influence us, in our whole conduct to God and man, we have the sure evidence of our integrity, and every reasonable ground of confidence towards God. An heart purified from all unworthy affections, enlivened and animated by the promises, habits, encouragements and prospects essential to true religion, is an habitation worthy the presence and comforts of God. It possesses all the dispositions of true happiness, fits men for the acceptance of the best of beings, and will finally secure them all those effects of his favour, which natural reason can encourage the hope of, and which are assured to us by the peculiar promises of divine revelation.

SERMON

SERMON XI.

The Importance of keeping our Hearts diligently.

PROVERBS iv. 23.

Keep thy heart with all diligence, for out of it are the issues of life.

IT is I believe impossible, in the present state of things, and in the manner in which we must here converse and live, so to guard our hearts, and maintain the purity and order of them, as to prevent all irregularities of imagination and thought from entering into them, and keep ourselves free of all those excesses of our affections and passions, which good men are never guilty of without regret, and wise men always endeavour to suppress and get the better of. So far indeed we are happy, that whatever is really involuntary, is not our sin. Whatever be the thoughts, that contrary to our own consent, force themselves into our minds, by mere surprize, and to which we are in no degree really accessary, we are no more accountable for, than we are

for

for the rovings of a delirium, or the monftrous
and abfurd imaginations, that are the frequent
effects of a frenzy ; and as to all involuntary ftarts of paffion, that are occafioned by
the mechanifm of our bodies, and the circu-
lation of our blood and fpirits ; that do not
proceed from ftrengthened habits, and continued indulgences ; we can be no more criminal upon account of them, than we are for
the accidental throbbings of the heart, or the
accelerated motions of the pulfe in a cold or
fever. Thefe things may give us pain, and
render neceffary the ufe of proper care and
medicine to remove the diforder, but in neither cafe can conftitute us guilty before
God.

But though this be true, and a very comfortable confideration to good men under the
neceffary imperfections, and unallowed infirmities of their prefent condition ; yet it is
no excufe for thofe *unhallowed imaginations*,
that *crowd* into the minds of men, and *dwell*
therein as in their proper habitation ; which
owe their rife to a long cuftom of finning,
and an heart fenfualized by criminal indulgences ; and if our paffions are eafily in-
flamable, and upon every occafion break out
into extravagant exceffes, as the confequence
of contracted and inveterate habits of vice
and wickednefs ; here we become guilty in
the nature of the thing, and in the eftimation
of God, our righteous judge. The plea of
human infirmity in fuch circumftances can be
of no avail ; for as habits are not natural, but
                                    contracted

contracted and felf-wrought, they cannot have
the character, nor deferve the indulgence of
mere natural infirmities; which are fuch, and
fuch only, as are the effects of natural conftitution, and to which we are unavoidably
fubject by virtue of thofe animal propenfities, which are inferted into, and infeparable
from the frame of our bodies, which we
bring into the world with us; and not fuch
as befet, and prevail over us by our own
faults, and which we might have prevented
by a due care over ourfelves, and the confcientious application of thofe means, to
which providence and grace have directed
us, to provide againft and fecure us from the
corruption of our natures, and the prevalence
of fenfual difpofitions and affections.

Were we as *careful* of our hearts, as we
fhould be, *much might be done* to guard them
againft the entrance of all thofe evil imaginations and thoughts, which too often crowd
into our minds, and are the fparks that kindle the fuel, which too often flames up, to
wafte and deftroy our integrity and peace; and
when they enter into us by furprize, without
almoft our knowledge, and contrary to our
confent; we may, by a due watchfulnefs
over ourfelves, at leaft hinder their abiding in
us. We may expel them as troublefome
intruders, and choofe whether we will give
them any countenance or harbour. 'Tis
owing to great negligence and incaution in
this refpect,

That

That men create within themfelves many kinds of wants, to which nature and reality never fubject them, and which are purely imaginary and artificial, the mere figments of vanity, luxury and pride, which prudence teaches them to guard againft, and of which we fhould immediately diveft ourfelves the moment we perceive them arifing within us ; becaufe if once we give way to them, and poffefs ourfelves with the imagination of their reality and importance, they will neceffarily excite within us thofe ftrong defires of fupplying them, that we fhall never eafily extinguifh, and which will powerfully prompt us to fuch meafures of gratifying them, as are inconfiftent with all our greateft obligations, and may involve us in difficulties highly prejudicial to our beft interefts in time and eternity.

If men would *confider the true ends of life,* and wherein confifts the right improvement and real enjoyment of it, they would not only fupprefs all irregular defires after that fictitious, fantaftick kind of happinefs, which poffeffes the imagination, and feeds the hopes of the generality of mankind, but direct their views to objects of fuch intrinfick worth, as well deferve their purfuit, and which if obtained will abundantly reward all their diligence and labour in fecuring them. The views by which men are influenced, and the ends they aim at, in great meafure characterife their actions, and denominate them,

in

in the moral fenfe, good or evil ; and therefore we ought carefully fo to obferve all that
paffes in our hearts, as to extinguifh every
mean, unworthy view of life, every falfe
motive of action, and efpecially every criminal inducement in the direction of our conduct, and to cherifh and govern ourfelves
entirely by fuch confiderations and aims, as
may render our behaviour to God and man
truly rational and worthy, may inftamp a
real dignity upon our actions, and entitle
them to the approbation of our final
judge.

Habits of action, whether good or evil,
create a ftrong propenfity to them, and faci-
lity of doing them, and render them fo familiar and natural to us, as that we wifh for
opportunities to repeat them, and cannot prevail with ourfelves to omit any inviting occafion of indulging ourfelves therein.   This
fhews the abfolute neceffity of *perpetual watchfulnefs* over our hearts, that we may not fuffer any abfurd, irrational, and criminal *habits*
from taking poffeffion of them ; fince if fuffered to grow inveterate, they will fubject
reafon and confcience, and every better fenfe
of duty and intereft to their influence and
power ; and becaufe the longer they are
indulged, they will grow the more obftinate
and incurable.   And therefore, if upon a
review of the ftate of our hearts, we find
that any finful difpofitions and habits have
been contracted by, and gained any afcendency
over

over us ; we fhould immediately refolve to
extirpate them out of our hearts, and give
them no reft 'till we have broken their
power, and refcued ourfelves from the tyran-
nical influence of them. To be carnally
minded, in fcripture, is to be wholly under
the power of fenfual difpofitions and habits,
in oppofition to the Chriftian temper, and
fpirit of the gofpel ; and this *carnal mind* is
exprefly declared to be *enmity with God*, irreconcileable with the purity of his nature,
and the great views of his moral government ; *for that it is not fubjeEt to the will of
God, neither indeed can be* ; the will of God,
and the perverted will of an habitual finner,
being directly contradictory, and in a ftate of
abfolute oppofition to each other. And therefore the Apoftle juftly adds : That they who
are in the flefh, or wholly enflaved to fenfual
affections and paffions, cannot pleafe God,
i. e. are objects of his high difpleafure ; their
temper and character are his abhorrence ;
and they are fo far from being the objects of
his approbation, as that they muft ftand condemned at his impartial tribunal. An accuftomed finner, in whom all the habits of
vice are in full power and exercife, is in too
wretched and impure a condition, ever to admit the prefence of God, and the joys of
his falvation. He is deftitute of every difpofition and genuine capacity for true happinefs. His own reflections will never produce
the teftimony of a good confcience, and the

rejoicings

rejoicings that flow from it. The fources of pleafure from which he draws his fatisfactions, are too grofs and polluted, ever to introduce into his mind the fatisfactions that flow from reafon, converfe with God, and the confcioufnefs of piety and virtue ; and fo entirely different from, and in their nature contrary to thofe that enrich and refrefh the future world of righteoufnefs and peace, that were he admitted to drink of them, he could never relifh them, but would be wretched and unfatisfied amidft all the plenty and fources of happinefs, even of Heaven itfelf. Here the exercifes of religion are difpleafing and tedious to them ; they abfent themfelves from them, becaufe they can find no entertainment in the ufe of them ; the very bleffings that are afked in the fupplications of religious men to God, are not fo much as the bleffings they defire ; the celebration of the divine majefty and perfections, the fongs of praife, and the facrifices of thankfgiving, in which true piety rejoices, are, in their account, either the practices of fuperftition, or dull, infipid employments, in which they can bear no part, becaufe the whole biafs and tendencies of their hearts have a quite contrary direction. And if thefe tendencies remain with them the fame in another world, as they are in this ; the fame averfions to the exercifes of piety will continue there as here ; and in the folemn afcriptions of glory and honour to him, that fits upon the throne, and the lamb for

ever

ever, they would remain entirely filent, or join in them unwillingly and by a kind of conftraint, and continue joylefs and unfatisfied, amidft all the triumphs and raptures of the fons of bleffednefs and glory. Search thyfelf therefore Chriftian. See if there be any remains of wrong affecticns and evil habits, that yet continue to influence thy defires and actions. Purge out this old leven. So watch over and keep thy heart, as to guard againft every tendency of them to enfnare, and defile thee. Supprefs them in their firft beginnings. Let every leffer and unpremeditated furprize and advantage they gain over thee be recollected with grief, indignation, and abhorrence, excite thee to a more faithful care of thyfelf for the future, and caufe thee with affection and fervency of mind, to pray in thofe admirable words of the Pfalmift: *Search me, O Lord, and know my heart. Try me and know my thoughts, and fee if there be any wicked way in me, and lead me in the way to everlafting life* *.

The beft of men, after all their moft careful infpection and watchfulnefs over their hearts, and notwithftanding the frequent victories they have obtained over all their paffions and affections, will find it difficult enough to keep them in the perpetual order, which they know 'tis their intereft, duty, defire, and endeavour to do. But oh how much harder a tafk is it for men, who have

* Pfalm cxxxix. 23, 24.

given

given themfelves up to perpetual, unre-
ftrained indulgences of fenfe and appetite,
without reflection, and care to lay them under
any reftraint, and in whom therefore the
habits of fin are confirmed and radicated,
and ftill continue in their full force and vigour !
How much harder a tafk is it, I fay, for fuch
perfons, to break the power of thefe habits,
to fhake off the chains and fetters with which
they have bound and entangled them ; fetters
to the fenfes not uneafy and galling, but foft
and pleafing, and which they can fcarce
perfuade themfelves, even to wifh to be delivered from ; and which, when convinced
of the abfolute neceffity there is of renouncing
them and becoming free from the bondage in
which they held them, they know not how
to recover themfelves from, nor how to attempt, nor by what powerful means to effect
their own falvation. And yet difficult as the
work is, it muft be done. Our everlafting
happinefs depends on the fuccefs of it ; and
by a due watchfulnefs over our own hearts,
and a perpetual guard fet upon our paffions
and affections, it may be finally happily ac-
complifhed. An abiding fenfe of the neceffity
of doing it ; the entering into ferious refolutions of immediately beginning it ; the checking thofe paffions in their firft rife and motions, that prompt to the ufual indulgences ;
the careful abftaining from all the occafions
and objects that may lead and tempt them
to it ; and make impreffions on the heart in
favour of it ; the exercifing a deep repentance

ance for having offended God, and injured
ourſelves, by the evil habits we have contracted ; the accuſtoming ourſelves to ſerious
reflection, and all thoſe important conſiderations that religion offers to our mind ; the
cheriſhing a real hatred and abhorrence of
ſoul of all our paſt ſinful gratifications ; the
exciting within ourſelves a due reliſh for the
pleaſures of reaſon and conſcience, of religion
and true virtue ; a diligent uſe of all the
means of converſion, to which God by Chriſt
hath directed us ; and the aſſiſtance of the
ſpirit and grace of God, obtained by daily
ſupplication and fervent prayer : Theſe things
will enable habitual ſinners to become ſuperior to all the greateſt difficulties they have
to encounter with ; will ſet them free from
the law of ſin ; and enable them, though
once they cried out from a ſenſe of their
danger : O wretched men that we are, who
ſhall deliver us from the body of this death !
to triumph in the words of the Apoſtle :
*Thanks be to God, who giveth us the vic-
tory through Jeſus Chriſt.* And in order
the more effectually to ſecure this victory,
we ſhou'd

3. *Give all diligence* ſo to keep our hearts,
as to *ſtrengthen and fortify them,* by *admitting*
into them the *proper guardians and ſecurities of*
our purity, peace and happineſs, and ſurrender-
ing ourſelves wholly to their protection and
cuſtody. An ungarriſoned fortreſs is a prey
to every invader, and requires no difficulty to
reduce ; and when thoſe who have it in poſſeſſion

feffion have none to oppofe them, their poffeffion will be fafe and undifturbed. If therefore we would preferve our hearts free from
the invafion of thofe enemies of our peace
and happinefs, that enter only to defile and
deftroy, or get rid of them if they have
formed admittance, it muft be by introducing
thofe friendly and powerful guardians, that
will be able to protect and defend them,
againft every hoftile atttempt, and effectually
prevent their ever gaining or retaining the fu-
periority over us. And

As the heart can never be well kept, and
duly governed without the powerful affiftance of *principles*, and the *firm belief* of thofe
important truths on which the being of religion, and the practice of all moral virtue is
fupported ; thefe principles fhould be rightly
underftood, their evidence clearly difcerned,
their importance fully attended to, and our
adherence to them ftedfaft and unalterable.
Confiderations of prudence may fometimes
produce a decency of conduct, and be a temporary reftraint from the indulgence of fome
particular bad habits and paffions. But it is
the force of good principles only, that can
reach the heart, that can ftrike at the root
of bad difpofitions and affections, and enable
men to keep them under perpetual reftraint
and government. When once we are divefted
of thefe, or look on them with indifference,
as precarious in their nature, and defective
in their evidence and importance ; the hearts
of men are immediately given up as a prey

to evil thoughts, and all the meaneft and vileft propenfities of their animal frames; and can have nothing in them to withftand the power of temptation, and prevent their being drawn in, to work out all iniquity with greedinefs. Here therefore we fhould be peculiarly watchful over our hearts, not to admit paffion and inclination to difaffect and prejudice us againft the principles of natural or revealed religion; for whatever plea of excufe for their unbelief fuch may have, who object to the fufficiency of evidence, after ferious enquiry; yet certainly that infidelity, which is owing to the prevalence of corrupt affections and paffions, is infinitely abfurd and contemptible, and renders men in the higheft degree criminal and obnoxious. For fenfe and appetite can furnifh no rational objections againft truth, and all conclufions, in reference to what we are to believe and do, drawn under their fuggeftion and influence, muft be delufive in their nature, founded on very incompetent reafons and motives, and highly dangerous in their confequences.

As there are fome original *natural fences,* implanted in our very frames, to fecure our innocency, and guard us againft the entire corruption and wafte of our minds, we fhould labour with the utmoft care fo to keep our hearts, as that we may *never lofe them,* nor fuffer them to be trampled down and wafted; for when thefe are broken up and deftroyed, the heart becomes quite defencelefs, and there is nothing left in it upon which the
beft

beft principles and moft powerful motives can
faften, fo as to have their proper efficacy and
force.   There grows up with reafon, when
it arrives to any kind of maturity, a ftrong
conviction and fenfe of the certain and original
difference between moral good and evil, as
clearly difcernible, and as plainly apprehended,
as the difference between natural contrarieties,
light and darknefs, or fweet and bitter, or
pleafure and pain.   There is, before men are
corrupted by practice, and hardened by example, a kind of fear and dread of entering
into the ways of vice, and efpecially of being
drawn into the commiffion of the greater
enormities and crimes of life.   The great
Author of our natures hath cloathed us, 'till
we have divefted ourfelves of it by indulgence,
with a kind of native modefty, fenfe of decency, and the feelings of fhame and confufion, that render the approaches to fin
difficult, and caufe men to ftart back at the
firft propofals of it, and reject the temptations
to it with abhorrence.   The love of character
and reputation, and being well thought of
and efteemed by the wife and good, is almoft
natural and effential to us as reafonable crea-
turs ; infomuch that he muft be a great
proficient in fin, and almoft divefted of humanity, that can perfuade himfelf to become
indifferent to character, and wholly regardlefs
of the opinion and fentiments of others concerning him.   The very power of reflection
creates a confcioufnefs of our own actions,

and every one finds himfelf accountable to
himfelf for his own conduct; and confcience,
if left in its natural ftate, and before it is
hardened and feared by long contracted habits of wickednefs, not only acquits and
commends us when we do well, but ho-
neftly accufes, reproaches, and condemns us,
when our actions are contrary to obligation
and duty, fills us with uneafy fears and apprehenfions, as the confequence of our tranfgreffions ; and frequently fo haunts and
purfues young practitioners in vice, when
led by inclination and folly, they are firft
learning the way to guilt, and initiated into
the execrable myfteries of debauchery, as
that 'tis not 'till after many ftruggles and
perfecutions of confcience, they are enabled
to fupprefs it, to fubdue it to inclination,
and fettle down without remorfe, in the
way of finners, and in the feat of the
fcorner. Now whilft the heart and mind is
poffeffed of thefe powerful prefervatives
againft the infection of vice and folly, the
corruption can never be total, nor the condition remedilefs and defperate ; and therefore we fhould fo continually keep and watch
over our hearts, as never to fuffer them to
be difpoffeffed of thefe powerful and friendly
forces, which whilft they are fuffered to
keep garrifon within us, will greatly affift
us in maintaining our liberty, in repelling
all hoftile invaders, and fecuring us to the
full enjoyment and firm poffeffion of all
the

the immunities, advantages, priviledges and blessings of our reasonable natures. I need only mention it, to shew you the unspeakable danger of his condition who hath lost all sense of the difference between moral good and evil, who is become fearless and intrepid in the paths of sin, who hath put off shame, and is incapable of blushing at the remembrance of the vilest and most dishonourable offences, who hath thrown off all regard to reputation and character, hath entirely suppressed the dictates of conscience, or so steeled himself, as entirely to despise and disregard them. That heart must be in the most desperate situation of corruption, which is thus despoiled of these excellent provisions of nature and providence for its defence and security, and that conduct be equally vile and profligate, that is dictated and directed by it.

As it is of great consequence to our welfare and safety, to prevent the entrance of all corrupt imaginations and thoughts, or immediately to expel them whenever they, unbidden, intrude upon us ; the best way of keeping the heart free from them in both respects, is *to accustom ourselves to considerations and reflections of a quite different nature ;* such as reason may suggest, or the principles, obligations, and advantages of true religion will furnish us with. Good and evil thoughts cannot dwell together at the same time in the same breast. If we receive the one, we

must

muſt reject the other, and there are no kind
of bad ſuggeſtions, that can proceed from
the heart, but may be counteracted and expelled by reflections of a quite different nature, which will eaſily occur to thoſe who
are duly acquainted and habitually converſant
with, the great things of true religion and
godlineſs. This is one of the beſt ſecurities
againſt the corruptions of the heart, and the
entrance and abiding of thoſe evil imaginations, which too often draw men into wrong
meaſures of conduct, inconſiſtent with their
preſent peace and final happineſs. Thus
ſhall we be able to ſilence the clamour of
all falſe and imaginary wants, to correct the
impulſe and cravings of wrong and impatient deſires, to diſpoſſeſs ourſelves of all
low, irrational, and criminal views, and ſecure ourſelves againſt theſe firſt occaſions
of ſin, which excite and enflame the worſt
paſſions and affections of our minds.

As our *paſſions and affections*, according to
the nature of them, are the great motives
and ſprings of action, there can be no better way of keeping the heart from the prevalence of bad ones, than by *rightly directing
all the natural* ones, and *introducing* thoſe
which are *more excellent and worthy* ; cultivating them with our utmoſt care, and re-
ſigning ourſelves wholly to their influence
and government. Our love and eſteem
ſhould be led to and terminated on the moſt
deſerving and amiable objects ; our confidence
and

and truft built on thofe foundations that are
ftable and permanent ; our fears regulated in
their exercife and degree, by the reality and
importance of the evils we dread ; our averfions and hatreds limited to what only is
odious and deteftable ; and our defires and
hopes, refpectively reduced and encouraged,
in proportion to the intrinfick worth of the
things they refer to, and the greater or leffer
neceffity and importance of them to our
true happinefs. Under this right direction
of our paffions, the contrary tendency of
them will gradually abate, and the exercife
of them can fcarce become irregular and intemperate. The natural paffions, in this view
of them, become real difpofitions of piety
and virtue, and are confecrated, fo as to become the genuine graces of the fpirit of God.
The reverence and efteem that we cherifh
for God, the affection and love that we
bear to Chrift, the truft we place in the divine perfection, power, goodnefs, and promifes, the refignation that we exercife to
the will and fovereign difpofals of providence,
the regard we pay to truth and righteoufnefs,
the hopes we place on the character and
mediation of Chrift, the promifes of his
gofpel, and the falvation and glory of the
world to come, the hatred we cherifh for
fin, the fear we cultivate of offending God,
and forfeiting his favour ; all thefe and the
like difpofitions, are not new created affections, but new directed ones, or the original

ones

ones newly biaffed, exalted, and enobled by
the objects on which they are terminated,
and which, when once they become habitual and prevalent, fortify the heart in the
moft effential and effectual manner againft the
entrance and power of every corrupt and criminal paffion whatever.

And in like manner, if we would keep
our hearts free from all irregular and criminal habits, or mortify and extirpate them,
if we have been fo unhappy as to contract
them ; this can never be effectually done
but by the prevalence and influence of the
contrary habits of piety and virtue ; firft
begun under the direction of our Chriftian
principles, and ftrengthened and improved
by daily exercife and practice. The heart
can never be divefted of pride, but by
making it give way to, and cloathing it with
humility.   Hatred and bitternefs of fpirit,
nothing can expell, but the fettlement of a
friendly and humane difpofition in the room
of it.   Paffion and anger will yield to nothing but the growth of a meek and gentle
fpirit.   Covetoufnefs is incapable of all cure,
but by the fole remedy of a prevailing
generofity.   The habit of intemperance can
never be broken, but by the regulations of
moderation and fobriety.   Every bad cuftom
yields only to its contrary ; and to fay all in
one word, every habitually wicked man will
continue fo, 'till he becomes an habitually
religious and virtuous one.   This is the proof,
and

and the only certain and convincing proof,
of a real converfion, without which all pre-
tences to it are hypocritical and delufive ; and
that heart can never be well guarded, and
rightly kept, which is not duly fortified by
eftablifhed and permanent difpofitions of
every thing that is truly virtuous and praife-
worthy ; nor can the powerful tendences it
hath contracted to fenfuality and vice ever
be overcome and expelled, but by fettled and
radicated propenfities to the practice of univerfal righteoufnefs.   This then fhould be the
care of every man that wifhes well to himfelf, and defires to keep his heart pure and
uncorrupt, to prevent bad habits from ever
poffeffing him, or to free himfelf from the
influence of them if contracted, to fortify
himfelf, and if I may be allowed the expreffion, to garrifon his mind with the united
forces of all thofe excellent habits of true
religion and moral virtue, which will effectually fecure it from all the internal propenfities to fin, and the fuccefsful influence of all external temptations to commit it.

And finally, what fhould never be omitted
on fuch a fubject, as *the preparation of the
heart in man is from the Lord,* he who would
keep his own heart in fafety and peace, *fhould
fecure the protection of the divine power and
grace,* by the moft *ferious and fervent fupplications* to God ; for though a *man may devife
his own way, it is the Lord who directs his fteps.*
Prefumption and felf-confidence little become
the

the prefent imperfect and frail condition of mankind ; and he, who diffident of himfelf, though not neglectful of his own duty and fafety, lives by faith in, and an humble dependence on the promifed aids and affiftances of his fpirit, is, upon the foundations of natural and revealed religion, the moft likely to fecure the poffeffion of himfelf, and to keep all the paffions and affections of his heart in that due regulation and order, as fhall render them moft fubfervient to his prefent ufefulnefs and comfort, and the fecuring his final falvation.

S E R M O N

SERMON XII.

All the Paths of the Lord are Mercy and Truth.

PSALM XXV. 10.

All the Paths of the Lord are Mercy and Truth unto such as keep his Covenant and his Testimonies.

IN the beginning of this Pfalm *David* acknowledges his dependance on God, expreſſes his truſt in him, and prays for the protection, mercy, and gracious conduct of God. *To thee, O Lord, do I lift up my foul *, O my Gód, I truſt in thee †. Shew me thy ways, O Lord, teach me thy paths ‡. Remember not my tranſgreſſions : According to thy mercy remember thou me §.* And to encourage his hope in the divine mercy and favour, he reflects upon the eſſential goodneſs of God, and his love of righteouſneſs, and from thence argues his readineſs rather to inſtruct and teach even ſinners how to repent and reform, than to

---

* Verſe 1.　† 2.　‡ 4.　§ 7.

deſtroy

deſtroy them for their tranſgreſſions. *Good and upright is the Lord, therefore he will teach ſinners in the way* ‖ ; *i. e.* lead them by his providence and word into the path of duty and happineſs. Much more ſhall the humble and meek be the objects of his care, and favoured with the kind inſtruction which they need. *The meek will he guide in judgment. The meek will he teach his way* *. All the methods of of his providence towards ſuch ſhall be conducted by mercy and faithfulneſs, and all finally contribute to their higheſt good. As in the words of my text. *All the paths of the Lord are mercy and truth, unto ſuch as keep his covenant and his teſtimonies* †. The paths of the Lord are the diſpenſations of his providence. All theſe ſhall be mercy and truth ; they ſhall be ordered in great goodneſs, with a kind and merciful intention, and conſiſtent with all the promiſes of God, which he hath made to the children of men. But then, they ſhall be mercy and truth only to ſuch *as keep his covenant and teſtimonies* ; *i. e.* to ſuch only who acknowledge and ſubmit to the obligations they are under to God, by a regular and conſtant obedience to his commands. *All the paths of the Lord are mercy and truth, unto ſuch as keep his covenant and his teſtimonies.* In which words are theſe two parts,

I. A deſcription of the *character of good men.* They *keep God's covenant and his teſtimonies.*

‖ Verſe 8.   * 9   † 10.

II. Their

II. Their *peculiar happiness. All the paths of the Lord are mercy and truth to them.*

I. The Pfalmift defcribes the *character of good and pious perfons. They keep the covenant and teftimonies of the Lord.* By the teftimonies and covenant of the Lord is meant the fame thing : *viz.* the divine law or will, folemnly publifhed and teftified to mankind.

The word rendered *teftimonies* comes from a root which fignifies *to witnefs* ; and is attributed to the laws or commands of God, becaufe of their folemn promulgation before proper and competent witneffes. Thus the law from Mount Sinai was very awfully publifhed by the miniftry of angels, and in the prefence of the whole camp of Ifrael; God teftifying or declaring his will by the moft evident and affecting figns. And under the gofpel difpenfation, God teftified his pleafure, and delivered the laws of his kingdom by his only Son ; and after him by his infpired Apoftles ; calling on the world to obferve the folemn evidence and confirmation of the truth of them, in the figns and wonders, and miracles and gifts of the Holy Ghoft, that attended them. The *teftimonies* therefore of God are thofe great and unalterable laws of religion and virtue, which he hath publickly declared and teftified to be agreeable to his will, and folemnly ratified by his fupream authority.

The *covenant of God* means, the conftitution of religion determined and fettled by his wifdom and mercy ; in which is particularly
explained

explained, and immutably fixed on the one
hand, what God expects from men as their
duty; and on the other, what they may
expect from God in virtue of his promise, as
the confequence of their fidelity in difcharge
of their duty. So that God's keeping covenant denotes primarily, his faithfulnefs and
truth in accomplifhing thofe voluntary affurances, which he hath granted men, of his
favour and bleffing, in confequence of their
compliance with the terms on which thofe
affurances were given. And mens keeping
God's covenant muft mean their performing
the conditions on which he hath covenanted
or promifed to beftow upon them the bleffings
to which thofe promifes relate; which conditions are, faith, repentance, and univerfal
piety and virtue. So that the fame laws of
God, which are called his teftimonies, are
alfo farther reprefented under the notion of
God's covenant by the Pfalmift; for thefe
two reafons : Becaufe they are an effential
part of the covenant which God hath gracioufly entered into with mankind; God
having made them the unalterable conditions
of his final favour and acceptance, and of thofe
invaluable bleffings he hath been pleafed to
grant us the promife of. And becaufe farther,
'tis the unqueftionable duty of all perfons, to
enter into this part of God's covenant, by pro-
mifing and performing an univerfal conftant
obedience to his will, as manifefted and revealed to them. Hence it is that obedience to
God's command, and keeping his covenant,

are

are in the facred writings equivalent terms : Thus God himfelf fpeaks to the people : *If ye will obey my voice indeed, and keep my covenants, then fhall ye be a peculiar treafure to me* *. And *David* defcribes *the mercy of the Lord to be from everlafting to everlafting, to fuch as keep his covenant, and remember his commandments to do them.* And on the contrary, to difobey the will of God, and violate his ftatutes, is to *break* God's *covenant.* If *ye will not hearken unto me, and will not do all thefe commandments, and if ye fhall defpife my ftatutes, or if your foul abhor my judgments, fo that ye will not do all my commandments, but that ye break my covenant : Then will I fet my face againft you* †. And that God's covenant doth not mean only, what God engages to perform in favour of men, but what he commands them to do in obedience to him, is exprefly afferted ; for thus faith *Mofes* to the people : *He declared unto you his covenant, which he commanded you to perform, even ten commandments, and he wrote them upon two tables of ftone* ‡. And therefore to enter into God's covenant, is not only to accept of God's promifes, but to bring ourfelves under folemn engagements to do whatfoever God hath commanded us, as the neceffary term of our having a fhare in the bleffings promifed. Thus *Mofes : Ye ftand this day all of you before the Lord your God* § — *that thou fhouldeft enter into covenant with the Lord thy God* ‖ — *leaft there fhould be amongft you man or woman, or*

---

* Exod. xix. 5.   † Levit. xxvi. 14, 15.   ‡ Deut. iv. 13.
§ Deut. xxix. 10.   ‖ 12.

tribe,

tribe, whose heart turneth away this day from the Lord our God, least there should be amongst you a root that beareth gall and bitterness *.　And he who cherishes this bitter root, and whose heart tnrneth away from God, doth not enter into covenant with him, but rejects God's covenant ; and should such a one blefs himself in his heart, saying, *I shall have peace, though I walk in the imagination of my heart, to add drunkenness to thirst* † ; 'tis an impious pre-fumption, and God hath declared that he will not *spare him, but blot out his name from under heaven* ‡.

From thefe paflages it appears that the de-fcription in my text, of thofe who keep God's covenant and his teftimonies, is a defcription of thofe who folemnly engage and covenant to obey thofe commands of religion and vir-tue, which God hath teftified or declared to be the ftanding and unalterable terms of our obtaining thofe bleffings which he hath fo-lemnly covenanted or promifed to beftow on them ; and who faithfully perform this their covenant engagement with God.　And

Under the Jewifh difpenfation, thefe laws of religion and virtue, which are the ftanding immutable laws of his kingdom throughout all nations, and periods of time, as they were publifhed with great marks of authority and majefty ; fo all the profperity of the nation was made to depend on the regular obfervance of them ; the higheft favours were promifed

* Deut. xxix. 18.　† 19　‡ 20.

to obedience, and the violation of them threatened with the fevereft penalties. And with refpect to particular perfons, we find the infpired Pfalmiſt conſtantly and invariably reprefents piety and virtue as indifpenfibly neceffary to the protection, guidance, fupport, and acceptance of God. Thus in the Pfalm where my text is. *The meek will he guide in judgment : the meek will he teach his way* *. *What man is he that fearcth the Lord ? Him ſhall he teach in the way that he ſhould chcofe* †. *The ſecret of the Lord is with them that fear him ; and he will ſhew them his covenant* ‡. And with refpect unto himfelf he prays. *Let integrity and uprightnefs preferve me. For I wait on thee* §. Let me by this fecure that protection and bleffing, which I humbly and heartily pray for from thee.

Under the *gospel, obedience* to the laws of God, in the regular and conſtant practice of religion and virtue, is made the *unalterable condition* of all the benefits of redemption ; the bleffings of the new covenant of grace being abfolutely confined to fuch who *cleanfe themfelves from all iniquity, and labour to perfect holinefs in the fear of God.* The great comprehenfive bleffing ſtipulated on the part of God, in the covenant he hath made with us by Chriſt is : *I will dwell in them, and walk in them ; and I will be their God* ‖. The fettled condition of this ineſtimable priviledge is. *They ſhall be my people. Wherefore come cut from*

* Verfe 9.   † 12.   ‡ 14.   § 21.   ‖ 2 Cor. vi. 16.

*amongſt them, and be ye ſeparate, ſaith the Lord,
and touch not the unclean thing : And I will receive you, and will be a Father unto you, and ye
ſhall be my ſons and daughters, ſaith the Lord
Almighty **. A proper covenant in its nature
is reciprocal, and neceſſarily implies mutual
obligations on the contracting parties. The
voluntary promiſe of God, which he hath
obliged himſelf to perform, is to be a God
and Father to us. But then the obligation
depends on this, that we become his people,
by ſeparating ourſelves from the corruptions
and vices of a wicked world, and yielding
ourſelves up to the practice of holineſs. Then
God will receive us as his people, and bleſs
us as his children. And without our coming
under this obligation, we have no part in the
covenant of God, nor any ſolid claim upon
his mercy and faithfulneſs.

This is the plain and natural account, why
the great duties of religion and virtue are
called God's covenant and teſtimonies, becauſe
he hath ſolemnly proclaimed them to be the
ſtanding unalterable laws of his kingdom,
hath inſerted them into his covenant of
grace and mercy with mankind, hath made
all the ſeveral promiſes of his covenant in
Chriſt abſolutely to depend on them, and
commands and expects from all mankind
that they ſhould heartily and willingly come
under theſe obligations, and in all parts of life
act anſwerable to them.

* 2 Cor. vi. 17, 18.

The

The character then of a truly good man, and a fincere Chriftian, is one who from a firm belief of the being and perfections of God, and a ferious, confcientious regard to his authority ; from a firm perfuafion of the truth of Chrift's character, as the meffenger of God, and the author of eternal falvation ; and from a fincere grateful acceptance of the promifes of God, and dependence on his mercy through him, keeps God's covenant and teftimonies ; who acknowledges the wife conftitution of this covenant, the reafonable-nefs and excellency of thofe eternal laws of truth and righteoufnefs, which are inferted into it, and become an effential part of it ; who from a fenfe of duty brings himfelf under the moft folemn promifes of obedience ; whofe habitual care is to anfwer thefe facred obligations from a full conviction of the in-difpenfible neceffity thereof, to his having an intereft in, and folid claim to the pro-mifed bleffings of eternal falvation by the Lord Jefus Chrift ; whofe regard to the laws of God and righteoufnefs is *univerfal*, ex-tending to the whole compafs of commanded duty ; *chearful and willing*, arifing from an intire approbation of the will of God ; *con-ftant and perfevering*, reaching to every condi-tion, and even to the end of life : Who, though he is fenfible of human infirmities, allows himfelf in no habitual courfe of vice ; whofe errors are his burthen and grief ; whofe repentance for every deviation from the rule of his duty is genuine and fincere, and

X 2 manifefted

manifested by a stricter guard over his temper and conduct for the future. In a word, he is one, who maintaining a sense of God's authority and Christ's love upon his heart, and desiring above all things to be approved and accepted by him through Christ, and to become intitled to the blessings of the everlasting covenant by him; purposes and resolves on an universal constant obedience, and gives the substantial proofs of his sincerity in this respect, by continually abounding in all those fruits of righteousness, which are by Christ Jesus to the praise and glory of God our Father. This is the person who is stedfast in God's covenant, and to whom all the ways of the Lord shall be mercy and truth. This leads me

II. To the second general, which is to consider the *peculiar happiness* of such persons as represented to us by the Psalmist in these words of my text : *All the paths of the Lord are mercy and truth.* And they teach us the following things.

1. That such as keep the covenant and testimonies of the Lord are in a *peculiar and special* manner the *objects of his care,* and for whose welfare and happiness he is more immediately and tenderly concerned. This is frequently asserted by divine revelation. *Thus the eye of the Lord is upon them that fear him, upon them that hope in his mercy* * : viz. to observe and guide, and *keep them in all their*

---

* Psalm xxxiii. 18.

ways.

ways. And again. *The righteous Lord loveth righteousness; his countenance doth behold the upright* †, i. e. with peculiar pleafure and approbation.

And this is highly confonant to the foundeft principles of reafon. For though it be certain, that God hath a real affection for, and wifhes well to *all* mankind, as they are his *creatures,* and his *children* by creation; yet fuch is the perfection and abfolute rectitude of his nature, that he *cannot approve and delight* in fuch of them, who debafe themfelves by criminal indulgences, and thereby render themfelves deftitute of that divine image, that moral refemblance to himfelf, which is their chief glory, and their only foundation for a fhare in the divine efteem and complacency. No. The approbation and difpleafure of God follows from, and is ever fuited to the moral character of men; and the fame unfpotted purity of his nature, muft always and every where render fin his abfolute averfion, and fecure to an unfeigned piety and virtue his fincereft affection and acceptance. And the certain, undeniable confequence from this is, the exercife of a peculiar care and providence over the righteous and good; for the affection which God bears towards them is not an impotent or indolent paffion, but an affection productive of its proper effects, and which manifefts itfelf in real and fubftantial inftances of benevolence and good-

† Pfalm xi. 7.

X 3   nefs

nefs. So that they who are confcious to themfelves of their integrity in religion and virtue, have all the reafon in the world to affure themfelves of a continued intereft in the friendfhip of God, and of fuch, a peculiar and diftinguifhing fhare in his efteem and love, as the reft of mankind never can have, nor reafonably claim or hope for. And

2. As the proof of this, *all the ways of God towards them fhall be mercy.* He will take them under the *peculiar care and protection of his providence.* As all the great concerns of their lives are fubject to his difpofal, he will conduct them for their benefit, and make them in the final iffue turn out to their advantage. Mercy and goodnefs fhall follow them all their days.

With refpect unto *temporal* bleffings, the truly good may expect fuch a fhare of them as they *really need,* and as will be *beft conducive* to their *final happinefs* ; and fhould God grant them more than this, fo much of worldly profperity as would prove a fnare to them, and draw them into deftructive courfes, this would not be a way of mercy, but of real difpleafure and indignation. And methinks this fhould be a confideration, that fhould form our minds into a ftate of the moft perfect contentment, under any of the difadvantages of the prefent ftate to which we may be fubject. Let but the Chriftian allow this, which is equally certain from reafon and revelation, and he could not fail of being

being eafy : The God whom I ferve is perfectly acquainted with the whole chain of
caufes and effects. He fully knows the particular inclinations, paffions, and appetites
that poffefs me.   The objects that would
excite them, and lead them into criminal
exceffes.   He forefees what inftances of
worldly profperity would betray me into fin,
and   finally ruin me ;   that this particular
bleffing I am fond of, and fometimes repine
for the want or lofs of, it would render me indifferent to religion and virtue, difaffect me to
my fupream happinefs, and make me carelefs in the purfuit of my eternal falvation.
And do I therefore wonder that 'tis denied
me ? Is not the great engagement of his
covenant with me, that all his ways towards
me fhall be *mercy* ? But would it be a pro-
ceedure of real mercy, to heap on me fuch
degrees of profperity in the prefent world,
as would ruin and deftroy all my expectations in a better ? No.   Let mercy purfue its
own courfe, and let nothing ever be vouchfafed to me, that is inconfiftent with the purpofes of the divine mercy in my eternal falvation.   This is the reafoning of a truly
wife and religious mind, that thinks rightly
of God, and wifhes well to its own beft
intereft.

However, the favours of God's external
providence are frequently multiplied upon
good men, as a prefent reward of their piety
and goodnefs.   He crowns their diligence
with fuccefs, and gives them not only the

necef-

neceffaries, but the conveniences of life. In circumftances of doubt and difficulty he directs their path, and teaches them to order their affairs with difcretion. In times of danger he protects them with his favour as with a fhield, and gives his angels charge concerning them, fo that no evil hath power to hurt them. If diftempers befall them, he fhews his goodnefs in healing their difeafes, and caufes them to return to life and health, that they may praife his name. In a word, as he bears them a fatherly affection, and rejoyceth to fee them happy ; he oftentimes fo overrules all his difpenfations of providence to them, as fhall moft effectually conduce to the increafe and eftablifhment of their prefent comfort and profperity.

But as profperity hath its fnares, and men are not always able to bear it ; God is oftentimes pleafed to fuffer thofe who keep his covenant and teftimonies, to fall into many, and thofe fevere and burthenfome afflictions. Now the way of God, even in thefe afflictive providences towards his people in mercy. *For whom the Lord loveth he chaffeneth, and fcourgeth every fon whom he receiveth* *. 'Tis through the dictates of mercy and love that he permits their befalling them. Was he indifferent to their welfare, and unconcerned about their happinefs, he would fuffer them to go on, without ever interrupting their flow

* Heb. xii. 6.

of

of worldly profperity, or endeavouring to bring them, by gentler chaftifements, to remember themfelves, their duty, and their falvation. But as he hath fet his heart upon them for good, rather than fuffer the world to ruin them, and permit them to go in an habitual courfe of wickednefs and vice, he will *vifit their tranfgreffions with the rod, and their iniquity with ftripes* ; thus like an indulgent parent chaftening them *for their profit, that they may be partakers of his holinefs, and that their afflictions may yield them the peaceable fruits of righteoufnefs.* This is the kind and friendly view of the mercy of God in the trials he permits to befall the righteous and good.

And as their afflictions are the appointments of unqueftionable mercy, in the great intention and view of them ; fo there will be farther proofs of *mercy* in the *circumftances, degrees,* and *duration* of them. They will be fuch in kind, as God knows we are beft able to bear, or as are moft conducive to exercife thofe graces we are moft defective in, to preferve us from thofe fnares we are moft endangered by, and to reform us from thofe particular fins we are moft fubject to the commiffion of. Perhaps we think the prefent burthen we labour under to be peculiarly fevere. But yet perhaps 'tis the only one we could have fupported with decency, or that in the end would have proved medecinal and healing. Other kind of afflictions might have driven us farther from God,

rendered

rendered us impatient and intractable, or failed of the cure which the mercy of Heaven intendethby them. Befides, the mercy of God appears in his readinefs to yield men the comforts and fupports which they need under them. If our afflictions are heavy, we may pray for, fo as to *obtain grace to help us in the time of need*; fuch meafures of *grace* fhall be fully *fufficient for us*; fuch *ftrength* from God as *fhall be made perfeEt in our weaknefs.* So that the aids of Heaven fhall be proportioned to our trials, and the confolation of God abound towards us for our fupport.

And, finally, if we are wife to comply with the defign of them, and when the ends of God's mercy in fending them is anfwered, we have reafon to expect that God will *put an end* to them, and gracioufly find a way for our efcape out of them. For *God doth not willingly affliEt or grieve the children of men,* or take pleafure in their diftreffes. And therefore as he never afflicts us but when there is need, either to promote his own glory, or our profit; fo there is reafon from the wifdom and goodnefs of God to reft affured, that when the defign of goodnefs intended by them is fully anfwered, there fhall be a final period put to them; either by the affliction's entire removal from us, or by the abatement of the painful fenfe of them, or by our removal from the affliction into that bleffed world, where we fhall enter into the reft of God, and enjoy the promifed reward of of our faith and patience. So that in every view of the affliction of the truly righteous and pious, they have reason to acquiesce in them as the appointments of real affection and goodnefs; and in whatfoever circum-ftances they are, or can be, to comfort themfelves with this confideration : All the paths of my God towards me fhall be *mercy and love.* And, laftly,

3. They fhall be all of them confiftent with the *truth and faithfulnefs of God.* The truth or faithfulnefs of God is often fpoken of in Scripture as an encouragement to the upright and good. *O Lord, thou art a God full of compaffion and gracious, long-fuffering, and plenteous in mercy and truth* *. And in the New Teftament. *Faithful is he that calleth you, who alfo will do it* †. Now this truth of God plainly refers to his covenant en-gagements with his people, or to his promifes of mercy and grace in which he hath caufed them to hope. And when the Pfalmift af-fures us, that *all the paths of the Lord fhall be truth to them that keep his covenant*, he means, that God will abundantly make good all his kind affurances in their behalf, and fo con-duct all the methods of his providence to-wards them, as fhall moft effectually conduce to make them partakers of the bleffings pro-mifed. Some promifes to the upright and faithful are more abfolute and exprefs : Such as the pardon of their fins, their acceptance

---

* Pfalm lxxxvi. 15.　　† 1 Thef. v. 24.

to favour, their fupport under temptation, the comforts and affiftance of his holy fpirit, and their prefervation by his power through faith unto falvation. Thefe are bleffings abfolutely connected with virtue and piety, and as God himfelf hath thus gracioufly connected them, he hath through an abundant condefcention and goodnefs, given every faithful Chriftian an humble yet ftrong claim upon himfelf, and they may plead even the juftice and faithfulnefs of the great and bleffed God for performance. *For God is not a man that be fhould lye, nor the fon of man that he fhould repent.* And how much furer a ground of comfort are fuch abfolute affurances as thefe from the beft of beings, than if we were left to the mere reafonings of our minds in cafes of fuch importance as thefe. I acknowledge that reafon would give fome ground for fuch expectations of good men ; but full certainty, fo as to exclude all doubt, muft depend upon promife and actual engagement. And therefore in proportion as certainty exceeds conjecture, and affurance is better than the higheft probability, fo much ftronger muft the encouragement be which proceeds from divine revelation, than any that could be given us by unaffifted reafon.

There are other promifes, as to which God hath left himfelf more at liberty, and the performance of which depend on his pleafure and wifdom, and from which men have no abfolute claim, any farther than as the granting them is confiftent with, and con-

contributes to the more effectually fulfilling
those divine engagements which are pofitive
and exprefs.   Such are all the promifes of
worldly favours and bleffings without exception ; bleffings which are not in their
nature effential to our true happinefs ; and
which oftentimes, were they given in abundance, would prove fuch ftrong temptations
even to good men, as would probably caufe
them to forfeit the nobler bleffings abfolutely
connected with fincerity and fidelity.   And
therefore the fame truth and faithfulnefs of
God that oblige him to perform the promifes
he hath given us a certain claim to, the
fame kindnefs and mercy of God from which
the promifes of pardon, grace, and eternal
life proceed, lead him to withhold from us
all thofe inferior bleffings, which we could
not enjoy with fafety, and of which the grant
would prove prejudicial to our higheft
eternal intereft.   So that even afflictions
themfelves, when they become neceffary to
reform, quicken, exercife, and preferve the
truly good, as they are arguments of the divine benevolence and care, fo are they the
folid proofs of the divine faithfulnefs and
truth.   For all the paths of God are faithfulnefs and truth, to them that keep his cove-
vant and teftimonies.

How ftrong an encouragement doth this
fubject afford us, for fidelity in the covenant
of God, and care to obferve the divine teftimonies.   Would any thoughtful perfon,
who confiders his dependance on God every
moment

moment of his being, the terrors of his anger, and the comforts of his favour, be excluded from a fhare in the mercies of his nature, and the promifes of his covenant in Chrift ? Would we have the paths of God towards us all anger and feverity, and inftead of enjoying the pleafing light of his countenance, difcern nothing in him but awful frowns, and the marks of his difpleafure ? Would we be willing to have the providence of God fet itfelf againft us, and all the methods of it confpiring to render us wretched ? Is there not fomething infinitely pleafing in the thought of having an intereft in the eternal and unchangeable mercies of God, and folid claim, for the̅ moft valuable bleffings we can wifh or want, upon the divine veracity and juftice ? This is the fure priviledge of thofe only who keep the covenant and teftimonies of God.

And are we confcious to ourfelves, that this is our conftant endeavour and care, what folid ground have we for fatisfaction and peace, and with what intire chearfulnefs may we commit the care of all our concerns in well doing to the conduct and difpofal of God's providence ? We have not only the mercies of God's nature but we have more. We have covenant engagements, we have folemn promifes, to plead and urge in our behalf, for every bleffing we really need. God himfelf hath affured us by immediate revelation, and the manifold experience of the truly good, that all things fhall be mercifully

cifully over-ruled for our benefit, and contribute to our final acceptance and falvation. And are not the promifes of the God of truth to be depended on ? Should we repine at any thing that he orders, when 'tis an orderance of mercy, and in purfuance of the promifes of his unchangeable grace ? No. Truft in him at all times, ye righteous, and let his word be the foundation of your conftant hope. For though the Heavens may perifh and wax old, his word is a tried word, of which not a tittle fhall pafs away, without its full accomplifhment.

SERMON

SERMON XIII.

Chriſt the Friend of his obedient Diſciples.

JOHN XV. 14.

Ye are my Friends if ye do whatſoever I com-mand you.

IT is eſteemed, and not without reaſon, a very high honour and priviledge, to be numbered amongſt the friends of perſons of great eminence, rank and ſtation ; and there can ſcarce be any character of higher diſtinction and dignity, than that of being the friend of the king ; the being owned and regarded by him as ſuch. The wiſe man re-preſents it in this view, when he ſays : *He that loveth pureneſs of heart, for the grace of his lips, the king ſhall be his friend* *. *i. e.* Inte-grity and candor of diſpoſition, and a graceful, polite converſation, have ſuch powerful charms in them, as will inſinuate themſelves into the minds of kings, and almoſt irreſiſtibly

* Prov. xxii. 11.

ſecure

secure their friendship. The Apostles of our blessed Saviour, as well as the rest of the Jews, expected that their master would be as the Messiah, a temporal prince, and that they should enjoy peculiar advantages under his government, and be exalted above others by the honours that should be conferred on them. And our Lord in my text assures them, that he would take them into the number of his friends, if they would obey his commands, and distinguish them as such by the favours he vouchsafed them. An admission into the counsels of princes, and the secrets of the cabinet, is a peculiar mark of the royal confidence and favour, and adds dignity to nobility and station. And in allusion to this, our Lord tells his Apostles in the verse after my text : *Henceforth I call you not servants, for the servant knows not what his Lord doth. But I have called you friends ; for all things that I have heard of my Father, I have made known to you* * : I have led you into the secrets of my commission from God my Father, and thereby treated you as my companions and intimate friends, and not as servants, who are not intrusted with the counsels and secret views of their master ; whose business is to obey orders, and not to enquire the reasons and motives of them.

But though our blessed Saviour honours his faithful disciples with the character of friends, he did not thereby intend to cancel

* Verse 15.

their obligations of ſubmiſſion and obedience to him. Thoſe whom earthly princes honour with the character of *friends* do not ceaſe to be their *ſubjects* and *ſervants*; and the higher they ſtand in their maſter's favour, and the more diſtinguiſhing marks of confidence and friendſhip they are treated with, they are bound to greater fidelity in their ſtations, and to exert themſelves with proportionably greater diligence in executing their commands, and ſupporting their authority, their honour and intereſt. And therefore our Lord, when he tells his Apoſtles, that he would not treat them as ſervants ſo much as friends; yet lets them know, that the very condition of his friendſhip to them, was their obedience to his commands. *Ye are my friends, if ye do whatſoever I command you.*

He here evidently aſſumes the character of their *Lord and Maſter*, aſſerts his right to command, and their obligations to obey, and to obey him in every thing he commanded them. The friendſhip between Chriſt and his diſciples is not that which ſubſiſts between equals, but between perſons infinitely different in rank, dignity, and perfection; which doth honour to them, and from whence no real benefit, or acceſſion of dignity can accrue to him; which ariſes ſolely from his condeſcenſion, and from no previous merit and worth in them; and which though it introduces them into the moſt valuable priviledges, and hath connected with it the

moſt

moſt valuable and durable bleſſings, yet abates
nothing of the diſtance between them, di-
miniſhes nothing of his ſupream authority
over them, admits them into no indecent
familiarities with him, allows of no neglects of veneration and homage to him, nor
exempts them from any ſingle inſtance of
obedience to him. His commands are all
ſacred to every one that he honours with
his friendſhip, and they count it their happineſs as well as duty to obey them.

Many were the *commands* which our bleſſed
Lord gave to his Apoſtles, and thoſe who
attended him during the exerciſe of his
miniſtry on earth ; not relating to ceremo-
nial obſervances, and external rites and forms
of religion, of which there is little or nothing
to be found in any of the inſtructions which
he delivered to his hearers ; but to the great
and weightier matters of the law of God ;
the *love of God with all the heart*, the *love of
our neighbours as ourſelves*, the regulation of
our paſſions and deſires, the exerciſe of all
the worthieſt affections of human nature, and
the bringing forth all the amiable and excellent fruits of righteouſneſs and true holineſs.
This muſt be ſaid in honour of the precepts
of Chriſtianity, and the doctrines of its great
author, that they are *comprehenſive* of the
whole of true religion and real virtue, in their
inward diſpoſitions, the external duties required by them, the ſacred principles that
excite to and animate them, and all the rational and weighty motives, that are neceſſary

to ſupport the practice of them. They extend to all ranks and conditions of men, to all their various ſtations and characters, to all the ſeveral relations of life they bear, to all the different changes, periods and circumſtances of their beings, inſomuch that it is not poſſible to add a ſingle precept of religion and piety, that hath any foundation in truth and reaſon, that is not plainly comprehended in the commands of Chriſt, or taught by his Apoſtles, under the direction and inſpiration of his holy ſpirit.

As theſe commands of Chriſt are *all* of them enforced by his authority, and are the precepts of the eternal God by him ; as they are commands of immutable truth and righteouſneſs ; all calculated to promote the happineſs of thoſe who obey them, and are neceſſary to the approving ourſelves the genuine diſciples of Chriſt, and the faithful ſubjects of his kingdom, our obedience to all of them is expreſſly required, and indiſpenſibly neceſſary to our becoming the friends of Chriſt. *Ye are my friends if ye do whatſoever I command you.* Faith gives no priviledge or diſpenſation to violate any of them. There are no freedoms of love, or grants of friendſhip inconſiſtent with duty. Zeal in leſſer matters will not exculpate for the neglect of greater, nor will a partial regard to ſome of the eaſier requirements of Chriſt, excuſe us for an habitual, wilful neglect of others more difficult, and therefore more unpleaſing. There can ſcarce be an inſtance of greater
preſumption

prefumption in a fubject, than to affume to himfelf a difpenfing power, and fo to diftinguifh between the laws of his prince, as to make his own inclinations and private views the rule and meafure of his obedience to them ; regarding fome and rejecting others, as beft fuits his intereft or pleafures. The authority of Chrift is in all inftances equally obliging, and his precepts have in every refpect the fame truth and reafon to fupport them, and are in their nature the very proofs of his friendfhip to them, and regard for their happinefs. And therefore every one who knows how to value this friendfhip of the Son of God, inftead of meafuring and abridging his duty by his inclination, will fubdue his inclination to principle and duty, and ftudy to approve himfelf to his great Lord and Mafter, by an *univerfal, unlimited obedience* to his will. Thus only can he maintain the confcioufnefs of his own integrity, and hope to be acquitted and rewarded as a good and faithful fervant, in the day when God by Jefus Chrift will judge the world in righteoufnefs.

And how unfpeakably great is the *advantage* of doing what Chrift commands us, reprefented by him in the words of my text. *Ye are my friends if ye do whatfoever I command you.* I will receive you into the number of them, treat you as fuch, and give you a fhare in all the priviledges you can defire or expect from me. How great is the *condefcenfion* and *goodnefs* of our bleffed Lord in

thus

thus admitting finful men into fo honourable, near and intimate a connection with himfelf, and how *fubftantial* is the *happinefs* arifing from it !

Friendfhip implies in its very nature *peculiar affection* and *diftinguifhing efteem* for the object of it. It hath its foundation in love, and cannot fubfift without it, and collects and unites all the powers and forces of it, that it may terminate the more warmly on the perfon who attracts it. And this is included in the friendfhip of Chrift to men, fuch efpecially as keep his commandments. He bears them the fincereft and warmeft affection. He tells his Apoftles, *as the Father hath loved me, fo have I loved you. Continue ye in my love. If you keep my commandments ye fhall abide in my love, even as I have kept my Father's commandments, and abide in his love* *. How ftrongly defcriptive is this, both of the fincerity and intenfenefs of his love. God declared him to be his *only begotten*, and therefore his *well beloved Son, in whom he was well pleafed* ; and if he loves us as the Father loved him, it muft be without diffimulation and hypocrify, it excludes every thing of indifference and coldnefs, every thing of humour, caprice, ficklenefs, and inconftancy, and muft be permanent and immutable. And though the words above-mentioned were fpoken immediately to the Apoftles, yet this affection of Chrift was not peculiar to them ; for he de-

* John xv. 9, 10.

clares

clares in general of *all*: *He that hath my commandments, and keepeth them, he it is that loveth me, and I will love him, and manifeft myfelf to him* *; hereby plainly making his love and friendfhip as extenfive as faith in him and obedience to his will. Of this love of Chrift it is impoffible we can ever doubt, when we confider that he left his original glory, fubmitted to all the infirmities of our mortal ftate for our benefit, went about doing good whilft he converfed on earth, and gave the laft proof of his affection and friendfhip to us, by dying, in order to obtain eternal redemption for us. And how pleafing and defirable a circumftance is it to be beloved of the Son of God! What are the qualifications of the perfons one would wifh to be efteemed and beloved by? I can fpeak for myfelf, and I believe for you alfo: Perfons of fuperior rank and dignity, purity of heart, fanctity of character, diftinguifhed wifdom and knowledge, amiablenefs of temper, extenfive ufefulnefs, and liberal fources to gratify the friendly, generous difpofition. All thefe characters meet in Chrift in the higheft perfection, and therefore to be beloved of him is the moft defirable circumftance of our beings, this is that affection we may well value ourfelves on, and juftly glory and triumph in if we can obtain it.

Friendfhip farther interefts itfelf in the *profperity and happinefs* of thofe whom it em-

---

* John xiv. 21.

braces,

braces, and is follicitous to promote their real welfare. It is fo kindly affectioned towards them, as to look upon their concerns as its own, to wifh them every thing they really want, or can reafonably defire. And how eminently doth this character diftinguifh, adorn, and enhance the value of the friendfhip of Chrift! He is a friend to our beft intereft in the prefent life, and to the health, perfection, dignity and happinefs of our reafonable fpirits. The generous concern that poffeffes him is, that we may here obtain mercy and forgivenefs from God whom we have offended, the treafures of all ufeful knowledge, fettled habits and difpofitions of genine piety and virtue, to render us partakers of a divine nature, the pleafures of integrity, the fatisfactions of a good confcience, peace with God, the joys of a well grounded, lively hope of glory, and a fure and eftablifhed intereft in his favour and acceptance. Nor is this regard of Chrift for us limited to time. His love to his friends hath no bounds to its duration. He wifhes their eternal intereft, and is follicitous to render them partakers of bleffings fubftantial in the kingdom and prefence of his Father and his God. Arguments thefe of the fervency and fincerity of his affection, that it is without any diffimulation to abate the value of it, and void of every circumftance that can lower the obligations arifing from it.

Again, *friendſhip* is of a very *tender* nature, hath quick feelings, ftrong fenfibilities, en-

ters

ters into the afflictions and diftrefles of thofe
it embraces, and kindly compaffionates and
pities them under them.   It is a very ftrong
expreffion of *Job : To him that is afflicted,
pity fhould be fhewn from his friend, but he for-
faketh the fear of the Almighty* * : Or as the
words fhould certainly be rendered : He who
is defective, or grows cold in his affection
to his friend in his affliction, even he for-
fakes the fear of the Almighty.   How far
was this from the character of Chrift ? In
goodnefs and compaffion, who is there that
can compare with the Saviour of mankind !
How numerous are the proofs of his tender
fympathy with thofe, whom he faw labouring under difficulties and miferies ! *When the
leper came to him, he·was moved with compaffion, and put forth his hand and healed him* †.
When he faw an *only fon* carrying to his grave,
and the *tender mother weeping* over him, he
kindly faid to her *weep not,* and inftantly *reftored* him to her joyful embraces ‡.   When
the multitude that followed him were fpent
with *fafting,* he faid to his difciples : *I have
compaffion on the multitude, for they continue
with me now three days, they have nothing to
eat, I will not fend them away fafting, leaft they
faint in the way* §, and immediately *fed* them
with bread of his own *miraculous* creation.
When he faw *Martha* and the Jews *weeping*
on account of the death of *Lazarus,* he entered into their forrows, he bore their griefs,

* Job vi. 14.   † Mar. i. 41.   ‡ Luke vii. 12—14:
§ Matt. xv. 32.

and

and *mixed his tears* with thoſe of the mourn-
ers *. When the Jews watched him to *ſee
if he would heal the withered hand on the ſabbath
day, he looked round on them with anger, being
grieved for the hardneſs of their hearts* † ; and
when he could do no more, and found that
the deſtruction of *Jeruſalem* was inevitable,
when *he came near and beheld it, he wept over
it,* and in the agony of his diſtreſs cried out :
*Oh ! that thou hadſt known, even thou at leaſt in
this thy day, the things that belong to thy peace !
But now they are hid from thine eyes* ‡. Indeed
his whole life manifeſted the tender goodneſs
of his heart, and the ſhare he took in the
afflictions of the miſerable and unhappy §.
*He was touched with the feeling of all our in-
firmities, and was in all things made like to his
brethren, that he might be a faithful and merciful
high prieſt, in things pertaining to God, to make
reconciliation for the ſins of the people* ‖. Even
his *exalted* and godlike ſtate in Heaven hath
not quenched his compaſſion for ſinful men.
He *pities the ſinner* that hath no pity for himſelf, and wiſhes his recovery and ſafety whilſt
he is madly inviting his own deſtruction.
*Having himſelf ſuffered, being tempted, he knows
how to have compaſſion on thoſe who are tempted,*
and from his own experience of the danger
of a tempted ſtate, is able and ſtrongly
prompted to ſuccour them that are tempted.
He knows all the diſadvantages of our preſent condition, and if I may uſe the expreſ-

* John xi. 35.   † Mark iii. 5.   ‡ Luke xix. 41, 42.
§ Heb. iv. 15.   ‖ ii. 17.

ſion

fion in a figurative fenfe, *weeps with his genuine difciples when they weep, in all their afflictions he is afflicted* *, and in his love and in his
pity, will fooner or later redeem them.
For,

Friendfhip is not only full of compaffion,
but ever *ready* and *propenfe to exert itfelf* for
the benefit and fafety of thofe who come
within the reach and influence of it, according to the power and ability it poffeffes.

It is an obfervation of the wife author of
the ancient bcok of Ecclefiafticus †, that
" fome men are friends for their own oc-
" cafion, and will not abide in the day of
" trouble. They are companions at the ta-
" ble, but will not continue in the day of
" affliction." But the Son of God can never
be a friend for his own occafion, as he cannot want any thing that we can give, nor
receive any advantage from the fervices that
we can pay him. He is a friend to us for
our own fakes only, and becaufe he knows
our diftreffes, and is willing to relieve us
under them. He can therefore never forfake
us when we need his help, never look cool
and indifferent upon us when we want his
affiftance, nor like the Pfalmift's lovers and
friends, *ftand aloof from our afflictim* ‡, when
we wifh him to be near, and a prefent help
in the time of trouble. His power is almighty and he can fave us ; his friendfhip is
ftrong and permanent, and will never defert

---

* Ifaiah lxiii. 9.   † Ecclef. vi. 8, 10.   ‡ Pfalm xxxviii. 11.

us.

us. He knows we are finners, came into the world to fave us, and died to purchafe our forgivenefs ; and if we are *weary and heavy laden* with the fenfe of our guilt, and the fears of a divine difpleafure, *he will give reſt to our ſouls* by reconciling us to God, fecuring us from condemnation, and caufing us to rejoice in the hope of glory. He is acquainted with the ficklenefs and inconftancy of human nature, and the continual need we have of divine fupports to fettle, ftrengthen and eftablifh us, in the difcharge of our duty, and the purfuit of our higheft happinefs ; and he is ever ready to vouchfafe us the affiftance of his bleffed fpirit *to confirm us blamelefs to the end. He was in all things tempted like as we are, though without fin, and will fuffer no temptation to befall us, but what is common to* and fupportable by *men,* and *will with every temptation find out a way for our efcape, that we may be able to bear it. He was exceeding forrowful even unto death,* at the profpect of his own fufferings, and well knows how liable we are to be *in bondage through the fears of death.* Let us but keep his commandments, and he will take away the fting and terrors of death, and enable us to await the hour of it, and bear its neareft approaches, not only with refignation, but with chearfulnefs and pleafure ; and what no created friendfhip can do for us, his will ; *reſtore us to a glorious and bleſſed immortality.* In a word, as *he is able to do for us exceeding abundantly above all that we can aſk or think,* he

will

will do for us every thing that we can hope or
wifh for from the moft confummate goodnefs, aided by the exertion of almighty
power.

It is a farther effential quality of *friendfhip*, that it *treats with great indulgence* the
faults and *errors* of thofe whom it receives
into its bofom, never imputes to them involuntary offences, never ftrictly animadverts on
leffer failings, hath *charity* enough to *cover
a multitude of fins*, gladly accepts the proper
acknowledgments for offences committed,
forgives when there is a becoming fenfe of
them, and rejoices to triumph over them by
renewed inftances of affection and favour.
Oh! how illuftrious an example of this have
we in the Son of God! *Peter* denied him
with oaths and curfes, and yet *he looked him
into repentance*, and not only *forgave* him, but
reftored him to his *office* and *dignity* as an
Apoftle.   Though *all his difciples forfook him
and fled* from him in the hour of his trial,
his love to them triumphed over their infirmities, and when rifen from the dead, without reproaching them for their deferting him,
received them again with his former confidence and affection.   He came to fave, and
he knew how to pardon, he profeffed himfelf the friend of mankind, though he knew
them to be finners, and will therefore never
condemn, where there is room to fhew mercy
and forgive.   Our involuntary errors he will
never remember againft us, nor fhall our
paft violations of his commands ever feparate

us

us from his love, if we turn to a better
obedience for the future ; for he can have
*compaffion on the ignorant and them that are out
of the way* ; or as the words fhould be rendered * : He can be equitably difpofed, or
affected with moderation toward thofe who
are ignorant and erroneous, who either know
not their duty, or wander from the path
of it.

Yea more than this, inftead of rigidly re-
marking our errors, or taking pleafure in reproaching us upon account of them, or renouncing his friendfhip towards us for the
many miftakes of conduct with which we
are chargeable, he approves himfelf our faft
and faithful friend, even by becoming *our patron* and *advocate*, and interceding for us with
his heavenly Father, *that we may obtain mercy,
and grace to help us in every time of need.* *Job*
in the agony of his diftreffes, and the full
conviction of his own heart of his innocence,
paffionately cries out : *Oh that one might plead
for a man with God, as a man pleadeth for his
friend †!* This is an inftance of a truly generous and cordial friendfhip, to apologize
for the errors of a friend, as far as they are
capable of an apology, to vindicate him
againft falfe or aggravated accufations, and
to employ the power and intereft it hath to
prevent or mitigate his condemnation. Bleffed
Saviour, how faithful, how affectionate is thy
friendfhip to the fons of men ! *If any man fin*

---

* Μετριοπαθειν.   † Job xvi. 21.

we have an advocate with the Father, even Je-fus Chrift the righteous, whofe blood cleanfeth from all fin, and he *is able to fave to the uttermoft all that come unto God by him, feeing he ever liveth to make interceffion for us.* How great is this benevolence, that he thus condefcends to act in Heaven itfelf as the protector of finful men, that he patronizes their caufe, that he pleads the merits of his own fufferings and death for their forgivenefs and reftoration to favour, and that though he fits at the right hand of God, he is there not forgetful of his friends on earth, but employs his intereft with God his Father for their benefit and falvation ! And what may we not expect, if we keep his commands, from an interceffion fo powerful and conftant ; from his advocacy, who is the well beloved Son of God, who is appointed by his Father's goodnefs to this high and benevolent office, and even *advanced by him to be a Prince and a Saviour, to grant repentance and the forgivenefs of fins.*

How *great* and *valuable* are the *bleffings* which he is empowered to beftow, as the *friend* and *advocate* of mankind, and which he is able to beftow, in *whom it hath pleafed the Father that all fullnefs fhould dwell.* With him are all the treafures of knowledge and wifdom, and friendfhip is in its nature communicative, and the friends of princes are admitted to their fecrets, initiated into their counfels, and made privy to the moft concealed meafures they purfue. And therefore Chrift tells his difciples in the verfe following

my

text : *Henceforth I call you not fervants ; for the fervant knoweth not what his Lord doth. But I have called,* i. e. owned and treated *you as friends ; for all things that I have heard of my Father I have made known unto you ;* as he revealed to them the . fecret purpofes of his Father in fending him into the world, and promifed them his bleffed *fpirit, that fhould lead them into all that truth* which it was neceffary for them to know, in order to fpread the knowledge of his gofpel amongft the feveral nations of the earth. And when he was on earth, how excellent and important were the fubjects on which he difcourfed with his Apoftles ! How ufeful the converfation he entertained them with ! How did he open their minds to knowledge ! How kindly did he remove their prejudices, and teach them gradually, as they were able to bear it, one truth after another, relating to the kingdom of God ! And though we have not the benefit of perfonal converfe with him, as his difciples had, and are not to expect from the advantage of his friendfhip any new difcoveries and revelations, as they had ; yet ftill he now liberally communicates to us, from his own fulnefs of grace and truth, by means of his gofpel, that facred repofi-tory of divine truth, all thofe eternal coun-fels of God, which they were commiffioned to publifh to mankind, that relate to the re-demption of a finful world, all thofe principles of divine truth that we are concerned to know, all thofe important duties, that we

are

are bound to practice, all thofe facred and powerful motives, that are proper to influence us, and all thofe realities and powers of the life and world to come, that may moſt effectually excite and eſtabliſh our hopes, fill us with comfort, and render our obedience to his commands an eaſy and delightful ſervice.   Nor will thoſe *ſecret aſſiſtances* of his *ſpirit* be ever wanting to good and upright minds, that are neceſſary to direct them in the purſuit of truth, to preſerve them from pernicious and deſtructive errors, and to ſecure the good influence of the principles they believe upon their hearts and lives.   And this is one peculiar advantage of a well choſen friendſhip, and of intimacy contracted with perſons of ſuperior wiſdom and underſtanding, that it is ſo highly improving, ſo communicative of knowledge, and conveys in the moſt eaſy and engaging manner the moſt valuable and beneficial inſtruction ; according to that certain maxim : *He that walks with the wiſe ſhall be wiſe* *.   And let us but walk with Chriſt, by obeying his commands and imitating his example, and he will make us wiſer than he who hath the heart to multiply his worldly treaſures, and than the mere Philoſopher, who hath the moſt extenſive knowledge of the ſyſtem of the univerſe ; even wiſe to the pleaſing our God, and the eternal ſalvation of our ſouls.

* Prov. xiii. 20.

As true *friendfhip* is thus liberal in imparting what it knows, and loves to fhare its fecrets with thofe on whom it terminates, it is *generous* and *free* in the communication of what it hath to give, and takes a pleafure in beftowing on them thofe favours which may contribute to their happinefs, or tend to their honour. All things are common amongft friends, is a known maxim, and there cannot be, in the nature of things, a genuine friendfhip that is ungenerous, parfimonious, illiberal and fordid. The Friendfhip of princes is for this reafon preferable to all other, becaufe they have more to beftow, and are known to be peculiarly bountiful to their favourites. When the officers of *Antiochus* perfuaded *Mattathias* to become a pattern of obedience to the king's command, by his conformity to the idolatrous religion of the Pagans, the powerful motive he offered was : " So fhalt thou and thy houfe be in the " number of the king's friends, and thou " and thy children fhall be honoured with " filver and gold and many rewards * ;" the royal bounty being the natural effect of the royal favour and friendfhip. But what are the riches and honours that earthly princes have to beftow, in comparifon of thofe which he who is *King of kings, and Lord of lords,* hath in his power to vouchfafe to his faithful fubjects, whom he dignifies with his friendfhip ! Theirs are all fading treafures, and tranfitory honours ; his fubftantial and

* 1 Mac. ii. 18.

durable·

durable. Theirs refpect the body only, his the immortal foul. Theirs are limited to time and the prefent world ; his reach to a future ftate, and are lafting even to eternity. He calls us brethren ; a title this that earthly princes conferred on others, when they would give them the moft diftinguifhing mark of their favour and friendfhip ; and a title, which, as conferred by Chrift, exalts us higher than the higheft of earthly monarchs can raife us. He introduces us into the houfhold and family of God, and gives us the liberty of freedom and accefs to the throne of his grace, whenever our wants or our inclinations lead us to approach it. Yea, *he makes us kings and priefts to his heavenly Father,* and allows us *to fit down in his Father's kingdom.* He cloaths us with raiment faiier and purer, infinitely richer and more valuable than human art can form, or the moft coftly materials on earth can furnifh out ; purity of heart, fanctity of character, and a robe woven with all the graces of the fpirit of God, and the facred difpofitions of piety and virtue, and by caufing us to appear in the very image of God, and to wear the refemblance of the moft high. He puts us into poffeffion of the true riches, thofe *which neither moth nor ruft can corrupt,* and which neither violence or fraud can diffeize us of ; riches of truth and grace ; *peace of confcience* and *peace with God*; *joy in the Holy Ghoft, and hope of glory,* and hath given us an unalienable title to *an inheritance incorruptible, undefiled, that fadeth not away, and that is re-*

ferved

ferved in Heaven for us. Thefe are thy gifts,
O Jefus, thou Son of the living God ! Thus
fhall it be done unto thofe whom thou ho-
noureft with thy friendfhip ! Admit us to
this honour, and we have all that our higheft
ambition can reach to, and are fure of every
thing our hearts can defire, or that can contribute to our happinefs ; for then *whether
Paul, or Apollos, or Cephas, or the world, or
life, or death, or things prefent, or things to
come, all fhall be ours, for we are Chrift's, and
Chrift is God's *.*

It is farther no fmall advantage that arifes
from the *friendfhip* of earthly kings and
princes, that it fecures thofe who enjoy it
an *admiffion into the prefence*, and intitles them
to the diftinguifhing liberty of *perfonal converfe.* This was the peculiar happinefs of the
Apoftles and difciples of Chrift, when he per-
fonally miniftered on earth, when they heard
his words, faw his wonderful works, had re-
courfe to him for inftruction, and received all
the confolation of his promifes and grace.
And though this be a priviledge now above
our condition, now he is in Heaven, and we
are fojourners on earth, yet ftill methinks we
may converfe with him in the hiftory of his
life, and the revelation of his gofpel, as though
we were actually prefent with him. When
we read the accounts that are left of him,
faith and meditation will renew thofe former
fcenes, and prefentiate to our minds thefe

* 1 Cor. iii. 22, 23.

paft

paft events, and with what pleafures may we imagine ourfelves his auditors, fitting at his feet, learning fiom him divine wifdom, and *bearing the gracious things that proceeded out of his lips!* How eafily may we follow him in our minds in all his travels, and rejoice with the blind man when reftored to fight, with the lame when recovered to the ufe of their limbs, with demoniacks when returned to foundnefs of mind, with the difeafed when healed of all their maladies, with the dead when raifed to new life, with the hungry, fainting multitude, when fed and fatisfied with heavenly bread, and with the confcious, trembling finner, when pronounced pardoned and accepted with his God. Can'ft thou not, Chriftian, I know thou can'ft, for thou haft often done it at *his table*, trace him yet farther, through all that dreadful fcene of fufferings that he endured, from the malice, rage, and impiety of his enemies, when his profeffed friend betrayed him with a treacherous kifs, all his difciples forfook him and fled, and God his Father feemed to have deferted him, and leave him entirely to the power and fury of thofe who had fworn his deftruction. Follow him to the chief Priefts and Rulers, to *Herod's* court, to *Pilate's* tribunal, to *Golgotha* the place of fuffering, and fee with what patience he endured the vileft indignities, with what intrepid refolution he owned himfelf the Son of God, and promifed Meffiah, and with what refignation he offered himfelf *as a lamb to the*

flaughter,

ſlaughter, without reproaching his perſecutors, and breathing his laſt with a generous prayer for their forgiveneſs, and a kind apology for their guilt, from their knowing not what they did. A ſerious believing mind will intereſt itſelf in all theſe tranſactions, and preſent them to itſelf, as though they were actually preſent. But thou wilt not I am ſure, Chriſtian, leave thy Saviour in the grave, nor let thy faith and hope there lie buried with him. See the trembling earth proclaim *his victory over death*, the angels of God declaring his reſurrection, the keepers of his grave aſtoniſhed and deſerting their appointed ſtation, the Chief Prieſts confounded and enraged, his diſciples rejoicing to ſee their maſter returned to a new life, and made witneſſes to his aſcenſion into the kingdom, preſence, and glory of his father. In all theſe tranſactions we may, by a ſerious review of them, become almoſt perſonally preſent, and by admitting the conſideration of them deeply into our minds, we may awaken all the ſame variety of ſentiments and paſſions, as though we had been actually witneſſes to theſe important and aſtoniſhing events. All this however doth not come up to the actual *admiſſion into his preſence*, and *ſeeing* and converſing with him in perſon, *face to face*. But rejoice, Chriſtian, this honour is reſerved alſo for thee, *if thou doeſt whatſoever he hath commanded thee*. Though now *thou ſeeſt him* not, thou *loveſt him*, and *rejoiceſt* in him. Hereafter thou ſhalt *ſee him*,

him, whom thy foul loveth, and love him more when thou rejoiceft in the neareft approaches to his perfon and glory. The day is coming when the Heavens muft reftore him, when *he fhall come in the clouds of Heaven,* encompaffed with his *Father's glory,* and furrounded with the *angels* of his prefence ; when *every eye fhall fee him,* and thine eye fhall behold him feated on his judgment feat ; when his mouth fhall *pronounce thee pardoned and accepted,* when his arms fhall embrace thee as his genuine difciple, and his reward diftinguifh thee as *a good and faithful fervant ; when thou fhalt fee him as he is,* and when thou feeft him, wonder to fee thyfelf *transformed into his image,* and appear in his glory ; when he fhall *prefent thee holy and blamelefs before his Father's prefence with exceeding joy,* and thy joy fhall be unutterable, to fee thyfelf thus honoured by the Friend and Saviour of mankind, and find thyfelf allowed to dwell *forever with the Lord.* Then fhall the mutual *friendfhip* between Chrift and his faithful followers, and between God and them, be confirmed, by the feal of Heaven, and rendered *immutable* and *eternal.* Then fhall the true worth, and infinite advantage of being the friends of Chrift be fully underftood, when all that Heaven can give us fhall be put into our poffeffion, and all that God can beftow advance our happinefs to the higheft perfection. Oh ! how honourable, how infinitely defirable is this friendfhip of Chrift ! Life is not life without it.

Better

Better be blotted out of being, than blotted out from the number of his friends. Would you live and die amongſt the favourite number? Do what he hath commanded you. He owns none as his friends but the *obedient* and *faithful.* For this is the conſtitution irrevocably fixed : *If ye keep my commandments, ye ſhall abide in my love, even as I have kept my Father's commandments, and abide in his love* *.

* John xv. 10.

SERMON

SERMON XIV.

Godlineſs explained and recommended.

1 TIMOTHY iv. 8.

Godlineſs is profitable for all things, having the promiſe of the life that now is, and of that which is to come.

WHO is not influenced by the proſpect of advantage, and what wiſe man is there, who will not purſue thoſe methods, which he looks on as conducive to his beſt and higheſt intereſt ? As it reflects no credit upon any man's underſtanding, not to know wherein his true happineſs conſiſts ; ſo 'tis no recommendation of his religion, that it makes him drop all regard to it, and works him up into ſuch an enthuſiaſm of diſintereſted zeal, as cauſes him to renounce all conſideration of his own welfare, as a motive to the ſervice of God, and the practice of virtue. Practicing virtue for *virtue's ſake*, and being religious out of a *ſimple* view to the *glory of God*, wholly abſtracted from the happy conſequences of them to ourſelves, are mo-

tives

tives very near a kin to each other, fupported by the fame kind of thin fpun arguments, and equally conducive to promote
the intereft of real piety and goodnefs.
And though chriftianity hath been reprefented, as a fort of *mercenary* fcheme, becaufe it allures men to embrace and fubmit to it, by the promifes of very great and
durable *rewards*; yet the objection would
have been much ftronger againft it, and
urged, I doubt not, with great affurance and
triumph, by the enemies of revelation, if
there had been *no recompence* infured by it;
who would not have failed to reprefent it, as
a cold and comfortlefs inftitution, without
power or efficacy to perfuade, and highly
unworthy to be embraced by men, in whom
the principle of felf love is effential, and infeparable from their natures, and who can
never renounce or facrifice the true intereft
of their being, without being chargeable with
fhameful ignorance, rafh prefumption, and incurable folly ?

The pretence for being religious merely for
God's glory, and without regarding the happy
effects of it in reference to ourfelves, is built
upon the falfe fuppofition, that the *glory of*
God and the *happinefs of his creatures*, may, or
do ftand in *oppofition* to each other. For if
they do not, then whatever contributes to the
one promotes the other alfo, and the ferving
God to promote his glory, is equally ferving
him for our own profit and advantage. Not
to add, that if the fuppofition of being religious

gious folely for his glory, excludes all regard
to his approbation, acceptance, and favour,
as this would be a real inftance of madnefs
and impiety, it is impoffible it can ever be
a real requirement, or recommendation of
true religion.   If on the other hand, we
may and ought to have refpect to the divine
acceptance and favour, the boaft of being
religious only for God's glory hath no reality
and truth to fupport it, fince the favour of
God is attended with the higheft advantages throughout every period of our duration.

In like manner, if *virtue* is to be practifed
for *itfelf*, the meaning muft be, if it be a
good one, becaufe of its intrinfick, unalterable, natural propriety and fitnefs, its eternal
excellency and worth, and becaufe it wants
nothing external to recommend it, nothing
but what arifes out of itfelf, and is neceffarily
connected with its effential principles and
duties.   On this fuppofition the *tendencies* and
confequences of virtue muft be taken into our
account, as the very propriety and excellency
of it can never be accounted for, but by the
effects of it, and its direct and certain tendencies to preferve the good order, peace and
welfare of focieties, and its influence to fecure the dignity, to promote the ufefulnefs,
to enlarge the mind, and to prepare for felf
enjoyment, to furnifh out the moft pleafing
reflections, and effectually to provide for the
entire welfare of every individual.   The confequence of which is, that to love virtue for
itfelf,

itself, is to love it because it is *beneficial* to ourselves ; and therefore every one may be very difinterestedly virtuous, or virtuous for the sake of virtue, who loves and practices it for the sake of those blessed consequences which it hath a certain tendency to produce.

No doubt, but that if the advantages and *rewards* that we propose as our great inducements to religion and virtue, are in their nature *mean* and *unworthy*, such as have no connection with, and do not arise out of these things themselves ; such as may be, and frequently are very powerful inducements to vice and folly, and such as ought to be sacrificed, whenever the interest of religion and virtue require it ; the acting merely upon such motives in those great concerns, is base and dishonourable, and argues such a mercenary and contemptible spirit, as is highly criminal in its nature, and entirely takes away every thing venerable, excellent, and sacred, from the most specious appearances of piety and goodness ; because in such cafes these appearances are not founded in truth, are consistent with the greatest corruption and depravity of heart, and will be of no longer continuance than the lucre that arises from them ; or when that draws a contrary way, will naturally lead into practices utterly inconsistent with and destructive of the obligations and duties of religion and virtue. On the contrary, when the *motives* to both arife from an inward approbation of them, a prevailing

vailing love to them, and the happy confequences that arife out of them, and that
are connected with that favour and friendfhip of God which invariably rewards them ;
thefe are evidently religious and virtuous motives, are dictated by principle, argue a prevailing integrity of mind, are reafonable in
themfelves, and therefore our acting under
the influence of them muft be acceptable to
that great and good being, who formed us
for happinefs, and is willing that we fhould
diligently purfue and finally fecure it.

It is upon this principle, that the Apoftle
in my text encourages us to the practice of
true religion, by the glorious encouragement
and affurance of its being univerfally beneficial to us, in every valuable intereft of
our being. *Godlinefs is profitable for all things,
having the promife of the life that now is, and of
that which is to come. Bodily exercife profits little.* Every thing external in or by which
men can bufy themfelves, is but of little
avail to their real happinefs. Should they
exercife themfelves, and even become victors
in the *facred games*, the reward, the prize of
victory would be infignificant in itfelf, and
but of fhort duration to the poffeffors. Should
they weary themfelves in external rites and
ceremonies, and practice the greateft bodily
feverities and abftinences, what would it contribute towards their acceptance with God,
or how promote their final falvation ? 'Tis
godlinefs and that alone, the thing itfelf, not
the bare name or fhew of it, the reality and
fubftance,

fubftance, not the fhadow or form of it, that is univerfally and invariably *profitable*; for befides its own natural tendency to fecure all the moft valuable interefts of our beings, it hath the farther *promife* from God *of the life that now is*, and *of that which is to come*. In fpeaking to thefe words I fhall confider,

I. The *nature of that godlinefs* of which our Apoftle fpeaks. And

II. Shew you how it is *profitable for all things.*

I. I am to confider the *nature* of that *godlinefs* which the Apoftle here fpeaks of. The original word properly fignifies the right or *true worfhip of God*, and therefore fuppofes fome acquaintance with and *knowledge of him*; fome juft conceptions of his nature, attributes, works and providence, becaufe genuine piety, and the rational, acceptable worfhip of God depend on, and can never be fupported without it. All the falfe objects of worfhip, during the prevalence of Heathenifm, and all the abfurd and impious idolatries and fuperftitions that obtained in the *Gentile* world, owed their rife and continuance to miftaken fentiments, and a prevailing *ignorance* of the true God; and the fame caufes will ever be attended with the fame effects; abfurd and miftaken notions of God neceffarily producing anfwerable abfurdities in the worfhip of him, and being deftructive of the fpirit of a pure, acceptable devotion and piety.

This

This confifts in the *right difpofition* and frame of the *mind* towards God ; fuch a difpofition, as the firm belief of his being, attributes, univerfal providence, and moral government, frequently attended to, and duly impreffed on the mind, will create and eftablifh, and which is generally expreffed in Scripture by the comprehenfive phrafe of the *fear of God.* Thus *Cornelius* is faid to be a *devout man,* or, fince the word is the fame as in my text, a godly man ; after which 'tis added, by way of explication, that *he feared God* †. And thus, what we juftly render from the Hebrew, *the fear of the Lord is the beginning of wifdom,* the Greek verfion renders : *Piety to God is the beginning of wifdom ;* as though piety, godlinefs, devotion, and the fear of God, were *equivalent* expreffions. And indeed they are fo ; for this *fear of the Lord,* which the facred writings fpeak of, as comprehenfive of the whole of religion, implies in it all thofe facred difpofitions and affections of foul towards him, which the confideration of his infinitely perfect and glorious character, and the various relations he fuftains in reference to us, fo juftly challenge and deferve ; that humble fenfe of our dependence on him, which becomes us as the creatures of his power, and abfolutely fubject to the difpofals of his good pleafure ; that holy reverence and awe, which the confideration of his infinite rectitude, majefty, and glory fhould ever

† Acts x. 2.

excite

excite and preserve alive in our minds ; that
filial affection and esteem, which is due to
him as our father, friend, preserver, and
bountiful benefactor ; that humble confidence
and trust in him, which his never failing
power, goodness, truth, and faithfulness render him so highly worthy of ; that submission
to his will, and unreserved resignation to the
disposals of his providence, that ought perpetually to possess us, upon account of his
constant concern for our welfare, and the
equity and unerring wisdom of all his dis-
pensations ; and, finally, that dread of offending him, and that sollicitude and care to approve ourselves to, and be accepted of him,
which the infinite importance of his favour to
our welfare, both in time and eternity, render both our interest and duty. These dispositions are essential in their very nature to
constitute true piety and godliness. It is
what our blessed Saviour calls, *worshipping
the Father in spirit and truth* ; *in spirit*, as it is
properly the worship of the reasonable mind ;
and *in truth*, as it is that worship of God,
which is founded in the eternal reason and
fitness of things, in opposition to all superstition and idolatry, and every external form
and ceremony that is not accompanied with
these internal sentiments and affections, in
which the life and power of true godliness
consist ; and what therefore is necessarily and
immutably the duty of every reasonable being, and for the same reasons, and upon
the same foundations, as any other moral
virtue

virtue or duty that can be mentioned. But then,

As all the internal difpofitions and affections of the mind, have their proper fruits, by which they difcover their life and influence; *godlinefs* therefore farther implies all thofe *external actions,* that are *exprefjive* of our *inward devotion* towards God, and to which the affections, effential to true godlinefs, when terminated on the great object of worfhip, do naturally and powerfully excite. Benevolence and charity, when real and prevalent, will exert themfelves in all fuitable inftances of actual goodnefs; and if juftice and temperance are formed within us into rooted and permanent habits, fobriety of life, and righteoufnefs of conduct, will certainly become an effential part of our character. In like manner, if *fentiments* of unfeigned godlinefs *pofjefs our minds,* and the principles and habits of genuine piety enter into and form our governing temper, there will be the *natural and proper indications* of them, and they will not fail to exprefs themfelves by all thofe inftances of reverence and devotion towards God, which arife out of them, and are infeparably connected with them; *by humbly adoring* his infinite majefty, *ferious prayer* for his protection and bleffing, *grateful thankf-givings* and affectionate praifes for the innumerable inftances of his goodnefs, *folemn recollections of the riches of his grace* in the redemption of the world by Chrift, and *attending* on all *thofe facred fervices,* in which thefe beft principles may be recalled to his confideration, imprefled on his mind, and rendered more effectual to confirm and eftablifh him in his own purpofes of fubmiffion and obedience to God ; and by which the knowledge and fear of God, and the practice of univerfal righteoufnefs may be beft promoted and kept up in the world, amongft all ranks and degrees of men. The queftion with a truly religious perfon will be ; not, of what benefit thefe and fuch like performances will be to God, for they need not be informed that they can be of none ; not, what alteration can they make in the purpofes of his will, becaufe they know he is abfolutely unchangeable ; but are thefe things *reafonable in themfelves*, are they *fuited to my character* and condition, as a dependent and greatly obliged creature, are they *enforced* by the *authority* and command of God, have they the *fanction* of the *greateft and beft examples* throughout all ages of the world, and are they in themfelves and natural tendences, likely and *probable methods of promoting in me* that difpofition and character, which are neceffary to my final happinefs in the favour of God ? If they are, as they certainly are, all objections againft them, are of no force, and ought to make no impreffions on the minds, nor to have any influence on the religious behaviour of wife and good men. But I would farther obferve on this fubject,

That every *focial, humane virtue* may be confidered as an *effential part* of the character
of

a *godly man,* and may be *exalted* by him into a real inftance of *acceptable religion* and piety. Although religion, properly fo called, both in temper and practice, may be certainly included under the general name of righteouf-nefs, or moral virtue, yet 'tis not true on the contrary, that every inftance of moral virtue is neceffarily and always an act of religion ; becaufe any fuch may be performed without any reference to God, and when they are to be performed, cannot be any inftances of reverence or devotion to him. But as perfons of real religion *acknowledge God in all their ways,* they dignify and exalt moral virtue, and confecrate even human goodnefs into a facred facrifice of genuine and acceptable piety ; becaufe they obferve all the great duties of morality, which arife out of their relation to and connection with men, not only becaufe they are ftrictly reafonable and fit in themfelves, but becaufe thofe relations, upon which their reafonablenefs and natural obligation depend, are of the creation and *appointment of God,* and becaufe thefe duties are for this reafon evidently *the ordinance of God,* and *agreeable* to his will. So that the fame action being performed, as reafonable in itfelf, and as an inftance of reverence to the authority and commands of God, is both *vir-tue* and *piety,* an inftance of true morality and genuine godlinefs. And indeed the *mo-rality* of all actions is *extreamly defective,* where there is *no* proper regard paid to God in the performance of them ; becaufe true

morality

morality takes in all the various relations of men, and the several obligations they are under, and by consequence their relations to God, and the obligations they are under to reverence him, and yield obedience to his will. Godliness therefore comprehends in it all the real instances of social virtue and moral righteousness, that are performed from a prevailing sense of deity, which the desire of approving ourselves to God, and the lively hope and full persuasion, that he *is a rewarder of those who diligently seek him.* This leads me

II. To the *second* general, which is to shew you the *unspeakable advantages* that are connected with and inseparable from *true godliness* ; or genuine religion in principle, disposition, and practice ; what are the profits and gains that arise out of real piety and virtue. The Apostle tells us, *that godliness with contentment is great gain* *, and in my text, *that it is profitable for all things, having the promise of the life that now is, and of that which is to come.* It hath a natural tendency to procure us every needed good, and is conducive to happiness in every circumstance of our being, and throughout the whole of our duration, and will invariably promote and secure it, if its influences are not, by weakness or wickedness, unnaturally prevented. Let it be considered here

* 1 Tim. vi. 6.

That

That *godliness* naturally *creates* and *fixes* the *genuine disposition for happiness* in every mind that submits to the power and influence of it. True happinefs is not the arbitrary creature of a capricious and fickle imagination, but hath its proper and certain caufes, from whence it flows as a neceffary effect and confequence. The fource of it is internal, feated originally in the mind, in the ftate of its paffions, and the nature of thofe affections and habits, that influence and govern it ; on which account the wife author of the Proverbs affures us, *that a good man is fatisfied from himfelf.* If the affections are mifplaced, irregular, intemperate, or unnatural, happinefs is fo far in the very nature of things never to be obtained, to be purchafed at no price, nor to be extracted from the moft valuable objects we can be in poffeffion of. If, on the contrary, the ftate of our paffions be regular, that they are directed to the moft excellent and deferving objects, if they are proportioned in their exercife and influence to the real worth of thofe things on which they refpectively terminate, if they are under due controul, and fubject to the unerring conduct of truth and reafon : In a word, if we indulge none that are unnatural and criminal, if thofe which are natural be kept within the bounds of moderation and prudence, and if there be none of thofe generous affections wanting, that reafon and principle excite and juftify ; happinefs is then near us, it dwells within our very bofoms, and we

A a 3   cannot

cannot poffibly mifs the invaluable treafure.
Now that godlinefs, which the gofpel of
Chrift recommends, as far as it influences
and prevails over men, will prove a fure and
friendly fource of the moft fincere and valuable happinefs , for it will abfolutely deftroy
and extirpate every unnatural and criminal
affection ; it being impoffible for any thing
of this kind to live and flourifh in that heart
that is confecrated by piety to God, and in
full poffeffion of thofe heavenly graces of
which true religion fuppofes and includes
the habitual exercife. And as it thus fubdues and eradicates every unworthy paffion
and affection, fo it regulates and moderates
all the natural and lawful ones, reftraining
them from fixing upon improper objects,
and from growing warm and intemperate,
where the due exercife of them is allowable
and ufeful ; for as religion elevates the affections to thofe things which are of the
nobleft worth and importance, and directs
their principal force and ftrongeft tendency
towards them, as their proper reft and center, their biafs towards every thing of an
inferior, fecondary nature and worth, muft
be proportionally lefs precipitate and violent.
And, finally, whatfoever thofe difpofitions
and affections are, from whence a truly rational, folid, and lafting happinefs can flow,
or which in the exercife of them can any
ways contribute to the dignity and proper
enjoyment of human life, religion neceffarily
excites, cultivates, ftrengthens, and preferves
them.

them. Faith and hope, truft and confidence, affection and complacency, benevolence and goodnefs; in a word, all the divine and human virtues, that are feated in the heart, and form the temper of a godly man, either produce that ferenity, calmnefs and peace of mind, which conftitute a gentle, eafy, flowing happinefs, or elfe that triumph and rejoicing of foul, which hath a fomewhat more impetuous pleafure attending it; and afford delights that are more warm and tranfporting, but which can never grow immoderate, or be attended with any danger of running into forbidden and criminal exceffes. So that *godlinefs* may with the greateft truth be faid to be *profitable for all things*, or conducive in every refpect to the advantage of mankind, as it univerfally and invariably *forms* by its own natural tendency, the *genuine difpofition* for our *higheft happinefs*, and will be *productive of it*, where there is nothing to check and prevent the influence and efficacy of it. But farther,

This *godlinefs* not only produceth the temper and capacity for happinefs, but alfo *fecures thofe invaluable advantages and fubftantial bleffings*, which nothing elfe can yield, and of which nothing can wholly or finally deprive thofe who are in poffeffion of them. Thefe advantages relate

To the *whole of our frame*, for the happy influences of religion reach to our bodies and fouls. It is friendly to the welfare and intereft of our *bodies*; as it is an effectual pre-

fervative

fervative from all thofe exceffes and violences
that tend to weaken and deftroy them, and
the fureft preventive of thofe pains and diforders, that weaken and torment them ;
as it powerfully calms thofe fears, and eafes
men of thofe cares, which prey upon their
vitals, deprefs their fpirits, and fometimes
overwhelm them with mifery and death ;
as it compofes the mind, and fubdues all
that inordinacy and violent agitation of the
paffions, which diforder the frame, and
thereby preferves and even encreafes the
ftrength and vigour of the conftitution. And
as to the *mind*, the benefits accruing to it
from the habitual prevalence of a godly difpofition, exerting itfelf in all the genuine effects, are of the higheft and moft valuable
nature. For it ennobles all the powers of it,
by directing them to, and employing them on
the moft excellent and worthy objects, con-
fecrates all the affections of it to the higheft
and beft purpofes, cultivates and perfects all
thofe heavenly graces, in the poffeffion of
which, the real dignity and amiablenefs of
it confift, fecures thofe pleafing reflections
that yield it the moft grateful entertainment,
introduces into it the pureft and moft fatisfying pleafures, flowing from the moft worthy and permanent fources, and as it opens
its profpects into the moft diftant futurity,
and ftrengthens the hopes of the moft durable
bleffednefs and glory. I add farther,

Godlinefs is profitable for all things, as the
advantages of it run through *every ftage*, and
enter

enter into every condition of human life ; for
there are no circumstances or periods of our
beings, to which the blessed influences of it
do not extend, and largely contribute to the
safety and comfort of it. If it enters into
childhood, as sometimes through the blessings
of God rewarding the care of a good education, it doth, what favour doth it conciliate, what tenderness of affection doth it
engage, what beauty and loveliness doth it
imprefs ! Like an early bloffom enriched and
impearled with the dews of Heaven, the
beauty of which is heightened and enlivened
by the luftre that fparkles in it, and which
breathes fragrancy and fweetnefs to all around
it. In *youth* it is a fure *preservative* from the
moft dangerous and deftructive fnares, the
fafeft guide into fuccefs and profperity, the beft
defence of innocence and integrity, the higheft
evidence of good fenfe and a found underftanding, the nobleft ornament to grace and
diftinguifh us, the wifeft method to fecure an
intereft in life, and maintain it, and the
only effectual means of a growing reputation
and increafing ufefulnefs.   In the middle
ftage of life, it is a permanent fource of
the moft valuable fatisfactions, fuitably employs and exercifes all the paffions, when
the youthful heat and warmth of them is
fubfided and fpent, adds a peculiar relifh to
every enjoyment, and,teaches how to ufe the
bounties of Heaven with a becoming moderation, gratitude and dignity.   In old age it
ftrengthens the foul under all the neceffary
decays

decays of nature, refreſhes and chears it, when the blood runs ſlow, and the pulſe begins to languiſh, feeds it with pleaſure by reflections on what is paſt, and delightful proſpects and anticipations of much better things to come, and renders it truly venerable in itſelf, amiable in the ſight of men, and pleaſing in the eſtimation of God himſelf. Like a tree bending under the weight of its ripened fruit, or a garden richly adorned, in which every flower and plant is grown up to full maturity and perfection. In proſperity it cloaths with moderation and humility, inſpires with benevolence and generoſity, excites to uſefulneſs and acts of kindneſs, warms the heart with gratitude, dictates adoration and praiſe to the fountain of all good, ſweetens every enjoyment, adds a reliſh to poſſeſſion, ſettles the mind by hope and truſt above the anxious fears of future diſappointment and want, and is attended with the chearful deſire and proſpect of a better and more durable inheritance. In all kind of afflictions it is the moſt effectual cordial, and affords the moſt ſenſible relief, produces patience under pain, ſubmiſſion and calmneſs under diſtemper, reſignation and hope under diſappointments and loſſes, light in the darkeſt gloom, intervals of chearfulneſs under the deepeſt melancholy, and in that moſt important and needful moment, when fleſh and heart begin to fail us, and we ſhall ſee an end of all created perfection, fetches in ſupports from him who is the eternal, uncreated

ated good, and thereby caufes the foul to triumph over death in its neareft approaches, and to rejoice in the near view of life and immortality, with a joy unfpeakable and full of glory. For,

In the laft place, the *advantages* of a real and undiffembled *godlinefs reach beyond the grave*, extend to the whole poffibility of our exiftence, and are commenfurate with eternity itfelf. We cannot indeed affure ourfelves from reafon, nor demonftrate by any train of certain confequences, that God is obliged in juftice to reward the temporary piety and virtue of any of his creatures, even fuppofing it blamelefs and perfect, with an *exceeding and eternal weight of happinefs and glory*. However, this is an inference of truth, that every man, rightly ufing his reafon, would naturally draw ; that the difpofition and life of genuine godlinefs muft be as acceptable to God, as well in the future, as in the prefent ftate ; and that as he cannot but approve it, he will not fail to diftinguifh and reward it by fome fuitable and peculiar marks of his favour. And therefore let the duration of our being be ever fo extenfive, that fincere piety and virtue which God approves, muft be of as lafting advantage to it, and the benefits attending it reach throughout every period of our exiftence. The *change of worlds* can make no *alteration* in the *nature and confequences of things* ; the religious temper, the affections of a mind devoted to and terminated on God, and the difpofition formed by
the

the love and fear of him, by faith and hope
in his power and goodness, and by that univerfal benevolence and righteoufnefs, which
imprefs us with a divine image and likenefs,
thefe things can never lofe their intrinfick
worth, wherever they dwell, and of how
long continuance foever they may be, will
ever remain the fame natural fources of hap-
els, and equally worthy the friendly re-
was and approbation of God. So that
godlinefs muft be univerfally profitable, as in
its own nature it tends to perpetuate our happinefs in every poffible ftate of our exiftence. And this fentiment is confirmed by
the doctrine of revelation, which affures us,
that *it hath the promife of the life that now is,
and of that which is to come.* It gives us
the affurance of immortality, and of *a bleffednefs incorruptible, and that fadeth not away.*
So that both the nature of the thing, and
promife of God confpire to eftablifh us in
this pleafing affurance, that a religious life
fhall be an happy one, and that the gains of
godlinefs are both temporal and eternal.

How glorious a recommendation is this
of Chriftian piety and virtue, when we thus
confider it in its immediate and certain con-
ction with all the moft valuable interefts
our beings in every ftate and period of
their duration. The love and defire of happinefs is natural to all men, and God himfelf is pleafed with our moft diligent purfuit
of it. How careful therefore fhould we be
to direct our views aright, and to feek it
from

from thofe pure and living fprings, from
whence alone we can derive it. How diligently fhould we cultivate all thofe facred
difpofitions towards God and man, of which our
certain relations to both demonftrate the reafonablenefs and propriety ! Efpecially when
we remember, that we are hereby ftrength-
ening the foundations and encreafing the
caufes of our own felicity, and more effectually fecuring the uninterupted and eternal
poffeffion of it. By this means every individual would be bleffed in himfelf, and focial
life, in the larger and leffer branches of it,
would be filled with innocence, purity and
peace. The bleffing of the Almighty would
fhine upon our tabernacles, every mind
would be full of joy, every family an habitation of comfort, and after the enjoyment
of thefe leffer tranfitory advantages, the fame
God, who hath trained us up for an immortal ftate, will bring us to the poffeffion
of that unchangeable world, where, from the
never ceafing communications of his bounty,
our happinefs fhall be fully fatisfying to our
natures, and permanent as that eternal fountain from whence it flows.

SERMON

SERMON XV.

Genuine Piety essential to present Happiness.

1 TIMOTHY iv. 8.

Godliness is profitable for all things, having the promise of the life that now is, and of that which is to come.

IF I was particularly to repeat to you all the several Passages of Scripture, that limit the hope and gift of salvation to the steady, habitual practice of righteousness, and that holiness of heart and life, to which our Christian principles lead us, and the example and doctrine of Christ oblige us ; and that expressly and peremptorily exclude from all the benefits of redemption, and the heavenly inheritance and glory, all the workers of iniquity, who have defiled themselves with the great transgressions of life, and lived in a course of wilful and presumptuous sins ; it would take up more time than is allotted for the present service ; for passages of this nature abound in every page of our bibles,

and

and there is nothing more frequently and
ferioufly inculcated in divine revelation than
this ; that the workers of iniquity fhall be
finally rejected from the kingdom of God,
and that 'tis neceffary we fhould *have our
fruit unto holinefs, that the end may be life
everlafting.*

But fo it happens, that fome of our *modern
fpiritual Phyficians* have a *quicker* way of healing their difeafed and miferable patients, and
an eafier method of faving the fouls of finners from condemnation and death. Let
them be loaded with ever fo many enormous
crimes, and have fpent their whole paft lives
in the practice of thofe wicked works, that
argue a fettled enmity to God, yet in a few
days they can wafh them as white as fnow,
fill them with affurance of falvation, even
when receiving the punifhment due to their
offences from human juftice, and give them
an immediate and fure paffage, through
every obftacle, to the heavenly happinefs and
glory.

'Tis but *believing*, it feems, and all is *fecure* ; and raifing in themfelves a firm perfuafion and confidence that they fhall be
faved, and they become inftantly heirs to
eternal life and glory. Chrift, they are told,
hath done every thing for them, and therefore all their paft vices and impurities, and
their having been entire ftrangers to the Chriftian temper and character, is no kind of
bar to their obtaining mercy ; for as to
their fins, the blood of Chrift will cleanfe
them

them from them all, and as to their want of all the graces and virtues enjoined by the gospel, and their having been defective in every instance of obedience to God, the *obedience of Christ* is to supply the room of it, and in his righteousness they are to be righteous, though they have been utterly destitute of all righteousness themselves.

If this doctrine could be true, you may *go on*, Christians, *in your sins* without fear, and live regardless of God and goodness without danger. In a few days, at the close of life, when you can sin no longer, you may retrieve all, and one act of faith in Christ, as your Saviour, if you can work yourselves up to it, will be a sufficient passport to his blessed kingdom and presence. And indeed there is but *one objection* to this comfortable doctrine, that is of any great importance, and that is : That *it is not*, and *cannot be true* ; or that if it be true, the doctrine of the *gospel* must certainly be *false*, and an heap of absurdities and contradictions ; which never makes faith in Christ, as that implies a *peremptory belief* and persuasion, *that we shall at all events be saved*, the one great necessary to salvation ; but such a *faith* as shews its life by *good works*, and *obedience* to God's commands ; or, in other words, such a life of uniform, steady piety and virtue, as is the effect of our faith in Christ, and is produced by our belief of and attention to the great doctrines of his gospel. To them, *who have their fruit unto holiness, the end shall be everlasting life*, is an essential fential truth of divine revelation ; and our bleffed Lord, who, one would think, fhould know the terms of falvation, expreſly declares, *that the dead ſhall hear the voice of the Son of God, and ſhall come forth, they who have done good unto the reſurrection of life, and they that have done evil unto the reſurrection of damnation**. And as to the promifes of God, my text informs us to what they are limited, and what the character of thofe perfons is to whom they are appropriated. *Godlineſs is profitable for all things, having the promiſe of the life that now is, and of that which is to come.*

The *godlineſs* here fpoken of, or, as the word fignifies, the *right worſhip of God*, fuppofes a *competent knowledge* of God, in his perfections, works, and providence, and conſiſts in the *right diſpoſition* of our minds towards him, and the *habitual exerciſe* of that reverence, affection, gratitude, humility, refignation, truſt, hope, and other graces of the good fpirit, which difcover themfelves by their proper and genuine effects, thofe of folemn adoration, ferious prayer, devout thankfgivings, frequent converfe with him by reflection and meditation, and attending on all thofe facred fervices, that are proper and neceſſary to confirm us in our beſt principles, hopes, and purpofes, and excite us to care and diligence in approving ourfelves to God, by the practice of all the fruits of righteouf-

---

* John v. 28, 29.

nefs. For in how contemptible a light foever fome may place the duties of *morality*, or the virtues of juftice, humanity, charity, temperance, chaftity, meeknefs, and others of the like nature, yet no man can be a truly godly man, that is not a moral one ; and when our good works, or the virtues we practice are performed out of reverence and love to God, and faith in our Lord Jefus Chrift for final acceptance and falvation, they then contract a double worth, and are inftances of *pure and undefiled religion,* and of genuine and acceptable piety to God, equally with any inftances of devotion, that we can engage in the performance of.

Now this *godlinefs is profitable to all things.* It hath *a natural tendency* to procure us every needed good, and is conducive to our happinefs in every circumftance of our beings. For it invariably *creates* and *fixes* the *proper difpofition for happinefs,* in all who fubmit to the power and influence of it. The happy influences of it extend to the *whole of our frame,* to all the *beft interefts* of our *fouls and bodies* ; they reach *to every ftage of life,* and enter into all the various circumftances, in which the providence of God can place us in the prefent world ; and reach to the *longeft poffibility of our exiftence,* wherefoever the goodnefs and wifdom of God may think fit to place us after our death ; becaufe the fame difpofitions, from which our happinefs flows in this world, muft produce the fame good effects in every other world, and becaufe that godlinefs,

godlinefs, which is honoured with the divine approbation here, muſt be equally pleaſing and acceptable to him hereafter.

But then, as the *natural* confequences of religion and virtue may be, and oftentimes have been *prevented* by *external* accidents, that it is not in human power and wiſdom to pre- vent, the Apoſtle adds, for our farther encou- ragement, *that godlinefs hath the promife of the life that now is* ; that is, the promiſe of God to fecure the true happinefs and enjoyment of it. And as death is the extinction of our prefent life, and *mere reafon* can never aſſure us of the reſtoration of it, and much leſs of our recovery to a ſtate of incorrupti- ble and never fading happinefs and glory, the Apoſtle farther adds, *that godlinefs hath the promife* of God, not only of the prefent life, but of *that which is to come.* So that in what inſtances foever, the natural confe- quences of godlinefs may fail to promote our true happinefs, in this or a future world, God by his promiſe hath engaged to ſupply the defect, and by his own power and good- nefs to fecure the real welfare of both. Let us confider thefe things diſtinctly.

I. *Godlinefs hath the promife of the life that now is.* It hath been frequently an objection againſt a religious and godly life, that it is really a very great obſtruction to mens pre- fent enjoyments, inconfiſtent with thofe plea- fures which the generality purſue, and fome- times cannot be perfevered in, without re- nouncing and facrificing all our moſt valuable interefts, relative to our bodies and the prefent ftate. And the objection undoubtedly is fo far juft, as that it muft be acknowledged, that there are many gratifications, which fenfual men eagerly purfue, which piety forbids the indulgence of, and that there may be, in fome particular feafons, very great inconveniences attending a fincere and fteady perfeverance in our Chriftian profeffion and practice.

And it is farther certain, that whatever be the meaning of *godlinefs having the promife of the prefent life*, the Apoftle could never intend to affure us, that *worldly riches, honours, and pleafures* fhould be the *conftant recompenfe* beftowed by God on true religion and virtue. This indeed fometimes doth happen in the courfe of God's providence, and confidering things in their natural connection, piety and true goodnefs is the moft direct and certain way to all that worldly profperity, which on the whole is beft for us, as well as the moft effectual method to render it fecure and permanent. However, there is no neceffary perpetual connection between a life of genuine godlinefs and temporal profperity, nor any promife from God, that I know of, always to fecure fecular advantages, in any remarkable manner, to devotion and the practice of righteoufnefs. The grand encouragements to this are derived from the objects of a *future* ftate, and the principle that is to direct our whole conduct here, is that of *faith* in the important realities of the unfeen and

eternal

eternal world. And the good things of the
prefent ftate are fpoken of rather under di-
minifhing characters, as fading temporary objects, that *perifh in the ufing*, that laft but for
a moment, that are attended with very dangerous temptations and fnares, and that oftentimes prove deftructive to the poffeffors
of them. And therefore revelation is fo far
from raifing any hopes, or giving any promifes of diftinguifhing worldly profperity, as
that it rather cautions us againft purfuing it
too eagerly, enjoying it too freely, and placing
our proper happinefs in it.

However, there is a real and important
truth in the words of my text ; that *godlinefs
hath the promife of the life that now is,* or that
God hath given many gracious affurances,
relative to the interefts and happinefs of the
prefent life, the accomplifhment of which
may certainly be depended on, and which
religious perfons fhall experience the truth
of, if they are wife to improve the means
he is pleafed to afford them, for their own
advantage and comfort. They may in a particular manner affure themfelves :

That their *lives* fhall, as to the *continuance*
and *fupport of them,* be under the *continual
care and protection* of God's providence, and
whilft they abide by their principles, and
remain fteadfaft in their duty, lengthened out
to their full period, *i. e.* till they have anfwered the great end of life, and whilft the
continuance of it fhall be for their real benefit and welfare. And this is all a wife man

would defire ; and to wifh to live, when God
knows that the gratification of fuch a wifh
would prove greatly injurious and deftructive
to us, is the greateft folly, as it is wifhing
to outlive the only valuable ends of life,
viz. the ufefulnefs and happinefs of it. Whether we are continued here a longer or fhorter
period, is in itfelf of little confequence, and
neither argues the favour or difpleafure of
God. The only circumftance of any real
confequence to us, and by confequence that
is defirable in its nature, is : *To live long
enough to approve ourfelves to God, to form
ourfelves into the right difpofitions for happinefs,* fo that if life be prolonged we may
fpend it worthily and comfortably, or if the
duration of it be fhortened, we may be
truly prepared for whatever fhall be the
events of the life and world that is to come.
If God preferve us here till this is done,
we may be well content, though we are
permitted to continue here no longer, and
to remove wherever the good pleafure of God
fhall fee fit to tranfplant us. And fuch an
affurance of life God hath really given to
piety and virtue in the gofpel revelation. This
is the exprefs promife of our Lord himfelf :
*Behold the fowls of the air, for they fow not,
neither do they reap, nor gather into barns, yet
their heavenly father feedeth them. Are ye not
much better than they ? Confider the lillies of the
field, how they grow, they toil not, neither do
they fpin. And yet I fay unto you, that even
Solomon in all his glory was not arrayed like one*

of

of these. Wherefore if God so cloath the grass of the field, which to day is, and tomorrow is cast into the oven, shall he not much more cloath you, O ye of little faith? Seek ye first the king-dom of God, and all these things shall be added to you *. In these words, God having made men of a *more excellent nature* than the lillies of the field and the fowls of Heaven, is laid down by our blessed Lord, as a *solid reason* and certain proof of their being under the *immediate* care and guardianship of providence, and that God would concern himself to up-hold them in life, and provide for them the necessary supports of it, whilst they are in the way of their duty, and 'till they have finished the service to which God hath ap-pointed them. And men of sincere piety have peculiar reason to assure themselves of a continued interest in the divine protection, for the security of their lives, more than all the rest of mankind, who governing them-selves by their passions and sensual affections, and walking in those paths of sin, which are his abhorrence, have reason to fear their being left to the consequences of their own follies, and that they shall fall a prey to those de-structive evils to which they voluntarily ex-pose themselves. Whereas righteous and godly men, may, from the general ends and reasons of providence, as well as from the especial promises made them, assure themselves of the security and continuance of life, whilst

---

* Matt. vi. 26.

B b 4

life is worth the having, as long as they are
capable of rightly improving it, and the farther continuance of it would not expose them
to any dangerous and destructive evils. So
that *godliness* hath the *promise of this life*, as it
is a real security to religious persons, that God
will never suffer them to be cut off by such
an *untimely* and immature death, as would
prove unfriendly to their best interest and
happiness; but amidst all the various dangers
of life, to which they may be exposed, will
either enable them entirely to escape these,
or preserve them from all their destructive
effects, 'till he knows it is for their advantage
to give them a final deliverance, by removing
them into that better state of existence, where
they shall never be molested or endangered
by them any more. With such a promise,
who need be anxious about life? " Under
the divine protection no destruction can come
near me. I know I shall live, and not die,
as long as I wish to live, *i. e.* as long as God
knows life is best for me, and longer methinks one would not indulge a single wish to
protract it." Again,

*Godliness hath the promise of the life that now
is*, as it is an effectual *preservative* from all
the *great occasions and sources of unhappiness
and misery*, and as it hath the assurance
of *God*, that he will be their *guardian* and
protector from them. From whence proceed the greatest distresses and uneasiness of
human nature? What is the real cause of
mens being involved in wretchedness and
                                    destruction?

deftruction ? Is it the arbitrary and fevere appointment of God ? Is it becaufe he takes pleafure in their anguifh and ruin ? Is it his agency and providence, that hath introduced fo many evils into the world, and expofed human life to fuch an infinite variety of calamities, that perpetually infeft it ? No. God is blamelefs. The fource of thefe things is to be fought elfewhere, and men are their own tormentors and deftroyers. God hath created all things for good, and if men would follow the direction of his providence and word, the miferies of mankind would in great meafure immediately ceafe, and happinefs foon return to us from her native heaven, to fmile on, and blefs again the inhabitants of our world. But if men will cherifh the caufes of their own unhappinefs, contrary to the will of God, how can they efcape that mifery which they thus bring upon themfelves ? If they will cherifh thofe corrupt paffions and affections, which they ought to fupprefs, they muft be drawn into thofe inconveniences and evils, which when they feel they would be glad to be delivered from. If they will indulge to criminal pleafures, and enter into all the methods of fin and folly, they muft feel, in their intervals of reflection, all that remorfe of confcience, and thofe cutting reflections of their own minds, which the fenfe of guilt naturally and conftantly produces. If they will needlefsly expofe themfelves to the danger of powerful temptations, they muft expect to

fall

fall by them, and reap the destructive consequences. If they will live without any
care to prepare for death, it is no wonder
they should be in perpetual *bondage, through
the fear of it.* In a word, the consequences
of sin and folly are, in their nature, unfriendly
to mankind, and if we cherish the causes of
our own misery, we put it, as far as we
can, out of the power of God himself to
prevent it. But now godliness hath the sure
promise of the gospel of being effectually
guarded from all these aggravated distresses.
It suppofes that the habits of sin are in some
good measure broken, and it hath the af-
surance, *that he who hath begun the good work,
will carry it on* to greater perfection, and fully
complee' it in the day of Christ * ; and as our
deliverance from these grows more intire,
the sources of unhappiness proportionably
diminish, and the mind becomes more and
more disposed to be comfortable and blessed.
Even men of religion and piety have their
errors to acknowledge, and that give them
some uneasy moments. But then they have
their relief from the divine promise, that God
will justify them freely by his grace, and
that being recovered from sin, they shall be
finally saved from condemnation, and therefore are free from all those aggravated terrors,
to which the sense of unpardoned guilt must
necessarily expose them. They are encom-
passed with temptations equally with other

* Phil. i. 6.

men,

men, from the fnares of life, and the circumftances of the world around them.   But
then 'tis their happinefs, that they are not
equally endangered by them.   For they have
the comfortable promife, *that God is faithful,*
who will not fuffer them to be tempted above
what they are able, but will with the temptation
alfo make a way for their efcape, that they may
be able to bear it * ; and being thus affured,
that *the grace of God will be fufficient for*
them, they chearfully commit themfelves to
the divine protection, fure either to efcape
the danger of temptation, or the guilt and
mifery that follows by being overcome, and
complying with it.   As *godlinefs* is the beft
ornament, and trueft improvement of life, fo
it is in its nature the *beft preparation for death,*
and the promife affures us, that he who lives
by the Chriftian faith *fhall not die eternally,*
is paffed from condemnation to life, and
being made meet for, fhall finally become partaker *of the inheritance of the Saints in light.*
So that he is relieved and comforted under
the thoughts and approach of death, and
can poffefs his mind in peace in thofe moments, when habitual and impenitent finners are deftitute of every confideration to
fupport them, and betray a thoufand uneafy apprehenfions of what fhall befall them,
in that future ftate of exiftence, into which
they are entering by death.   In a word, godlinefs is effectually fecured by the promife of

* 1 Cor. x. 13,

God

God from every real evil to which human
nature is incident, and that can be finally deftructive of its proper happinefs. Again,

   Godlinefs hath the promife of the prefent life,
inafmuch as it hath the affurance, that all
the *various events* of it fhall be fo *over-ruled
by the providence of God*, as to contribute to
the prefent comfort and happinefs of thofe
who follow after and practife it. In many
refpects, as to external circumftances, *all
things happen alike to all*, and the good as
well as the bad experience promifcuoufly the
different effects of profperity and adverfity;
the worthieft Chriftians being fometimes under great trials and afflictions, and others of
them in poffeffion of all the valuable advantages of the prefent ftate, juft as other men
are, who live entire ftrangers to the life
and power of godlinefs. But how great are
the advantages enfured to true piety, in
thefe various conditions, by the exprefs promife of God, in which thofe of a different
character have no intereft whatfoever! For
to thefe latter profperity is a fnare, brings
them into powerful temptations, that corrupt
and prepare them for deftruction, alienate
their hearts from God, and render them
utterly thoughtlefs of, and unprepared for
eternal falvation. And when they are in
circumftances of affliction and diftrefs, they
have no confiderations to relieve them, no
profpects to revive them, no promife of God
to take refuge in, no heart or knowledge
rightly to improve them, nor any reafon to
                                 promife

promife themfelves, that the event fhall be
comfortable and happy to them. But what
faith the promife to religious and good men?
Can there be a more comfortable affurance
than that of the Apoftle? *All things work together for good to them that love God* *. And
what pleafure may we take in the various
circumftances of life, in which providence
hath placed us, under the influence of this
bleffed perfuafion, *that neither death nor life,
nor things prefent, nor things to come, fhall be
able to feparate us from the love of God which
is in Chrift Jefus* †. So that if God fhould
pleafe to bring them into circumftances of
great profperity, it fhall not prove a fnare
and a curfe to them, and God will enable
them to ufe it with innocence and dignity,
and to improve it to the beft purpofes, the
benefit of others, and the increafe of their
final reward from God. And as to thofe
afflictions that may befall them, however
grievous they may be in fome refpects, the
intention of them is friendly, and the effect
of them fhall be beneficial, as they fhall be
rendered by them *partakers of God's holinefs*,
and prepare them *for a far more exceeding
and eternal weight of glory*. Well therefore
may *godlinefs* be faid to have *the promife of the
prefent life*, in that it hath fo kind an influence upon all the various circumftances of
our being, and fince there is nothing can
poffibly happen to us, but what God will

* Rom. viii. 28.   † 38, 39.

make

make some way or other contribute its share to our real welfare and happiness. Again,

Godliness hath the promise of this life, as it hath the *assurance* of the *constant assistance of the spirit and grace of God*, to establish and perfect it, and to aid those who love it and are partakers of it in the discharge of all the important duties of their Christain call-ing, and enable them to secure their own eternal salvation. Life is of very little im-portance, considering it only as our capacity for *animal* services, and the enjoyment of merely sensual satisfactions and pleasures. In this view, it is just upon a level with the life of brutes, and answers no more worthy and valuable ends than theirs. What ren-ders us superior to the beasts of the field, and better than the fowls of the air, is our capacity for *rational services*, our being formed for the exercises of religion, for the practice of righteousness, for usefulness in our stations, and for the exalted happiness of a future everlasting existence. And he pos-sesses life in the best manner, and hath infi-nitely the highest advantage from it, who employs it for these excellent purposes, and improves the season of it in the cultivation of his own mind, serving the most valuable interests of others, approving himself to God, the great author of his being, and *laying a good foundation against the time to come*, in order to secure the possession of eternal life. And what mighty encouragements have sincere Christians to engage them to diligence and
activity

activity in the difcharge of their duty, and the
purfuit of their happinefs, from the promifes
of God in the gofpel ? If they are confcious
to their own imperfections and weaknefs,
and find themfelves too unequal to the important fervices required of them, yet the
promife is fufficient to infpire them with refolution, *that God will work in them both to will
and to do of his own good pleafure.* If their
duty be attended with any peculiar difficulties, the promife of God will render them
fuperior to them all, *that his ftrength fhall be
made perfect in their weaknefs, and that he will
eftablifh and fettle them.* If at any time they
are under uneafy apprehenfions with refpect
to their final fafety, and afraid leaft they
fhould be perverted from the path that leads
to happinefs, and incur the forfeiture of eternal life ; their courage will revive, and their
hopes grow chearful, when they recollect
the grace of that promife, that *God will never leave them nor forfake them, but preferve
them* by his power, *through faith unto falvation.* And thefe promifes of revelation are
agreeable to the perfections and character of
God, the beft of beings, and are vouchfafed
us, for our comfort and fupport under all the
difadvantages of the prefent ftate, to affift us
in purfuing the great ends of our beings, and
render our enquiries after, and purfuit of happinefs finally fuccefsful.   And laftly,

  *Godlinefs hath the promife of the life that now
is,* as it fhall certainly prove the means of
fecuring the true poffeffion and enjoyment of it,
whilft

whilst it continues, and be a *preparation* and *introduction to the blessings of a better*. They who live in a perpetual dissipation of thought and time, who have no principles to govern them, no good dispositions to influence them, no services of reason to employ them, nor better hopes of futurity to enliven and animate them, do not live, *i. e.* do not properly enjoy life, and cannot have the highest and best relish of it. The happiness of *reasonable* beings must be derived from *reflection* and *disposition*, from right action, from the esteem of those beings with whom we are connected, and on whom we are in any manner dependent for the continuance of life, and the welfare of it. This happiness can only be secured by religion and virtue, and the promise of God gives us full certainty, that happiness shall be the certain consequence of governing ourselves by the principles and rules of them. The comprehensive blessing of human life, and that on which all the real enjoyment of it depends, is the friendship and favour of God, with which every other kind of real good is connected. And this inestimable blessing God hath assured religious persons they shall never be deprived of. *All things are yours*, saith the Apostle, *for you are Christ's and Christ is God's*; through him we are interested in God, as our reconciled God and Father; and he hath said, *I am your God, and you shall be my people*. Now the sense of the *love of God shed abroad in our hearts*, and the well grounded persuasion,

that

that we fhall never be forfaken of his goodnefs, is a circumftance of all others the moft
grateful and pleafing, and will caufe the
moments and hours of life to pafs on with a
chearfulnefs of foul, that can arife from no
other reflection whatfoever. This belief and
affurance will make follitude unfpeakably
more pleafing than all the gay affemblies
for vanity and amufements. This will fecure integrity in the conduct of all the fecular concerns of life, and that prudence in
the management of them that is neceffary to
fuccefs, and that folid comfort that flows from
them both. It adds a relifh to profperity
itfelf, when it is confidered as the effect of
divine goodnefs, and an earneft of future and
higher favours. It produces contentment in
humbler circumftances, when regarded as the
difpofal of a wife and faithful friend, who is
engaged to order all things for our benefit
and welfare. Under afflictions it produces
patience and acquiefcence in the will of
God, and thus takes away the bitternefs of
them, and prepares and opens the heart for
the confolations of God, that are not fmall.
In the laft moments of life, the apprehenfion
and perfuafion, that we ftand well with God,
and are through Chrift the objects of his favour, will fpread a chearing light *throughout
the valley of the fhadow of death*, caufe us to
pafs through it with refolution and hope,
and look forward to the end of it with joy
unfpeakable and full of glory. In a word,

C c   the

the truly religious perfon, whatever be his
fituation in life, is fitteft to have the trueft
enjoyment of it. His own principles, his
governing difpofitions, his future profpects
and his intereft in God, and the good promifes he hath given him, all confpire to
render the prefent life a blefling to him ;
for on all thefe accounts the work of
righteoufnefs fhall be peace, and the effect
of righteoufnefs quietnefs and affurance for
ever *.

From what hath been faid we may well
infer, of what unfpeakable confequence to
the happinefs of human life the *promifes of
God by revelation* are ; which fo clearly afcertains the doctrine of providence, fets it in
fo clear a view, reprefents it in fo comfortable and friendly light, and affures religious perfons of a conftant intereft in the
care of it, and all the affairs of their whole
exiftence fhall be under the direction of infinite wifdom and goodnefs, and ordered for
our prefent and future advantage. This makes
life, with all its inconveniences, a real blefling,
and is the beft ingredient that I know of in
the happinefs attending it. If I know that
providence will be my protection and guide
during the few uncertain years I am to
abide here, and that the feafon of life, well
employed and improved, will be my introduction into a more perfect and durable

* Ifaiah xxxii. 17.

one;

one ; 'tis comparatively of but fmall importance, what our external circumftances are,
or how long or fhort our duration is in this.
This knowledge we can derive only from revelation and promife, and our beft reafonings
without this aid will be uncertain and unfatisfactory. Let us therefore be thankful
for, and cordially embrace thefe promifes,
and under the influence of them be careful
to *perfect holinefs in the fear of God.*

SERMON XVI.

Glory, Honour, and Immortality, the Object of the Chriſtian's Purſuit.

ROMANS ii. 7.

To them, who by patient continuance in well doing, ſeek for Glory, and Honour, and Immortality, eternal Life.

NO man hath, properly ſpeaking, the ordering and fixing his own circum-ſtances in life; but whatever his condition may be, if he is a wiſe man, he will make the beſt of it, and improve it to the moſt valuable purpoſes he can. That all think life a bleſſing, is evident from their being ex-treamly loth to part with it, and from the care they take to preſerve and prolong it ; and there cannot be any thing more contrary to reaſon, and all the rules of true prudence, than for any one voluntarily to ſhorten the period of his own life, and thereby cut himſelf wholly off from all that happineſs, which, with a right improvement, it might be made to yield him.

If

If our preſent lives were to determine our exiſtence, and we had no future expectations whatſoever, and it was in our power to paſs the time of them with reputation, comfort and happineſs, by living as the law of our natures, and the unbiaſſed judgment of our minds ſhould direct us ; though the real importance of life would certainly leſſen, in proportion to the ſhortneſs of its duration ; yet it would certainly be a reaſon why we ſhould protract it to its utmoſt length, and guard againſt every accident that would tend to impair or deſtroy it ? for it is certainly better to be happy, for a comparatively little while, than never to be happy at all, and never permitted to have any exiſtence, throughout the whole immenſity of duration ; and therefore to be happy as long as we can, without defrauding ourſelves, by any wilful imprudence, of any part of the ſeaſon of enjoyment, that nature or providence might think fit to allow us.

But of what *infinitely greater importance* and worth is *human life*, if it is intended by the great Author of it, as an *introduction* into a more *durable* ſtate of exiſtence, and if there be in our nature ſuch an active principle, as is capable of, and form'd for an *everlaſting* duration ; of ſurviving the ruins of the body, and exiſting, exerciſing its rational powers, enjoying its reflections, and ſharing in a much ſuperior kind of happineſs than what the preſent world can afford, and that ſhall be commenſurate with eternity itſelf ? How highly would this illuſtrate and recommend

the

the benevolence and grace of the Almighty Creator; if his own great view, in calling us into being, fhould be our finally fharing *eternal life*; and if he hath made it the one great bufinefs of our tranfitory continuance here, to feek for a glorious and bleffed immortality, hath by his *own promifes*, excited and encouraged this bleffed hope, and given us the cleareft and fureft *directions* how we may finally obtain it. If thofe reafonable fpirits that are within us have no principle of corruption and diffolution in them, the diffolution of the body cannot at leaft affect their exiftence; they may, and they muft live, when the tabernacles they now inhabit fhall be levelled with the duft, and continue to exift 'till the great Father of them by his infinite power fhall think proper to annihilate them. But as there is nothing in reafon to juftify fuch a fuppofition, I think the conclufion, from God's having created the fpirits of men for an immortal duration, is certain and indifputable, that his *original intention* in thus forming them, was their obtaining immortal happinefs. And indeed, I fhould fooner believe, that men were produced by fatality or chance, though nothing can be more abfurd than fuch a fuppofition, than that they were made by an infinitely wife and good Being, with the original view to their being neceffarily and eternally miferable; becaufe I cannot difcern either the wifdom or goodnefs of fuch a difpenfation.

And we may, I think, learn with the greateft certainty what the *original end of creation* was,

by

by confidering what was the certain and avowed *end of God's sending his Son into the world,*
which was *not to condemn it, but that the world
through him might be saved* ; not becaufe he had
appointed mankind to wrath, but from the
determined purpofe of his goodnefs, that *all*
who would believe and obey the gofpel fhould
obtain redemption by him : For thefe two
great works of God cannot be repugnant to
each other, but muft neceffarily coincide with
and be fubfervient to one another, in the
fcheme of God's moral providence and government. But as no two purpofes can be
more inconfiftent with and oppofite to one
another, than thofe of *deftruction* and *redemption* ; it appears to me felf evident, that as
benevolence was the great motive in the divine mind to call mankind into being, and
mercy the all powerful motive that formed
and executed the plan of their redemption,
the original intention of *creation* muft be *happinefs,* and the capacity for happinefs granted,
not cruelly to difappoint, but with a god-like
generofity to oblige and fatisfy it, becaufe it
certainly is the end of redemption.

The *feeking after eternal life* is reprefented
by our Apoftle as what fhould be the great
view of *mankind in general* ; for he tells us,
*that God will render to every man according to
his deeds ; to them who by a patient continuance
in well doing feek for glory, honour, and immortality, eternal life.* Now if it be every man's
duty to do well, and continue patient in well
doing, it is by this doctrine of the Apoftle,

equally

equally his duty to feek after that glory, honour, and immortality, which God hath determined fhall be the final reward of it.   But
it can be no man's duty to *feek after glory,
honour and immortality,* if it be what he can
never poffibly obtain ; and therefore not any
man's duty *to continue patient in well doing,* who
is unavoidably cut off from all fhare in the
recompence attending it.   If he is to feek for
eternal life by conftancy in good works, it
can be no more impoffible for him to obtain
eternal life, than to abound conftantly in good
works, and if God expects that he fhould feek
after it, it is a demonftration that God is ready
to give eternal life, and will finally beftow it to
all, who by a fteady perfeverance in Chriftian
piety and virtue render themfelves capable of
obtaining it.   Oh ! how great and excellent
is the Chriftian vocation ! How high and dig-
nifying the work of life ! What can be a
nobler purfuit than immortal glory and honour ! What more worthy and rational method of purfuing, than by ftedfaftnefs and perfeverance in well doing ! Let us here confider
thefe two things,

    I. What *that glory, honour, and immortality*
        are, which are propofed to us, as the
        great object we are to purfue ; and
    II. What *the feeking after them* implies.

    I. Thefe words reprefent to us, in a very
pleafing view, the *important bufinefs* of human
life, that every man fhould be perpetually
employed in, and to which he ought to make
                            his

his whole conduct subservient. 'Tis nothing less than *glory, honour and immortality*. Creation was not the work of humour and caprice, nor of a sudden, accidental dictate of unpremeditating benevolence ; but of mature counsel, directed by infinite wisdom, and intended for the best and noblest purposes. The desire of life, in living, rational beings, is inserted by the God of nature into our frames, and we cannot extinguish it if we would ; and the belief of a future state so naturally arises out of the due exercise of our reason, and is so connected with the belief of a God and his providence, as that it hath universally obtained in all ages, and men find it impossible ever wholly to get rid of it, but either by stupifying their minds and consciences through the excess of vice ; or by endeavouring to persuade themselves that there is no God, which is the excess of folly ; or by denying the exercise and inspection of providence, which is the greatest absurdity, upon the supposition of the real existence of an infinitely wise and gracious God. And if this belief of a future state be so natural to the mind, and thus arises out of the inward convictions of their reason, and their discerned connections with the great Author of nature ; is it not a real proof that he intended men should form this belief, and be led into it by a right and impartial use of their reasonable powers and faculties ? And after all is this belief a false persuasion, when it thus arises out of truth ? Are our best reasonings all fallacious ? Wherein then can we

ever

ever truft them ? Or hath God deceived us, and given us reafon and judgment only more effectually to impofe on us, and neceffarily to conftrain us to believe what after all our beft convictions there really is not any foundation for believing ? This appears to me to be a moft unworthy fentiment of God, and fo difhonourable to his perfections and character, as that it is impoffible I fhould ever be per-fuaded to receive it.

Befides, let it be confider'd, who are the perfons that in all ages have thrown off the belief of a future ftate, or rather endeavoured to perfuade themfelves that there is none ; and they will generally be found to be fuch, whofe characters procure lide credit to their opi-nions, and who give no reafon to fufpect a very rigid impartiality in their reafonings con-cerning them. It will not be an invidious re-flection to fay, that not one of them can have any fentiments or real fenfe of religion, and that far the greateft part of them are men of liberty and pleafure, to whom the belief of a future ftate is not very pleafing or favourable, who are too much under the power of in-clination to weigh in an equal ballance reafons that would lead them into a perfuafion of the truth of undefirable principles ; the belief of which would either make them uneafy in their methods of life, or force them to forfake thofe practices, from which they do not fo much as wifh to be reformed. Now when men of this caft and character ridicule, or indulge to fcepticifm about a future ftate,

or

or take upon them to deny it, and the great events that are to take place in it, respectively according to the difference of men's actions ; their very characters discredit their sentiments, and shew they are the result, not of maturer judgment, but of an irrational biass, and a real prejudice against truth and righteousness ; or, in a word, unbelievers through conveniency and choice. On the contrary, the higher men's sentiments are of God, the more firm their belief of his providence, the more seriously they worship him, and the greater friends they are to the practice of universal righteousness and virtue, the more disposed they are to the belief of a future state, and the more certain and pleasing their expectations of happiness in it. 'Tis one of the first principles with them, that God is a rewarder of them that diligently seek him, and they cannot help connecting piety and virtue with the hope of a recompence from him. Now whence is this connection ? Doth it not arise from the nature of God, and the most certain nature of things ? Is it not therefore a connection made by God himself, as he hath so formed us, as that we cannot help seeing and rejoicing in it.

The conclusions of infidelity and vice are often seen in the most convincing manner to be groundless and false, when the charm of pleasure is broken, and the amusements and deceits of folly forsake them, and the intervals of sober and calm reflection come in

the

the room of them. But fo far is the belief of a future ftate, and a bleffed immortality from deferting or appearing falfe or precari- ous to fincerely religious and virtuous men, that in thefe very feafons and intervals, when infidelity fneaks away from the heart, fcourged out of it by the furies of remorfe and ter- ror, and the vices that occafioned it become the abhorrence of thofe who practifed them ; this belief frequently rifes into the fulleft affurance, and their profpect of a bleffed re- compence from God becomes more certain and delightful. Tell me then ye fons of vice, whence comes this mighty change in your convictions and principles frequently at the clofe of life ? Or whence is it, that you become as thorough believers, in fpite of yourfelves, as thofe you have ridiculed for fu- perftition and credulity ; and believers too, without dignity, unwillingly, and utterly de- void of comfort ? Why do ye not always die as firm unbelievers as you have lived, and make the bold trial of eternity with an un- daunted courage, and an intrepid contempt of every thing that may happen in it ? Alas ! for them, confcience recoils, reafon forbids it, contrary probability ftares them in the face, and even full conviction of its folly and madnefs is the dreadful cure of all their un- belief. But whoever faw or heard of an ha- bitually religious and good man turn unbe- liever, when he came to die ? Did fuch a one ever repent of his piety to God, the virtues he hath practiced, or the good works

he

he hath been enabled to abound in ? Did he
ever grow pale at the conſciouſneſs of having
been juſt and chaſte and temperate, benevolent and kind and merciful ? Or ſtart back at
the thoughts of death, at the remembrance
of having maintained *a conſcience void of offence
towards God and man* ? Or renounce his hopes
as vain and criminal, or die convinced that he
lived a fool, by living under the influence
of faith and reaſon ? Whence is it, that no
one inſtance of this ſhould ever happen ? It
cannot be from any real rational convictions,
that there is any truth in the principles of
religion, or the doctrine of a world of future
recompence ; if, as unbelievers and libertines
would endeavour to perſuade us, all theſe notions are founded only in imagination, childiſh
prepoſſeſſions, miſtaken education, and the
glooms of melancholy and enthuſiaſm. If
this be the caſe, it may be as reaſonably expected, that believers ſhould at leaſt ſometimes
turn infidels, religious men deride their own
practice as ridiculous and ſuperſtitious, and
virtuous men laugh at the diſtinction between
good and evil, in the cloſe of life, and when
they are going out of being, as they imagine,
into non-exiſtence ; as that ſcepticks ſhould
turn believers *, profligates ſhould curſe their
former follies, and hardened ſinners relent,
profeſs their repentance, and promiſe amend-
ment, if they recover from the danger that

* Sed. Vid. Plutar. vit. Bruti et Flor. l. 4. c. 7. circa finem.
Plutar. de Superſtit. p. 165. a Dion. Caſſ. p. 47. § 49. fin. 36.

threatens

threatens them. This latter cafe frequently happens.; the former never ; and the reafon is evident, becaufe infidelity is generally the hafty unripened conclufion of felf-prejudice, of corrupt inclination, and the habitual love of vice ; made in a fort neceffary for vindicating themfelves to their own confciences, or to ftifle and extinguifh the painful reproaches and remonftrances of them. And therefore the profpect of death, which fhews them clearly to themfelves, introduces reafon in the room of paffion, awakens confcience to give its impartial teftimony, and makes men weigh things, not in the deceitful ballance of inclination, but of fober, cool and deliberate judgment ; which ftrips vice of its delufive and enfnaring drefs, and reprefents it in all its native and genuine deformity, and makes them, in fpite of their own wifhes, apprehenfive that there is a fomething to come, for which they know they are but ill prepared, after they go down to the grave ; I fay the profpect of death, when the enchantments of pleafure are now no more, and the delufions of fin can no longer impofe on them, forces them to renounce their former fcepticifm, to confefs the truth of the principles they once derided, and turn cowardly penitents, through the dreadful, but juft fears of a future damnation. Whereas virtuous and good men, who embraced the principles of religion and morality through rational conviction, without fuffering inclination and the love of vice, to bribe them againft truth and righteoufnefs,

righteoufnefs, and who through the influence of their principles have *lived foberly, righteoufly and godly in the prefent world,* can never change their principles in the laft period of life, from any conviction that they have embraced them upon any dishonourable and fenfual motives, nor ever repent for a fingle moment, that they have purified their hearts, and preferved themfelves free from the corruptions of the world, by their obedience to the truth, but die as they have lived firm believers, and rejoice that as they have *fought after glory, honour, and immortality, they shall obtain eternal life.*

. The words we render *glory and honour* are joined together by the beft writers, and though there is a great fimilitude of meaning in them, yet it is very far from being exactly the fame *. The firft denotes the good efteem and reputation that any man hath with others, upon account of any real or fuppofed excellencies he is poffeffed of, or any peculiar priviledges or diftinguifhing favours conferred on him, the original word frequently denoting opinion, and from thence by an eafy figure that reputation, refpect and praife, which follows, from the good opinion of others. Thus it is faid of fome of the *chief rulers* of the Jews, *that they believed in Chrift, but becaufe of the Pharifees did not confefs him, leaft they should be put out of the Synagogue ; becaufe they loved the praife of men more than the praife of God* †. *i. e.* good efteem and applaufe of men more than the com-

---

* δ.ξα.   † John xii. 43.

mendation of God.   The other word *, we render honour, properly denotes thofe marks of favour, that are beftowed by others, efpecially by a fuperior, either as the reward of another's merit, or to teftify a peculiar regard and affection to him, and thereby to elevate him above the common rank, and place him in circumftances of diftinguifhed dignity. Thus, *a prophet hath no honour in his own country* †.   They will not give him the facred title, nor the efteem and reverence that is due to it; and our Lord tells his Apoftles : *If any man ferve me, him will my father honour* ‡; advance him to a ftate of the higheft dignity, and diftinguifh him by the peculiar favours beftcwed on him.   So that the great employment and comprehenfive fervice of a Chriftian, as fuch, is to purfue the higheft reputation, and the moft durable and fubftantial honour.

1. He is to feek after *glory*, and peculiarly *that glory which comes from God*; that praife and commendation which he beftows on all thofe who approve themfelves to him, by always doing the things that pleafe him. There is a kind of natural inftinct in men, that powerfully leads them to wifh the good opinion, and defire to be efteemed and well fpoken of by others.   Even virtuous minds cannot diveft themfelves of the love of praife, and no man can help feeling a very fenfible pleafure from the cordial commendation of

---

* τιμη   † John iv. 44.   ‡ xii. 26.

thofe

thofe he loves and honours, and every wife and good man will endeavour by a right behaviour, firſt to deferve, and then fecure it; and he who cares not what the world fays of him, hath put off decency, and forfeited the common civilities of mankind. This good opinion of others will be proportionably more valuable, according to their fuperior characters and ranks, their diftinguifhing titles, their ſtations of honour, and efpecially their moral qualifications and endowments, fanctity of behaviour, fhining abilities, and amiable difpofitions and affections. And therefore the commendation and praife that comes from God is of all others the moſt defirable, as it is not the effect of partiality and prejudice, hath nothing of affectation and flattery in it, nor is given upon a miftaken opinion of the character of thofe who are the objects of it; but is founded in truth, upon the poffeffion of fome real excellency, fomewhat that is truly praifeworthy, and eftimable in the infallible opinion and judgment that he forms of perfons and things; and whofe praife therefore is not like the fickle, unmeaning applaufes and miftaken commendations of ignorant or deceitful men, that often mean nothing, and are no proof of any real excellency, or commendable quality in the perfons on whom they are beftowed, but is given by him as his teftimony to real worth, and renders the perfons who receive it worthy the affection, efteem, friendfhip and honour of the whole reafonable creation. This, Sirs, is a *blessing worth your pursuing.* You can live for nothing greater or better.   Secure this, and you have all that heaven and earth can bestow.   *The praise of God* is of infinitely more value than all the treasures of the universe, and will add a greater sanctity, lustre, and dignity to their characters, than should angels and men, and thewhole creation join in the applauses they give you ; *for not he who commendeth himself, or is commended by others is approved, but he who the Lord commendeth* *.   The *characters* of thefe are expreſſly *declared in Scripture,* and if we can obferve them *in ourſelves,* with what pleafure, with what thankfulneſs to the grace and mercy of God, ſhould we reflect on our happy condition, in that amidſt all the imperfections that accompany us, yet we are in our prevailing temper and character of the number of thofe *excellent ones of the earth, in whom he delights,* whom his countenance *beholds with pleaſure,* whom he hath fet apart for himfelf, whom he approves by the voice of revelation, and who ſhall finally receive his commendation, in the moſt authentick, publick and honourable manner. *For there is a day approaching, when God by Jeſus Chriſt,* will folemnly, and in the view of the whole rational creation, *pronounce* every fincere and faithful Chriſtian, *acquitted* from every charge againſt him, publickly *declare him a good and faithful fervant, and command him to enter into his maſter's joy.* Thus

* 2 Cor. x. 18.

ſhall

shall it be done to those, whom God delights to honour. Who would not wish to be of that diftinguished number ! Who would not be glad thus to have his fidelity acknowledged ! What mufick will that *well done* of the Son of God, be in thine ears, Christian, if thou shalt hear it fpoken to thyself ! Sweeter than the melody that the moft exquifite ftrains of earthly fkill can form, or the harmony of the heavenly choir of angels themfelves can poffibly entertain thee with. Oh ! feek after this glory, and God by Chrift will hereafter beftow it on thee. And this is the more valuable, as,

2. This commendation of God hath *the higheft priviledges and honours attending it.* Mere commendation hath little fubftantial in it, and praife that hath nothing valuable attending it, is but an infignificant breath, that minifters but little to the true enjoyment and dignity of life. It is but thin food, and though it may give a momentary pleafure, foon leaves us empty and unfatisfied. The *praife that comes from God* is not only *highly honourable* in its nature, but its *confequences* the moft truly *glorious*, and worthy to awaken and animate the warmeft ambition of our minds. There is nothing efteemed amongft the fons of men more than conqueft and victory. Thofe whom God approves fhall obtain the moft difficult and glorious *victory* of all others. They not only conquer themfelves, their criminal paffions and affections, and the corruptions and temptations of the finful world in which they

dwell,

dwell, and of the powers of darknefs, who
have in every age fubdued and enflaved fo
great a part of mankind to their ufurped and
lawlefs dominions ; but what is more, they
fhall *triumph over death and the grave*, from
which the heathen world imagined there was
no poffible redemption, and the conqueft of
which nothing can fecure us, but the power
and grace of God in the gofpel of Chrift
Jefus. To trample this enemy under our
feet will be a victory indeed, in which we
may juftly boaft. This will render us in the
literal fenfe *more than conquerors*, infinitely fuperior to all the boafted heroes of the earth,
who after they have won battles, and fubdued
kingdoms, and obtained the moft fplendid triumphs, have yielded up their laurels, and
become captives to the irrefiftible power of the
common enemy and deftroyer of mankind.
In confequence of this victory over death,
how rich will be the *crown* that fhall incircle
them, the *crown of glory, life, and righteoufnefs*, and how bright the robes of victory,
with which God fhall cloath them ; when
this *mortal fhall put on immortality, this corruptible fhall put on incorruption, when we fhall be
equal to angels* in our external appearance, by
being formed into the moft perfect *refemblance
of the Son of God* himfelf, and thus fitted to
enter into the manfions of fupream blefled-
nefs and glory. For this is a farther circumftance of honour, that we fhould keep in
conftant view, and diligently endeavour to
purfue ; *an admiffion* into that blefled world,
which

which is the *peculiar habitation of* God himfelf, where the Saviour of mankind *fits inthroned at the right hand of God* his Father, where all the flower of the creation, angels and arch-angels, thrones and dominions, principalities and powers, have their everlafting dwelling, and enjoy eternal felicity, in the prefence and full enjoyment of him, who is the true fountain of honour, and whofe favour is the fource of uninterrupted and incorruptible bleffednefs. To be admitted as affociates with them in their celeftial enjoyments and fervices, how ineftimable the priviledge, how high the honour! 'Tis to this, Chriftians, you are to afpire. 'Tis this you are to make the object of your perpetual purfuit; and could any defcription of mine help to awaken and fix your ambition to fecure this heavenly glory and honour, how happy will be your condition, and with what joy unfpeakable fhall we meet together in the day of Chrift ! And what compleats the whole, is

3. That the great object of our purfuit is *immortality*, as well as *glory* and *honour*, i. e. this glory and honour that we are to aim at is *incorruptible* and *immortal.* The original word denotes incorruptibility, or what will never corrupt and decay ; is not liable to fade and perifh. For this is the invaluable difcovery, that hath been made us by the doctrine and mediation of Chrift, *who hath brought life and immortality*, i. e. *immortal life to light by his gofpel*, and affured all his faithful difciples,

D d 3   by

by the moſt exprefs promiſes from God his Father, that it ſhall be finally conferred upon them. *My ſheep,* ſays he, *hear my voice, and I know them, and they follow me, and I give unto them eternal life, and they ſhall never periſh, neither ſhall any pluck them out of my hand. My Father who gave them me is greater than all, and none is able to pluck them out of my Father's hand* *.

This is the mortifying circumſtance which lowers the value of all earthly good things, that they are frail, uncertain and periſhing. What is *life* itſelf ? How comparatively ſhort in its longeſt duration ? How ſoon liable to be cut off ? How certainly will the hour come, that puts an everlaſting period to it ? How little are *health* and *ſtrength* to be depended on ? How ſoon weakened by diſtemper, or impaired and waſted by increaſe of years ? How frail a flower is *beauty* ? Of little more ſtability than the painted bubble that dies away almoſt as ſoon as it riſes, that wanes by a ſickly blaſt, or envious beam, that often changes into deformity by a cruel diſeaſe, the bloom of which is every day, though imperceptibly for ſome time, wearing off, and that frequently entirely departs, without leaving any traces, by which the remembrance of it may be preſerved. Our *riches,* how often do they treacherouſly deſert their envied poſſeſſors ! *Moth and ruſt corrupt them, and thieves break through* and plunder them. *Fame* and

* John x. 27, 29.

glory,

glory, how thin and empty is the foundation that fupports them, fickle as opinion, various as fancy, capricious as humour, unfubftantial as a vapour, that droops at the breath of calumny, that dies away with change of fortune, that a fingle imprudence often blafts, and that is much oftener uttterly deftroyed by the malignity and treacherous practices of reftlefs envy, impatient difappointment, and implacable malice. Even earthly *majefty* itfelf hath the fame marks of inftability and corruption engraven on it, that all other worldly perfection hath, the crown will fooner or later drop from the wearer's head, the fcepter fall from his hand, his titles be tranf-ferred to another, and all the pomp of human grandeur be levelled with the grave. So true is that divine admonition of the infpired writer : *All flesh is as grafs, and all the glory of man as the flower of the grafs. The grafs withers, and the flower thereof fadeth away* * ; but, O glorious confolation ! *the word of the Lord endureth forever ;* the *promifes* of God by Chrift are *yea and amen ;* abfolute in their grant, and infallibly certain in their performance. The great promife of the gofpel *is eternal life,* and that life endowed with incorruptible glory and honour. The approbation that God will beftow, will be a *permanent* blefling, and *immutable* as his love of righteoufnefs and truth, that can never decay in the importance and worth of it, will cloath

* 1 Pet. i. 24, 25.

D d 4

us with a dignity that can never ceafe, that will render us unchangeably refpectable amongft all the orders of the heavenly hierarchy, and the infinitely valuable effects of which will be lafting as eternity.   For

The honours conferred in confequence of this final praife that comes from God, are not only the moft valuable, but *permanent* in their nature.   The fplendor of our celeftial bodies, when once invefted therewith, fhall be *incorruptible* and *immortal ; our dwelling eternal in the heavens* ; our accefs to God ever free and open ; our conformity to him perfect and immutable ; his nobleft image upon our nature fixed and indelible, and the luftre of that *crown of righteoufnefs* and life, *which the Lord, the righteous Judge, fhall give to fuch as love him*, at the fecond appearance of the Lord Jefus Chrift, fuch as *fhall never fade away.* 'Tis a very pleafing account St. Paul hath given us of this important truth, in that paffage, where comparing the Chriftian life to a race, he fays, *Know ye not that they who run in a race, run all, but that one only receiveth the prize* * ; viz. he who outftrips the other, and comes firft to the gaol that is before him.   *So run you*, adds he, *that you may obtain.   Now they do it to obtain a corruptible crown, but we an incorruptible one ; fo we run, not as uncertainly,* whether we fhall ever get the prize, but fure of receiving it, if we run *lawfully*, i. e. with patience and perfeverance,

---

* 1 Cor. ix. 24, 25.

for how many foever there are who run this race, *none* of their labour *shall be in vain in the Lord*, but the crown of life and glory be diftributed equally to them all. Such is the infinite liberality, and the diffufive bounty of God, the great Inftitutor and Lord of the Chriftian race, that he holds out to every one of us the incorruptible crown, bids us feize on the glorious prize, bear it off in triumph, and wear it as our own forever. Well may the Chriftian ftand aftonifhed at this amazing offer and promife of the grace of God, and cry out in the furprize of his foul : *Immortal life and glory for me !* For me, who am but of *yefterday*, and taken out of the duft ! For me, who am a *finful* creature, and have forfeited the prefent life, and all the happinefs of it ? Shall I awake out of the duft, triumph over death, rife in my Saviour's image, and fhare in all the joys and glories of eternity ! Yes, this is the affurance of him, who can beftow this bleffednefs, and whofe goodnefs is infinite and will finally vouchfafe it. *O the riches of the grace of God !* How undeferved, how free, how large and permanent the effects of it !

But it muft be *won* before it can be *worn*. *Glory, honour, and immortality* are too valuable bleffings to be beftowed, where men throw contempt on the offer of them, value other things in preference to them, and will not ufe the proper methods to obtain them. They will never be had without *diligently feeking them*. We muft *feek after glory and honour,*

and

and immortality, by conflancy in good works, if
we would finally inherit *eternal life.* And
furely,

The *importance* and *worth* of them deferve
to be the frequent fubject of our moft *ferious
confideration.* It is one great excellency of
the Chriftian doctrine, that it raifes the minds
of men above all fenfible and terreftial objects, elevates them to the contemplation of
future invifible realities, tranfports them into
eternity itfelf, and makes them, even in the
prefent life, in fome of the moft pleafing
hours and feafons of it, the inhabitants of
the celeftial world, converfant with fuperior
fpirits, and fhares with them in their higheft
fervices and enjoyments; yea even caufes them
to approach the eternal God, and prefents to
their view the glorified Redeemer in all the
majefty of the Son of God, and all the grace
of the Redeemer of mankind, and their benevolent Interceffor and Advocate at his Father's right hand. In thefe things we are
nearly interefted, and as 'tis an inftance of
high impiety not to have God in all our
thoughts, fo it is of the moft criminal negligence and folly never to think of that future world, for which we are evidently made,
nor of that better life, and more glorious condition, into which the future ftate will introduce all who believe and obey the gofpel.
Every one fees it impoffible to feek after what
never engages our thoughts, and what therefore never can be the object of our view. If
immortal bleffednefs be indeed the great end
we

we aim at, it will certainly employ some of our most serious moments, and we shall never suffer, either the interests of the present life, or the love of pleasure, perpetually to exclude all that concern about it, which its infinite importance deserves, as though we did not at all believe the reality of it, or esteemed it of less value, than the transitory enjoyments of the present life. Indeed if we would weigh things impartially in the balance of reason and truth, the incorruptible glory and blessedness of the heavenly world, as described and promised by the gospel revelation, is of that infinite superior worth in itself, and consequence to us, as that every thing that can be named of temporal prosperity and glory will appear to be as nothing, yea less than nothing and vanity. Strange, that every trifle should have a share in our thoughts, and immortal life and happiness so seldom be admitted into them, and make no more lasting and pleasing impression upon us ! Hardly can he be said *to seek after glory, honour, and immortality,* who is wholly engrossed by other views, and hath no inclination or heart to consider the mighty sum of happiness they include, and by what means they may be most effectually secured.

If we in good earnest set ourselves to pursue this immortal glory and blessedness, it will be the object of *our high esteem,* we shall value it in proportion to its worth, and *set our affections on it,* as the one great comprehensive blessing of our being. It will excite

our

our warmeft defires of obtaining it, and fill
us with the ftrongeft ambition of being finally
accounted worthy to receive it. This is the
advice of the Apoftie. *If ye then be rifen with
Chrift, feek thofe things which are above, where
Chrift fitteth at the right hand of God. Set
your affections on things above, and not on things
on the earth* *. And when he writes to the Co-
rinthians to comfort them under their fufferings for Chrift, and to direct them from
whence they muft derive the fupports they
wanted, he informed them, it muft be by
habitually *looking, not at the things which are
feen, which are temporal, but at thofe which are
not feen, which are eternal* †. And indeed the
more converfant we are with the promifes of
the gofpel, the more we enter by faith and
meditation into the nature and circumftances
of the happinefs and glory that fhall hereafter be revealed, the more will it appear to
deferve our preference, above every thing elfe
that can come in competition with it, the
more ardent will be the defires of our hearts
after it, and the ftronger our ambition finally
to fecure it. If thou haft a generous mind,
I know that the commendation and praife of
the impartial and good, when attended with
the inward confcioufnefs of having done well,
and deferved their efteem and friendfhip, muft
give thee a pleafure, the moft grateful in its
nature, and that will greatly heighthen the
relifh and enjoyment of life. But now re-

* Colof. iii. 1, 2.   † 2 Cor. iv. 18.

fle&t

flect but for a moment ; if thou art a lover
of praise, and that thou mayeft be without
vanity or guilt, the praife that comes from the
greateft and beft, and that hath the moft
folid advantages connected with it, muft be
the moft defirable. Could'ft thou obtain the
commendation of God, fhould he by an au-
dible voice diftinguifh thee, and declare thee
to the reft of the world ; this is the man that
I approve and honour, and own as my friend
and favourite ; with what dignity of character
would it cloath thee ! What refpect would it
conciliate from the world ! How truly venerable and facred would it render thee !
Why, this is the very honour that awaits thee
as a Chriftian. Before a grander affembly
than the whole earth can form, thou fhalt be
pronounced by the mouth of the Son of God,
before angels and men, *a good and faithful
fervant,* be diftinguifhed as fuch by the rewards of heavenly life and glory, and be put
into the full poffeffion of an *incorruptible and
unfading inheritance.* Oh what joy will tranf-
port the heart at this awful tranfaction ! How
will the fons of light congratulate thee, on
the teftimony of God himfelf to thy integrity
and fidelity ! How will thy fellow faints rejoice with thee, in thus mutually fharing the
commendation of your God and Father !
With what fatisfaction will the benevolent
Saviour conclude the folemnity of the univerfal judgment, when from his high tribunal
he fhall thus determine your everlafting ftate :
Come, ye bleffed of my Father, inherit the kingdom
prepared

prepared for you from the foundation of the world.
Here is the hope, this the ambition of the
faints of God, that fhould continually poffefs and influence them. If our affections are
thus engaged, I fhall only add :

That the final obtaining this immortal
glory and honour will be regarded by us, as
the *great end of life,* and all our actions will
be made fubfervient to this, as the firft and
higheft intereft of our beings. The feeking
after this immortal bleffednefs doth indeed by
no means imply that we are never to think of
any thing elfe but this, or that we are to
grow negligent of and indifferent to all the
interefts of the prefent life, and have no
refpect to things vifible and temporary, the
more effectually to fecure things invifible and
eternal. Superftition may teach this, but true
religion never can, and the gofpel of Chrift
no where doth. A reclufe may poffibly be a
good man, but then his goodnefs will be as
unprofitable to men, as it is to God, and
therefore be in proportion of lefs value and
confequence to himfelf, becaufe his very
faith wants one thing effential to recommend
it, as it doth not, and cannot *work by love,*
and his piety, if he hath any, doth not fo
fhine before men, as to excite them *to glorify
our Father who is in heaven.* Such is the goodnefs of God, that he allows us to be wife for
ourfelves in time as well as eternity, and we
may be feeking after immortal glory and bleffednefs, even whilft we are properly in queft
of the comforts and conveniences of the prefent

sent state. He who is travelling may be very diligently pursuing his journey, even when he doth not actually think where he is going, but is taken up with the objects of the road through which he passeth ; and may have one principal design he is habitually carrying on, though many intermediate affairs may happen, which require some degree of attention and care. A wise and prudent man will always prefer his true interest to all others, and a sincere Christian, whatever are his engagements in the present state, will never forget those which relate to a better. He will in general never pursue the advantages of time by such measures, as will incur the forfeiture of the blessings of eternity ; and if these two interests should at any time interfere, he will drop the lesser, and pursue that which is the most worthy his regard, and will best reward it. He fixes this as the governing principle of his conduct, that as God hath graciously offered immortal glory and blessedness, he will at all hazards secure the possession of it, and loose every thing rather than be deprived of it. And therefore he will *transact all the affairs* he is concerned in here, so *regulate his pleasures,* as to the nature of them, and the manner of indulging them, and so comply with the customs and practices of the world he lives in, as *not to prejudice* his hopes of, and title to the nobler services and enjoyments of an *happier and better world.* And being firmly persuaded, that *he who walketh uprightly walketh surely,* and that
the

the path of true religion and virtue, is the only path that leads to life and happineſs, he is determined ever to purſue his nobleſt hopes *by a patient continuance in well doing ;* knowing from the reaſon of things, and the conſtitution of God by Chriſt, that if he *gives all diligence to add to his faith virtue, to virtue knowledge, to knowledge temperance, to temperance patience, to patience godlineſs, to godlineſs brotherly kindneſs, and to brotherly kindneſs charity ;* he ſhall contract the beſt meetneſs for that incorruptible happineſs he cheriſhes the hopes of, and at laſt *have an entrance adminiſtered to him abundantly into the everlaſting kingdom of our Lord and Saviour Jeſus Chriſt.* But this immediately leads me to the ſecond general, of which in the next diſcourſe.

SERMON

SERMON XVII.

A Patient Continuance in well doing explained.

ROMANS ii. 7.

To them, who by patient continuance in well doing seek for Glory, and Honour, and Immortality, eternal Life.

OH how happy is it for men, that they are sure to obtain eternal life by seeking it ! How tempting is the object that invites our pursuit ! How pleasing and honourable the means to be employed in order to our obtaining this invaluable blessing ! How worthy of God to ordain ! How suitable to our nature and condition diligently to improve ! It must be sought after, and will certainly be secured by a patient continuance in well doing. I shall therefore now proceed

To consider the second general head of discourse from these words ; or how this invaluable prize of glory, honour, and immortality is to be pursued and finally secured ; viz. *We shall seek it by a patient continuance in well doing* ; or as the words would have been

better, and more nearly to the original rendered ; *the perfevering practice of every good work* ;
or as others think ; through the patience or
perfeverance of the good work. Agreeably to
this verfion, they explain this *good work of
faith*, which our blefled Lord calls the *work
of God*, and which is fometimes called the
work of the Lord, and *the work of Chrift*. And
thus the fenfe will be ; that to them, who by
patience and perfeverance in the faith of
Chrift, feek for glory, honour, and immortality, God will give eternal life. And this
contains a very juft and important truth ; for
patience and perfeverance in the faith of
Chrift, implies *fidelity* and *conftancy* in our
Chriftian profeffion, by ftedfaftly *adhering to
the truths* of his gofpel, and under the influence of our Chriftian principles, *habitually
practifing all the virtues and important duties*,
that are peculiar and effential to the Chriftian
life. But though there be no objection againft
this doctrine, yet it doth not appear to be
the real fenfe of the place ; for there is no
inftance in which *faith* is ftiled thus defcrip-
tively *the good work*, and when we read of *the
work of faith*, it doth not mean faith, as
wrought in us by the power of God, but thofe
good effects, which faith works or produces, where-
ever it is genuine and influential. Thus St.
Paul tells the Thefialonians, *that he remembered without ceafing their work of faith and labour of love* * ; i. e. that good effect which

* 1 Thef. i. 3.

their

their faith produced, and that diligence in
doing good to which their affection excited
them ; or as the Apoſtle expreſſes it to the
Galatians : *Faith which worketh by love* *.
And that by perſeverance of the good work
in my text, he means, as our tranſlators have,
with great propriety rendered it, *patient continuance*, or ſteady perſeverance *in well doing*,
is evident by his *oppoſing* it to *diſobedience to
the truth*, and *obeying unrighteouſneſs*, and *working evil* ; and aſſuring us, *that God will render
glory, honour, and peace to every man that worketh
good* †. So that the doctrine of my text is
this : That the approbation of God, and the
honours of the heavenly ſtate, and the everlaſting continuance of both, are to be purſued
and finally ſecured by *an habitual courſe of
good works*, or by a ſteady perſeverance,
throughout the whole of life in all Chriſtian
piety and virtue. Let it be obſerved here

1. That the *good works* here ſpoken of, include the *whole of our Chriſtian practice and
duty*, and comprehend in them all the inſtances of piety to God, all the obligations
of juſtice, equity, and goodneſs to others, the
regulation and government of all our paſſions
and affections, diſcovered by a perpetual temperance, ſobriety and moderation in the management of ourſelves ; *whatever things are
true, venerable, juſt, pure, lovely, reputable, virtuous, and praiſe worthy. Theſe are the things,*
which as Chriſtians, we are *to think of,*

approve and do, if we would have the blessing and presence of the God of peace with us.

The gospel of Christ is not only a system of *doctrines*, but of *good morals* too ; it not only contains a charter of priviledges, but a code of laws, and a directory of duty ; not only sets before us *exceeding great and precious promises*, but the *commands* of God, and the precepts of *universal righteousness* ; never recommends *faith* to the exclusion of *good works*, but as the very *root* that produces, cherishes, and perpetuates them. And to shew of what importance they are in Christianity, the Christian blessedness is frequently represented in the sacred writings, under the notion of a *recompence* and reward, which necessarily supposes somewhat *done by us*, as the object of the reward ; *viz.* our fidelity to God and Christ, by a persevering belief of and obedience to the gospel. Hence our life and duty as Christians is compared to a race, and we are exhorted *to run, so as that we may obtain* ; because as in this ancient exercise or game, perseverance in running was necessary to obtain the prize, so it is with respect to the Christian life ; we must *continue*, with an unbating vigour and resolution, in that way of religion and virtue, duty and obedience to God, which the gospel chalks out to us, if we would finally *lay hold of eternal life*, which is the inestimable *prize of our high calling of God in Christ*. This is what the Apostle calls *our meetness for the inheritance of the saints in light*,

our

our direct and immediate preparation for and, title to the Christian reward. This is the doctrine of our blessed Lord, and his Apostles. *He that heareth*, i. e. obeys my word, *and believes on him that sent me, hath everlasting life, and shall not come into condemnation* * ; in which words he puts faith and practice on the same foundation, and makes them equally necessary to salvation. And he tells his disciples : *Hereby is my Father glorified, that ye bear much fruits ; so shall ye be my disciples* †. And St. *Paul* in the close of his discourse concerning the resurrection, exhorts us : *Be ye stedfast, immoveable, and always abounding in the work of the Lord, forasmuch as you know that your labour shall not be in vain in the Lord* ‡. And after St. *Peter* had been exhorting the people he wrote to, to behave worthy the precious promises of the gospel, by uniting all the most excellent virtues in their character ; he adds this consideration as the great encouragement and motive to it : *If ye do these things ye shall never fall ; for so an entrance shall be ministered to you abundantly into the everlasting kingdom of our Lord and Saviour Jesus Christ.* But that *unless these things be in us and abound, we shall be barren and unfruitful in the knowledge of our Lord Jesus Christ* §, and that if we are defective in them, *we are blind, and cannot see afar off*, i. e. like short sighted persons, cannot see the most important objects clearly, and distinctly, and *have*

---

* John v. 24.   † xv. 8.   ‡ 1 Cor. xv. 58.   § 2 Pet. i. 10, 11

forgotten

forgotten that they were purged from their old fins, or that the great defign of the promifes given them, was to enable them to efcape the corruptions of the world, and renounce their former fins, and recover them to the practice of the moft amiable virtues.

Yea, of fuch importance are good works in the Chriftian fcheme, as that in the future judgment our everlafting ftate will be determined and fixed for immortal life and happinefs, if we fhall be found to have diligently practifed and abounded in them. Will you believe Jefus Chrift on this article, who is to be your judge and mine at the laft great day ? He fays in general, *that the Son of Man fhall come in the glory of his Father, with his angels, and then he fhall reward every man according to his works* *. But he fays more than this ; that *they who are in their graves fhall hear his voice, and fhall come forth ; they that have done good unto the refurrection of life, and they that have done evil to the refurrection of damnation* †. Agreeable to this is the doctrine of St. Paul immediately after my text. *To them that are contentious, and obey not the truth, but obey unrighteoufnefs, God will render indignation and wrath ; tribulation and anguifh upon every foul of man that doth evil ; but glory, honour, and peace to every man that worketh good ; for there is no refpect of perfons with God.* And indeed this is the doctrine that runs through the whole New Teftament, that the great things

* Matt. xvi. 27.　　　† John v. 29.

that

that will be cognizable at the tribunal of Chrift will be the actions of all men, and that they will be acquitted or condemned, rewarded or punifhed, as their *actions*, i. e. their prevailing behaviour through life, fhall be found upon trial to have *been good or evil.* In our Saviour's words, *the wicked* and uncharitable *fhall go into everlafting punifhment, but the righteous into life eternal.*

And indeed this is placing the glory, honour, and immortality of the future ftate, upon its rational and folid foundation. For men are, what their actions and habitual conduct denominate them to be, and if they are judged at all, it muft be by their moral character, and can be by nothing elfe ; and if they are judged by this, if their moral character be found evil, they muft fall under condemnation ; for God cannot approve fin, nor juftify the doers of it ; and if their actions fhall appear to have been in a prevailing manner influenced by Chriftian principles and motives, and agreeable to the main effential precepts of Chriftianity, they will thus far be approved, and the perfons who do them be accepted *as good and faithful fervants*; and the fins and errors from which they have been recovered by repentance will obtain *remiffion, through the redemption that is in and by our Lord Jefus Chrift.*

To render indeed any of the actions of our lives in a moral fenfe good, eftimable in their nature, and commendable by a wife and righteous God, they muft be dictated by,

and

and proceed from proper *principles of truth*,
and the difpofitions of a *good and worthy heart*.
The very fame actions in one man may have
great moral dignity and worth in them, that
in another perfon may have little or nothing
to recommend them, and which though
they may intitle them to great efteem and
affection from others, who cannot know the
motives from which they flow, and the real
temper of heart that influences them, may
be found extremely defective, and altogether,
or almoft utterly deftitute of every circumftance of real worth, when *weighed in the balance of the fanctuary*, and viewed by his eye,
which penetrates into the inmoft receffes of
the hearts of men. *Education* and the general cuftoms of the nations we live in may
reconcile and habituate men to the external
forms and ritual obfervations of religion. Mere
good nature, and a difpofition originally friendly
may prompt fome to the moft kind and generous behaviour. A fenfe of decency, a regard to *reputation*, and the love of the praife
of men, may be the views by which others
act in the good works which they perform ;
whilft fome, and thofe the moft deteftible of
all others, appear ferious, devote, and extreamly godly, the better *to promote their
worldly intereft*, to infinuate themfelves into
the favour of thofe, whom they have an intereft to deceive, and whom they intend to
make the prey of their own neceffities, extravagances or avarice. In thefe circumftances,
actions good, as to the matter and appearance
of

of them, may be extremely bad as to their moral nature and qualities, and all their beſt works may in this view be juſtly called *ſplendida peccata, ſplendid crimes,* incruſtated with the paint, and decorated with the gloſſy colours of piety and virtue, though abſolutely void of the reality and truth of them : But the good works in which ſincere Chriſtians perſevere, and ſeek for glory, honour, and immortal life, are as much ſuperior to theſe, as the ſubſtance to the ſhadow, as real beauty is to that which is fictitious, and as the ſterling gold to the baſer metal which imitates and reſembles it. They proceed from *principles* of the moſt certain and important truth ; *faith in God, as the rewarder of them that ſeek him ; faith in Chriſt,* as the great Inſtructor, Pattern, Saviour, and Judge of all men ; and *faith* in the future inviſible world, and *the recompence of reward,* finally to be diſtributed to all that believe and obey the goſpel. They are the reſult of the *beſt* and moſt excellent *diſpoſitions* of mind, a due reverence for God's authority, the deſire to approve ourſelves to him, and the governing ambition of ſecuring his favour, from the love of Chriſt, and a prevailing gratitude to him for all the benefits of redemption, from a warm deſire of reſembling him in the perfection of his character, and all the amiable virtues of his example ; of being owned by him hereafter as his genuine diſciples, being publickly acquitted by him before his awful tribunal, and *admitted* to enter *into his joy,* and dwell for ever in his

kingdom

kingdom and prefence, from a real and cordial fpirit of benevolence and humanity, the inward approbation and love of juftice and righteoufnefs, and that habitual integrity and candour of heart, which prompts to all focial duties, renders perfons always defirous, and even fometimes anxious to do that which is right, and which is a perpetual excitement in all things to act, as our profeffion, characters, relations, and engagements in life require. And will any perfon venture to call fuch actions as thefe *fplendid fins?* Thus to debafe the effential duties of the Chriftian life, to reproach them as worthlefs, and of no efficacy and influence, of no confideration and value in the laft great day, when they are declared to be *profitable to men, and acceptable to God through Jefus Chrift?* The real foundation upon which our final acquittance in judgment, and our admiffion into eternal life, is expreffly made by Chrift himfelf to depend?

'Tis true, that the very *beft works* of the beft of men are very far from rifing up to the full ftandard of *perfection*, and that was the *reward* of Chriftian piety and virtue to be abfolutely *limited* by the *meafure* of any human goodnefs, our hopes would fink to a very *low* degree, and the future happinefs arifing from this plea would be extreamly imperfect and fhort lived. But then it fhould be remembered, that *imperfection* in goodnefs is the very condition and one of the moft *effential characterifticks* of the prefent ftate of mankind,

mankind, fince there *is not one that liveth and finneth not.* If this was not the cafe, where would be the neceffity or ufe of the fcheme of redemption by the fufferings and death, the interceffion and advocacy of Chrift; which fuppofe men not to be free from fin and blame, but is founded on the reality of all men's being finners, and their confequent need of the falvation of God by Chrift. But then there is nothing more eafily reconcileable, than that *glory, honour, and immortality,* may in one view be confidered and promifed under the notion of the *reward of a patient continuance in well doing* ; and in another as the effect of *the riches of God's grace through the redemption* obtained for us *by Jefus Chrift.* For though a reward always implies fervice done, it by no means implies, that the fervice is equal to the reward, and gives a claim in ftrict equity and juftice to the recompence promifed and conferred. He who only doth, what his duty obliges him to do, may expect protection, but cannot deferve peculiar favours; much lefs if he be deficient in his duty, or in any confiderable inftances hath acted contrary to it ; and though there may be a propriety, arifing from the character of a fuperior, and the ends of government, in conferring benefits on one who hath no ftrict claim in juftice to receive them, and a real meetnefs and difpofition in him to receive fuch benefits, arifing from an ingenuous acknowledgment of his faults, a defire to amend, and a future care to approve himfelf

faithful

faithful in his ftation ; yea, though a fuperior
may encourage offenders to return to their
duty, and behave fuitable to their obligations,
by the promife of fome peculiar and diftinguifhing recompence : Yet every one fees,
th,a in all thefe cafes the benefits vouchfafed
are the real effects of goodnefs, and the recompence of grace, and not of proper debt
and merit.   The propriety of beftowing it,
and the meetnefs of the perfon to receive it,
demonftrate the wifdom of the giver, but doth
not leffen the freedom and grace of the gift, nor
create the leaft merit in him that receives it.
The favour might have been withheld without any impeachment of juftice, and had the
recompence never been promifed, no injury
would have been done to him, who had no
original right to demand it.

All men are the fervants of God by nature, and born under immutable obligations
to yeid him the moft intire and chearful obedience of foul and body to all his commands;
and had they never deviated from their alle-
giance and duty, they might certainly have
expected from the equity of their wife and
good creator, his protection, and all thofe
marks of favour, that were fuitable to their
nature, and neceffary to their happinefs, whilft
he was pleafed to continue them in being.
And this is the utmoft they could have claimed either in equity or juftice.   Whether God
would perpetuate their beings, or not, depended on the refolutions of his own wifdom
and goodnefs ; for his giving them being was

no

no reafon in itfelf, why he fhould render them
immortal, and though that might be no forfeiture of being by fin, yet as there could be
no natural obligation upon God to perpetuate
it, there could be no injury done them in
his refuming it; for fuppofing their obedience ever fo perfect, it would be no more
than what they owed him in ftrictnefs of
duty, and there can be no proportion between
the fervices of men, which are repaid by the
bleffings of life every day, and the gift of
everlafting life and bleffednefs; which though
it be confiftent with the goodnefs of an infinitely benevolent being to beftow, it is infinitely beyond the worth of any created goodnefs to deferve.   But how infinitely more
abfurd is the plea of right to glory, honour,
and immortality from any of the children of
men, in their prefent *imperfect* and *finful* condition.   Who of us can pretend to *innocence*,
or if recovered from a finful courfe, to an
after *finlefs and perfect obedience?* It would be
affronting their own good fenfe and experience, fhould I attempt by any arguments to
convince you, that you are offenders againft
God, and a compliment which you yourfelves
would think founded in the moft criminal
and palpable flattery, fhould I addrefs you,
and encourage you to hope for eternal life,
as perfons who had never forfeited the favour of God, and in no one inftance incurred
his difpleafure.   To you therefore and me,
merit in us, with refpect to God, and the gift
of everlafting happinefs, muft be deemed as
nothing

nothing better than the dictates of ignorance, the excrefcence of folly, and the offspring of the moft criminal prefumption. It is true, that God hath been pleafed to encourage our repentance, our return to our duty, and our perfeverance in well doing, by the promife of forgivenefs, the reftoration to his favour, and the recompence of everlafting life and bleffednefs. But is not this an encouragement of *mercy*, a recompence of undeferved grace and favour, that difcovers our unworthinefs, at the fame time, that it proclaims and illuftrates the riches of the grace of God. So that though the terms on which the blefsing is beftowed is an habitual practice of all good works, yet ftill the blefling is by us unmerited, and can be claimed only by virtue of the conftitution of the gofpel grace, and the voluntary promifes of God by Jefus Chrift.

In thefe good works we muft *patiently continue, never be weary of well doing*, nor yield to the influence of any temptations to prevent our progrefs, and turn us afide from the path of our duty. In the firft ages of Chriftianity, the difficulty of perfeverance in the faith of Chrift and obedience to his gofpel, was exceeding great, and the fevereft terrors of perfecution threatened and endangered the refolution and conftancy of the Saints of God. But they ftood their ground, and triumphed in their victory over all their enemies. Strengthened by their principles, and animated by the prize of heavenly life and glory, that they

kept

kept continually in view, and *laying aside every weight* and incumbrance of fenfual affections, and criminal paffions, and every *fin that eafily befat them, they ran with patience* the arduous *race that was fet before them, looking unto Jefus, the author and finifher of their faith, who for the joy that was fet before him endured the crofs, and defpifed the fhame, and is fat down at the right hand of God,* and having *overcome* they *fat down with him in his kingdom, even as he overcame, and fat down with his father in his kingdom.* Our difficulties and temptations are of another kind, and arife not from the terrors of perfecution, but the *fnares of profperity,* the *cares of life,* the *perpetual hurries and engagements* of fecular *bufinefs,* the *infatiable thirft of riches,* the eager promptings of *ambition,* the immoderate love of *pleafure,* and the growing inclination of *conformity to the world* in all their gratifications, cuftoms, and manners whatfoever. And how fatal are the effects of thefe difpofitions to the intereft of all true religion and men's conftancy in Chriftian piety and virtue, wherever they prevail! They make men gradually forgetful of all their beft principles, weaken by continual encroachments all their beft refolutions, extinguifh the worthieft affections of their hearts, fupprefs thofe fentiments and convictions of their confciences they once cherifhed as their treafure and joy, create an indifference to and incapacity for all ferious and religious reflections, leffen their regard to all the inftitutions of piety and devotion, make them

give

give way to the amufements and cuftoms of
thofe, who make no profeffion of Chriftian
godlinefs, lay them open to innumerable fnares,
and by chafing away the guards of innocence and virtue, render them impotent and
defencelefs ; or, to fum up all in thofe affecting words of St. Paul, throw them into
fuch *temptations and fnares, thofe many foolifh
and hurtful lufts, that pierce them through with
many forrows, and finally overwhelm them in
deftruction and perdition.* But thefe things, O
ye fervants of God ! and heirs of immortality,
you muft *carefully flee, and follow after righte-
teoufnefs, godlinefs, fidelity, love, patience, and
meeknefs, that fighting this good fight of faith,
you may finally lay hold of eternal life* *.

They who defert the path of well doing,
defert the path that leads to and ends in a
glorious and bleffed immortality ; if they tire
and give out, before the race is finifhed, they
renounce all title to the heavenly prize. The
Chriftian race never ends but with life itfelf,
and well doing is the Chriftian's duty, 'till
he is actually put into poffeffion of his reward. And what is there, that can be, in
the reafon of things, of weight enough to
tempt a wife and confiderate man, to give
over this facred purfuit of incorruptible glory
and bleffednefs, and abandon that path of
well doing, that will bring us finally to the
poffeffion of it ? Compare *time* and *eternity*
together, and the former will appear but as a

---

* 1 Tim. i. 2, 10, 12.

moment,

moment, a mere point in comparifon of the latter. Weigh in an impartial balance the glare of wealth, and the fhew of riches, and what proportion will there be between thefe perifhing treafures, which may be loft in the purfuit, and which, if obtained, muft foon be parted with ; and thofe which are incorruptible, from which the poffeffor never dies, and which fhall never treacheroufly forfake, or difappoint the largeft expectations of him who gains them. Let ambition purfue its views. Only let us wifely fix the object of it, and carefully regulate the meafures of obtaining it. But how low is that ambition, which reaches no higher than the advantages, honours, and interefts of a world, the fafhion of which is perpetually paffing away, and we ourfelves as conftantly paffing out of it ! 'Tis an ambition truly honourable and worthy, that enobles the mind which cherifhes it, and that fhall fooner or later be gratified in its full extent ; to excell in every thing that is great and good, that imitates the conduct of the eternal God, that aims at the neareft and faireft refemblance to him, that hath for its object his final and publick approbation, the robes of celeftial glory, the crown of righteoufnefs, and the reward of life and happinefs incorruptible and heavenly. Here thy ambition, Chriftian, let it be ever fo warm and intenfe, can never be a fin, becaufe the means of gratifying it are prefcribed by God, comprehend all the effential duties of human life, and a fteady perfeverance in them, throughout all the various ftations, circumftances and changes of our prefent beings, and confift in thefe things, and in thefe alone.

This glory, honour and eternal life we muft *conftantly aim at* in all the virtues we exercife, in all the fervices of life we engage in, and every good work of chriftian obedience that we perform. For this is doing them with an eye *to God's glory*, which can never be inconfiftent with the happinefs of men, and which is beft promoted by the diligent difcharge of our duty to him, and the endeavour of being finally approved and accepted by him. If it was poffible we could feparate thefe things in our own minds, and live the chriftian life without propofing to ourfelves his favour, as the grand inducement to it, it would be an extravagant folly in its nature, a criminal fuperftition, the greateft excefs of diftempered enthufiafm, and what would greatly diminifh the intrinfick worth of the beft fervices we could perform. To be indifferent to the commendation of God, and the reward of his infinite goodnefs, is unnatural, and indeed abfolutely impoffible to one who knows what God is, and under the prevalence of right difpofitions and affections to that moft excellent and bleffed being. No. *To be accepted of God* fhould be uppermoft in our hearts, and the generous ambition, that we fhould live every day under the powerful influence of. Seeking after glory, honour, and eternal life, is to aim at this bleffednefs in all we do,
and

and to make all the actions of our lives subservient to our securing it.

If this be our aim, let us farther seek after it, *by cherishing the lively hope and assurance of it*, whilst we continue stedfast in the way of our duty, and *giving all diligence by well doing, to make our calling and election sure.* Take, says the Apostle, *for an helmet the hope of salvation;* and he exhorts the Hebrews, that as *God is not unrighteous to forget their work and labour of love, which they shewed towards his name, they should shew a constant diligence* in all the services of goodness *to the full assurance of hope to the end, and that this hope they should retain as an anchor of the soul, both sure and stedfast, and which enters within the veil* *, hath its fast and firm holding in the very sanctuary of God, where it is impossible it can be moved, or ever fail them. The consciousness of well doing naturally excites somewhat of hope in God; but as he hath connected with it, by the constitution of his own mercy in Christ, the grant of everlasting life and happiness, we should not allow ourselves, whilst *we are stedfast and immovable, and always endeavouring to abound in the work of the Lord,* to suspect or question the readiness of God to fulfill his own promises, and give us eternal life, as the gracious recompence of our faithfully pursuing it. Hope animates to diligence, quickens us to the practice of virtue, renders superior to the difficulties of

---

* Heb. vi. 10, 11, 19.

F f 2

our duty, and is one of the beft motives to
ftedfaftnefs in the practice of it.

And finally, by a fteady, patient continuance in well doing, we are *increafing our meetnefs* for, and thereby ftrengthen the foundation of our title to the inheritance of eternal
life, and thereby feeking after it, in the moft
effectual manner we can poffibly take to obtain it. Good difpofitions grow ftronger and
firmer by thofe actions to which they lead
us ; and on the other hand, as thofe difpofitions take deeper root in us, and grow more
influential by cultivation and improvement,
they heighten the regard to, and increafe
the ability for all thofe good works, to which
they naturally and powerfully excite us ; fo
that they reciprocally affift each other, and
are mutually fubfervient to their refpective vigour and increafe. And how can we more
effectually feek after the glory and bleffednefs of the heavenly world, than by continually increafing our meetnefs for it, and per-
fecting thofe facred affections of mind, which
are the only ones that prevail amongft the
happy inhabitants of the celeftial regions ?
How can we be more directly purfuing the
recompence of eternal life and glory, than
by abounding in thofe good fruits of the fpirit, and exercifing thofe virtues of the
Chriftian life, to which that recompence is
promifed and fecured ? Every duty we perform from faith in, and love to God and
Chrift, and every good work that we do, out
of obedience to God, and that we may ap-.
                                        prove

prove ourfelves to Chrift, is increafing our ftock of riches for eternity, and *laying up in ftore* a more abundant provifion *againft the time to come.* It proportionably afcertains our title to all the bleffings contained in the promifes of God, and that have been purchafed by Chrift for thofe who believe and obey his gofpel. The increafe of grace, by increafing purity of heart, vifible in the growing holinefs, virtue, and ufefulnefs of our lives, is a real advance in true happinefs, as it multiplies the inward fources of happinefs, and prepares us for the higheft advance and full perfection of it. What can we imagine conftitutes the felicity of Heaven itfelf? What, but the utter abfence of all unnatural, criminal affections, the full maturity, and the eternal exercife and improvement of all the beft and worthieft difpofitions, and the being for ever employed in thofe pure, facred, benevolent, and friendly fervices, in which all, without exception, are there engaged; without which Heaven would loofe its beft joys, and the glories of the place would never render us compleatly happy. Thus then muft you feek after glory, honour, and eternal life, by perpetually cultivating and improving the temper of heart, that is peculiar to that bleffed ftate, into which you hope to be admitted, and living as the inhabitants of it do, and like them, as far as you can unblamable, in the practice of all the great duties of fubftantial godlinefs and virtue. Thus will you be advancing towards their perfection, anti-

cipate

cipate the joys of Heaven, enter into the genuine work and employments of it, and finally be received as the bleffed inhabitants of it yourfelves, and have your full fhare in that *fulnefs of joy* that is *in his prefence*, and *in thofe pleafures that are at his right hand and laft for evermore.*

And indeed this divine connection between patient continuance in well doing, and the immortal glory of a future life, is neceffary and immutable. God will give eternal life to Chriftians of this character, and to them alone. Immortality is no bleffing in itfelf, but as it is well circumftanced, and unlefs there be a proper difpofition for enjoying it. Immortality for the fake of vice, one would think could only be the wifh of a devil. Immortality only for the fake of fenfual enjoyments, the defire only of a brute. It can in no other view be a real bleffing, but as it opens to us an endlefs purfuit of wifdom and knowledge, as it introduces us into the prefence, and fecures us the perpetual favour of God our happinefs; as it forms us into the moft perfect refemblance of his perfection and rectitude, as it is dignified with the peculiar marks of his goodnefs, raifes us above the need and defire of all fenfual gratifications, fits us for the fociety and friendfhip of perfected fpirits, and perpetuates our capacity for loving, ferving, and enjoying God, the permanent, eternal fource of all perfection and bleffednefs. Eternity of duration thus endowed is infinitely defirable. " In the queft of

of fuch an immortality, by conftancy in well
doing, under the facred influence of the principles of truth and righteoufnefs, would I live
and die, and I fhall never queftion the power
of God, or his readinefs and inclination to
beftow it. In this fearch would I wifh you
to be habitually employed, that you alfo may
fhare in this *heavenly gift*, and to fee you
partakers of it will add to my joy, and make
Heaven itfelf to me more fenfibly pleafing
and delightful."

END of the THIRD VOLUME.

E R R A T A.

Page 40, line 23, for *there* read *thefe.* p. 64, l. 22, for
wherever read *whatever.* p. 108 in margin, for *virtuous joys*
rea_ *all thefe delights.* p. 131, l. 6, dele *of.* p. 225, l. 7, for
irfidelity read *infelicity.* p. 239, l. 1, for *immediately* read *me-
diately.* p. 240, l. 26, for *certanter* read *certainly.* p. 246, l. 1,
for *he* read *be.* ditto, l. 8, dele *a d.* p. 249, l. 22, for *is*
read *are.* p. 250, l. 5, read *after bad. as in this life.* p. 312,
l. 25, for *in* read *is.* p. 314, l. 7; dele *for.* p. 356, l. 9, for
which read *with.* p. 402, l. 11, for *who* read *whom.* p. 409,
at bottom, read *diligently.*